POISONING

The Purgatory Poisoning is Rebecca Rogers's debut novel and won the Comedy Women in Print Unpublished Prize 2021.

Rebecca grew up in Birmingham on a diet of *Blackadder* and *Monty Python*. For a long time, she thought Michael Palin was her uncle (he's not). Now a civil servant by day and writer by night, she's a proud mum to two grown-up boys and lives in the glorious south west of England.

@rebeccasrogers
@Rebecca.rogers.writes

The Purgatory POISONING

REBECCA ROGERS

HarperCollins*Publishers*

HarperCollins*Publishers* Ltd
1 London Bridge Street,
London SE1 9GF

www.harpercollins.co.uk

HarperCollins*Publishers*
Macken House, 39/40 Mayor Street Upper
Dublin 1, D01 C9W8, Ireland

First published by HarperCollins*Publishers* 2023
1

A catalogue record for this book is available from the British Library

ISBN: 978-0-00-855302-9 (PB)

This novel is entirely a work of fiction.
The names, characters and incidents portrayed in it are
the work of the author's imagination. Any resemblance to
actual persons, living or dead, events or localities is
entirely coincidental.

Typeset in Minion by Palimpsest Book Production Ltd, Falkirk, Stirlingshire

Printed and bound in the UK using 100% Renewable Electricity
by CPI Group (UK) Ltd

This book is produced from independently certified FSC™ paper to ensure
responsible forest management.

For more information visit: www.harpercollins.co.uk/green

For my dad

Prologue

Dave knew where he was before he opened his eyes. It was the smell; so distinctive that he remembered it after all these years: damp clothes, bleach, and burnt fish fingers.

He was in the youth hostel at St Ives, and it was 1992.

Or was it? Because a minute ago, he had *very* definitely been in his friend's dining room in North London, and it had *very* definitely been 2019.

With his eyes still firmly shut, he took a moment to steady himself. He remembered that he had felt unwell after the main course – sick as a dog, in fact. He'd never been a huge fan of prawn curry but it had never, *ever* had such swift repercussions before. He ran his tongue over his teeth for clues, but found nothing. Even those troublesome gaps between his molars were clear. All he could taste was the minty sweetness of a fresh breath that had evaded him for much of his adult life.

He was lying in a bed. Not his own double bed with an expensive memory foam mattress and pillows – this mattress was paper-thin and he could feel the springs in his back. His right hand was resting on something cold. Was that a zip? Was he in a sleeping bag?

But the strangest thing of all was that he felt . . . great. Better than great. It felt like someone had cleared forty-five years' worth of dead leaves from his brain, and the normal fog that usually greeted him when he woke up just wasn't there. His mind felt clean, clear and – well, new, somehow.

And yet there was that unmistakeable smell. The zip. And somewhere, someone was playing 'Could It Be Magic' by Take That.

There was only one explanation: he had suffered some sort of stroke at the party (doesn't that make you smell weird things?), he was now in hospital, and was high on morphine.

Only one way to find out. He opened his eyes.

Shit. He was lying in the bottom bunk of a wooden framed bunk bed, in the youth hostel at St Ives, and it was 1992.

1

The Holiday

Summer, 1992

If you'd have asked Dave that morning what his memories were of the summer of 1992, he'd have said this: he went on holiday to Cornwall with his parents and younger brother, Andrew. Andrew was eight and Dave was ten. Andrew was a pain in the neck and they had spent much of the holiday arguing. There was an incident in the water – something to do with Andrew not wearing his arm bands – but he was saved, and no harm was done. His parents were cross with Dave for a while, probably for not looking after him as a big brother should. And that was that, apart from fragmented recollections of rum 'n' raisin ice cream dripping down soft ice cream cones, and huge, salty waves that puckered their skin.

Memories are curious. The brain skews memories of events to protect us.

The truth about that holiday was this. David and Andrew's relationship was already on the rocks – partly because young brothers always hate each other to a greater or lesser degree, but mostly because Andrew had got travel sick on the way to Cornwall and had vomited all over David's superhero Top Trumps. The Silver Surfer would from that day carry an orange stain and an unpleasant aroma of acidy chicken Kiev.

After an eternity of driving from Croydon, the family had arrived at St Ives Youth Hostel at the golden hour, when everything was washed with rose-gold by the setting sun. The building was low and white and faced the sea, hugging the hillside. It was lit up with flickering strip lights which had caught harvester spiders and moths in their casings.

David's dad – Colin – turned the family Vauxhall into the hostel's driveway and parked behind a high wall that shielded the building from the sea. As they opened their car doors, they could hear the distant crash of the Cornish waves.

'Bring your things, lads,' said David's mum, Ann. 'We're here.'

Colin sold bathrooms for a living but he hadn't done so well that year (he'd only managed to sell seven bathroom suites, three high-flush loos and a single solitary bidet, and really you couldn't count the bidet as he'd thrown it in for free) so money was tight. A repeat of last year's swanky holiday in a three-star hotel in Newquay was out of the question, but Ann had insisted on going somewhere, so a compromise had to be made.

'What about camping?' Ann had helpfully suggested one

day, imagining hot coffee and bacon rolls in the morning sunshine as the boys played happily with other children around the tent.

'What? With my lumbar issues?' Colin was aghast that Ann would even contemplate for one moment him sleeping on an airbed. Just the thought of it made him wince.

'For the love of God, Colin. You've got piles. I've seen them dangling in all their glory. Stop pretending that your back hurts.' Ann sighed and went back to her copy of the *Radio Times*, circling '2:40 p.m.: *Shirley Valentine*' so hard that her pencil broke.

Later that week, in a chance meeting with Sue from up the road (whose court shoes were the subject of Colin's regular lapses in concentration) Colin mentioned that he was under pressure to find a low-cost family holiday destination. Sue suggested the youth hostel at St Ives.

'I mean, not that you and Ann are "youths" now – HAHAHA – but my niece said she had a smashing time there with her little ones a couple of years ago.' And then, quietly, close to Colin's ear, 'Of course it's not Butlins, but we can't all live like kings and queens, can we?' Colin shivered a little and looked at Sue's feet.

They were shown to their family room by Tim, a bronzed young man in his twenties wearing a shark's tooth necklace and no shoes.

'Dudes – bathroom is down the corridor, although you've got your own sink here, of course,' he gestured at the cracked basin as if showing off the crown jewels, 'and we do serve a continental breakfast but only between seven and seven fifteen a.m.'

Ann was indignant. 'That's not very long!'

'Yes, and I like to have time to read the paper,' Colin grumbled.

Tim shrugged. 'There are waves to catch,' he explained, smiling rakishly. 'Come with us if you fancy. Got a board?'

Ann suddenly wished she had a board. She also wished she could swim, had packed a slightly more revealing costume, and hadn't eaten that extra Battenberg slice at the services on the A303.

Meanwhile, David and Andrew were fighting over the top bunk. It was obvious to David that he, the older sibling, and therefore the superior being, should have first dibs. However, he had made the fatal mistake of not immediately claiming his territory when they walked into the room, having instead been hypnotized by the partial view of the shimmering sea from the window. By the time he turned round and had come to his senses, Andrew had climbed up the ladder and set up camp.

David was not going to be outwitted by his younger brother. He edged halfway up the ladder and leaned across Andrew, grabbing him by the collar and pulling him so hard that Andrew's head hung backwards over the bed.

'GETOFFGETOFFGETOFF. I'M FALLING!' shrieked upside-down Andrew, desperately clawing at his brother's face, trying in vain to gouge one or both eyes out to persuade him to loosen his grip.

'You're in MY BED,' stated David calmly, and pulled harder.

As he did so he was aware of a ripping noise and a bit more give than there should have been in Andrew's shirt. If David had known the word 'shit', he would have said it. In the event, all he could muster was, 'Oh – poo.'

Ten minutes later and Andrew was happily sitting cross-legged in the top bunk like a king. He was surrounded by his teddy courtiers, as well as his books and his special blanket that he picked at and then stuffed the fluff up his nose. David, however, was skulking in the bowels of the lower bunk; he lay on the bottom bed looking mournfully at the underside of the mattress above, stinging from his mum's reprimand and from his dad's clip round the ear. He sniffed his beloved Top Trumps. They still smelled of his brother's sick.

David had been sent to bed without any dinner. Not that any of them had any dinner, but at least the other three had enjoyed the remnants of the day's tuna paste sandwiches and orange Club biscuits. All David had was an old lemon sherbet that he'd found in a side pocket of his rucksack from their last holiday, a year ago. He unwrapped it quietly and licked it, wanting to make it last.

Big, fat, globby tears formed fast in David's eyes. This was going to be a terrible holiday. He hated his brother. He hated his mum. And his dad. He despised everyone, actually. Everyone who ever lived. Ever. And he felt very lonely indeed.

Desperate for someone to talk to – to tell how unfairly he had been treated – he remembered what his teachers always told him: God is listening. God would be a great person to talk to, because, David remembered, God's got the whole world in his hands. And he's got a hammer. David wished he had a hammer – he'd hammer all over Andrew in the morning, and in the evening.

So David clapped his tiny child-size hands together and silently prayed.

A bulb lit up on God's switchboard.

2

Purgatory

Twenty-seven years later and Dave – now beer-bellied and six foot tall, but with the same mop of unkempt dark hair – was once again in the bottom bunk. He stared at the underneath of the mildly stained mattress above and gingerly moved his right arm, then his left. All in working order. His legs seemed to be moving normally too, although they were constricted by a fetching green sleeping bag, half zipped up. Perhaps not a stroke then. He tried moving his mouth from side to side. All appeared normal. Christ on a bike – had he really been so drunk that he'd got in his car after the party, driven down the M5, found a youth hostel that he'd all but forgotten about from his youth, forced his way in, found the bunk bed that he slept in as a child and *had not even managed to get into the top bunk*?

Someone somewhere was still playing Take That.

He sat up and cracked his head on the bed frame above.

'SHIT! MOTHERFUCKING WANKFEST!' His swearing had come on over the years.

'Shhhh! If he hears you, he'll mark you down. Be quiet!'

A pair of slippered feet appeared by his head. Dave swung his legs, still in the sleeping bag, over the edge of the bed and gingerly unhooked his head from the bed frame. His eyes travelled up and he saw an old man in his pyjamas and dressing gown, looking agitated. Behind him were four other people, similarly dressed. Everyone was staring at him.

'Look,' Dave said, holding a hand up in apology. 'I'm really sorry if I woke you last night. I was pretty drunk, I think – although bizarrely no hangover today – must be my age. If you could just point me towards some breakfast then I'll be off and leave you in peace.'

The old man looked straight at Dave. 'Oh, but you can't leave,' he said. 'There's no way out. We've looked.' The small group behind him muttered their agreement.

'This is ridiculous.' Dave unzipped himself and staggered to his feet, noticing as he did so that he was wearing similar pyjamas and dressing gown to the old man – a 1950s-inspired combo of light blue cotton PJs and a thick, brown robe. He was suddenly embarrassed, and whispered to him, 'Sorry if you had to get me undressed last night. I must have been in a right state. I'll get these washed and back to you as soon as I can.' He looked the old man up and down and then back at his own pyjamas. 'I'm surprised these fit you to be honest. Are they yours from when you were younger and thinner and . . .' he paused for a second '. . . about six inches taller?' He scratched his head, confused. Perhaps the old man kept them as a special guest PJ set for strangers. 'Also, did I borrow your toothbrush?'

The old man looked confused. 'Toothbrush? I think we need to explain . . .'

'If you could just remind me of the way out?' Dave asked. He looked around for the exit. There didn't seem to be any doors, or at least not in the places that he remembered. Odd. Perhaps they'd redecorated?

A woman with shoulder-length dark hair, also wearing the regulation pyjama/dressing gown set but in a fetching candy pink, stepped forward. 'What's your name, love?' she asked softly.

Dave looked at her. 'Dave,' he answered blankly.

'Dave, sit back down, and mind your head.' She spoke to him as if he was her teenage son.

He sat back down on the bunk, reluctantly. 'Look, I don't want to make a fuss. I just need to go. I've got a long drive ahead and I've got an important meeting later.' He looked at his wrist where his watch used to be. 'Hey – have one of you lot nicked my watch?'

'Dave,' she said gently. 'Dave. No one has nicked anything. Time is just a theoretical construct created by humans. It doesn't exist here.'

He stared at her. 'Thing is, love, you're obviously out of your mind. No offence or anything. I mean, I'm big on mental-ness – I've done a course at work – and honestly, if I had a bit more time I'd love to chat about it, but I'm in a bit of a rush, so if I could just . . .'

Her eyes hardened and her voice was suddenly stern. 'You can't leave.'

Dave didn't like shouting at women but he felt like he was

losing control. 'Who do you think you are – my mother?' She narrowed her eyes at him. 'Look, love, mind your own business, won't you? I'm sorry, I know you're all old, or mad, or . . .' at this point he looked at a young man sitting quietly at the back of the group '. . . mute, but you're starting to PISS ME RIGHT OFF.'

As a single entity, the group gasped and physically took a small step backwards. The old man threw his hands over his mouth.

The woman sighed and softly touched his arm. 'Thing is, Dave . . .' she took a deep breath. 'You can't leave because . . . you're dead.'

3

The Holiday

Summer, 1992

Their first morning in Cornwall dawned as every day does in a British summer – lashing down with rain. The whole family – Colin and Ann in a creaky iron-framed double bed, and Dave and Andrew in their respective bunks – were awake long before the 7 a.m. breakfast alarm. Raindrops sounded like they were being fired at the rattling window with an air gun and the wind whooped and bellowed down the chimney breast.

'Welcome to Cornwall,' muttered Colin, turning over and pulling the blankets off his wife. Fifteen years of marriage had taught Ann that she'd never get those covers back, so she picked up the towel from the floor (placed there the night before for such a purpose), covered herself as best she could, closed her eyes and eventually fell back to sleep, dreaming of Mediterranean beaches and bare-chested surfers.

David woke up early too, having also had pleasant dreams; the difference being that his were about injecting his little

13

brother with the plague virus. As he opened his eyes, he suddenly became aware that Andrew had negotiated the ladder and was standing an inch from his face.

'What do you want?' David hissed.

'What's the time?' Andrew hissed back.

'Time you learned to tell the time.' David smiled and inwardly high-fived himself. Insult number one of the day. Excellent job.

Andrew tugged at the sleeve of David's pyjamas. 'Is it time for breakfast? I'm hungry.'

David looked across at his parents – Dad had fallen back to sleep and was snoring; his mum was restless under her pink beach towel – but he could see light around the edges of the curtains.

'Fine.' David was hungry too. 'Let's go. We'll see what we can find in the kitchen.'

Unfortunately for the boys, the rain had stopped, throwing the whole house into an eerie quietness. Everything they touched, creaked. The bed, the floor, the door; even their own bodies made creaking and clicking noises that seemed unbearably loud in the deathly calm of the Cornish morning. Andrew's shoulder clicked rhythmically as he walked. David stopped and turned.

'Turn your shoulder off,' he whispered.

'I can't,' whimpered Andrew, 'it's just how I was made.'

'Well – stop moving your shoulders. Walk like this.' Dave demonstrated a hands-by-the-side walk.

Andrew giggled. 'Penguin,' he said.

'That's right, Andrew. Be a penguin. A silent one.'

Andrew shut his mouth firmly and waddled after his brother down the dusty corridor.

'Keep up!' muttered David, abruptly arriving in the huge, shabby white kitchen. As he turned the corner, he became aware of an unfamiliar, looming figure silhouetted against a big, bright window at the end of the room. David stopped, suddenly, and Andrew – concentrating hard on his emperor penguin walk – careered into him from behind. They both stared at the imposing man in front of them.

'W . . . who . . . are . . . you?' stuttered David.

'My name is Go— hang on, no, it's . . . Michael. Yes, that's it. Michael.' He had a beautiful voice, reminding the boys of ice creams and snowmen and gold stars and bedtime stories. His silhouette was outlined in silver, as if someone had drawn a dot-to-dot around him with a sparkly pen. As he was in shadow, they couldn't see his mouth move, but they caught a glimpse of his eyes; something flickering, a light with great depth, a candle in utter darkness. Hope.

Neither boy could speak for a few seconds. Eventually, David roused himself and coughed.

'Where is . . .' David fought hard to remember the surfer dude's name.

'TIM!' shouted Andrew. 'It's Tim!' And then, to Michael, 'I liked Tim's necklace.'

'All right! No one likes a show-off, Andrew,' David seethed. Michael smiled. The boys emitted a tiny gasp. His teeth shone through the darkness like he was off the telly.

'Tim is sleeping. He had a late night. I'm in charge of breakfast this morning, so . . .' at this point Michael stepped away from the window into the light, and gestured towards the cooker and the cupboards '. . . what will it be? Pancakes with syrup? Milkshakes?'

David and Andrew nodded, open mouthed, eyes wide. Now David could see him properly, this person was some sort of mega cross between James Bond and Luke Skywalker and . . . someone else he'd seen on telly but couldn't put his finger on. He was handsome and tall and suave wearing a bright white suit with a thin tie that glittered like an oil slick; hundreds of colours shimmering in the sunlight.

'Sit down then, little ones.' Little ones? Dave wasn't sure he liked being called a 'little one' – after all, he was the second tallest in his class – but he was willing to let it pass on the promise of pancakes. The boys sat down at the large, rectangular kitchen table, stupefied. Andrew whispered, 'Am I dreaming?'

David whispered back, 'I don't think so.' His stomach felt queasy, and you didn't feel sick in dreams, did you? It wasn't that he was scared, exactly, but now that Michael had come out of the shadows, David suddenly realized how tall he was. In fact, it wasn't just that he was tall, but he seemed to fill the room and be everywhere, all at once. He was quietly closing the kitchen door and cracking eggs and crushing fruit and laying the table and whisking milk, all at the same time.

'And there we have it.' The words glided out of Michael's mouth as he gestured to the table, now groaning with pancakes and milkshakes and fresh fruit and maple syrup.

'Ohhhh, thank you,' spluttered David, eyes bright, before picking up a pancake with his fingers and ramming it into his mouth, whole.

'Rfnfnghoo,' managed Andrew, already a pancake ahead of Dave, strawberry milkshake running down his chin and dripping on his pyjamas.

Michael stood at the other side of the room watching the boys eat. 'You know, boys?' he said softly. 'I really like cooking. I really do. I don't get much of a chance to do it in my day job.'

'Oh, that's a shame. You're ever so good at it,' snuffled Andrew. David nodded in agreement. Mum made pancakes on Pancake Day but they were always very thick and had lumps of flour that stuck to your teeth. These pancakes were . . . heavenly.

'They taste like clouds,' said Andrew, his cheeks full. Michael smiled but said nothing.

A door creaked open in the corridor beyond the kitchen. Michael looked up. 'Right, so nice to meet you both, must be off. I'll be seeing you again.' David looked up and caught Michael's eye just for a moment. His eyes were so, so blue. David suddenly felt like he was falling in space.

The kitchen door flew open.

'Hey guys! You're up early. And already fuel-loading, I see – good job!' It was Tim.

'It wasn't us who made them – it was Michael,' Andrew spluttered through the last of his milkshake.

'Who's Michael, little dude?' Tim asked. *Little dude*. Dave rolled his eyes. What was it with these people? They really weren't *that* small.

'He's . . .' Andrew looked around for Michael, but he wasn't there.

'That's weird,' said David, 'he must have gone back to his room.'

'Don't know anyone called Michael staying here,' said Tim whilst cracking eggs into a large bowl. And then, in a conspiratorial whisper, 'Is this your cover story for getting up so early and using the kitchen? Don't worry, boys – your secret is safe with me. I'm known for keeping secrets. Although that's mainly because my memory's so terrible I just forget them. But still.'

He looked at them. 'Also, thanks for doing the washing-up. I would *never* have done that at your age.' He punched Andrew's shoulder as he walked past to get to the cutlery drawer. 'Good men.'

'But we didn't—' Andrew began.

'SHH!' hissed David. 'He'll think we're mad. At the moment he thinks we're just . . . tidy. Let's go outside and look for Michael.'

'Did you see his eyes?' whispered Andrew.

'Yes. I saw them.' David thought for a moment. 'They looked like big blue exploding—'

Andrew interrupted. 'Planets,' he said, with wonder. 'They looked just like exploding planets.'

David felt a rush of excitement, and took Andrew's hand. 'Let's find him,' he said.

4

Purgatory

'Dead?'

Imagine this: a stranger has told you that you're dead. You're obviously not dead, because, well – you've heard them say it, you can see them, your cognitive functions are good. But there is a problem. You're inexplicably in a place, or very similar to a place, that you stayed in when you were ten. You can't remember how you got there. You're wearing someone else's pyjamas and have no idea where your clothes, your phone or your wallet are. You're being watched by three very old people, a middle-aged woman, and a youth.

You feel absolutely amazing, by the way.

So how do you respond?

You become hysterical.

'A-HAHAHAHAHAHAHAHAHAHAHAHAHA.' Dave looked around to see if anyone else was laughing. Not a glimmer, not a hint of a smile, not even a sneer. Just mild concern.

'Dave. We know. It's impossible to take in.'

'A-HAHAHAHAHAHAHA.'

'It's OK, Dave. We've all been there.'

'A-HAHA. Ha. Oh.'

'We'll give you a bit of space.'

They all retreated into the corners of the room. The old man sat on a single bed, looking at him. The two old women sat together at a small table, talking quietly. The younger woman who had spoken to him said something to the sullen boy, who briefly smiled and turned to look at a blank wall.

Dave's brain was busy trying to fit round pegs into square holes. *OK*, he thought. *Perhaps I'm not in hospital. Perhaps I just took some drugs at the dinner party. I mean, I've never taken drugs before – apart from that one time I went to Amsterdam and someone made me eat that cake which doesn't really count – so it would be out of character. But you're never too old to try something new, right? Perhaps that was it? That must be it.*

I've just got to roll with it.

Dave looked at the boy who was staring at the wall. 'What are you doing?' he asked. 'Watching TV,' the boy replied. Dave looked at the wall. There was nothing there except for peeling cream paint and Blu Tack stains.

Dave studied him carefully. His face was reacting to some-thing; a half-smile, a shake of the head, the occasional nod. Dave asked the brown-haired woman with the kind face,

'What is he doing?'

She took some time before answering, appearing to be weighing up her response. Eventually she said, 'I know this sounds weird, Dave, but he's watching TV. In 2004. *Friends*, probably. He loved that series.'

Right, thought Dave, *I've had enough. 2004? Watching walls? Accusing people of dying?*

'What's your name?' Dave asked the woman.

'Laura,' she replied.

Dave looked her straight in the eye. 'Laura, has someone played a joke on me?' he said softly. 'Is it my brother? It's just that – I don't mind admitting it – I'm getting a little anxious. A tiny bit stressed. Did he slip something in my drink – you know, for a laugh?'

Laura looked concerned. 'I don't really want to be the one to tell you this – usually we leave it up to—'

'LAURA! Don't beat around the bush! Just tell me. Where. The Hell. Am. I?'

Laura's eyes narrowed and she took a step forward, invading Dave's personal space, her nose an inch from his. Dave forced himself to stand his ground, expecting to feel her breath on his face – but he felt nothing.

'I'll lay it all out for you,' Laura said. 'You're in Purgatory, Dave. You're in the balance between Heaven and Hell. Waiting for judgement. And every time you swear, you step a little bit closer to Hell. You're welcome.'

5

The Holiday

Summer, 1992

Tim unbolted the front door for the boys and they ran out onto the gravel drive, barefoot. No time for shoes. They didn't notice the chill in the air.

'Michael!' they called, desperate to see him again, but not fully knowing why. Where could he have gone? And why did he leave so quickly? They searched the front of the hostel, looking in salty windows where curtains were drawn back. They could hear Whitney Houston on a radio; someone, somewhere, had a window open.

David stopped, breathless. 'Andrew, did that man – Michael – remind you of someone? Someone off a film, or the telly?'

Andrew paused. He thought for a moment, then said confidently, '*Time Bandits.*'

Yes, thought Dave, someone in *Time Bandits*. They'd seen the film for a friend's birthday on video last month. It was old but it had been brilliant; Jess had ruined it though by kicking his chair the whole time, making him spill his Coke. Girls were irritating.

'Do you think he's a real Time Bandit?' Andrew asked hopefully.

'Don't be a wally! They don't exist. It's just a film, all made up. He just looks like one of the actors in it.' David scuffed his feet in the gravel. 'Anyway, do you want to find him or not?'

Andrew nodded enthusiastically.

'Right then, you go round the building that way,' he gestured off to the left, 'and I'll go the other way. Look everywhere. I'll meet you round the back.' They ran around the entire building looking in all the hidey holes and ditches they could find. No sign.

They met again, panting, at the side of the building. 'Maybe he went out of the front gate!' said David. They returned to the front and tracked around the high stone wall that encircled the hostel at the front, obliterating the sea view. There was an ornate iron gate, but it was locked. Sticking their faces through the gaps in the ironwork, they could just make out a sliver of green-blue waves rolling into the cove, and hear the low rumble of the sea.

'We've lost him,' murmured Andrew sadly.

David felt an aching disappointment that ran through his whole body. He shook himself. 'He's probably just over there.' He pointed over the wall. 'Help me climb it.'

'But you can see through the gate,' replied Andrew.

'If you're on top of the wall, you can see more. Besides . . .' David whispered conspiratorially into Andrew's ear, 'he might be hiding behind the wall.' David stepped back. 'Let me stand on your shoulders.'

'NO! It might hurt. And you'll get my pyjamas dirty. There are puddles.'

'Don't be a wuss. Come on. I'll be, like, five seconds. The mud will brush off. Mum will never know.'

'But you might hurt me.'

'Andrew, stop being a baby and hold still.' David grabbed Andrew's top and tried to push him down so that he could stand on top of him.

'NO, NO, I DON'T WANT YOU TO DO THAT!' shouted Andrew, twisting out of David's grip. 'MUM! DAD! David's hurting me!' But their parents were way out of earshot.

The boys grappled with each other and David, the stronger of the two, pushed his brother face down on to the gravel and wrenched Andrew's right arm behind his back. Andrew, frustrated, angry, and in pain, started to cry. 'You're hurting me. Please stop,' he spluttered through his hot tears.

David wasn't old enough to realize that the anger he felt was all tied up in the unfairness of Top Trumps and bunk beds – as well as his unfounded belief that Andrew was his parents' favourite. All sense of consequence went out of the window when he felt the adrenaline buzz of his brother's distress; David was owed this, somehow. Andrew was always forgiven, never blamed – even when it was obvious that he had broken every single rule. Just because he was younger, and put on 'that' face in front of Mum and Dad, making them feel sorry for him. No matter what Andrew did, no matter how obvious it was that it was his fault – David got the blame. Every single time.

Making his brother cry was sweet payment, long overdue.

*

David was not a naughty boy. He wasn't born evil. When he was six, he stole a single Bazooka Joe bubble gum from Mrs Stokes who ran the local corner shop – and was so scared and ridden with guilt by the whole ordeal that he couldn't step back inside the shop for a full two months, and even then he wasn't able to look Mrs Stokes in the eye. And one Saturday when he was eight, he attempted to extort his weekly pocket money out of both his mum *and* his dad, separately, only to regretfully realize that, despite appearances, they did actually talk to each other occasionally, and had told each other what had happened. He wasn't given any more pocket money for six months.

But these two occasions of wayward moral compass were the exceptions rather than the rule. And so, when he saw tears running down his brother's face and suddenly realized that he was actually inflicting real pain, he let go.

Andrew got up slowly and backed away like a wounded animal. He was covered in dirt and the right knee of his pyjamas was ripped, his skin grazed.

'I hate you. I HATE YOU. I'm telling Mum and Dad what you've done.'

'Shut up. What are you doing? I haven't hurt you! It's just dirt. Come back. ANDREW. COME BACK.'

But Andrew had run back into the building. And David knew that he was in trouble.

Sure enough, it wasn't long before his dad came striding out on to the drive, towelling dressing gown flapping in the breeze, showing off his underpants. David looked at the ground, waiting for the telling off, fearing the possibility of a swift slap round the head, and hoping above all else that this would be the end of it.

One look at his dad's face told him that this wouldn't be the end of it.

'David! First the fighting over the bunk bed, now this. Your brother is covered in muck and scratches. He says you pushed him over and held him down whilst you tried to climb on top of him. Did you? DID YOU?'

Oh, this was bad. He would have to start doing that trick that he did. The thing where he stopped listening and retreated instead to his safe place, inside his head, the quieter place where no one was shouting at him and he didn't have a brother but he did have his Top Trumps and none of them smelled like vomit. In fact, they all smelled like his mum's pink talc that she kept on the bathroom windowsill. And Michael, that man with the colourful tie, was there, and he was saying that everything was going to be al—

'. . . so I'm stopping your Top Trumps subscription AND I'm taking away your holiday money.' David snapped back for his dad's finale.

David was horrified. 'No, Dad! You can't! You can't do both! I won't be able to buy more Top Trumps and my ones are ruined because . . .'

'Well, you should have thought of that before you ground your brother into the floor. Just look at him!' He gestured to the window, where Andrew, safely inside away from the drama, was watching. David looked grudgingly at his brother. He had never seen anyone look so sorry for themselves. David's blood boiled.

'If you can show us that we can trust you, you can have your holiday money. But not until then.'

'But, Dad, it's not f—'

'Don't you dare say it's not fair.' His dad grabbed David's pyjama collar and dragged him back through the front door into the hostel. 'We have warned you over and over again. Go back to the room and sit on the bottom bunk and think about what you've done. I'm going to have breakfast with your mum.' With that, his dad disappeared into the kitchen, leaving a sad, barefoot little boy in his pyjamas in the cold stone-flagged hallway.

David reluctantly walked back to their room and slumped on his bunk. He could hear Andrew sniffing loudly above him.

'You shouldn't have told on me. No one likes a dobber.'

Andrew's sniffing increased.

'Look, I'm sorry. I'm sorry, OK? It's just that I really, really wanted to see that man Michael again. I thought that if I could just see over the wall, we might have been able to see which way he went. You know, so we could follow him.'

Silence from above. *Well,* thought David, *at least the sniffing has stopped.* 'Are your legs OK?'

A little upside-down tear-sodden face appeared suddenly from the top bunk. 'Bit sore.'

'Dad isn't going to give me any holiday money. I won't be able to buy any new Top Trumps now.'

Andrew looked at David and for a moment, David thought that Andrew might take pity on him, might share his pocket money, might actually offer to buy him the Top Trumps himself.

Andrew breathed in. Here it comes. David smiled inwardly. Here comes the sympathy.

'Good,' said Andrew. 'I hate you.'

And with that, Andrew's face disappeared, and David could hear him settling back into his top bunk kingdom.

Not as much as I hate you, thought David.

6

Purgatory

Dave stared at Laura. Purgatory. Purg-a-tory. He rolled the word around his head searching for a frame of reference. Purgatory. Something to do with Catholics? A holding place where you wait for . . . what did she say? Judgement? Surely something just made up to put the fear of God into you?

Laura seemed to read his mind. 'Not made up, Dave. Real. Well, real in the Heaven and Hell sense. Not in a biological sense. You don't really exist. It's complex.'

'I mean, I don't understand. Obviously. I don't understand. I feel great! How can I be dead?'

'I know this is hard to take in. I mean, it was difficult for Edie, and she's a Catholic, so she was expecting it.' She gestured to an elderly lady sitting in an armchair, whose mint green pyjama bottoms were rolled up to her wrinkled knees. She appeared to be listening to some music. Was she also listening to Take That? Whatever it was, the old woman was tapping her bare feet and humming tunelessly along, a touch of a smile on her thin lips.

'Dave, what's the last thing you remember, before you woke up here?'

He tried to recollect what had happened at the dinner party. It was surprisingly difficult to hold on to any memories, like clutching at pipe smoke.

'I know there were six of us: my brother Andrew, Jess, Hannah, Rose – that idiot, Ian – and me. But I can't remember any details. Why is that? I can't seem to quite . . . grasp anything.'

'Don't worry. We were all like that at the beginning. We haven't worked out why it happens, but it's something to do with the process of passing through the veil.'

'Through the veil? Are you a Victorian hymn book?'

Laura sighed. 'Get used to it, Dave. These Victorians knew a thing or two about death. They got a bit caught up with decay and eventide and failing light, but they knew that there was something else, you know, afterwards. Anyway, the memories will come back gradually. I'll warn you now – they may be a bit . . . alarming.'

'They can't be any more alarming than realizing that you're dead and you're in a holding cell waiting for some deity to choose your path of eternal light or eternal damnation.' He paused for breath. 'Who are you, Laura? Or who were you? How long have you been here? Waiting, I mean.'

Laura sat down next to Dave on his bunk. He felt the warmth from her body which was at once comforting and confusing. How could she radiate heat if she was dead?

'I was an engineer, believe it or not. Successful, too. I had two happy kids. A husband I loved.' She looked at Dave, eyes full of . . . what? Regret?

'I'm not sure how I died,' she continued. 'I think I had a stroke – my left side wasn't working properly one morning after I'd had a shower. I told John, my husband, I was going back to bed. And that's the last I remember.' Laura sighed again and Dave thought that he had never seen anyone look so sad. 'I don't know if I'll ever see them again. I've come to terms with it, though. No more tears left.'

But she didn't look like she had come to terms with it at all.

'I'm sorry,' offered Dave simply. What else could he say?

Laura arranged her face in a tight smile. 'It comes to us all. Death, I mean. It's just that mine – and yours – came too early. Were you married? Kids?'

Dave shook his head and made a face. 'Me? No. Kids! Not for me. Although I did have a girlfriend who put up with me for a long time. Rose. She was at the dinner party when I passed . . . "through the veil". We were in love. Or at least, I thought we were, until she told me that she'd been seeing that Ian bloke behind my back.' He looked up at Laura. 'I probably deserved it. I'm not the easiest person to be around.'

They sat together quietly. 'Could It Be Magic' was still playing.

'Do you have any other music? I'm fed up of Take That.'

Laura smiled. 'Is that what you're hearing? Sorry, Dave. That will be on for a while. You're lucky – my track is "Song Sung Blue" by Neil Diamond.' Dave looked confused. 'They pick a track from the year of your POD – your Point of Decision – and they play it over and over again.' *Point of Decision? What the hell? Oh God, don't swear, for fuck's sake, not even in your head. Fuck.*

31

He composed himself. 'Point of Decision?'

'It's the time in your life when you first made an important decision, of your own accord, that significantly affected another human being. Could be in a positive or negative way. That day is marked by – well, by God – and if you end up in Purgatory, your own personal purgatory will reflect where you slept that night.'

'So my Point of Decision happened sometime when I was on holiday?' He shrugged. 'If you don't mind me saying – how bloody ridiculous! I was ten, for fu— pete's sake! How am I supposed to remember that far back?'

7

The Holiday

Summer, 1992

The atmosphere was frosty when their parents came back to the room from breakfast. David was sulking and melancholy, sorting his Top Trumps into two piles; 'smells of sick' and 'doesn't smell of sick'. At the sight of his mum and dad, Andrew started whimpering again, complaining about his scratches and telling his mum that he thought his back was broken. Ann simultaneously made sympathetic noises to Andrew whilst looking daggers at David. 'We'll pop into town and get some Savlon, Andrew, and then, if everybody *behaves*,' she threw another terrifying stare at David, 'we'll go to the beach.'

The beach. The beach! Suddenly, the world was a better place in which to be a boy. It was as if someone had thrown a candy floss blanket over them. Andrew stopped moaning, sat up and started hunting through his bag for his trunks and inflatable ring, inexplicably forgetting about his horrific injuries. David's fog of guilt and anger suddenly lifted, his head filled instead with the salty promise of towering Cornish waves, gritty sand and rock pools.

Until last year, the Walsh family had travelled to Sidmouth for their summer holidays, every year without fail. Granny Walsh had owned a huge tumbledown Victorian house not far from the seafront, and the family could comfortably stay there for two weeks and not be afraid of making too much mess or noise (as Granny Walsh was fond of both mess *and* noise). Dave and Andrew both loved Sidmouth, with its wide pebble beaches and shops selling fishing nets and magnets, and deckchairs on the prom and mint choc chip ice creams. But Granny Walsh had died in 1990 and the house was bequeathed to the Sidmouth Squirrel Sanctuary, so the boys no longer had their favourite granny or their holiday.

What was left of Granny Walsh's legacy was spread thinly between nine siblings, but it was enough for Colin to buy a new Vauxhall Carlton, and to treat his family to a proper three-star hotel holiday in Newquay. David had loved that holiday. Not only had he been quick enough to claim the top bunk, but the wide, curving, shell-strewn beach was just twelve steps from their room, and David and Andrew spent every day jumping or diving into the rolling Cornish waves.

In fact, they had all loved Cornwall so much (David thought that he saw his mum crying and stroking the minibar in their room fondly just before they left) that every day for weeks after they got back, Colin searched high and low on Teletext for a budget version of the holiday they'd just had. He was about to give up and suggest a day trip to Bognor instead, when Sue had suggested the youth hostel in St Ives. And here they were, almost exactly a year later, arguing and fighting and falling out, just as a thousand families were doing, all over Cornwall.

Two hours later and trip to the chemist done – although Andrew's injuries had all been forgotten since the mention of a trip to the beach – they collected all the beach paraphernalia from the car ('I'll have to come back for the windsock, Colin, I've only got two hands') and walked the 100 yards or so, down the tiny, twisted roads, to Porthmeor Beach. Andrew tried to engage David in conversation, but David couldn't bear to look at his brother, never mind speak to him. How could Andrew have grassed him up? They were brothers, and brothers always supported each other. Brothers in arms. All for one, and one for all.

David scraped his spade along the road as he walked, happily thinking about all the ways in which he could wreak revenge on his brother. Guillotine. Rack. Removing the stickers on his Rubik's Cube. He was so deep in thought with his head down that he didn't hear his mother say softly, reverently,

'Oh Colin, it's beautiful.'

He did, however, hear his brother letting out a yelp of excitement. David looked up to see Andrew dropping his bucket and spade in a heap and running down to the water's edge, kicking up sand and spraying grit over the sunbathers unlucky enough to be in his way.

'CLOTHES OFF!' yelled Ann, as it looked like Andrew was going to catapult himself into the sea fully dressed. But he stopped at the point where the water met the sand, and turned to face the family with a questioning thumbs up. Colin responded with a double thumbs up, shouting 'GO! GO! GO!', and delightedly, Andrew tore off his clothes and ran full pelt into the sea. He was laughing, and laughing, and laughing.

Andrew's delight chipped a little bit of malice from David's thoughts and he couldn't help feeling a little lighter of heart. So he dropped his beach junk, threw off his clothes and shoes and – unashamedly wearing nothing but his pants – ran to the waves to meet his brother.

'Just paddling!' shouted Ann. 'Andrew hasn't got his armbands on.'

By the time Colin and Ann had collected the scattered items and set up camp – a 360-degree windbreak with a small opening towards the sea, inside which were two deck-chairs, towels, books, sun cream, and a bottle of Lilt, buried in the sand to keep it cool – the boys had ventured back from the water, ready for something to eat. They tried to enter the windbreak den but Colin blocked their way. 'Not till you're dry, lads. We don't want you dripping all over your mum's ham and cress sandwiches,' he said, and threw two beach towels at the boys, who were goose-bumped and shivering. They wrapped themselves up and sat on the sand in almost companionable silence, waiting to warm up in the weak August sunshine.

After a short while, a foil-wrapped missile landed in David's lap, and then another in Andrew's. 'Lunchtime!' came a voice from behind the canvas wall. A large hand appeared under the gap between the canvas and the sand, holding two white plastic cups full of Lilt. The boys snatched at them greedily. David drank his in one gulp – he hadn't realized how thirsty he was – and then let out such a large belch that he was sure he propelled himself backwards a little.

'ANDREW!' shouted his mum from behind the screen.

'IT WASN'T ME!' exclaimed Andrew, hurt. 'You always think it's me!' And then, quietly, 'Mine sound different.' David smiled to himself and slowly unwrapped the foil of his sandwich.

They sat in slightly less companionable silence until they had finished the sandwiches of too much marge and not enough ham, and tossed the empties back over the wall. 'OI!' shouted their dad. 'Oooh, Colin, that landed right in my tea,' they heard their mum say.

Best to move out of trouble quickly, thought David. He had an idea.

'Fancy a sandcastle challenge?' he asked his brother.

'Yes, please! Ace!' said Andrew, suddenly animated. He happened to be sitting right next to the biggest bucket and spade, and grabbed them. David's face dropped. Why hadn't he planned this better?

'They won't help you,' he muttered. He was unhappy to be left with the smaller set, but he didn't want to let on. He knew that his superior engineering skills would easily beat his brother's weaker efforts, and already had a complex design in mind.

Gauntlet thrown down, the boys, separately, set to work. David chose his spot carefully, and then made a start. Every so often he would throw Andrew words of advice, like biscuits to a dog, learned from his many long, hard summers of sandcastle construction. 'Wet sand, Andrew, but not too wet. Don't over-pack your bucket. Remember to pat it with your spade to get it out.'

Andrew wasn't listening. He was so happy. He wasn't being car sick. He wasn't being beaten up by his brother. He was just sat in his pants, on a warmish day at the seaside, belly full of curly white bread, ham and Lilt, mucking about with his bucket and spade – bliss. He both under-filled and over-packed his buckets. Some of his castles were only half there, some of them had mysterious extra bits ('lean-to's,' Andrew said to himself). He lay flat on the sand to gouge out his moats, and ate grit by mistake. He didn't care. At one point his mum came and smeared sun cream all over his back, and he barely noticed. He was an artist at work, sculpting, imagining, creating.

Sometime later, after he'd built not only the castle, but also the stables, gatehouse, formal gardens and outer boundary, he was aware of a shadow looming over him. He looked up and saw his dad admiring his build. 'Well Andrew, I never knew you had it in you. It looks like bloody Hampton Court! Ann! Come and have a look at this!'

Andrew looked back at the circular windbreak and saw his mum rise up from the middle of it, stepping out in her flowery swimming costume with matching swimming cap. She gasped. 'Andrew! That is . . . brilliant! Colin! Get the Kodak!' Andrew swelled with pride. The phrase 'Get the Kodak' was only uttered on exceptional occasions, and had never been used in connection with anything he had done before.

At this point, David looked up from his castle – a fine construction, all castles perfectly formed, some decorated with cockle shells, the beginnings of a moat – to see what was going on. He got up, careful not to damage any of his buildings, and walked over to Andrew. Before he could stop it, a small gasp came out of his mouth. He couldn't believe what he saw. It was a masterpiece.

For years afterwards, David would say that what happened next was an accident, pure clumsiness on his behalf, an over-balance, just a moment of childhood klutz. Andrew would claim that David simply couldn't cope with his younger brother's Kodak moment, and that a huge emerald wave of jealousy had risen in his brother, which he just couldn't control. Whether by accident or design, the result was the same – David's leg knocked against Andrew's main structure, and one of the magnificent towers collapsed.

The rest of the family stood in horrified silence for a couple of seconds. David thought he could hear a siren somewhere, but soon realized that the sound was coming from his brother, and it was growing in volume. Andrew's eyes were blazing and David, already regretting his actions, prepared himself for a physical onslaught. But Andrew didn't move towards him; instead he ran, shrieking, to David's perfectly formed castle, looked at David, grinned maniacally and kicked the living daylights out of it. Andrew was so feverish about the annihilation of his brother's work, he created his own sandstorm around him, making him almost invisible within his own sandy cloud.

David hadn't expected such a vehement response. There was a moment where, taken by surprise, he was impressed by the potency of his little brother's reaction. But after a second or two came the realization that his own perfectly built castle had ceased to exist, and David felt cold, clear anger rising inside him.

Colin gave Ann a warning glance, which they both understood meant 'there may be trouble ahead'. Ann cleared her
throat in preparation for shouting; Colin stretched and flexed,
ready to pull the boys apart.

But something unusual happened. Watching David, they
saw him pause, close his eyes and breathe in deeply. His face
wore an oddly thoughtful expression. And most disturbingly,
they both watched while David stepped hesitantly towards
Andrew – who had just about finished returning David's castle
to the ground – with his arm out. Not to hit him, but to shake
his hand. A sign of peace.

'Sorry,' David said, hand outstretched.

Andrew looked at his hand mistrustfully.

'It's just that I damaged yours and you destroyed mine, so
that makes us kind of quits, doesn't it?' David explained.

'Does it?'

'Sure. Shake on it.'

Andrew hesitantly raised his tiny hand and David grasped
it, squeezing hard. Andrew made a small meowing noise and
tried to shake David off, pulling his arm back as hard as he
could. But the more Andrew pulled, the more David squeezed.

Ann was just about to intervene when David let go
suddenly, throwing Andrew off-balance, forcing him to wind-
mill his arms just to stay upright. After steadying himself,
Andrew looked down at his hand which had a clear white
imprint of his brother's grip. He rubbed it gently, willing the
colour to return.

'David!' Ann scolded. She knelt in front of Andrew, kissing
and fussing over him. He was trying hard not to cry, but a

single tear had escaped and ran down his cheek. Ann turned to reprimand David, expecting him to be full of apologies, but was shocked to see that he was just standing there, hands on hips, looking out to sea and smiling.

David's memories after that point were much more vague. He only recalled that the afternoon spun out initially, at least, without a hitch. He had been forced to apologize to Andrew and the boys played together for a while, building a joint sandcastle that wasn't, truth be told, quite as impressive as either of their original creations. There was some kind of drama – he couldn't quite remember what – when Colin and Ann allowed the boys to swim on their own in the sea. David hazily recalled something about Andrew losing his armbands amongst the waves and having to be rescued by Colin. And Colin, not the fittest of fathers, was taken to hospital with chest pains, and was held there overnight for tests.

What David did remember vividly was the next day, having been diagnosed with mild angina and discharged from hospital, Colin saying cheerily to his family, 'Don't worry, everyone! This is what a British family holiday is all about!' and they all vowed to give the beach a wide berth for at least the next couple of days.

8

Purgatory

Dave stared at Laura.

'How do you know so much? About Purgatory, I mean.'

She smiled. 'Partly because I've been stuck here for so, so long, and I've picked up bits and pieces. But mainly because I've read this.' She slung a battered, laminated piece of card filled with close typewriting towards Dave. He looked at it.

'"Purgatory – what to expect".'

'It's worth a read. It will tell you the basics.'

Dave looked at the sheet. The plastic on its corners was peeling and grubby. 'Isn't it due a revamp?'

'Bit tricky. They don't have laminating machines here so it has to be done back down . . . there. Limited scope to do that, I think.'

Dave looked back at the sheet.

Purgatory – what to expect
Welcome to Purgatory! People are dying to get in here!

This is a handy guide which will tell you:

- *What Purgatory is!*
- *Why you're here!*
- *How long you'll be here!*
- *How you're judged!*
- *What steps you can take to help you progress to the next level!*

What is Purgatory?

Purgatory is a sort of holding place where we sort out what will happen to you in the next life. You're here because you've been both bad and good whilst you've been on Earth. Don't worry – you're not alone! Approximately 85 per cent of the human race end up in Purgatory. About 8 per cent go straight to Heaven. And about 7 per cent go to Hell. That's right – the good guys have it!

You'll probably be familiar with your environment. Your personal Purgatory is fixed the day that you arrive at your POD – your Point of Decision. This is a day in your life, typically when you're between seven to ten years old, when you make your first conscious decision that significantly affected another human being. This is the day in your life when judgement kicks off.

Examples of a POD

- *Handing in a lost wallet to a police station*
- *Giving (pocket) money to someone who is homeless*
- *Doing something really horrible whilst on holiday in Cornwall.*

Dave recoiled in shock and he dropped the sheet in horror. 'But how . . .?' he looked up at Laura.

'Ah. Is your POD on there?'

'I'm not sure. I mean – I destroyed my brother's sandcastle. And I hurt his hand a bit, I think, when I shook it too hard.' He paused. 'But is that enough to influence . . .' His words trailed off as he felt a whisper of a memory at the back of his mind. Something about the waves. And his brother.

Something dark.

He shook his head, forcing the jagged piece of memory away.

'Anyway,' he said. 'My POD can't possibly be on there. This is a really old sheet! Used by everyone.'

'I know, Dave. But it changes.' She shrugged. 'You know how people who are still alive—' Dave winced '—are worried about Facebook and Google invading our privacy, tracking us with cookies and personalizing every piece of marketing we read? They've got nothing on Heaven. In fact, I wonder sometimes if Mark Zuckerberg has a direct line to God. It would explain a lot.'

Dave picked the sheet back up and continued to read.

Depending on where you slept on your POD night, you may find others in your Purgatory space. They will have had PODs at a different time to you, so will be experiencing a slightly different environment. For example, they will hear different music, and may have access to other equipment which you won't be able to see or hear. This can be unsettling at first, but you will get used to it.

'Is that why that kid over there—'

'Louis,' Laura interrupted.

'Louis, is that why Louis is watching the wall? He can see a telly?'

'Yes. He was in the same youth hostel with his family when he was nine, and there was a TV in the room then.'

Dave looked gloomily at his surroundings. His room was very similar to how he remembered his room in 1992, but there were some differences. It was bigger for a start, with more beds, and more people. There were no doors. A sad little bookcase sat in the corner nearest him, with some well-thumbed I-Spy books, a stack of *Good Housekeeping* magazines and a Gideon's bible. The same pair of red, black and grey curtains hung by his bed, but when he had drawn them earlier, expecting to see an optimistic flash of sunshine, there was nothing there but peeling cream wall.

He didn't have a TV.

'Christ, I wish I had a telly.'

'Don't say that word, Dave. It will cost you marks. Keep reading.'

Why You're Here

Typical reasons for being in Purgatory include:

- *Not believing in God*
- *Being mean a lot and not saying sorry*
- *Lying and not saying sorry*
- *Murdering someone and not saying sorry*
- *Supporting Chelsea FC*.*

*Joke! This is of course not a reason on its own for being in Purgatory.

> - *Very few people are let straight into Heaven. Maybe nuns and NHS staff and I believe David Bowie had a free pass.*
>
> *We won't cover Hell in this document.*

Dave looked up. 'That's a shame. I'd quite like to know more about Hell as I think I have a reasonable chance of ending up there.'

Laura leaned in conspiratorially. 'I think it's because they don't want to scare us,' she whispered.

'I'm already terrified,' Dave confessed.

Laura nodded. 'I know.'

He looked back at the document.

> *But don't be frightened!*

That was odd. Had that just been added in, somehow? This document seemed to respond to his thoughts. But that was impossible!

> *During your stay you'll have a chance to top up your Heavenly points.*
>
> **Want to touch the hem of God? Top tips to top up your Heavenly Quota!**
> - *Don't swear*
> - *Be kind, patient and loving if there are others in your Purgatory group*
> - *Repent your sins (hint: this is important)*

Christ, thought Dave, before he could stop himself.

Remember – God knows what you're thinking!

CHRIST! thought Dave,

So you'll need to really try very hard indeed.

This was not going to end well.

How Long Will You Spend in Purgatory?

Longer than you can ever imagine!

It will feel like you are here for ever. Purgatory is a punishment, not a holiday. Every minute will feel like an hour, every hour like a day, every day a year. There is not much to do here – you are restricted by what you had in your room on your POD night. If you had a TV, a computer or even Wi-Fi, you are lucky! However, you are encouraged to ruminate on the life that you lived, rather than fill the time playing Minecraft. Remember – truly repenting your sins improves your score.

It will be difficult to keep track of time because time does not exist here. Having said that, you will have plenty of opportunity to increase your score (see next section).

You will not need to sleep or eat or drink or even go to the toilet, because – well, you're dead! Lucky you.

How Will I Be Judged?

God uses an objective marking sheet for judgement. There

is a benchmark number of points that everyone must get before passing into Heaven. We are unable to provide you with the whole document as it is many hundreds of thousands of pages long – however, here are some random examples of how we score people's Purgatory Points.

- Being baptised: +200 points
- Helping an old lady across the road: +2 points
- Giving 10 per cent of your salary to the church: +40 points per annum
- Ignoring someone in need: -11 points
- Stealing a Bazooka Joe bubble gum from Mrs Stokes' corner shop: -4 points.

Dave didn't even raise his eyebrows. *I'm no longer surprised by this*, he thought.

At the end of your 'time' in Purgatory, we add up your score and, if it's over the benchmark, you're in.

How Can You Help Yourself To Move On?
Onwards and upwards! To get to Heaven, keep doing more good things. Think positive. Read the Bible (we've left a Gideon's copy in your bookcase). Do good deeds if you get the opportunity. And most of all – repent!

Questions?
We've tried to cover everything but if you still have questions, be sure to ask Angel Gobe when he pops in to see you.

Dave put the sheet down on his bed. 'Who is Angel Gobe?' he asked.

One of the old ladies piped up from a Scrabble game, 'It stands for Angel Go-Between', she explained. 'He's a sort of middle man – middle angel – between Heaven and Earth.'

'That's right,' the other old lady chipped in. 'He makes sure we're settled in and answers any questions. He's lovely, isn't he, Edie? He looks like that smashing Michael Palin off the telly.'

The one who must be Edie nodded. 'Oooh, yes. Very handsome he is too. And no off-putting wings or anything too celestial. He looks almost human.' She shook the Scrabble bag. 'Do you play?'

Dave was unsure what to say. 'I have played . . . once. I wasn't very good.'

'We'll teach you, won't we, Edes!' said the other woman.

Edie nodded enthusiastically. 'Plenty of time to learn!' Then she turned to Dave and whispered furtively, 'Also, we don't have a dictionary so you can make up whatever you like.' She gestured to her sister. 'She hasn't tagged on yet.'

'I can hear you and of course I've tagged on,' the other lady said. 'I just can't be bothered to challenge you any more. Anyway – I do the same.'

'You do what? You—'

The two old ladies started shouting at each other incoherently, Edie picking up her letters and throwing them at her sister.

'Best let them get on with it,' said Laura. 'They'll blow themselves out after a while.' They left the women chucking Scrabble tiles at each other, and went to sit on Laura's neatly made bed. Proper sheets, Dave noticed covetously. He sat awkwardly, not being used to sitting on women's beds.

'Angel Gobe,' Laura had to raise her voice a bit to be heard over the caterwauling on the other side of the room, 'is a bit like God's HR department. He comes down and visits every so often to remind us what we should be doing. Come to think of it, he usually turns up at around the same time as a new arrival, so he should be here soon.'

Oh goody.

'Before he appears, let me introduce you properly to everyone,' suggested Laura. 'You met Wilf when you got here.' The old man grinned enthusiastically from his chair. 'And over in that corner are Edie and Freda.' The two older ladies, who were sweeping up Scrabble bits, waved absent-mindedly without looking up. 'And finally, there's Louis, watching TV.' Louis turned his head. '*Friends*?' Dave asked. Louis nodded silently and turned back to the wall.

'Poor lad. He's young. What did he die of?' Dave whispered to Laura.

'I'll let Louis tell you himself, when he's ready.' She turned and looked at the two old ladies. 'Those two, Edie and Freda, are sisters. Their POD involved each other – they rescued a man who'd been thrown from a horse. This place was a farm-house then, their family home.'

'What about Wilf?'

'He doesn't talk much, so I don't know much of his story. His POD must have been here but he won't talk about it with anyone – even the sisters. I've got a feeling he might have been evacuated here. He's been stuck here the longest.'

Dave sank back on his bed. He was dead. And this was it. This was the afterlife. A sort of purification holding bay in the guise of a youth hostel he visited when he was ten. It was . . . unbelievable.

'What's the purpose of this, Laura? I mean, why not just send everyone to Heaven or Hell, and skip this bit out?'

'We've talked a bit about that. We reckon that if Purgatory didn't exist, the vast majority of people would go straight to Hell. Think about it – it's a bit like a last chance saloon for people who I guess are essentially good but have . . . misunderstood the rules. Isn't that right, Wilf?'

'EH?' Wilf cupped his ear.

'WE THINK THAT WE'RE IN THE LAST CHANCE SALOON.'

'THAT'S RIGHT. GIVING US ALL A CHANCE TO REPENT. PRETTY DECENT OF HIM!'

'Or her,' muttered Laura.

'Her?' Dave was surprised. 'Do you think God's a woman?'

'I think so. Would a male God give us all a second chance?' she smiled wryly.

9

The Holiday

Summer, 1992

That evening, at visiting time, Ann settled David and Andrew in the hospital ward's family room with cups of warm lemon squash and a big bag of chocolate buttons each. The boys were unusually quiet after the day's excitement, and they sat mutely on the sticky hospital chairs, eyes glued to the TV, chewing their straws. She knelt down in front of them. 'I'm just going to see your dad,' she said, smoothing down Andrew's T-shirt and kissing him, then David, on the forehead. They both gave a small nod and David, leaning alarmingly out of his chair said, 'Mum! You're blocking the telly!'

Smiling, she stood and slipped out, padding down the corridor to the side room where Colin had been given a bed.

She paused at the entrance. A huge window flooded the small ward with golden light. Colin was in the bed in the far left-hand corner, his head back and mouth open, seemingly asleep. He shared the room with two other men, all considerably older, but hooked up to the same wheeled machines.

The man opposite Colin was being kept company by his wife, who was knitting in the chair next to him. The man in the bed closest to Ann was surrounded with his extended family, noisily sharing stories. There was also an unoccupied bed, and Ann took a moment to admire its crisp hospital-cornered sheets. She must talk to someone about how they make the beds so beautifully here.

A nurse appeared by her side, making Ann jump. 'Alright, my love? Need anything?'

'No thanks,' said Ann. 'I'm just here to see . . .' She nodded over at Colin, her eyes brimming with tears.

'I know.' She gave Ann's shoulder a gentle squeeze. 'He's going to be absolutely fine. Doctor's been and he said there's nothing to worry about. We'll just keep him in for observation overnight and, all being well, you can carry on with your holiday tomorrow.'

Ann smiled weakly and turned to thank her, but the nurse had moved on and was already making a fuss of the patient with the knitting wife, propping up his pillows and pouring him a fresh glass of water.

She's an angel, thought Ann, as she sat down quietly in the chair next to Colin, resisting the impulse to lean over and close his gaping mouth. He had a strange blue gown on, open at the front, revealing chest pads and tangled wires that connected to a machine on the other side of the bed.

He must have sensed her presence, because he stirred and turned to look at her.

'Hello, you,' she said.

'Hello, you,' he mumbled. He sat up clumsily.

'How are you feeling?' she said.

'A lot better than a few hours ago,' he said. It was true, she thought. He had colour in his cheeks. 'They say it's just angina. Not a heart attack after all. So I've just got to just take it easy.' He reached out for her hand and brought it to his chest.

Ann felt her whole body relax. 'Thank goodness.' She looked at Colin. 'Perhaps that will teach you to not play the white knight in future.'

Colin smiled. 'What can I say? I'm a superhero! I can't stop myself from rescuing people – it's in my DNA.'

Ann laughed and leaned over to kiss him gently on the cheek.

'You know Colin, today has been really . . . horrible. The boys . . . What David did to Andrew . . . I'm worried that – well, that there's something wrong with—'

Colin navigated his arm through the wires and put his arm around her shoulders, drawing her closer. 'Don't worry, love. I'm sure he didn't do it, or not on purpose anyway. We've got the rest of the week to redeem the trip.' He licked his index finger and held it up. 'And guess what? The weather is set fair!'

Ann smiled and shuffled her chair closer to Colin. They turned their faces to the orange light streaming through the window, and watched the magpies circling, silhouetted against the evening sun.

10

Purgatory

Dave's unexpectedly high-pitched noise, coming from a place of absolute terror, startled the whole room. Standing right next to his bed, looking down at him, was a man wearing slacks, a linen shirt, and a Panama hat. All in white, but with a very colourful tie. An Englishman abroad.

'Hello!' said the man cheerily. 'I'm Agent . . . sorry, Angel Go-Between. Welcome to Purgatory!'

'I . . . er . . . I guess . . . well, thank you.' Dave stared at him. Was this really a genuine, bona fide angel? Standing right in front of him, within touching distance? And they had been right – he *did* look like Michael Palin. The absolute spitting image. And he sounded like him, too.

'Yes, I do look and sound like Michael Palin. No, I am not Michael Palin. You will be pleased to know that Michael is very much alive and kicking and no doubt in the process of writing another hugely successful travel book.' Dave breathed a sigh of relief. Thank God. That WAS good news.

'You're now wondering why I look like Michael Palin.' (*Gosh, that's right.*) 'Well, the truth is, David – and get ready for this, because it's mind-blowing – it's actually Michael Palin who looks like me! The other way around! Do you see?' Dave found himself nodding along. But he didn't see. He didn't see at all.

'You don't see. Fair enough. It was the Angel of the Year competition. God runs it every year, of course. And in 1943 ... well, I don't like to boast, but I'll just say it the once – I WON IT! I'm not sure why – I mean, I knew I was nominated for the work I did in northern France, but I was just one of many –' he suddenly became very interested in the non-existent creases of his shirt, '– and anyway, the prize is to have a human made in your image. And Michael is marvellous, isn't he? I'm so very proud of him.'

'I love – loved – Michael Palin,' whispered Dave, suddenly wishing he was back on his sofa, watching *Monty Python* or *Ripping Yarns*.

'Yes, well, there it is. Who knows? You might very well see him again sometime! In the flesh! Well, not in the flesh, but in Paradise!' He looked down at the clipboard he was now suddenly holding. 'Although it looks like you've got some ground to make up.' He paused and looked straight at Dave. 'No one expects the Spanish Inquisition!' And then he laughed like a drain.

Dave had temporarily lost the power of speech. He suddenly realized that, as well as being frozen with terror, his mouth was open so wide that it was in danger of unhinging itself. At the same time, he was rather impressed by the celestial being in front of him. An angel who looked like Michael Palin and was a *Monty Python* fan?

'Oh, I haven't watched it. I'm far too busy. No, I just knew you'd like it if I said it.'

Dave's face dropped.

'Sorry to disappoint,' Gobe said briskly. 'Now, on to business. You've seen the laminated information?' Dave nodded sadly. 'Any questions?'

'Yes, lots actu—'

'Jolly good, plenty of time for that. Let's just get you settled in. I think Laura's been through the main points with you: you're here because of your POD – yours was rather interesting, gave us all a bit of drama at the time – and now's your opportunity to repent, be good, and pave your own way to Heaven. That's it in a nutshell. You won't need to eat or sleep or go to the loo. You'll probably feel better than you have done for a long time, and you won't ever get ill here. There's not much to do except for . . .' he consulted his clipboard '. . . play board games and cards. Oh – and read the Bible, of course.' Angel Gobe looked like he was preparing to disappear.

'I would like to know one thing, actually, before you go.'

'Ah yes. I thought you would.'

Dave hesitated. 'How did I . . . die? I mean, I was only in my forties, wasn't ill as far as I knew. Did I choke on something? Have an accident in the kitchen?'

Gobe turned to look at him and sighed. 'All right then. Is this yours?' gesturing to the bottom bunk.

'Well yes, I suppose so.'

'Right-o.' Gobe climbed in and lay on the sleeping bag. 'Come on.' He patted the nylon.

'What – get in next to you?'

'Absolutely. Where else are we going to have a private chat?'

Dave climbed in and lay on his side, facing the angel. Gobe's heavenly Palin-face was three inches from his. Dave could feel his breath on his cheek. It smelled of his mum's perfume.

Gobe waved his hand at the people on the other side of the room and their chatter ceased. 'Wow – how did you do that?' Dave asked.

'I thought it,' Gobe spoke softly.

'Is it magic?'

'No. It's just the power of God. I add in the hand-waving thing because I know you humans love it. Bit wizardy.'

'I see,' said Dave, but of course he didn't.

'Now then, David. I fear this will come as a bit of a shock.' He cleared his throat. 'The thing is . . . well, we think you were . . .' he paused, then whispered, 'murdered.'

'MURDERED?'

'I'm afraid so.'

'Holy shi . . .' Dave caught sight of Gobe's disapproving look. 'Are you sure? Who on earth would want to kill me? I've done nothing to nobody.'

'David, I've looked at your judgement sheet and that's not quite true, is it?'

'What do you mean?'

'I mean, there's a looooooong list.' Dave saw the angel look up and to the left, as if he were remembering or accessing something from his mind. 'Working backwards from Time of Death: finding that ring outside Sainsbury's and not handing it in to someone in a position of authority.'

'Ah yes, but . . .'

'Multiple blunders at work blamed on younger members of the team.'

Dave cringed. 'But how do you know about . . .?'

'Helping to carry Mrs Piecroft's shopping home and then stealing that bottle of whisky from her.'

'Now that was different,' spluttered Dave. 'She told me to take a little something.'

'Not a bottle of finest single malt, David! All she had to live on was her pension and she'd been saving up for that for six months.' Dave shrunk a little.

'Do you want me to go on?'

'No thanks. I get your drift.'

'The thing is, David, that most people have done bad things to other people. You might not perceive them as terribly hurtful, but others might. Mrs Piecroft, for example, was very upset for . . .' he was accessing something again, 'two weeks and four days.'

'That's very specific. Did she buy herself another bottle and feel a lot happier?'

'No. She died.'

'What? Because I'd taken her whisky??' Was that tantamount to murder? Or manslaughter, at least.

'No, no – she got pneumonia. Don't worry.' Dave sighed with relief. 'That's not to say that a little drop of whisky might not have eased her passing, though, David.' Gobe flashed him a remonstrative look. Dave noticed how blue his eyes were. Like big, exploding . . .

'You're HIM! You're Michael! From 1992! You made us pancakes!'

Gobe clapped his hands together excitedly. 'Yes, David! You remembered! Clever you!'

Complimented by an angel! Dave puffed his chest up. Things were looking up. But . . .

'Hang on. Why were you . . . why did you visit me? Us? Do you do that to everyone?' He paused. 'You must be *very* busy.'

Angel Gobe smiled. 'No, David, I only visit special cases.'

Dave felt himself swell again. First clever, now a special case!

'Don't be immodest, David. It's unbecoming.' Dave let his breath out in a whoosh. 'The thing is, we knew that your POD was going to be unusual.' Dave made a small noise as if he was about to speak. 'Don't ask questions, David, because I know what you're thinking, and I'll answer them if I can. It's just annoying to be interrupted all the time. OK with you?'

Dave nodded, mute.

'Right, so, we can't see into the future *per se*, but we do have an inkling of what is to come. A bit like looking through a very old window – all bubbly and dirty. We knew that your POD day was going to have a big impact on several people. We also – and I hope you don't mind me saying this, David – we also had a few doubts about you. You carry a lot of . . . fog . . . with you. We thought you might be . . . from the Nethers.'

'Nethers?' Dave couldn't help himself.

'Netherworld. Place of Torment. Abaddon.' Dave frowned. The angel sighed. 'For goodness' sakes – did you not listen in RE? Hell, David. Hell.'

'Sorry, I think I must have misunderstood you. Are you saying that you lot thought I was some sort of . . . demon?'

'You mustn't get offended, David. Some people generate a sort of haze, an opaqueness, so we can't clearly make out what's going on. In these cases I come down and take a little look.'

'You come and "take a little look"? In other words, you came to spy on me?'

'Well, if you put it like that . . .'

'Yes, I do! I do put it like that! You thought I was a demon and you came to spy on me!'

'Well, David, you've got to admit, as a child you had . . . rages. A violent temper. And you come from . . . unusual . . . stock.'

'"Unusual stock?" What on earth . . .?'

'Your mother, David.'

'Mum?' Dave suddenly had a clear image of his mum wearing a pink cardie, lying on the floor in her hallway just after her stroke, her grey hair beautifully set, her panic alarm just out of reach. She'd been there five hours before he'd found her, bewildered and confused. His eyes stung.

'Yes, David. Your mother is – was – a Diabolist.'

Dave's jaw dropped for the second time. Now this was just a step too far. Dave had accepted the fact that he was dead. He was also coming to terms with the fact that he was conversing with an angel who looked like Michael Palin. But being told that he'd been murdered AND suggesting that his own mother – his gentle, kind mother with dementia who had recently moved into Sunnyview Care Home – was a Devil worshipper?

He looked the angel straight in the eye. 'My mother,' he said calmly, 'who as I'm sure you know, is very ill now, is the kindest human I know.' Dave hesitated. 'Knew, I mean. She was brave and resourceful. She nursed my dad when he was ill, never resenting him, even when things got difficult. And she loved me and my brother unconditionally.' He felt tears welling up in his eyes and blinked them back, embarrassed and furious.

'Oh, I don't doubt it! She loves her family. But it appears she also loved the Devil, David. Well – at least, until she married your father. Not her fault, of course. Her parents . . . well, let's just say that they had a love of . . . candles.'

'Granny and Grandpa Cronk? In their terraced house in Dunstable? You have got to be kidding!' His dear old grandparents – Devil worshippers? Dave balled his hands into fists so tightly that he felt his fingernails cut into his palms. This . . . 'angel' . . . was playing him for a fool. The most devilish thing that he had ever seen his grandparents do was to put a bag into their neighbour's bin when theirs was full.

'I know you don't believe it, but it's true, David. Your grandparents came from a long line of necromancers. The Cronk family name is—'

The tiniest of bells rang, somewhere outside of the room and yet inside as well.

'Ah, for whom the bells tolls, amirite? That's for me. Sorry, David, I have to be elsewhere.'

'Hang on!' sputtered Dave. 'You can't just leave! You've just told me that you spied on me when I was alive because you thought I was Damien from *The Omen*, and that my mother's family were all Devil worshippers! As well as the small item of me being murdered! There are things I need to know – what was my Point of Decision? Surely it wasn't to do with destroying my brother's sandcastle?'

Gobe looked impassive, his face perfectly blank.

Dave cranked up the volume a notch and leaned forward, now just a couple of inches from the angel's face. 'And who, might I very politely ask, murdered me?'

Gobe remained calm and still, apart from maybe a hint of a smile at the corners of his lips.

Dave's voice turned sulky, like a child trying to negotiate with a parent who is sticking firmly to their guns. 'The least you can do is stick around to explain a bit more.'

'No can do, my friend,' Gobe touched Dave gently on the shoulder. 'Other fish to fry. Back soon.' And just like that, with a small fizzing noise, the angel disappeared.

11

Dave's Diabolist Grandparents

Dunstable, June 1958

For twenty-eight years, Betty and Eric Cronk were joint Chairs of the Dunstable arm of the First Satanic Society. Betty, a Satanist by marriage, treated their monthly diabolic gatherings as she would any WI meeting: her primary concern was buying enough bread for sandwiches, baking scones with a good rise, and making sure that the loo was clean. Eric took it all a bit more seriously, having come from a long line of largely unsuccessful Satanists. So seriously, in fact, that one afternoon, Betty walked into her living room to find that Eric had pushed the sofa to the edge and painted a pentangle on the floor. At least, Eric thought it was a pentangle.

'I think that's a rhomboid, love,' said Betty, as kindly as she could. Eric's face fell. 'Shall I put the kettle on?' she said, patting his hand lovingly.

In the event, Eric left the rhomboid in place, feeling that the Devil would understand, and anyway – his knees wouldn't take all the rubbing out.

At the monthly meetings, they had tried to do some summoning, of course. But possibly due to the rhomboid, or the fact that they couldn't get hold of any sandalwood and used a piece of balsa wood instead, or maybe due to a hundred other things that weren't quite right, they never seemed to have any success.

The lack of demonic apparitions didn't seem to affect the positive mood of the assembled characters. In fact, Betty often wondered, if they did accidentally summon a demon, what on earth would they do with it? The oddball members of the Dunstable First Satanic Society, she thought, were mostly there for the scones, sandwiches and a break from a lonely life.

Satanists can surprise you. Not really in what they do (the clue being in the name), but in who they are. Gathered on Eric and Betty's sofa for the July meeting was old Miss Plotts from the Post Office (liked to use her stamp heavily but otherwise appeared to be a lovely old lady, hair still peculiarly blonde despite being in her seventies); Dot and Arthur who they'd met at Bridge Club (diabolic at bridge but not in that way); Charlie, Frank and Harold from the local steam railway club ('Damn good with a sooty rag, those three,' Eric had once said to Betty) and lastly, young Jimmy, a seventeen-year-old Mod who just turned up one day and everyone was too frightened to ask where he'd appeared from. He wore a pork pie hat, rode a Vespa and swore. Betty was sure she'd seen him spit once too, in her roses.

Eric and Betty's only child, Ann, had as usual been sent to bed early with cocoa and a hard biscuit. And, as usual, she had gone to bed unwillingly and complaining that she wasn't tired; she was after all eleven years old and practically an adult.

It had been a hot day. So hot that Betty had not worn tights. Eric had wanted to leave the windows open, for 'the breeze', but Betty had said, 'What if the neighbours hear?' and so they were firmly shut. The temperature played havoc with Betty's scones and they lacked their usual bounce.

The air inside the house was still and close when the members started to arrive, and they all commented on it. 'Like an oven,' said Frank, taking off his tie and undoing his top button. 'Sorry,' said Eric, 'it's because of the neighbours.' He gestured next door. 'Don't worry – we've got lollies for later.'

Once everyone had taken a plate of sandwiches and a scone, Betty served tea (Jimmy brought his own home-brew, which had a mysterious green tinge to it) and lit the candles on the rhomboid. Frank, who had smoked a pipe since he was twelve, started to cough, gently at first, but soon he was doubled over, hacking and barking like, well, like a seventy-eight-year-old who had smoked for sixty-six years. The noise filtered upstairs and woke Ann, who had only just got off to sleep.

She opened her eyes and heard calls of 'Get him some water!' and 'Don't worry, Frank, just cough this up and you'll be right' and 'Oh Bets, he's blown all the candles out.' Ann had always been told, very firmly, that she should stay in bed on these evenings, whatever she heard filtering up from down-stairs. These were grown-up dinner parties, and not for children – ever. She was used to waking to the sound of chanting and finding its rhythm so soporific that she would fall back asleep within minutes. But Frank's coughing alarmed her and she was suddenly wide awake, fully tuned into the commotion filtering up from below.

There was a spot on the stairs where one of the banisters was missing, thanks to Eric's sloppy handling of the stepladder when decorating many weeks before. If you crouched on this stair at a certain angle, and the living room door was ajar, you could see a slice of the activity in the room, as well as clearly hear what was going on. Ann had sat there one day when she'd heard her parents arguing in the living room. It transpired that her father had brought home seven dozen eggs that had apparently 'fallen off a lorry'.

'If they'd all fallen off a lorry, Eric, they'd all be smashed to smithers,' her mother had yelled. 'Now get them out of my house!' Through the open door, she had seen her mother slip one of the egg boxes into her apron before pushing the rest towards her father.

So Ann took her place on the stairs, and listened to the coughing subside. When Frank was settled, no one said anything for a while, and there was the occasional sound of cutlery scraping on a plate, or a teacup being placed gently onto its saucer. Then someone said, 'You've outdone yourself this time, Bets. These scones are *heavenly*!' Which was followed by a loud chorus of agreement.

She could just see her father get up, and he 'a-hemmed' importantly.

'Right-ho, everyone. As is usual, we will start by making the sign of the horns to show respect to our Satanic master. All together!' Eric punched the air with his right hand, his index finger and little finger aloft, and his other two fingers tucked into a fist under his thumb. The whole group stood up and echoed his tribute, apart from Frank, whose arthritis meant he couldn't bend his fingers. His resulting gesture looked unfortunately like a Nazi salute. He saw Eric staring at him and looked abashed. 'It's not my fault! I can't bend my fingers!'

Someone pushed the door to, so Ann could no longer see what was going on, no matter how she twisted her head to find a clear view. She briefly considered putting her head through the banisters but rejected the idea, remembering when she had done this aged six and got stuck, and her mother had to use copious amounts of margarine to slide her out. It had taken two weeks of rough carbolic shampooing to get rid of it all.

Ann had just decided to go back upstairs to bed when she heard her father say,

'Everyone! Settle down, please. We have reached number fifty-four in the Diabolic Spell Book.' [rustling of pages of a book] 'Whilst we may not have overtly seen the results of our past spells, I believe that they are lying latent, ready to fire when our Master feels that the time has come!' [mutterings of 'yes' and 'hear hear' and someone saying 'Bets – is that scone going free?'] 'Incantation fifty-four is a protection spell. Betty and I have gathered the necessary ingredients' [cough from someone] 'sorry, and a big thank you to Charlie who brought the hazel stick which he found on his last dog walk – it is a rather marvellous specimen. Betty will now bring in the cauldron.'

Ann shrank back into the shadows as her mother walked into the hall and then disappeared into the kitchen, reappearing almost immediately with their cast-iron casserole dish. It looked heavy.

There were mutterings of appreciation. 'Take the lid off, Bets – let's have a look.' A pause and then a collective gasp. 'Oh Eric!' an old lady's voice. 'Can I give it a stir?' 'No, Mrs P, we've got to do it just like it says in the spell, otherwise it won't work.'

'As usual, Betty has typed up the spell so we can all read it at the same time.' [rustling of paper] 'Betty – have you got the biscuit tin and the whisk? Right then. Everyone set? No, Miss P, we're not doing the Latin this time. I can't get my tongue around it. Not too loud, please, everyone! I know it's exciting but we don't want to wake Ann. Count us in, please, Bets.'

Ann heard a soft, metallic, rhythmic sound – presumably the whisk being drummed against the biscuit tin – and her mother's voice counting in time. 'One, two, three, FOUR.'

And then a collection of low voices chanting.

> *Demonic force of Beleth:*
> *Prince of dark and angel fallen*
> *We, your earthly servants call-en*
> *Commit to you our life-long duty*
> *Our loyalty and faith are absolute-ly*
> *In this life, we follow your spell*
> *To tread our satanic path to Hell.*

A pause. Faint coughing.

'Everyone all right to progress? Mrs P? Good. Again, please, Bets.' The drumming again.

'Incantation fifty-four. Protection of blood relatives against the enemy. Altogether:

> We, *The Nine From Dunstable (near Luton),*
> *Worshippers of Lucifer*
> *Dark Angel and Soon to be Lord of All*
> *Call upon Beleth, mighty and powerful warrior*
> *To protect those precious to us and related in blood*
> *Against enemy forces*

[Her father's voice: 'Wave the wand, Charlie! Wave the sodding wand!']

> *Throughout their lives*
> *Block out intruding eyes*
> *Keep them in shadow*
> *Allow them to continue our work in your shade.*

Silence. A woman's voice, 'Did you feel anything?' 'Well, my cough's a bit better.' There was the sound of muttering and eventually of the lid being returned to the casserole. The door opened and Betty appeared, returning the pot to the kitchen.

With her mother's back turned, Ann gingerly stood up on the stairs, trying to avoid the creakers, which she knew were numbers three, eight and nine. Standing on step seven, she lifted her right leg high and pushed hard on the banister so that she could skip to number ten. But as she did so, in a state of imbalance, something caught her eye and she turned just in time to see a shadow rushing along the wall towards her. Simultaneously, a terrible sadness filled her body with concrete, turning her insides out — she felt it engorging her fingertips and her toes and seeping into her brain. Emptiness and loneliness suffocated her.

She was drowning.

She tried to cry out for her mother but her mouth was dry and her lips seemed sewn together. Her hand lifted from the banister and she desperately clawed to find it again. Her eyesight turned black. She was aware of falling, and the thumping sounds as her body hit stair number three. And then, nothing.

'Annie! Ann! She's coming round, I think. Can you hear me, Annie?' It was her father's voice. He was slapping her face. *Get off*, she thought. One of her ankles hurt. Actually, it hurt *a lot*. She wasn't sure which ankle it was as they seemed to be tangled together. That emptiness though, the darkness — that was gone. She felt light, and alive.

More slapping. She opened her eyes.

'Oh Annie! Thank goodness!' A painful hug from her mother. Stirrings of relief from the assembled crowd.

'One of my legs hurts,' she mumbled.

'Stop slapping her and get some ice, Eric,' ordered Betty. 'Or if we haven't any, use the frozen carrots.' And then, softly, 'It's OK, sweetheart, I think it's just a sprain.' Ann felt her mum gently untwisting her legs and she winced with pain. 'Sorry, darling. Can you tell me what happened?'

'I couldn't sleep so I sat on the stairs for a bit.' Ann looked up. 'I know I shouldn't have, but I listened to you all saying the . . . spell, or whatever it was. And after you'd finished it . . . I don't know . . . I remember a shape rushing towards me on the stairs, and a blackness, and I felt so empty and sad. I think it pushed me, Mum. Or pushed through me. I was so scared!' Miss P gasped. Dot reached for Arthur's hand. Frank's throat rattled. Even Jimmy the Mod made a small squeaking noise.

Eric came rushing in with frozen carrots. 'Did I miss something?' he said.

Her mother was still for a few seconds. 'Beleth,' she whispered, under her breath. 'He came.'

'But I feel fine now, Mum. Good, actually. Apart from my leg. Also my cheeks sting a bit.' Betty looked accusingly at Eric, who shrank back a little.

'Let's help you back to bed, love,' Betty said. Eric stepped forward, gently lifted her up and carried her back to her room.

'Sorry about your cheek,' he whispered, tucking her in. 'I was worried you were . . . you know.'

'I know, Dad.' She yawned. 'Don't worry – I'm fine. I feel absolutely fine.' And she did. She felt splendid. Ann kissed him on the cheek. 'Night night, Dad. Sorry for causing a fuss.'

'Night, sweetheart. Don't you worry at all.'

She closed her eyes, turned over and immediately fell asleep.

Eric looked at her for a moment – what had they done? Something about his daughter – something he couldn't quite put his finger on – had changed. She looked different – older, suddenly. He touched her cheek gently, before turning off the light and walking carefully down the stairs, avoiding the squeakers.

The Dunstable Nine had gathered back in the living room. Fresh tea had been made. Everyone was energized and enthusiastically chattering to each other, and Charlie's cough had miraculously disappeared. Amongst the affray, Betty watched Miss Plotts heave herself out of her armchair and walk slowly over to the wand, which had been left on a side table. She picked it up gingerly, studying it with a beady eye, and Betty thought for a moment that she saw the stick glow faintly red in her hands.

'Everything OK, Miss P?' she asked. Miss Plotts hurriedly put the wand down.

'I just wanted to . . .' but she was cut off by Frank, suddenly at her side.

'The spell – I think it worked, Miss P! I can't wait to see if it's had an effect on my Philip.'

'And my mum!' Dot called out.

'And . . .' And so on. Distracted, Miss P sat back down and joined in with the hubbub. Betty looked down at the wand – just a knobbly old stick resting on a tea-stained table – and wondered if all the excitement had sent her imagination into overdrive.

Eric stood at the door. He had never really thought that any of their spells would work, having always been a bit of a disappointment to his Diabolist parents. The Cronks had worshipped the Devil for hundreds of years; his female forebears had a proud tradition of being burned at the stake, or drowned in village ponds strapped to ducking stools, and his male ancestors had done a lot of gloating about how they could turn rabbits into hares. His mother and father had been revered in their home town of Aylesbury; Eric remembered regular comings and goings of odd visitors, money changing hands and more than once, police at the door. His father's study had been full of 'things' in jars preserved in formaldehyde. His mother had grown unusual herbs which she had burned regularly to ward off 'the old enemy'. It had been a home of smells and drama and, once or twice, accidental kitchen fires.

Eric had managed nothing demonic thus far in his life, yet had come to enjoy the Dunstable Nine meetings as an excuse to massage his fragile ego and to eat Betty's delicious scones. But tonight, it looked like they had succeeded. He knew he should be delighted but the gnawing at his stomach wasn't going away. What in Hell's name had they done?

There were only three more meetings of the Dunstable Nine. The first was full of excitement, story-swapping about relatives who'd had strange experiences on the night of the spell-casting – although Betty was doubtful that anything had actually happened to them given that the stories revolved around 'not wanting her usual cup of tea before bed' and 'suddenly having the energy to go to the pub'. Building on the success of the last meeting, they tried to cast an animal transformation hex on Charlie's gerbil, but it didn't work. Jimmy the Mod thought it was because they didn't use the wand from last time; Betty and Eric had searched everywhere for it, both secretly blaming the other, thinking they'd put it on the fire by mistake. At the end of the evening, Jimmy had excused himself to go to the toilet, and Betty had found him in Eric's study, leafing through his paperwork. He said he was looking for the wand. Betty told him to get out.

The second meeting was less joyful than the first. Betty had told Eric about Jimmy, but Eric had dismissed her concerns. 'He's young and curious,' he said. 'Probably just interested in how a mature man runs his accounts.' Betty thought this was ridiculous, and kept Jimmy within sight at all times. There was still no sign of the wand.

At the third meeting, Ann had, as usual, been sent to bed early. Just as she was falling asleep, she heard the creaker on the stair. Something about the sound of the unfamiliar gait put her on guard, and she glanced at her wardrobe where she had hidden the wand – she wasn't sure why – making sure the doors were firmly shut. Then, without thinking, she rolled out of bed, picked up a pair of 8mm knitting needles from her dressing table and waited behind the door. While she stood there, holding the needles above her head, she reflected that these were not the normal actions of an eleven-year-old girl.

The handle started to turn.

Her father's voice, coming from the stairwell but still loud and clear, made her jump. 'WHAT ARE YOU DOING?' The handle stopped turning and Ann heard a hollow thumping sound, followed by a muffled OOF noise and then, 'I was only . . .'

Jimmy.

An argument ensued, and she heard Jimmy run down the stairs and straight out of the house. Ann rushed to her window to see him rev up his scooter and accelerate away, followed by her father chasing him in his slippers. When he got halfway down the street, Eric collapsed, his hands clasped to his chest. Ann pressed her hands to the window and screamed.

'DADDY!'

Hours later, with both her parents whisked away in the ambulance, Ann was still awake at midnight when the house phone rang. The muffled, low voice of the neighbour, Mrs Perkins, who was keeping an eye on Ann, drifted upstairs. Ann caught the occasional phrase – 'terribly sorry, Betty' 'I won't wake her' and 'I'm happy to stay for as long as you need me.'

Ann pulled the sheets over her head and curled into a ball, hugging her knees to her body.

That was the last meeting of the Dunstable Nine.

12

Purgatory

As soon as the angel disappeared, the murmuring of voices recommenced. Dave could hear one of the old ladies arguing with the other about whether the American spelling of 'color' should be allowed.

'Well, if we're going to allow that, why don't we allow words in German? Swahili? Celtic? Makes a mockery of the whole thing!'

Laura was playing peacemaker, trying to calm the situation. It sounded like she was used to it. Tired of it, perhaps. Wilf sat silently, his eyes closed. It was hard to read his expression, but that might have been because he looked so ancient that his face had fallen in on itself. Louis was still watching the wall, occasionally a faint smile warming his melancholy face.

Dave lay on his back and stared at the familiar underside of the top bunk. It's not every day you find out you've been murdered, he thought. Or that your mum came from a family of – what did he call them? Diabolists? Or that the angel at God's right hand was the image of Michael Palin.

At this point, you might think that Dave's brain would be going haywire, trying to work out who had murdered him out of the five other guests at his brother's dinner party. Or that he might be trying to recover memories of Granny and Grandpa Cronk for evidence of evil doings. Or even, perhaps, thinking back to his POD day to try to remember whether something else happened between him and his brother.

But actually, all he could think about was the day that he stole Mrs Piecroft's cherished bottle of whisky.

13

The Incident Involving Mrs P's Whisky

It had only been a few months ago. A hot, dead evening. He had spent a good forty minutes drinking in someone's armpit on the Northern line and had run out of Wood Green station, gasping for air.

What a terrible day. It had started like every day since Rose left him two weeks ago; his alarm had gone off, and he had reached out to touch Rose's arm, only to find cold bed sheets and be reminded once again that she wasn't there.

Then there was the presentation at work. His boss was at fault, of course. Jim should have known better than to ask Dave to present to the board. He was a software developer, not a candidate for *The Apprentice*. Admittedly, Dave could have practised more and papered over some of those gaping cracks ('So, Dave, how does this process change benefit the company, exactly?' was, on reflection, an obvious question he could have prepared for). Dave's stuttering attempts to answer this and other straightforward questions had drawn disdainful looks from some quarters, and smirks from others. Only Jim's face had remained stony still.

Farewell, sweet, sweet promotion.

He was only 100 yards from his house when, on the opposite pavement, he'd spotted old, round Mrs Piecroft struggling home with two immense shopping bags. She was wearing one of her usual flowery kaftans that threatened to trip her up on every step, and he could hear her panting heavily. He desperately wanted to get home but he and Mrs Piecroft had history; she was a good friend of his mother's, as well as his History teacher at school. So there was only one thing to do.

'Mrs Piecroft! Need a hand?' He crossed the road and waved to her.

'OOF!' she said, as she hefted her bags to the floor. Her face was round and red like a party balloon. 'David! You are a good boy! Always were. Apart from when you stuck that pencil in Alice's ear that time.'

Dave rolled his eyes. 'You bring that up every time, Mrs P! I was eleven years old! Anyway, she deserved it.'

'So you say, David. I'm not so sure.' She paused. 'Well, what are you waiting for? Pick 'em up, my boy!'

It was a short walk to Gloria's front door, but the weather was so close and sultry that Dave could feel rivulets of sweat dripping down his back, soaking his pants. 'Come in and shut the door!' ordered Gloria. 'I've got some squash.'

'Mrs P, I haven't drunk squash since I was eight,' Dave said, flopping onto her Seventies green corduroy sofa which he noticed was covered in crumbs.

'Nonsense! If it's good enough for Roger Federer, it's good enough for you.'

He couldn't argue with this logic, and he took the glass of weak orange squash from her gratefully. 'Just need a wee!' she called, already halfway to the loo. And then, from behind the closed door: 'Not been feeling myself today.'

'Can't stay for long, Mrs P – got to head back and do some work from home.' It was a lie. At that moment, he hated everything about his work. He hated his boss. He hated that project. The team. Even the crappy building. 'I'll put your shopping away before I go.'

'That's kind of you, love,' he heard from the toilet. 'Help yourself to a little something.'

He carried the bags into the kitchen and put them heavily on the worktop, noticing that Gloria's breakfast things hadn't been cleared away. 'You been feeling OK, Mrs P?' he called, methodically putting away the mixed herbs, the salt, the stewing steak, and the packet of fondant fancies.

'No, I told you! Been a bit funny,' came the answer, followed by a long, loud fart. 'I'm on the toilet, so it's allowed,' she called.

'You'll probably feel better after that,' shouted Dave, coming to the final item to tidy away. This was unusual. He gently lifted the small, shining, golden bottle. A beautiful single malt. His mouth started to water. He wasn't usually a big drinker – confined to pub visits only with friends – but today had been a bastard of a day. He just needed a little something to take the edge off this . . . self-loathing. What if he just smelled it? That would be OK, he thought. He would have to break the seal, but Mrs P would think that it was done in the shop.

So he snapped the seal and opened the bottle, bringing the whisky close to his face so he could inhale those bewitching fumes. And before he knew it, the neck of the bottle was in his mouth, and the whisky was burning the back of his throat.

The sound of the toilet flushing broke his reverie. Panicking, he twisted the cap back on the bottle, ran into the sitting room and thrust the bottle in his bag. 'Got to run, Mrs P,' he shouted as he opened the front door.

'Thank you for your help, David,' he heard before he let the door close. 'I'm going to visit your mum next week. Will you be coming to see—'

But Dave had already closed the front door and was running down the street. Something strange had come over him. He suddenly felt different – elated. *HAHA! Silly old woman! I always hated History, anyway*. He ran back to his block of flats at full pelt, sweating profusely, and bounced up the stairs two, three at a time. Once inside with the door shut, he took the golden bottle from his bag, sat in his favourite chair, leaned back and dispatched half of the whisky in three immense glugs.

He wiped his mouth with the back of his hand, feeling the heat of the alcohol settle in his belly. He was tired, all of a sudden. The gentle heat of the evening sun warmed his face, and his eyes closed.

When Dave awoke, hours later, it was fully dark. He reached over to the light switch, fumbling to find it for a moment. As he switched it on, he caught a shadow moving swiftly across his field of vision, right to left. He turned his head to see it properly, but whatever it was, it had gone.

It was cold, but a trail of sweat was lazily running down his forehead and into his left eye. It stung. Foggy headed, it took him a minute to remember what had happened with Mrs P. What had he done? The realization seeped through him and he buried his head in his hands.

It felt like he had stolen from his own mother.

He resolved there and then that he would visit Mrs P the following day with a new bottle of whisky, flowers and an apology.

Of course, he never did.

14

Purgatory

Until now, Dave had successfully managed to parcel up his guilt into a box and shove it high up on to a shelf in a dusty, remote area of his mind. But scratching over the memory of that day catapulted Dave back into full-on abhorrence for his own behaviour. How could he have done such a horrible thing? To Mrs P, of all people?

And was Mrs P, who had died so recently, in her own version of Purgatory now? Or maybe she'd be sent straight to Heaven? Unlikely, as she'd never mentioned God or the Church and in her youth had done some 'dubious' things in the name of the Croydon Trotskyists and nuclear disarmament (he never found out what, exactly). He hoped she was somewhere nice, and that there was plenty of whisky and ice for her to enjoy.

He felt something sharp and salty again in his left eye, a tear this time. It quickly bubbled over and ran down his cheek, then on to his cotton sheet.

THE PURGATORY POISONING

'I'm sorry, Mrs P,' he whispered.
A light fizzed on God's switchboard.

15

Heaven's Hub

'Isn't there anywhere else we can go, Arial? It feels like we're being spied on.'

Gobe and his apprentice, Angel Arial, were in Heaven's Hub, standing beside an apparently infinite vertical bank of light bulbs, which stretched higher and wider than either of them could see. Most were illuminated. Some blinked on, or off, as they watched.

Heaven's Hub was enormous, of course. I mean, not just horizontally – think of a cross between a warehouse and an eighteenth-century ballroom – but vertically too. It wasn't exactly white, but a palette of whites and soft golds, silvers and greens. There was no visible ceiling.

God's switchboard covered one wall. Rows and rows and rows of small light bulbs with gold fixings, rising as far as even an angel's eye could see. This was where all of human life was monitored, interpreted and answered if the occasion called for it. To you or me, the flashing lights would make no sense; even the finest codebreakers in the world, given infinite amounts of time and tea, wouldn't come anywhere close to cracking the cipher. They might be able to tell, eventually, that one gold illuminated light represented a human prayer. And they might possibly conclude that two gold lights lit up next to each other represented a minor human action that had an impact on the individual's afterlife. And if they were at the top of their game they *might* be able to tell that three lights of a certain colour depicted a major action that would have a significant effect on what happens to humans after death.

But there was no way they could deduce that a single white light was a thought, a feeling – even a dream – registered by Heaven and stored, ready for judgement when the time came. And that a complex and quick succession of lights represented a myriad of pathways; thought, deed, thought, feeling, deed.

Human beings were complex creatures and it needed the most complex of systems to keep an eye on them. This was it: the spy centre of the universe.

The two angels that Gobe was referring to were Facility Angels called Zaqiel and Penemue, two of Heaven's oldest angels. Facility Angels were caretakers of the bulbs on God's switchboard. It was their very important role to fix any faults or issues (like occasional burnout), and to dust and polish and generally keep the switchboard in tip-top working order. They had enormous, powerful wings to help them reach even the highest lights on the board; their flying skills were legendary, and at the Angel Olympics, held every hundred Earth years, they unfailingly won gold halos in all the airborne sports.

Zaqiel and Penemue were standing not far from Arial and Gobe, whispering to each other, their huge wings at rest. Occasionally they looked up at the other two, and then whispered some more.

'Couple of old gossips. Haven't they got anything better to do? Like DO THEIR JOB?' Gobe barked the last three words loudly. The two other angels suddenly broke away from each other and flew off vertically, high up the switchboard, busily immersing themselves in important bulb-polishing duties.

Gobe turned back to Arial and hissed, 'Houston, we have a problem.'

'Did you know, sir, that the original quote from the spacecraft was "Okay, Houston, we've had a problem here," but that it wasn't snappy enough for the film, and so—'

'Yes, yes, Arial. Please save your Wikipedia lesson for later when we've both got nothing better to do. Listen – I got the report about the murder. David Walsh. Remember?'

'Of course, sir! Three emerald lights on the board.' Arial took particular interest when green lights showed up on the switchboard; they always meant foul play. Instances of three green lights together – signifying murder – were unusual and Arial, with his analyst's brain, remembered every single one of them.

'Good. Well, I've watched the playback and I can't see the murderer. In fact, I can't see anything. It's completely fogged.'

Arial rubbed his hands together. If there was one thing he loved, it was a mystery. And a murder mystery to boot. 'Let me take a look, sir. It probably just needs some adjustment.'

He closed his eyes for a moment and Gobe watched his face twitch subtly. He was getting pretty good at this.

Arial was an apprentice Switch Angel, working under Gobe who had now really moved into the people-management area of Switching, as well as running Purgatory. Less hands on than he used to be, and by God he missed it some days. Switches were highly skilled – the only angels in Heaven who could interpret the complex coding of God's switchboard. They had no wings and so couldn't fly, but they had incredible sight, able to see bulbs thousands of feet above them. They could also feel vibrations from the switchboard through their bare feet, giving them additional insights and further helping their analysis.

But a great Switch was not all technical aptitude and no socks. To be a fully rounded Switch you needed to have natural empathy with, and interest in, the human race. This couldn't be taught – you had it or you didn't – and Arial had it in spades. He had many human obsessions and fascinations, including medieval weapons, steam travel and, above all, Eighties cop shows.

This level of insight, combined with his technical know-how, vast personal computing power and Gobe's hands-on mentoring meant that Arial was one of the best Switches around. In fact, he had long surpassed Gobe in many of his Switch abilities. And what he was particularly good at, was Playback.

Switches could replay scenes from Earth that had already happened. Apart from God, they were the only entities who could do this, and were therefore in great demand. Arial's To Do list was enormous, but when Gobe asked him to do something, he knew better than to say no.

As Arial concentrated on his task, eyes now open, a three-dimensional scene appeared between them. It was milky, like looking through a steamed lens. First, a kitchen scene where a woman with long golden hair surrounded by cooking carnage was slopping food onto six plates. Arial flicked his wrist and the scene moved to the dining room, where they could just about make out five other people sitting around a table, talking.

Gobe tapped Arial on the arm and gestured to Zaqiel and Penemue, who were now hovering within spitting distance, their ears quivering for gossip, then gently pulled Arial around so that their bodies hid the scene from the two other angels.

'Can you see?' Gobe said, leaning so far into the scene that his head actually became part of it. 'It completely mists up around about . . . here.' He fast-forwarded the players to a point where the woman in the kitchen was bringing the plates through to the dining room, where the scene blanked, as if someone had videoed a piece of white card.

'So it does,' said Arial. 'That's odd. Does it stay like this the entire time?'

'Right until after his death. Then it lifts.'

'Hang on, sir.' Arial strode over to his podium; a small, movable stand-up desk with sides, like a tiny choir stall. It was covered in golden knobs and levers, numbered buttons and what appeared to be a small millwheel on the side. Gobe had once asked Arial what this was for and Arial had replied, 'nothing – I just like the look and feel of it' – a perfect answer for a Switch.

Arial wheeled the little podium over, its castors squealing

on the marble floor. He stood inside it, facing the misty scene, and started pressing buttons. Gobe noticed that as he did so, his mill wheel started to turn. Neat. He must remember to refer to that when writing his next report.

'What is it, Arial? The interference? It's all around David, like a heavy coat.'

Arial continued to tune his knobs and whistles and said nothing. Gobe thought he hadn't heard.

'Arial. ARIAL. I need to know. Is it . . . Him?'

Arial knew who he meant.

'Can't really say at this stage, sir. It's highly unusual, certainly. Could just be an electromagnetic spike.' He walked around the projection and scratched his chin. 'Let me see what I can do with it, clean it up a bit.'

'"Clean it up a bit?" This isn't CCTV, Arial. Have you been watching *The Bill* again?'

Arial blushed.

Gobe continued. 'Now don't get touchy, but I have to ask – are you absolutely sure it was murder? Perhaps the switch-board is faulty?'

Arial looked horrified. 'The switchboard faulty? *God's* switchboard? Not possible, sir. The way it was crafted, how it is maintained . . .' he glanced up at the Facility Angels, who were pretending to dust. 'It's as perfect now as the day it was created.'

Gobe looked at the vast switchboard. It really was impressive. Looking a touch retro these days, yes, but it had been telling the truth for thousands of years and he supposed there was no reason for it to be going haywire now.

'So, our five dinner party guests are all suspects. I'd like to be briefed on them all.'

Arial brought a small notebook out from under his robes and took a pen from his breast pocket. Having a breast pocket sewn into angel robes was quite a statement.

'Can you go back to when everyone started arriving?' Gobe asked.

Arial made a swooping gesture with his hand and the scene rewound to a static picture of an empty hallway in a large Victorian house. Gobe said, 'Before we start, remind me how the guests know each other?'

Arial paused, retrieving information.

'So – we've got Andrew, David's younger brother.'

Gobe nodded. 'There's just two years' difference, isn't there? That would make him thirty-five when his brother died. And who else?'

'There's Rose, David's ex-girlfriend. She's a musician. A cellist.'

'A cellist? How wonderful. Although – and I am trying not to stereotype here, Arial – I can't see a cellist in a romantic relationship with David, can you?'

'Perhaps that's why they're not together any more, sir.'

'Hmm – perhaps. Who else?'

'Ian, Rose's current partner. He's a bit . . . well, let's just say that I don't like the look of him.'

Gobe raised his eyebrows. 'It's not our place to judge, Arial. There's a time and a place for that and it's not now.'

'No, sir. Sorry, sir.'

'That's quite all right. Then there's Jess, isn't there? I seem to remember . . .' Gobe scratched his chin. 'An old friend of the brothers. Their mothers were close when the boys were young. Jess is an artist now, I think? Fond of wearing black. And lastly . . . what's the host's name again? Hannah?'

'That's right. A friend of Rose, I think – she got to know David and Andrew through her.'

'Thank you, Arial.' Gobe turned to the paused scene in front of him. 'Watch it with me, please. Make sure I don't miss anything.'

'Yes, sir.'

At first, it was like watching an episode of *Through the Keyhole*. They were viewing through the lens of a celestial drone camera, initially flying at first-floor level outside the front of the house, and then diving through the seemingly fluid front door.

'This is a fair-sized house for this area of London, Arial. Must be worth a fortune. Did you say this was Hannah's?'

'Her parents', actually. Her dad's ill. Her mum's away, I think – Sorrento.'

Gobe smiled nostalgically. He loved Sorrento. When was it he was working around there? AD 79. Some volcanic disaster. Terrible mess. Mind you, the lemons there were to die for.

He drew his focus back to the scene. As his thoughts settled, the volume rose within the tableau and they heard the doorbell. A girl in a long, flowing white dress answered the door. She looks angelic, Gobe thought. 'That's Hannah,' Arial said.

'Does she have any . . . celestial connections?' Gobe asked.

'Not to my knowledge. She looks different though, doesn't

she? Something unusual about her. She's got a lovely way of walking.'

Way of walking? What a strange thing to say. Arial was right though. She had an unusual gait: flowing, gliding, minimal.

'Shall I do the full background check?'

'Yes. And please stop using terminology you've picked up from *Line of Duty*. Honestly.'

Arial coughed. 'Sorry. It's just that I've heard you sometimes call yourself Agent Go . . .' he tailed off as he noticed Gobe's eyes burrowing into him. 'Right. Sorry, sir. Level Two *Tessera iudicium* as follows.' He closed his eyes.

'Hannah Taylor. Born 1986, currently thirty-three. Baptised early – lovely Christening photos by the way – standard upbringing, church school, blah blah blah. Positive Point of Decision – helping an older couple fix their tent after a night of heavy rain at a campsite in Pembroke.'

'Yes, yes, this is all very fascinating, but can I just have the relevant info? Pertinent to the murder, I mean?' Gobe saw Arial flinch and checked himself. He was unusually irritable today. 'So sorry, Arial, I don't mean to be snippy.' He pulled at his collar. 'This little scenario has me a bit rattled.' He patted his fellow seraph on the shoulder. 'You're a good chap.'

Arial, not used to his boss suddenly being so brusque, and then so apologetic, felt himself momentarily at a loss for words. He wondered whether Gobe was feeling all right. Then, realizing that Gobe could tell exactly what he was thinking, he quickly shook the thought off. 'Thank you, sir. I'll be as quick as I can.' He closed his eyes once again.

'So . . . Hannah knows David through his ex-girlfriend, Rose. Hannah and Rose met fairly recently – we don't know how. In fact, we don't know much at all about Hannah.'

Gobe was silent. There was something about Hannah that was familiar, something he couldn't quite put his finger on. If he could only—

Arial interrupted his thoughts. 'Hold on. There's something strange here. I can't seem to tap into . . .' His hands and body started to shake, and he suddenly opened his eyes. They were wide and glassy.

'What is it?' asked Gobe. He touched Arial's sleeve.

'I can't go any deeper with Hannah. There's a huge Block, a wall. It's beautiful but . . . slippery. It's impossible to get over it.'

'What? Let me try.' Gobe knew it was a long shot – Arial was the best analyst they had. But he'd been a pretty good Switch himself back in the day, so perhaps, given a different technique . . . 'You take a look at the others whilst I'm gone.'

He closed his eyes and dived in to Hannah, looking for all connections to David or to any of the other guests. He travelled through her working life – some sort of office – her pub trips, a weekend to Menorca with friends, gym trips, cycling . . . but every time he tried to approach her connection to David, he was faced with an enormous obstacle. It reminded Gobe of a huge inflatable slide, the kind that has bumps in it and foam tumbling down it, higher than he could see.

Throughout his long life he had occasionally come across Blocks like this. They were not common because the skill needed to place one in a human history was immense. Blocks were used to hide information and were tools used by both sides, for camouflaging motivations or even cloaking actions, if the Block was sophisticated enough. A long time ago, he'd been involved in an operation to unravel the Block of a demon who had attempted to cover up his misdoings in order to visit his sister in Heaven. They'd successfully breached that particular Block, but much of the time, if placed correctly, it was difficult to find a weakness and a way through. The Block placed in Hannah was unfortunately well conceived and beautifully constructed. He tried every mental gymnastic trick he could think of to get round it, through it, over it. Everything failed. It was impenetrable.

Gobe opened his eyes. He felt something salty on his top lip. Sweat? That was new.

Arial was staring at him, concerned.

'You're right, Arial. It is well placed.' He paused. 'How did you get on with the others?'

'I've looked at them all. Rose and Ian are fine. Their playbacks are, with one exception, pretty much normal. But Andrew, Jess and Dave are full of Blocks – different to Hannah's, more rudimentary, and stretching all the way back to when they were children together. These Blocks aren't beautiful, sir – not like Hannah's at all. They're sinister and a bit . . . well, they're unnerving. If you get too close to them, they feel unbearably hot. And . . .' Arial struggled to find the right word '. . . cruel.'

Gobe conjured a small white dining chair from the air and sat down elegantly, crossing his legs.

'Go on,' he said.

'And the weird thing is, although Rose and Ian are generally pretty normal, whenever their lives intersect with either Jess's, Andrew's or David's, they become inaccessible, too.'

'Show me,' said Gobe. Arial nodded and pressed a large orange button followed by some smaller yellow ones and finally pushed a slider thing upwards. The scene in front of them changed. Rose and Hannah appeared to be in a restaurant waiting for Jess to arrive. When she finally showed up, she took off her coat, hung it on the back of her chair, and bent to give Hannah a kiss on the cheek. As soon as she did this, the screen fogged and they could see no more.

Gobe sighed and shook his head, puzzled.

'One more,' said Gobe, and Arial's fingers skittered over the buttons once again, bringing up a scene with Ian, drinking on his own, in a pub. He was sitting nervously in a wing-backed chair by a log burner set in a large stone fireplace. Brass ornaments hung around it. There was no one else about except for the bartender who, Gobe noticed, was helping himself to a double whisky. Dave appeared from another room, having to duck under a low, beamed door. He looked around the room and saw Ian, who had his back to him. Dave asked the barman for 'one of those whiskies that you're having' and he walked stiffly over to Ian, sitting down in the chair opposite. As they started to talk, the sound stuttered and blurred, and the scene misted up. By the time Ian had finished a sentence starting, 'Thanks for coming, Dave', Gobe and Arial were watching a blank, silent screen.

'Fascinating. When was this?' Gobe asked, leaning forward,

still staring hard at the screen despite it showing and telling nothing.

'About a week before the murder.'

Gobe sat silent for a while, and Arial knew better than to interrupt. He was used to Angel Gobe's thinking sessions. One time, Gobe was thinking for so long that Arial managed to watch a whole series of *Columbo* before Gobe was ready to speak again.

On this occasion, Arial pretended to busy himself with his manuals, and he got one out from under the desk that he'd been studying earlier – 'Practical Wireless for the Car Radio'. He'd just got to a good bit about dual conversion receivers when Gobe broke his silence.

'Two things, Arial. One: that meeting between David and Ian is fishier than a cat's bowl that hasn't been cleaned for a week. And two: these Blocks. They're coming from two different sources. Hannah's is beautiful, elegant, refined. The Blocks in the others are rough and jagged and I don't like the look of them one bit. But the strangest thing, Arial – I've got this really peculiar feeling that I've seen them before.'

'There was one other thing, sir,' said Arial, appearing not to hear. 'I saw it when I was looking at Jess.'

'Go on.'

'I think you already know that Jess's mother – she's called Elvis, by the way – was friends with David and Andrew's mother, Ann; that's how the three of them met. The history is scratchy, opaque – but the two mums definitely met up regularly at each other's houses.'

Elvis? 'Well?' said Gobe. 'What happened when they met?'

'I can't see. They drew the curtains.'

'Figuratively "drew the curtains"?'

'No, sir – I mean they would go into the house and always draw the curtains in every room. From that point I couldn't get in to see any more.'

'So the act of closing the curtains formed a Block against us? Against the light?'

Arial nodded. 'It looks that way.'

Gobe sighed and put his head in his hands. 'I think I'm having my first headache. Is this how it feels?'

'Would you like me to find you some . . .' Arial searched for the word, 'paracetamol?'

'Don't be ridiculous.'

Arial perched awkwardly on the side of his podium.

'Are you going to tell God?'

'Of course.' A short pause. 'Maybe.'

Gobe sat thinking for a minute. Arial sat next to him, quiet and unsettled. He had never seen his master so rattled before.

Without warning, Gobe sat bolt upright. 'Arial,' he said brightly, 'I have a plan. And this is it. I will go and talk to God. While I am doing this, I want you to flex that bulging analytical muscle of yours – do all that you can to draw out any information about the relationships between these people. Because knowledge, dear boy, is power. And after we have gleaned all that we can, then . . . well then, I'll come up with another plan.'

'So basically, your plan is for me to get on with my job.'

'For now. Let me see your To Do list. Actually, don't. Drop

everything else. I feel that this, whatever it is, is the ugliest challenge we have faced for a while. I can't see David clearly. I can't see the murder. I don't know who did it. And I've got to tell God that I haven't a clue what's going on.'

16

Ann and Elle

In the spring of 1990, two years before the holiday to Cornwall, Colin – David and Andrew's dad – had found a new job selling bathroom suites in Croydon, so the whole family upped sticks to be closer to his work. 'The opportunities for selling bathrooms are better for me in Croydon, boys,' their dad had told them enthusiastically. 'And you know what opportunity means – more toilets, more treats!'

Their new home was a Seventies box with a brown front door and a flat brown front lawn, and it sat amongst other similar boxes on an endless brown housing estate. Ann hated it but tried her very best to look on the bright side. She could paint the door, water the lawn, and she was sure the neighbours would be nice once she got to know them – even if they had refused to answer the door to her so far. And a big plus was that St Mungo's Church of England Primary School, one of the best in the area, was just a ten-minute walk away.

It was the first day of the new September term, and Ann

was struggling. Colin had left early ('Might not be home for tea, love – got a multiple bidet bite in Bromley'). The boys, having seen none of the promised treats all summer, were in foul moods. David, aged eight and perfectly able to dress himself, had put his jumper on back to front and had tied his shoes together. Andrew, aged six, had hidden his school uniform in the kitchen bin the night before, only discovered after Ann had covered it with the remains of the morning's porridge.

Eventually, Ann managed to herd the boys to the school gate, Andrew in his crusty jumper and David with one shoe on and dragging the other behind him. David was picking up conkers and alternately putting them down his pants, then into his mouth, to 'keep them safe'; Andrew was crying, waving a huge stick around and shouting that he 'wanted to stab everyone lots and lots to death'. Ann was trying to laugh this off whilst simultaneously hissing at Andrew to keep quiet and foraging around in David's pants and mouth to clear him of nuts.

The bell went to signify the start of school. All the other parents had left, except for one mother who had just come back out into the playground. Ann could feel her eyes pricking. 'Andrew – shush, please – put that stick down – David, you'll choke, give me the—'

'Want a hand, love?' said the woman. She held out a hand. 'I'm Jess's mum. I think she's in . . .' she looked at the two boys, '*his* class.' She pointed at David.

Ann shook her hand enthusiastically. 'I'm Ann, and I'm at the end of my tether. Thank you so much . . .'

'Elle.' Elle moved closer. 'Actually, my full name is Elvis. Please don't tell anyone.'

Ann could have hugged her. 'Elle . . . thank you. You're a lifesaver. Can you take this one in for me?' She looked at David, whose hamster cheeks were filled with conkers.

Elle knelt down to face David. 'Now then – David, isn't it? Can you spit your missiles at me? See if you can reach me.' She started backing towards the classroom door. 'Come on, hit me with them!'

David couldn't believe his luck. Being ordered to spit conkers at an adult? Brilliant! Out they came, along with lots of child-goo: POP POP POP POP POP.

'That's it, David. Almost got me there. Come a bit closer . . .' She'd just backed over the school threshold. 'Tiny bit more – AGH! YOU GOT ME!' David was now in the building. 'All missiles launched? Well done! Have a great day.' She shimmied past David who, having lost all his mouth nuts, was ferreting in his pants for more ammo.

'He's all yours!' Elle called to the nearest teacher, Mrs Armstrong, who at 8.50 a.m. already looked persecuted. Elle swiftly closed the classroom door and trotted into the playground to meet up with Ann, who had successfully managed to snap Andrew's stick in half and drag him into his class by his sleeve. She could still hear his wailing as she walked briskly back through the school gates with Elle.

'Are you OK?' asked Elle.

'I'm all shook up.'

Elle grimaced.

'Sorry' said Ann. 'Thank you so much for your help. Come back to mine for a cup of tea?'

Elle smiled. 'Love to,' she said.

They walked the half-mile or so back to Ann's house. Ann saw Elle look around, eyebrows raised, at the identikit houses, built from sandy brick, with frontages half covered in vertical dark brown tiles, small bay windows with white scalloped edges, beige garages. Marigolds and roses in the front gardens. Tidy and neat, neat and tidy.

Before Elle could comment, Ann jumped in. 'So,' she said, as they approached the front door. 'I've got to ask. Why Elvis?'

Elle sighed. 'I'm a massive fan, always have been. When I was seventeen, I changed my name by deed poll.'

'Who were you before?'

'Brenda.'

Ann smiled, thinking she was joking. Elle's face clearly showed she was not. Ann hurriedly let them in and they took their coats off, Ann hanging hers up carefully on one of the hooks in the hall, and Elle throwing hers on the stairs. 'Life's too short for hooks,' she said, with a wink.

Over the next hour or so, they drank numerous cups of tea and made their way through half a loaf of homemade banana bread that Ann had been saving for the boys. They talked and talked about their families, and holidays, and previous lives. Before they knew it, it was lunchtime.

'Want to stay for a bite to eat?' said Ann, opening the fridge door. 'I've got . . . curly bacon gone green at the edges and some suspicious-smelling chicken slices?'

'You make it sound so appealing,' said Elle, 'but I've got a better offer at the dentist.' She opened her mouth and pointed to somewhere near the back. 'Rotten to the core.' She smiled, then winced. 'Could do tomorrow though? I'll bring my own soup.'

They met again at Ann's for lunch the following day, and then at Elle's for elevenses the next. Her house could not have been more different to Ann's. Elle lived in a red-brick Victorian end of terrace, with peeling window frames, and a huge magnolia tree in the front garden, its buds so close to the house that they tapped on the windows when the wind blew. Her front door was black with a large, rusty knocker in the shape of some sort of – Ann squinted at it – troll?

'Like it?' asked Elle. Ann nodded. She really did.

Inside, it was dark but cosy. The magnolia blocked out much of the light, but irregularly spaced table lamps gave out a comforting glow. A shabby green velvet sofa was draped with old blankets and an old wicker chair, full of holes and blackened in places, sat by an open fireplace. In the kitchen, shelves were filled with glass jars full of herbs and condiments and cereals and some other things that Ann didn't recognize. A huge, tarnished copper kettle stood proudly on a gas stove.

Instinctively, Ann let out a little whistle.

'Bit different to your place, isn't it?' Elle said, smiling.

Ann drank it all in. 'It's wonderful,' she said. 'I'm jealous. It's so . . .'

'Witchy?' Elle asked. Ann looked at her. 'It's all right,' said Elle. 'That's the look I'm aiming for. I've always had an interest . . .' she waved at the bookshelf in the corner, which was crammed with books on witchcraft and wizardry '. . . but have never really taken it seriously.' She looked at Ann. 'I'm not a crackpot or anything, Ann. I've never done spells. Ha!' She snorted, as if it was the most ridiculous idea. 'As if!'

The kettle started to whine. Ann had known Elvis no time at all, but there was something about her – she felt comfortable in her presence, and safe.

'Well, it's funny you say that, but I've had some . . . experience with witchcraft,' she said slowly, carefully. *Do it*, she thought. *You've been longing to tell someone your whole life.*

'Really?' Elle took the kettle off the hob and opened one of the glass jars, picking out teabags and placing them into large red mugs. 'I hope you don't mind me saying, but you don't look like someone who is interested in the dark arts.' Elle was right. Since her mum died, Ann had tried to hide it, forget about it.

Elle opened a cake tin, revealing a tea loaf. She hit it with a knife, making a strange metallic sound as if she'd hit a steel pipe with a spanner. She shrugged apologetically. 'Cake making is not my forte.' Elle took out a bread knife and started sawing. 'But witchy stuff – that's a different matter. Love potions, curses, voodoo dolls – what I'd have given to be able to cast a decent spell at various times in my life. And covens. I like the idea of covens. Women getting together and cooking round a pot. Sharing recipes. Also cats – I'm a big fan of cats. And hats. Pointy ones.' She handed Ann the slice. 'Mind you don't crack your teeth on it.'

Ann accepted it gratefully and unsuccessfully tried to break a piece off using brute force. 'Thing is,' she said, resorting to sucking the cake like a boiled sweet, 'my parents . . . well, there's no easy way to say this . . .' She looked at Elle uncertainly. She suddenly felt a bit unwell. 'Thing is, Elle . . . they worshipped the Devil. They were Satanists.'

Elvis put down her tea abruptly and her jaw slackened. 'Really?' Ann could see a solid lump of cake in her mouth.

'Yes.' And then, in a rush, 'They weren't very good. In fact, we think they only ever managed to conjure one spell that worked.'

'Reeeaaallly?' Elvis was actually drooling. 'That's amazing!'

'Yes.' Ann hadn't expected such a positive response. 'Um . . . do you want to see their stuff?'

Elle jumped up and grabbed her jacket. 'Do I? I haven't been this excited since Elvis's Comeback Special. Can we go to yours now?'

Leaden loaf cake abandoned, the two women made record time to Ann's house. Once in the house with the door shut, Ann immediately drew the curtains. All of them.

Elle watched curiously. 'Why are you doing that?' she asked.

Ann paused. 'I'm . . . I'm not quite sure,' she said. Why *was* she closing the curtains? 'It just seems like the right thing to do.' She shivered suddenly.

'Someone walk over your grave?' asked Elle.

Ann nodded, but it was more than that. 'I suddenly feel a bit . . . haunted. No, not that. More . . . hunted,' she said to Elle. 'Do you feel it?'

Elle shook her head. 'I just feel a bit hungry,' she said. 'And mildly pre-menstrual.'

Ann smiled, and shrugged. 'Perhaps that's what it is,' she said. 'Stay here – I'll pop up into the loft and see if I can find the box.'

Ann disappeared into the attic and after a lot of shuffling and scraping, brought down three large, stained cardboard boxes. She set them down on the sheepskin rug. Elle, sat in Colin's recliner, was the opposite of reclined. She could barely contain herself.

'What's inside?' she said, straining forward.

With some difficulty, Ann opened the first box and brought out a large glass jar with an ornate stopper. It was half full of something green and dried. She looked at the faded label, written up in a calligraphic hand.

'Desiccated . . . something. Can't read it.' She handed it to Elle, who took it as if she was receiving the Holy Grail. Reverently, she took off the stopper and gave it a sniff.

'I'm not getting anything.' She looked disappointed.

'Seriously?'

'If anything, it smells a bit like my mixed herbs from Kwik Save.'

'That's probably exactly what it is. I wouldn't put anything past my parents. They had a knack for suburban sorcery.'

Ann carefully unpacked the boxes on to the living room carpet, rug, shelves – anywhere they could find a space. Within an hour, they were surrounded by glass jars of all different sizes, most of which looked like they contained supermarket herbs, but some were more interesting: 'Bat Poo', read one label, although the jar had only the tiniest brown ball-bearing in the bottom; one said 'Eagle Feathers', but plainly contained pigeon feathers, probably found in the garden; another was 'Witch's breath' (Elle opened it, turned it upside down and gave it a shake – 'Bloody empty,' she said, disappointed. 'Doesn't even smell of witches.')

'Blimey – no wonder this one was so heavy,' said Ann, as she lifted her mum's orange cast-iron casserole dish from the final box.

'Was that the cauldron?' Elle was fast becoming disillusioned. 'It's a bit small. And not very black.'

'They made do with what they had,' said Ann absent-mindedly, rummaging around. 'We're missing the most important bit.' She opened the lid of the box wider to allow in more light. 'It must be in here somewhere.' She took the box over to the window. 'Come on . . . Where is it?'

'What are you looking for?' asked Elle, hoisting herself off the recliner and joining Ann by the window.

'The wand. Well, a stick that my dad's friend found. I think it's the one remotely magical thing they ever used. And now it's disappeared.'

'Maybe it got thrown away. If it was just a stick?'

'Possibly. But I was so careful with it.' Ann was running her finger around the inside edge of the box. 'Ah! Of course! Hang on a minute.'

She'd noticed some sort of cardboard flap running along the bottom of the box. Hooking her index finger under it, she managed to lift it and bend it over. And underneath was – yes! There, lying diagonally, was the hazel wand.

'Is that a false bottom?' Elle was peering into the box. 'That's a clever bit of engineering.'

Ann picked up the wand and held it to the light. 'I think I knew how important it was to hide it properly. How could I have forgotten about it?' She turned the wand in her fingers. The bark was green and shiny, as if it had been ripped from the tree that morning. It felt unnaturally warm. Perhaps it was something to do with the loft insulation they'd installed.

'I remember,' she said softly. 'Mum and Dad both died prematurely. Dad had a stroke when I was nine, and Mum and I sort of formed a team. Unbreakable. We were each other's armour. But when I was eighteen she died suddenly. She was only forty-six, and I never got to the bottom of what happened. Something to do with her heart.' She put the wand down carefully on the window ledge and looked at Elle. 'I still miss her every day.'

Elle touched Ann's arm tenderly. 'I'm sorry,' she said, simply. They stood in silence together.

'After that, I packed the wand away. I think . . . maybe I thought that the wand had been bad luck for us. That it had somehow caused their deaths. I even tried to break it once, but couldn't.' She flexed her right arm, like a body builder. 'Puny muscles, see?'

Elle laughed and squeezed Ann's bicep. 'Feels like a mouse's duvet.'

Ann smiled, wiped her nose with her sleeve and looked at Elle, straight in the eye. Which was tricky as Elle was under five foot tall.

'Tomorrow,' she said, 'want to cast a spell?'

Elle smiled. 'I thought you'd never ask.'

17

Purgatory

Dave lay in his sleeping bag, fiddling with the zip and thinking about being murdered. He knew who had done it, of course. That unhinged idiot who insisted on wearing flares and a neck scarf as if he were some artistic flaneur from the Seventies. That bastard who had managed to crowbar Rose from him and now, because he and Rose had become friends again, his shrivelled manhood of an ego couldn't cope, so he had killed Dave in a fit of jealousy.

Ian. It had to be Ian.

The question was – how did he do it?

As a teenager, Dave had devoured Whodunnits by Conan Doyle, P.D. James and Agatha Christie, but by the time he was an adult, the stories were out of favour, made into tired dramas for daytime TV. He'd always had a soft spot for the books though, occasionally dipping back into his collection for a gruesome murder mystery fix.

Six guests. A dinner party. Plenty of food and the guests

were awash with alcohol. Of course, if it was a Christie novel, the murder weapon would have to be poison. Arsenic, probably. Although could you buy arsenic these days? Does Amazon sell it? Or Boots, maybe?

If only he could remember something about the evening – he might be able to recall what it was that tasted odd, or perhaps whether Ian was acting strangely. He found himself worrying about how he died. Did he expire with gravitas: a dramatic but elegant fall to the floor with some beautifully crafted last words? Did he say 'Live Long and Prosper?' like he had always planned to on his deathbed?

Or did he simply let his face fall into his food and then let out a final, trouser-ripping farewell fart?

He sighed and wondered if and when his memory would resurface. Also, Take That were driving him insane. He had no idea how long he'd been in that bunk, but 'Could it be Magic' must have been on its 100th – or 200th – play. He put his fingers in his ears to try to block the noise.

'It won't work!' Wilf shouted, gesturing to his own ears. 'It seeps in! Don't know how. It's bloo . . . it's torture! I wish we'd known about this in the war!'

Louis stopped watching the wall for a minute. 'Don't worry. Your ears get used to it eventually. A bit like tinnitus. Just when you think you're going to go mad, your brain equalizes things for you. Clever really.' He resumed wall-watching.

Dave glanced over at Edie and Freda, who had stopped playing Scrabble and appeared to be in some kind of trance, staring at each other. Louis caught his eye again. 'They're repenting,' he said.

'They're what?'

'Repenting. It's what we're all here for. They're thinking about what they've done and they're saying sorry in a meaningful way. It's really the only way we're going to get up there.' He pointed towards the ceiling.

'By saying sorry?'

'By saying sorry and meaning it,' replied Louis. 'You've got to mean it. No point in just saying it with no weight behind it. God will know.'

Dave thought for a minute. 'But how do you remember all the things that you've done wrong? I mean, I've done a lot of stuff that I'm not proud of. There's no way I'll be able to remember it all.'

Louis smiled. 'It sort of . . . comes to you. I think Angel Gobe wants to make it as easy as possible for us to get there. I mean, he's odd, no doubt, but he's a good guy. I think he gives us as long as he can to repent before we have to move on.'

Dave got up out of his bunk and walked over to Louis. 'How long have you been here?'

'Absolutely no idea. At first I tried to count the number of times I'd heard 'Who Let the Dogs Out' but lost count somewhere in the sixties.'

'"Who Let the Dogs Out"? Woof. That's rough.'

'I honestly don't hear it any more. Like I said, something's adjusted. So now I concentrate on repenting. And on *Friends*.'

They were quiet for a while. Then Dave asked, 'What are you repenting at the moment?'

'The same thing I'm always repenting.' Louis looked at Dave square on. He sighed. 'Murder. Well, a sort of murder. I killed myself.'

If Dave's heart were beating, it would have stopped for a moment. He gurgled something and then cleared his throat. 'I'm sorry,' he said.

'Me too.' There was an uncomfortable silence, when Dave wished above all things that he was elsewhere. In life he had successfully avoided 'difficult' conversations like this, preferring to scoot along in his own unbreakable bubble and deflect any sad news that threatened its integrity. But in this room, there was no escape.

Dave noticed his fingers were drumming on his legs, and stopped them.

'Don't worry, you don't need to say anything. It's shocking, I know.'

Louis managed a half-smile and Dave tried his best to return it. He wanted to respond, somehow. So he put out his hand and sort of half patted, half held, Louis' shoulder.

'Thanks,' said Louis.

Dave shuffled on his seat. He noticed that Laura was watching them intently. 'I am so sorry, Louis. I don't know what to say. I don't know anyone who's . . . well, who's killed themselves.' He realized too late what he'd just said and snorted with laughter at his own ridiculousness, then apologized profusely to Louis, not wanting to offend him.

Dave needn't have worried. Louis was smiling. 'You know, Dave, I wasn't that sure about you when you first arrived. But you're actually OK. I'm glad you're here. I hope we both make it,' he gestured upwards, 'up there. But I think we've both got a hell of a lot of work to do.'

And with that, he turned his head back towards the wall.

18

Heaven

Angel Gobe stumbled out of God's chamber feeling like he'd been trampled all over by winged horses. He'd known it would be a difficult meeting but he hadn't realized that God would be so . . . angry, if not *at* Gobe, then in Gobe's general direction. And so full of questions. Usually, God had no questions. Usually, at these regular status meetings, Gobe stood before God with a pencil and paper, and just wrote down decrees, or orders. The chain of command was very clear. But this time God didn't have many – any – answers, only questions. What was causing the mist? Who had put the Blocks in? What was so special about David and the rest of this group? How did he die? Gobe tried to fill in with best guesses and probabilities and platitudes, but God was having none of it.

God didn't like not having the answers. It was unusual, unnerving and infuriating. Gobe was celestially ejected from God's authority with a metaphoric boot up the arse and the echoing and sinister order: FIND OUT OR THERE WILL BE

HELL TO PAY. Gobe choked back an unfamiliar feeling in his throat and was surprised to notice something cold running down the centre of his back. Sweat? Again? Angels don't sweat. Neither do they breathe, or sleep, or go to the toilet, or do any of those irritating biological things that humans do. So why was he . . .?

He shook the thought from his head and ran down Heaven's corridors to Heaven's Hub where he burst in on Arial, who was sitting on a chair placed in the centre of the room. He was staring at the lights, flashing on and off. He also appeared to be wearing what looked like a Walkman. Gobe's heart sank. This did not look good.

'Well?' he asked. Arial's face turned, surprised, and Gobe realized that he'd been deep in a trance, working.

Arial stood up, blinked several times and said, 'It's Spandau Ballet, sir. Rather good, actually. Although I've no idea what Spandau Ballet actually means. Have you got any—'

'Not the music, Arial. The murder!'

'Ah yes, of course. Right, sir. Well – good and bad news. The good news is, I've run some numbers and done the analysis, and I've managed to find out who put the Blocks in to Dave, Andrew and Jess. I also think the same someone misted up the murder scene so we'd be unable to see it.

Gobe waited. 'Well? Who was it?'

Arial did a sweepy gesture with his robe. 'It was . . .' He paused for effect.

'You're not a magician about to reveal the secrets of how he saws a woman in half, Arial. Get on with it.'

'Sorry, sir. It was . . .' Arial looked around the room to

check that any other angels were far enough away not to overhear. An apprentice Facility Angel, Medida, was busy polishing bulbs about thirty feet above them. He lowered his voice to a whisper, 'Beleth.'

Gobe appeared not to hear.

'Sir? I said it was—'

'Yes, Arial, I heard you.'

Gobe's face had turned ashen and he looked unsteady on his feet. Arial, not quite understanding the sudden change in his master, grabbed the chair that he'd been sitting on and placed it behind Gobe, nudging him gently in the back of the knees. Gobe sat down heavily, his head in his hands.

'Beleth. Of course it is. I had an inkling a few years ago but—' Gobe shielded his eyes from his apprentice.

Arial, not the most comfortable or experienced in dealing with awkward social situations, leaned forward and patted his master on the top of his back. He had seen humans do this to other humans on the TV when one of them was upset, and it had always fixed the problem. He had been patting for what seemed like a very long time indeed before Gobe looked up, managing a half-smile.

'I think that's quite enough, Arial, thank you. Full marks for being comforting. I mean, if I were human I'd have huge bruises and little skin left on my shoulder by now, but I'm not, so bravo for trying. A1 for effort.'

Arial wasn't sure what 'A1' meant but Gobe seemed better, which meant that the patting had worked.

'Do you know him, sir? Beleth, I mean?'

'I have . . . some contact with him, now and then. In the

beginning, our paths crossed frequently. We had some things in common, you see.' Gobe appeared to be lost in thought. 'But I haven't had any dealings with him directly for many, many years.'

Arial didn't know what to say to this. He had never met a demon. His life in the Hub meant that he led a pretty sheltered existence. He loved his job, and he knew he was good at it, but he longed for some 'on the ground' experience in the world, and maybe even underneath it.

He was itching to ask more questions about Beleth and the demonic plane when Gobe cut him off.

'Still, at least we know who – what – we're dealing with. And he – it – is not insurmountable.' He held his hand out to Arial who pulled him up from his chair with a not inconsiderable amount of effort. 'Good work!'

'Thank you, sir. I've also found weaknesses in the foundations of Beleth's Blocks that I might be able to exploit.'

'Excellent, Arial. And what about the white Block? The one in Hannah?'

Arial shuffled uncomfortably. 'That is proving more tricky. It's troubling me, sir. I've tried all sorts of different pathways and diversions but I can't penetrate it. And there are no clues to who put it there.'

Gobe's collar seemed remarkably tight all of a sudden. Instinctively he undid his top button. This was a white Block and so it was probably created by one of his colleagues in Heaven. And such a complex Block indicated the involvement of someone high up. Someone *very* high up indeed. Whatever was going on was well above his pay grade.

'Hmm. And what about the mist? Around the murder? Have we got anywhere with clearing that?'

Arial was apologetic. 'Sorry, sir. But if that Block is Beleth's doing then I think he's had help. From what I've heard he's not clever enough to have engineered something like this. I've never seen anything like it.'

Gobe considered this for a second. He looked around to make sure that Medida and any other snooping angels weren't within hearing distance. He said softly,

'This isn't Beleth's doing, Arial.' He cleared his throat. 'Is there anyone you trust? Anyone who can help without making a fuss? Without telling tales?'

'Telling tales, sir? Oh, you mean like a snitch?'

'A "*snitch*"? What have you been watching this time?'

Arial looked at his feet and mumbled something which sounded to Gobe like 'The Sweetie', or 'The Sweeney' or something similar. Then he said, 'Thing is, sir, I don't know many other angels. It's not that I don't try to make friends but – well, I don't seem to be able to connect very well. And quite a lot of them are very loud.'

Gobe could certainly relate to that. 'Between you and me, my boy, a lot of them are all wings and no trousers. Don't you worry at all. You and me – we are the . . .' he searched for a reference that Arial might understand '. . . *A-Team*. We'll crack this together.' He gave Arial what he hoped was a reassuring smile.

It seemed to do the trick, because Arial rewarded him with a bobby dazzler of a grin.

'Now, Arial, what equipment will we need? I'm thinking

flipcharts. Marker pens. A coffee machine. One of those trans-parent walls that you can write on and stick things to.'

'But sir, we don't . . .'

Gobe waved him away. 'Well, order in whatever you think we'll need. I'll sign it off. No need to worry anyone else with this.'

Arial's day was getting brighter by the second. If there was one thing he loved above data, it was stationery. And a coffee machine! He might even get away with one of the fancy ones with a milk frother . . .

'Now,' mused Gobe. 'What we need is to do a spot of clue-hunting. I think what is required is a "site visit". Ever been down to earth, Arial?'

It was as if all of Arial's Christmases, Epiphanies and Advents came at once. At last! He would meet Columbo, Cagney, Lacey and Morse!

'Not yet, sir. But I've always wanted to. Always.'

'Well, grab your black tie and some sort of wreath. Because we've got a funeral to go to.'

19

Purgatory

Rose

Dave had been trying to convince Freda to play Uno with him, to no avail.

'You'll not have me playing those new-fangled games. Besides, I'm too old. Dead, in fact. I haven't got the brain space to learn anything.' She grinned mischievously. 'Another game of Scrabble?' Dave sighed and reached into the bag to pick his seven letters.

He'd just pulled out his third 'U' when it struck him like a truck. A memory. About Rose.

He looked up at Freda, mute, 'U' still held aloft. 'Well?' she said. 'What is it?'

'I remembered something, Freda. It's Rose. Something she said to me.' He gulped. 'Something important.' He couldn't believe it. Had she really said that?

'Oh, that's wonderful! Here, everyone! Gather round! David has remembered something!' His Purgatory friends stopped what they were doing and shuffled over, looking at Dave expectantly.

'It's Rose,' he said again. 'The day before I . . . well, I . . .'

'You got murdered,' said Edie, ever practical. Freda shushed her.

'Yes . . . that,' said Dave.

Freda gently took the Scrabble tile out of Dave's hand. 'Come on, then – tell us what you remember,' she said.

'It's fractured,' he said. 'The memory, I mean. I'm not sure I can put it all tog—'

'Start from the very beginning,' Freda interrupted. 'You might find that when you get to the good bit, it all drops into place.'

'Also,' said Wilf. 'A good story fills the time.'

There was a lot of nodding and murmurs of agreement, and everyone gathered around Dave, like scouts round a campfire. Dave, haltingly at first – having never told a story in his life – started to tell the story of him and Rose.

Dave had literally fallen in love with Rose at first sight, having spotted her on the other side of a university bar one night, and stumbling over feet and table legs to get to her. Even now, Dave remembered exactly how she'd looked; she'd been wearing what looked like his parent's hall carpet, sewn into loose dungarees; her dark hair was backcombed into some sort of hay bale, and her green eyeshadow caught the strip lights like cat's eyes on the M25.

She was beautiful.

Over the next few weeks he found out that she was a music student (first instrument – cello), had a penchant for Pernod and black and – crucially – was single.

Occasionally, opposites attract, and so it had been with Dave and Rose. They'd graduated and moved in together, in a tiny flat in Putney. Dave fell into a good, steady job with a company that developed workflow software, and Rose picked up gigs where she could, playing occasionally as fifth cello, so far to the rear of the orchestra that once she actually fell off the back of the stage.

Time passed. Rose was offered a permanent job with an orchestra and played in concerts almost every evening. Dave fell into a slightly more important job at work because there was no one else to do it, and he often came home late. If they were lucky, Rose and Dave would have one or two evenings each week when they would cross over for ten minutes or so – a quick peck on the cheek and a 'how has your day been' – and then Rose would have to go.

On Sundays, the only day when they were both free, Rose would be keen to do something together, but Dave preferred to play on his PlayStation. It was his way of relaxing, but he saw now – too late – that he should have done more, tried harder. Asked her how she was, helped with the washing, used those National Trust memberships that she'd forced him to buy. Rose eventually gave up trying to coax him out on day trips, and instead of talking to each other, they started to communicate by Post-its left on the fridge.

One evening, about four years after they'd moved in together, Dave ate his TV dinner and played his computer games, watched the news and went to bed. His normal routine. It was only when he went to turn his bedside light off that he noticed Rose's lamp wasn't on. Because she wasn't home.

She'd gone to her parents, who were all too please to let her stay, having never approved of Dave. 'Please don't have babies with him,' he'd overheard Rose's mother say to her daughter once. 'He's got as much creativity in him as a brick.' Dave, initially offended, concluded that she was probably correct. Besides, creativity doesn't pay the bills.

He thought that Rose would come back by the time the next month's rent was due, but she didn't, so he had to pay it. He had to pay the next 119 months' rent too, because she stayed away for about ten years. In fact, she went abroad with her orchestra – an opportunity that she had tried to talk to him about when they were together, but Dave had ignored. Over the following years, her friends told Dave that she was living in Paris, then in Berlin, then Barcelona.

Dave put a map of Europe up on his wall, and stuck small coloured stickers to those cities. He often sat in his gaming chair, staring at the dots wondering how she was, what she was doing, and who she was with. He felt stuck; he had no motivation to move on. Occasionally, he forced himself to go on a date, but he felt like he was wasting everyone's time, as he was only interested in one girl.

Then, out of the blue and almost ten years to the day after she'd left, he answered a knock at the door and there she was. She looked radiant and gorgeous but smaller than he remembered, overwhelmed by bags and boxes and, of course, her cello. He blushed, still in his underpants and the flat a mess behind him. She kissed him and told him she was back for good.

Unable to say anything sensible, Dave said, 'You smell different,' because she did. Rose took one step into the flat and sniffed. 'You don't,' she said.

Rose laid down the rules. 'It will be different this time,' she said. 'I want children. Do you?' Dave just made a gurgling noise. He didn't want children – he was only in his thirties for God's sake – practically still a child himself. But he attempted to move his head in a manoeuvre that he hoped would be construed as a nod, but he could later say was actually a shake, if challenged.

It was lovely to have Rose back – and not only because she tidied up the place. Dave hadn't realized how much he'd missed the sound of her: her voice, her clattering about in the kitchen, her strange classical playlist, her cello practice. They immediately set to work on having a baby, but despite trying different positions, downloading apps and buying hormone trackers, nothing worked. Dave could see that each month passing with no blue line chipped a little bit from Rose's heart.

She was still out most evenings with the orchestra, and she started to go to the after-show parties – something she had never done before. Even Dave, a man not known for his insight, could see that she was keeping busy so that she didn't dwell on their inability to get pregnant. She started to bring friends home after the concerts, late at night when Dave had his pyjamas on. He didn't like it much but didn't want to challenge Rose, in case she left him again. So he kept quiet, said 'hello' to everyone, then excused himself and went to bed with his earplugs in.

One evening, she brought her usual friends, plus someone new. Dave was brushing his teeth when they all fell through the door, and he mumbled his usual 'hello' through the froth. He noticed three things immediately about the new friend that he didn't like. Firstly, he wore tweeds, a flat cap and some sort of 'neckerchief'. Secondly, he put his feet up on their coffee table. And thirdly – he was a man.

The next day he asked Rose who this person was. She just shrugged and said, 'Ian, I think.'

And Dave thought nothing more about Ian until one day, a few weeks later, when Rose announced that she was leaving him. Again. But this time, for Ian.

Edie interrupted. 'She left you *again*?' Freda gave her a kick.

Dave hung his head. 'Yep,' he said. 'I was absolutely devastated, truth be told.'

The group were silent for a moment, as though giving the lost relationship a respectful pause.

'But what was the thing you remembered?' blurted Edie, twitching away from another kick from Freda.

'Well, I haven't been able to remember anything about Rose since that point, until just now, this one, crucial thing . . .' He paused.

'Get on with it – we haven't got all day,' Edie cut in again.

Freda shot her sister a look. 'Edes – what are you talking about? We've got a bleedin' eternity!'

They shrieked with laughter.

127

'Come on, Dave.' Laura patted his hand. 'What have you remembered?'

'Well. Rose and I were back in my flat. Our flat. I'm not sure when, but I think it was months after she'd left me and maybe just a few days before my murder. She was unhappy, and she wanted to leave Ian. She told me that he – well, that she was scared of him. That he often got angry, smashed things up, and had even threatened to hit her on more than one occasion.' There was a collective gasp. 'She wanted to give us another go, but she was afraid to leave him in case he hurt her. And she said – she said that she loved me. That she'd never stopped loving me.'

20

The Funeral

They stood behind a rose bush in the Garden of Remembrance, watching the mourners arrive. Arial thought that the weather was 'absolutely marvellous', not having seen heavy rain from the other side, as it were. Gobe was just glad that by good fortune someone had left an umbrella on a bench close by. He tried hard not to worry about his trousers getting splashed.

It was Arial's first proper visit to the terrestrial sphere. Gobe had been forced to explain to him that it wouldn't be appropriate to go to a funeral dressed entirely in white, and so they had both toned down their appearance by wearing muted shades of grey. Arial had insisted on wearing a trench coat and hat, which Gobe had initially mocked, but now wished he was wearing too as the blustery showers snuck under his umbrella and started to soak his jacket.

'If you don't mind me saying, it's an ugly looking church, sir.'

'It's not a church, Arial. It's a crematorium. Some people

call these buildings "chapels" but they're nothing of the sort. They're unconsecrated buildings, they all look like tiny factories and they're all built on roundabouts.' He looked at Arial. 'I am very disappointed with humans on this matter.' He disliked visiting crematoria. Everything about them: the architectural design, the uncomfortable chairs, the bareness of the walls, the 'one in, one out' attitude, the stiff curtain, the tinny sound system. Why did they not hold David's funeral in church? A proper send-off with hymns and candles and an organ and pews. And a vicar.

'Who are those men in uniform, sir?'

'Police, Arial. They probably became policemen because they loved *Columbo* too. Actually, it might be worth one of us talking to them to find out what they know.'

Arial looked blankly at him.

'Well, go on!'

'But I've never . . .'

'You're an angel, Arial. An angel who's obsessed with crime dramas. If anyone can wring information out of a policeman, it's you. Now go!'

Arial scurried off and Gobe watched him charming the constables at the entrance. As they talked, a woman in a long, flowing dark blue dress passed them and walked into the building. Her skirt flapped in the wind and she pulled it to her to keep it under control. Her long blonde hair was tied up in a complex style, like the Edwardians Gobe had once known, and secured with pins dotted with pearls. She glanced up and Gobe saw that her face was tear-stained – or was that rain? This was Hannah. She was beautiful, but there was something odd about her. She was timeless, or time-full; her dress sense was influenced by half a dozen centuries, and yet equally she was so . . . contemporary. What was it about her that made her so unique?

He was just about to get up from his hiding place and follow her inside, when he saw a couple arrive, hand in hand. Actually, now he looked closer, not hand in hand at all. The man, dressed in tweeds and a bizarre Sherlock Holmes-style deerstalker, was gripping the woman by the top of her arm and pulling her forwards. The woman was leaning away from him; not struggling exactly, but obviously not happy to be with him. She was wearing enormous sunglasses, the kind that women wear when they are covering something; tears, probably, thought Gobe. Her hair was loose around her face, the rain plastering it to her pale skin. She didn't seem to notice. The two of them found cover under the porch of the main building, and he smoothed down her hair, whilst she looked away. Rose and Ian. Gobe found himself wishing he had a notepad and a pencil to lick.

Gobe came out from behind the rose bush and strode confidently over to the couple. He was just a couple of paces away when he remembered that it was important to look sad at funerals, and so swiftly changed his gait and his expression to one of sympathetic melancholy.

'Hello,' he said, as bleakly as he could manage. 'My name's . . . er . . . Matthew. I'm David's uncle.'

Rose managed a little smile. 'Hello. David never said he had an Uncle Matthew. But then, he wasn't great at keeping up with his family.' She held out a damp hand. 'My name's Rose. And this is Ian.'

'Her boyfriend,' Ian said, unnecessarily. Gobe shook Rose's hand and then took Ian's, even though he hadn't offered it.

'Did you both know David well?' Gobe said, pumping Ian's hand up and down several times and noticing with some interest that Ian was trying to crush his own hand with his powerful and manly grip. Gobe restrained himself from applying even just a fraction of his strength, which he knew would shatter Ian's hand into a thousand pieces.

'I was his girlfriend,' said Rose. Ian shot her a look. 'Sorry, ex-girlfriend. But we were . . .' she glanced at Ian, who looked more sour than a truck full of lemons. 'Oh, never mind.'

Rose looked over Gobe's shoulder and gave a sad little wave to a couple who had just arrived. 'Excuse me,' she said, and walked slowly over to them, bent over, the weight of the world on her shoulders. Ian turned to Gobe and said, quietly and conspiratorially, 'I don't want to talk ill of the dead, but Dave led her on a bit, you know? You're his uncle, blood is thicker than water and all that – I get it – but I have to tell you, Dave really treated her badly.'

'Oh dear. Did he?' said Gobe.

'I'm afraid so. But I've been there for her to scrape her off the floor, as it were. Truth is, she was too good for Dave anyway. No offence.'

'None taken.' This wasn't strictly true. Angels, for the most part, didn't offend easily, but in this case, Gobe chose to take offence. Truckloads of it. He looked back at Rose, who was waterlogged and completely miserable. *We will have to watch out for her.* He made a mental note to check in on her when all this murder business was resolved.

A group arrived who looked like they'd come straight from the office – men in shiny blue suits and women in high-necked blouses and pencil skirts. One of the women was crying, and a friend gave her a grubby tissue. A couple of the men were playing games on their mobile phones. Gobe made a point of remembering their faces.

'Here come the stars of the show!' Ian said, slapping Gobe on the back. Gobe was considering slapping him back, with the full force of an angel's fury, when the funeral cortege pulled up. White flowers spelling out the word 'brother' sat wedged between the coffin and the hearse's window. A smartly dressed man – Andrew – got out of the black car that parked up behind the hearse, and he put up a white plastic umbrella, holding it above the open car and proffering his hand to the figure inside. A woman dressed in a black trouser suit and wearing what Gobe believed were called 'DMs' on her feet got out unsteadily. That must be Jess, he thought. They cut very different figures; he was tall, straight, broad-shouldered and confident. She, in contrast, was like a bird – tiny, bent, hesitant. She held a handkerchief to her face, and Andrew said something to her before putting his arm around her shoulders. They waited for the coffin to be ceremoniously unloaded onto the shoulders of the undertakers, Jess's body lurching occasionally with involuntary sobs, and then followed the pallbearers into the crematorium with their heads bowed.

There was something strangely familiar about them both. Andrew bore little resemblance to David, so it wasn't a genetic similarity that he was seeing. Besides, Jess wasn't related to either of them and she – well, she had it too. Whatever it was.

It was almost like they were bound together – David, Andrew and Jess – by an event, or a person or a . . . He tried to put his finger on it, but failed.

Gobe put up his found umbrella and ran to where Arial was still chatting to the policemen ('Do you get to use your baton much?') and hissed at him, 'We've got to take our seats!' Both policemen stopped short and looked at Gobe in awe.

'You're – you're that guy from the telly! What's his name, Pete? That one from *A Fish Called Wanda*. And Monty Thingy. Palin! Michael Palin!'

His friend – PC Pete, presumably – joined in. 'I can't believe it. I loved your travel stuff. So . . . English! Here, Michael – can we have a selfie? My mum won't believe I've met you.'

Gobe had made a mistake. This Michael Palin thing was always tricky to plan for when he came to Earth, but in the midst of all the brouhaha up in Heaven, he had forgotten to take adequate camouflaging steps before he left. He quickly pulled himself together.

'Officers – can I rely on your discretion?' They both nodded. 'This is an upsetting time for me and my friend here and I wonder if we could please save the photograph for after the proceedings? You do understand, of course.'

The policeman appeared admonished. 'I'm so sorry, Mr Palin. Of course, sir. You can rely on us.' PC Pete tapped his nose conspiratorially. 'We're sorry for your loss, aren't we, Steve?'

'Yes, sir. So sorry.' PC Steve tipped his hat and shuffled uncomfortably from foot to foot.

'Thank you. Come now, ummmm, Eric.' Arial looked at

him as if to say – who, me? Gobe took him roughly by the arm and marched him into the building, taking Arial's hat off his head and pulling it on to his own, pushing it as far down as he could so that his eyes were only just visible under the brim.

'My need is greater than yours. I'm in disguise,' he said to Arial, by way of explanation.

The two angels glided in softly and sat at the back and to the side, in the hope that everyone would be fixated on the coffin and curtain in front, and not turn around to point and stare. Gobe quietly put down his umbrella. 'Nimrod' was playing through the tinny sound system.

'Now Arial, if I could die and therefore have a funeral, I should like 'Nimrod' to be played. What a glorious piece of music. Heaven sent, I believe.' He paused. 'What would be your choice, Arial? Your final piece of music?'

Arial thought for a while – longer than strictly necessary. He was taking the question very seriously indeed. Eventually, he said, 'Occasionally we get some interference on the switchboard, due to weather conditions or crossed wires or something – no one really understands why. Sometimes we hear snippets of people's phone conversations, or the bleeping of hospital machinery, or a radio or TV programme. One time, I heard what I thought was the most beautiful piece of music ever played. I was captivated by it, sir. In fact, I recorded it and played it back again and again. It made me feel . . . alive.'

Gobe looked at him, astonished. 'That is wonderful, Arial! That is what music is supposed to do! What was the piece? Bach, or Mozart, perhaps? I wonder if I know it.'

Arial looked embarrassed and mumbled something under his breath.

'What?' Gobe leaned in a little.

Arial cleared his throat. 'It was the theme to *Fame*, sung by Irene Cara. Have you heard it sir? The lyrics are remarkable.'

Gobe closed his eyes and leaned back on his chair. Sometimes he wondered whether anything he said was having any effect on Arial at all.

His thoughts were interrupted by the pleasant voice of a kind-looking woman in a navy suit, who had appeared at the lectern at the front of the room.

'We are all here today to celebrate the life of David Damion Walsh, brother of Andrew, and beloved son of Colin and Ann. Sadly, Colin has passed and Ann is not able to be with us today.' Gobe knit his brows together. That's a bit rum. Surely someone would have made the effort to bring his mum here from the care home?

The celebrant's gentle and soporific voice faded into the background as Gobe looked around the room. The coffin – oak, Gobe noted with approval – rested on what appeared to be a Seventies divan, frilled around the edges with burgundy velour. Matching curtains hung lifelessly from the pelmet, framing the scene. Spiders had cleverly made lacy equilateral triangles by web-weaving at both corners.

He studied the backs of those seated in front of him. The fact that he couldn't see anyone's face didn't trouble him. He was extremely good at 'seeing through people'; all angels had the gift, of course, but Gobe's ability was sharper than most. It wasn't that people went physically transparent, exactly, but rather that their true emotions were exposed. In Gobe's case, he saw human emotions as colours, and through a millennium of practice, he'd learned to interpret and translate them with some degree of accuracy.

He was seeing a lot of green in the room, which was expected, as green generally dovetailed with sadness. And funerals were sad, generally. The men who had been on their phones were colour flaring; in other words, having little peaks and troughs of excitement, anxiety, happiness and disappointment. He couldn't see, but Gobe would stake his reputation on the fact that they were still playing some game or other. He prickled – then reminded himself that he wasn't there to enforce civilized human behaviour. He was there to solve a murder.

He found the backs of heads of the five guests that he was interested in, all sitting in a line at the front of the room. First, Rose. She sat, back ramrod straight, still. Unlike other mourners, she did not dab at her face with a hankie, or bow her head. She shone with emerald-green. Genuinely sad. But around the edges, she also sparked red and orange, like tiny fireworks. She was angry too – interesting . . .

Sitting next to her was Ian, his hand still fixed to Rose's arm. He was thoroughly brown. Not a conker brown, or even a chocolate brown. Just a sort of dried horse dung brown, with no interesting coloured flashes or variations. This meant he was thoroughly bored. What sort of person is bored at a friend's funeral? A bit of a shit. The type of person who wouldn't think twice about committing a heinous crime.

Hannah. He had a soft spot for her and he didn't quite

understand why. Was it simply because she had worn a white dress at the dinner? Was he so easily influenced? She was radiating pale green. He wondered if that was her natural state; she wore the colour easily, like a comfortable coat. But like Rose she carried other colours – less central, but still there. In fact she had a rainbow of colours, signalling a huge spectrum of emotions. This woman can really *feel*.

He reluctantly tore himself away from Hannah to look at Jess and Andrew, who were sitting nearest the celebrant. Maybe just a trick of the light, but he couldn't immediately see any colour at all, from either of them. Gobe shifted his position, trying to get a better view. When he was happy that he could see them perfectly, he tried again. Nothing. Just the blue and black of their nylon jackets.

'Arial!' he whispered urgently. Arial was humming along to 'How Great Thou Art', and didn't immediately hear him. Gobe stuck his elbow into Arial's ribs and Arial looked at him, alarmed.

'What's wrong?'

'Do me a favour. Take a good look at Jess and Andrew. They're sitting right at the front. Then tell me what you see.'

'Do you mean have a go at EMG, sir?'

'Yes Arial. Emotive Gazing. You've learned about it before, haven't you?'

'Well yes, sir, but I've never done it for real before.' Arial looked worried.

'Don't be anxious. You have to jump in some time. Just try your best. It will be a great help.' Gobe nodded and smiled encouragingly.

Reluctantly, Arial stared at the backs of Jess and Andrew. After a while, Gobe noticed that his eyes had turned leaden and his face was an odd shade of puce.

'Arial! What are you doing?'

'I'm concentrating, sir. Hard.'

'And . . .?'

Arial's body collapsed with relief. 'No luck, sir. Can't see a thing. Sadness elsewhere though. Oh – and those men over there,' he pointed, 'are playing on their phones.'

'Very good, Arial. A-star. Now put your finger away. What do you make of it? More Blocks?'

He shrugged. 'Has to be, sir.' Gobe sighed. 'But sir – have you seen . . . him?' Arial pointed to an old man sitting on his own at the far side of the room, partly obscured from Gobe's view. Gobe leaned forward for a better view and could barely contain his astonishment.

'Good Lord, Arial! It looks like he's burning!' Arial had to agree. The man was flashing red and orange from his brogue shoes to his pork pie hat. 'Any idea who he is?'

'No, sir. Want me to check him out?'

Gobe thought for a second. 'Leave him for now, Arial. There's only two of us and we've enough on our plate without running round after strangers. Probably a dead end. A red herring, as it were.'

'A wild goose chase?' suggested Arial.

Gobe smiled. 'Bravo, Arial! Your colloquial language is coming on a treat. Exactly that. A wild goose chase.'

Arial felt extraordinarily pleased with himself. 'Can we go now, sir? All that – looking – took it out of me a bit.'

'Not on your nelly.'

Arial looked confused. 'Not on your . . . nelly?'

Gobe waved dismissively. 'I want to get closer to those two – Jess and Andrew, I mean. Talk to them. Gather some clues.' He looked at Arial. 'Are you with me?'

'Always, sir,' croaked Arial wearily.

'How Great Thou Art' had finished and people were settling back down on their uncomfortable chairs. The smiley celebrant lady took to the podium again, thanking everyone for their robust singing (tuneless, in Gobe's opinion) and said that David would have been able to hear their marvellous voices from Heaven (how little you know, Gobe thought). After a small pause she looked over to Andrew and said, gently, 'And now, David's brother Andrew will say a few words.'

Andrew walked over, a folded piece of paper in his right hand. He tapped the mic and opened the paper. The angels sat forward, attentive. *He looks like a thinner, more attractive, more successful version of David*, Gobe thought.

'Thanks so much for coming, everyone. So lovely to see so many familiar faces. Dave would have been really pleased.' He sniffed and looked towards the back of the room. Gobe pulled his hat further over his eyes, but he needn't have worried – Andrew was looking at PCs Pete and Steve, who were loitering by the back door.

'Before telling you all about Dave and what a great brother he was to me, I wanted to say something about the nature of his death.' Everyone in the room held their breath. Was he about to reveal something?

'The fact is – well, the fact is . . .' Andrew seemed to be

struggling. He took a hanky from his pocket and blew his nose. 'It's just that . . . Dave was everyone's friend – I simply cannot believe that anyone would have wanted him dead. The results of the post-mortem won't come through for a while, but I'm convinced that they will reveal that the police . . . (he glanced again at the uniformed officers at the back, who looked uncomfortable as the majority of the mourners turned to stare at them) . . . have made a huge mistake, and that he died of natural causes.'

He paused, and coughed, and then looked down again at his crumpled sheet. Andrew took his hanky out again, this time to dab at his eyes. A few seconds of silence passed, and people started to look at each other. Jess got up from her chair.

He looked at her. 'I'm fine,' he said. 'Fine.' She sat back down.

'So anyway,' Andrew seemed to visibly pull himself together. 'Many of you knew Dave well, but for those who didn't, let me tell you about the man he was. He is summed up by his favourite joke, which he made up and told to me when I was eleven. A man walked into the doctor's with a lettuce in his bum . . .'

Gobe half listened and half watched as Andrew delivered a eulogy that was more suited to a best man's speech at a wedding than his own brother's funeral. He was playing to his audience and, after a few minutes, had them laughing out loud. Even Arial perked up. Only the celebrant had the decency to look awkward, and Gobe noticed the police were not laughing either. Shock and grief can do funny things to people, but delivering a comedy sketch at your brother's funeral is, at best, odd. He watched the reaction of the other four suspects and noticed that Ian was laughing loudest and longest. *I have your card marked*, he thought.

Andrew's speech was drawing to a close. He had – thank goodness – returned to his initial sombre mood.

'. . . and as Gandalf said, "The journey doesn't end here. Death is just another path, one that we must all take."'

'Amen,' said Gobe and Arial together. PC Steve looked quizzically at them, and Gobe sank down under Arial's hat.

Andrew took his seat and one of the smart work-dressed women was invited to read 'Do Not Stand at My Grave and Weep'. She had sweat patches under her arms and knocked the microphone off its stand as she was collating her papers.

'Sorry, so sorry,' she muttered into the mic, and the celebrant reassured, 'Don't worry, dear, it's fine, it's all fine.'

The woman was so nervous that she read the lines in the wrong order, making Gobe tut before he could stop himself. Arial looked at Gobe quizzically. 'I don't understand it, sir,' he whispered.

'You're not the only one,' said Gobe.

'Thank you, Sophie,' said the celebrant softly, and she smiled kindly at Sophie, who was now quietly sobbing. 'And now,' she addressed the crowd, 'it's time for us to say goodbye to David.' She nodded over the heads of the gathering to someone unseen in a booth at the back.

A whirring sound signalled that something important was about to happen. 'That sound,' said Arial, 'it's exactly the same as when the baggage reclaim carousel starts up at airports.'

Gobe was just about to ask how Arial knew that, when his attention was taken by the stiff burgundy curtains jerking into life, and haltingly moving towards each other. After what seemed like hours – Gobe overheard PC Pete saying, 'could have solved the Jack the Ripper case in the time it took for them to shut' – David was finally hidden from view.

Gobe glanced over at the five friends in the front row. Jess, Hannah and Rose were talking together quietly but intensely. Hannah, Gobe noticed, was holding Jess's hand. The celebrant had walked over to Andrew and was bending over to talk to him. Ian, the odd man out, stared at the curtain, his hand still clamped to Rose's arm.

'Always Look on the Bright Side of Life' started playing through the tinny speakers. Gobe saw PC Steve turn to him and give him the most enormous wink. Gobe smiled back, weakly.

'I need to get close to the coffin,' Gobe muttered under his breath as the rest of the mourners were leaving.

'But it's . . . he's gone, sir! They'll have roasted him by now.'

'Don't say "roasted", Arial, it's not a nice thing to say.'

'Cooked?'

'NO, Arial. Humans say "cremated" when describing the . . . burning up . . . of bodies. It's all about respect. And the idiosyncrasies of the English language.' Gobe saw that Arial was full of questions about this point, so he cut him off quickly.

'The staff here have up to three days to cremate David's remains. Hopefully they're still doing paperwork . . . or having a smoke. While I'm doing that, I need you to talk to

Andrew and Jess. And see if you can find out more about the others, too. Remember, Arial – they're *all* suspects. All five of them.'

He could see panic in Arial's eyes. 'Me, sir? But I'm . . . I'm not trained.'

'I'm not asking you to make a citizens' arrest, Arial. Just talk to them. You're good at that!' He gave Arial a little shove towards the group. 'Go on! I'm going to have a poke about behind the scenes.'

Before Arial had a chance to reply, Gobe swept off and slipped behind the curtains. Arial dusted himself down and took a deep breath. *You are an undercover spy*, he told himself. *You are MI6's best agent. You can do this.*

He saw that Andrew was saying goodbye to the celebrant and walked confidently over to him.

'Andrew? My name's . . .' Arial paused – what was his name? He looked around, searching for inspiration. '. . . Dusty, and I'm a friend of – *was* a friend of David's. Dave's.' Oh dear. This was not the best start.

Andrew looked momentarily surprised but then stuck out his hand. 'He never mentioned you, Dusty. Did you work with him?' Andrew was looking intently into Arial's eyes. 'Yes. And no. Not directly. We share an interest in . . . human engineering. Not *human*. I mean, obviously human. Just engineering.' Andrew's stare was really discombobulating. Is this what grief did to people?

'Well,' said Andrew, finally severing his stare, 'thank you for coming.' He looked at Jess, who had just stood up to join them. 'We need to go.'

She looks so tired, Arial thought. Wrung out and empty. Without thinking, he said, 'Are you OK?'

She raised her eyes, heavy and red-lidded, and said, 'What do you think? My best friend is dead, and I've broken a promise to . . .'

But they were interrupted by the celebrant, who had re-joined the little group. 'I'm terribly sorry, but the cars are waiting for you. And . . .' she coughed, embarrassed, 'our next one is due in five minutes.'

And before Arial could ask 'Wait! What? A promise?' the group had swept out of the room, Andrew leading confidently. Only Hannah glanced back, looking at Arial, a small smile on her lips.

Gobe wasn't going to be happy with him. He'd let the suspects slip through his fingers. What had he learned in that short meeting? No, wait – what could he *deduce*? That Andrew had an unexpected confidence and bravado about him. That Jess was extremely upset about Dave's death and had broken a promise – but to whom? And Hannah's smile . . . what did that *mean*?

Arial shook his head as if to mix up all the clues, hoping they'd settle in some sort of order. But they didn't. So he took out his notepad and scribbled down what he could remember, and then set off to find his master.

21

Beleth's Second Coming

Elle practically skipped home from Ann's house, the promise of spell-making the next day having been sealed over half a cup of overly strong tea and the crusty end of the banana bread. Ann was fizzing, too. That evening, she sat down with Colin in front of the TV, wishing that she could tell him what had happened. But the words died on her lips. After all, didn't he hate 'that illusion stuff', calling it all 'smoke and mirrors'? Hadn't he told her to throw away her parents' demonic 'claptrap', and hadn't she ignored him and hidden it all, even mislabelling the box on purpose as 'Ann's old clothes' so that it would be put straight into the loft without being opened after they moved house? Why had she done that?

There was another thing worrying her, too. Since holding the hazel wand – no, since even just *thinking* about it, she'd felt . . . exposed, all of a sudden. Like she'd been under a blanket for years and suddenly someone had ripped it off, shouting FOUND YOU at the top of their voice. She felt unsafe. Watched.

She told Colin nothing, and they sat through *EastEnders* in silence. After the closing credits, she reached for Colin's hand. He looked momentarily surprised, but then squeezed her hand back and said, 'Pop and get me a snowball will you, love?' And, glad to have something to do, she did.

The following morning, on the school run with the boys, she felt anxious. She'd had a sleepless night and didn't even notice when David tripped Andrew up on purpose, or when Andrew poked David in the eye in revenge. At the school gate, she absent-mindedly shooed both crying boys towards their class, where a bewildered teaching assistant calmed them with tissues and stickers.

Elle tapped her on the shoulder. 'Ann,' she said, having watched the boys from a different part of the playground. 'What's wrong?'

When Ann turned round, Elle was shocked. Her new friend seemed to have aged ten years overnight.

'What is it, Ann? What's happened?'

'Nothing,' said Ann. 'Nothing, yet. But I feel . . . I feel like . . .' She stopped suddenly. A man was walking down the road to the school, fighting his way through the throng of parents on their way back home. He stood out as he was wearing a thin tie, a parka and shades, but it was the pork pie hat that sent electricity up Ann's spine.

'Move,' she hissed.

'What?' said Elle, confused.

Ann took her firmly by the arm. 'Out the back gate. Now!'

She pulled Elle firmly through the empty playground which wrapped round the school building, only looking behind her just as she was about to round the corner and lose sight of the front gate.

Jimmy the Mod was standing at the entrance to the school with his back to them. She watched as he put his hand in his pocket and pulled out something rectangular and golden. A small hand movement, and a flame appeared. Her racing heartbeat slowed – it's a cigarette. He's just lighting a cigarette.

'What's going on?' said Elle, as Ann practically dragged them through the top gate.

'That man,' said Ann, panting. 'Did you see him?'

Elle nodded. 'The guy who looked like he'd time travelled from the Fifties? With the funny hat?'

'That's him.' She paused. 'Can we go to yours? The long way round. I need some time to think.'

Elle found it extremely difficult to keep her mouth shut during the twenty minutes it took to walk back to her house. She had so many questions but could see that Ann was struggling to work something out in her head. It was only after they had made it safely through Elle's front door, and she had put the kettle on, that she dared to say,

'Right. I can't stand it any more. Out with it.'

Ann took a deep breath. 'OK. So, since yesterday, I've been feeling weird.'

Elle reached up to the shelf and retrieved a large green teapot, its lid shaped like a witch's hat. She blew the dust from the top. 'I only use it for special occasions,' she murmured. While she warmed the pot and made the tea, Ann told her all about that evening at her parents' house when the Dunstable Nine had successfully cast the protection spell on her, and how she had felt almost superhuman for months after. She knew that the wand was just a stick that they'd picked up from the forest floor, but it had taken on powers that no one understood. It had lain dormant for years in that cardboard box until they had re-discovered it yesterday.

'Elle, I know this sounds unbelievable – I mean, it all sounds unbelievable, doesn't it? – but when we found the wand again yesterday, it felt like a beacon had been lit under me, lighting up the location of the wand to whoever is looking for it.' Ann's hand was shaking as she picked up her teacup. 'And if they find the wand, they find us too.'

Elle's eyes were wider than the enormous chocolate cookies she had placed on a plate in front of them. 'And that weirdo at school – he's one of them? A seeker?'

Ann nodded. Elle picked up a biscuit. 'It's a bit of a stretch, Ann, isn't it? I mean – perhaps that geezer is a bona fide parent? Or he just looked a bit like your man?'

Ann took a deep breath. 'That man is Jimmy. Jimmy the Mod. He was part of the original Dunstable Nine. I remember him clearly, Elle, from that night – I remember how he looked at me, and at the wand. He *desired* it. Even though I was very young, I knew that we had to hide the wand from him. I think he always suspected I had it but he never harmed me – maybe because he was frightened by Beleth. Beleth became part of me for a while, you see. Maybe he's still there,' she pointed to her chest, 'protecting me from all sorts of things – including people like Jimmy.'

'But I don't get it,' Elle said, confused. 'Jimmy's a baddy, right? So he's on Beleth's side . . . no?'

Ann shook her head. 'It's not that simple. I get the feeling that Jimmy wants the wand to – I don't know – use it for his own selfish reasons. To become some kind of evil superhero, like . . .' she struggled to bring to mind David's Top Trumps, 'the Basilisk, or something.' Elle nodded, not understanding what was going on at all but quite enjoying the ride. 'I think Beleth wants me to keep the wand. Or at least, wants me to keep it hidden from others.'

'OK,' said Elle, warming up to the conversation, cookie now in hand, 'but you're all good, because Beleth is protecting you, yes? So why are you worried?'

'Because Jimmy came to the school.' Ann had tears in her eyes. 'It's the boys, Elle. Somehow, he knows where the boys are. And the boys don't have protection.'

'Oh.' Elle swallowed hard, trying to keep up. 'So you think he'll use the boys to get to the wand? Following them here? Or kidnapping them?' She gulped, reaching out to clasp Ann's hand.

'I don't know.' Ann withdrew her hand. 'But I do know that I'm damn well not going to give him the chance. He'll probably be there at home time – maybe he'll try something then. I can't risk that.' She paused, gazing into the middle distance, before her eyes snapped back to Elle, alight with intention. 'I'm going back to the school right now to pick them up.' She pushed back her chair. 'You wanted to cast a spell? Well, come with me. I'm going to protect my boys with the only spell that ever worked – the protection spell. Let's see how Jimmy the Twat deals with that!'

Elle fist-pumped the air – whether because they were going to cast a spell, or because Ann had sworn, she wasn't sure.

In no time at all they had collected the boys – and Jess too (Elle waved away the idea of doing the school run for a third time that day: 'My body isn't meant to be put through such strenuous exercise'). The women marched back from school with military efficiency, Ann positioned at the front of the group, and Elle at the back. Both were on high alert. They took a long way back to Ann's house and the walk, normally a peaceful affair punctuated only by the boys hitting each other, consisted of an unstoppable flow of etymological entertainment from Jess.

'Andrew and David – do you know what Miss Tucker said? She said that I was the best at putting my hand up ALSO Sam did a wee and it missed the toilet and he got in trouble ALSO it was pie for lunch and the meat looked like soil ALSO Alice's skirt got stuck in the hedge and Peter kissed her and ran away and she couldn't do anything ALSO I found a piece of plastic under the desk and Sara dared me to eat it but I said no ALSO we had PE and I did a roly poly ALSO I'm hungry have you got any snacks ALSO ugh what's that? ALSO Pam went to Disneyland and met Mickey Mouse can we go ALSO Mr Pearson said we can ride our bikes to school ALSO where are we going again? ALSO I quite like this dress but Sara's got a pink one with stars on ALSO what is a "family e-sergency?" . . .'

Did all little girls talk this much? Jess didn't seem to pause for breath. Ever. But Ann's boys were loving it. Andrew, a little younger than Jess, walked solemnly and silently next to her, hanging onto her every word and occasionally nodding to show he was listening. David, a few months older and there-fore practically an adult, busied himself with picking up sticks and thrashing undergrowth with them.

Ann resisted the strong urge to stick her fingers in her ears.

When they arrived back at the house, Ann settled the chil-dren in front of the TV with hastily made peanut butter sandwiches and strict instructions not to disturb the adults. They all nodded, mute, eyes already glued to the screen. She closed the curtains again. He'd know that they'd collected them from school . He'd have felt the change. He'd be looking for them now. They didn't have much time.

She bustled into the kitchen where Elle was waiting impa-tiently. 'What about the ingredients for the spell?' she asked. 'We didn't have time to do any proper witchy shopping.'

'I think we'll be OK,' Ann said. 'Last time, we hardly had any of the right ingredients on the list and it still worked. But I do have one or two items that survived the move . . .' She opened the freezer and pulled out the bottom drawer. At the back, hidden underneath a large packet of oven chips, was a freezer bag full of – well, Elle wasn't quite sure. It looked like—

'Is that a pig's trotter?' she asked, taking a step backwards.

'It is,' said Ann. 'Well, it was. It's been with me for quite a while now. Best hold your nose – I'm about to heat it up.'

Elle grimaced but watched rapturously as Ann got to work. She put the kettle on. Put the stove on. Put the casse-role on the stove. Put the trotter in, along with some other hastily measured and unidentifiable ingredients. Gave it all a cursory stir.

Meanwhile, Elle did the only thing a sane person would do in such a stressful situation. She made a pot of tea. And fashioned a face mask out of a hankie to try to avert the awful stench emanating from the hob.

'OK,' said Ann. 'We're almost there. Can you get the spell book for me? It's on top of the bookcase.' Elle dragged a kitchen chair over and climbed up, searching for the book with her fingertips. She touched something leathery, unfamiliar and weirdly warm, and pulled it down carefully. It was a large, ancient, leather-bound book, cracked and blotched. Large gold lettering adorned the front.

SPELIS

'I . . . I've never seen anything quite . . .' Elle stuttered, cradling the book tenderly and tracing the tiny hills and valleys of the cover with her fingers. She noticed her hands were shaking.

'Yes, yes, Elle,' Ann said impatiently. 'I'll show you properly later. There's no time now.' She held her hands out for the book. Elle passed it to her grudgingly, eyes glued as Ann placed it on the countertop. It fell open at the protection spell, of course.

'You're going to need to get Jess away from my two,' Ann said. 'I've got some colouring pens and paper in that drawer – girls love colouring, don't they?' Elle nodded. 'Sit her down at the table and keep her busy while I . . . you know.'

Elle was put out. 'But I want to see what happens!' she said.

'Please!' said Ann. 'It's important. I don't want her seeing this.'

Elle hesitated for a moment, and then called out, 'Jess!

153

Jessie! Come here! Look what Auntie Ann has found for you!'
She spread the colouring pens and paper around on the table,
and looked up at Ann. 'Do it,' she said.

Ann, clutching the casserole and with the wand in her back
pocket, passed Jess on her way to the sitting room. 'What is
it, Mummy?' she heard her say, excited, as she ran into the
kitchen. The boys were sitting together on the sofa, watching
Dr Who. Andrew's hand was holding David's arm. They were
beautiful, Ann thought. Perfect. Was she doing the right thing?
Perhaps it *was* coincidence that Jimmy had appeared by the
school gates that day. Perhaps his children *had* moved to that
school. And really, when she thought about it – what proof
did she have?

She opened the curtains, just a crack. And there was the
proof. In the distance, at the top of the road, was the unmistakeable loping figure of Jimmy the Mod. He was walking
slowly, looking intensely at each house before moving on to
the next. Her heart quickened. There really was no other way.
She forced herself to breathe deeply and did a quick calcula-
tion – if he took a similar amount of time looking at each
house, she had about ten minutes before he reached them.

She put the casserole down on the coffee table.

'All right, mum?' said David casually. 'That smells.'

'Poo,' said Andrew, holding his nose.

There wasn't time to explain to them what was going on.
This is to protect them, she said to herself. And maybe countless others – who knew what Jimmy could be capable of if
he found the wand? She grasped the wand firmly and started
to read out the spell.

22

Purgatory

Photographs

Dave yanked the zip of his sleeping bag. It had got caught – yet again – in the nylon. Was this his Purgatory punishment? Being forced to fix this zip a thousand times, over and over again?

He had almost got it free using a combination of brute force and cunning, when he heard a noise in the bunk above him. He gave the underside of the thin mattress a soft punch with his balled fist and heard a yelp. Suddenly, a strange upside-down face appeared, pale and large like a full moon, eyes wide and dark hair dishevelled. He was smiling.

Dave, who had assumed it was Louis on his top bunk playing silly buggers, sat up in surprise and banged his head on the bedframe.

'Don't swear, David!' said the stranger jovially. He disappeared for a moment and then reappeared the right way up, jumping down to the floor with surprising agility. He was wearing creased white robes that had frankly seen better days, and had a pencil behind his ear and what appeared to be a large ink smudge on his cheek. His robes ended at his shins and Dave could see that he was wearing Adidas trainers.

'Allow me to introduce myself,' said the stranger. 'I'm Arial, Angel Go-Between's number two.' He gave a stiff bow. Shouts of 'Hello, Arial!' and 'All right, fella!' came from the others, and Arial turned to deliver the same peculiar bow. 'I saw this in Hercule Poirot,' he confided in Dave.

'Hello, Arial,' said Dave, rubbing his head and then continuing his attempt to fix his zip. 'Nice to meet you.' Nothing surprised him any more.

'Want some help with that?' Arial asked, nodding to the sleeping bag.

'Well, I . . .' began Dave, but before he could finish, the zip moved freely and smoothly under his fingertips, as if he'd slathered it in WD40 and lard. The relief was palpable.

'Thank you,' said Dave.

Arial smiled. 'Glad to be of service!' He sat down on the bed next to Dave. 'But that's not the reason that I'm here.'

'You do surprise me,' said Dave.

'Do I?' said Arial. 'Jolly good. We saw that your memories are coming back.' Of course they did. They can see everything. 'And . . . well, don't laugh. I watched this programme from your BBC TV channel about how to jog memories. Human memories, I mean. Angels' brains are so enormous that we can remember absolutely everything.'

'Of course they are,' said Dave, under his breath.

'Right, anyway, they suggested using photographs as a method to help memory recall. And I happen to have one of these in my collection.' He reached into an inside pocket and pulled out what looked to Dave like an Instamatic camera.

'Is that . . .?' he began to ask.

'It certainly is! Polaroid 600 square!' said Arial, extremely animated now, handing the camera to Dave.

'Nice,' said Dave, absent-mindedly turning the camera over in his hands. 'But why do you need me to recall my memories? Is it to do with my murder? Surely you've got records?'

Arial hesitated. Gobe hadn't specifically told him not to say anything to Dave about the Blocks or the funeral. On the other hand, he knew that revealing too much was going to get him into hot water. He didn't want to get told off by Angel Gobe or, more worryingly, someone higher up in the organization for being a blabbermouth.

He paused for so long and was so still that Dave was just about to ask if he was OK, when Arial said very slowly and carefully, 'I don't know who murdered you.' This was true. 'It's above my pay grade.' Which was also, theoretically, true. 'But I will ask Angel Gobe to come and see you.' He would mention it to Gobe next time he thought they couldn't be overhead.

'And anyway,' Arial said, happy to change the subject, 'I've managed to take these.' Out of another pocket he pulled out a handful of photos and, one by one, he fixed them, with the use of something sticky that he took from somewhere under his robes, to the bedframe above Dave's head. Dave craned his neck to look at them. There, plain as day, albeit yellowed around the edges, were Andrew, Jess, Rose, Ian and Hannah.

Dave's stomach lurched. 'Oh my G . . . iddy aunt,' he

whispered. He looked at the pictures, one by one. 'I think I'd forgotten what they truly looked like.' His eyes rested on Rose. The photo was of her playing the cello at a concert, her eyes shut, her hair loose, fully enveloped by the music. She was beautiful. He touched the picture and felt a strange emptiness inside that reminded him of a feeling he'd had, a long time ago.

'I miss her,' he said simply. Arial stood looking on, hands clasped in front of him like a priest, and gave him a sad smile.

He forced himself to look at the other photos; Andrew first – a picture of his brother in the pub, a pint of Salty Sea Dog in his hand. Like Dave, he had dark hair, but Andrew's was greying at the temples, despite him being the younger brother by two years. Dave had to concede though that Andrew was the better-looking brother; he was taller, fitter, more coordinated. He even had whiter teeth – git. He was smiling, showing them off, carefree as always, and pointing at something off camera. *No doubt taking the micky out of someone*, Dave thought. *Probably me*. He said quietly, 'All right, mate? Hope you're OK down there.' They'd fought like cat and dog when they were children but as adults they had settled into a fondness and understanding that only siblings can have. Although he'd never said it out loud, Dave loved his brother, and was sure that Andrew felt the same.

Then there was Jess, sat at a table, pots and pans hanging on hooks in the background. Was that her kitchen? Dave couldn't remember, or didn't know. Had he even been to her house? He looked closer, but nothing else gave him any clues. She wasn't smiling. He couldn't say for sure if she had smiled at all since they had left the safety net of primary school. He felt real affection for that melancholy face, framed in a severe bob, painted with heavy eyeliner and bright red lipstick. The make-up couldn't hide her sadness. In fact, it accentuated it. Why did she feel like that? Had he known, and had just forgotten?

Then Hannah's picture. All the photos were a bit fuzzy ('Retro!' Arial had announced with pride) but Hannah's was particularly blurry, as if taken through mist. She was sitting on a grey sofa, turned to the side, talking to someone. Despite the poor quality of the photo, you could tell that she had cheekbones you could cut glass on and a cool beauty, like a Nordic supermodel. But try as he might, Dave couldn't summon any form of emotional connection to her. He knew that she had hosted the dinner party, and had a vague recollection that she lived in a big house – but apart from that, he was drawing a blank.

'Anything?' asked Arial hopefully. Dave shook his head.

'Never mind. It might come back.' Arial pointed at the last picture. 'Try this one for size,' he said.

Ian. There he was, the absolute bonehead, standing outside the front door of a pub, cigarette in his hand. He looked cold, or nervous, perhaps. Dave didn't immediately recognize the pub – it wasn't one of his locals – and he squinted closely at the pub sign. 'The King . . .' What was that last word? The colourful sign showed a picture of a horse and its rider, the rider appearing to clutch something near his eye. Wait a minute. Something flickered in Dave; a tiny ember glowing amongst the ash of his memory. Hang on a second. The ember started to burn. That was the King Harold in Epsom, and that was the night that—

And suddenly he remembered. That was the night after Rose had told him that she still loved him. The night that Ian had demanded a meeting with him and Dave, like a fool, had agreed. It came back to him in a flood – he had been raging after Rose had told him how scared she was of Ian. He had wanted to go round there and then and 'smash his face in' which Rose, thankfully, had dissuaded him from doing. She knew that Dave had only ever been in one fight and that was aged nine, over another boy's enormous Jupiter marble that he'd taken and refused to hand back. And even that hadn't ended well for him.

But when, remarkably, Ian had phoned Dave the following morning and asked for a meeting in the pub, Dave had felt the rush of fury again. He couldn't wait to see Ian and crush him, if not with his fists, then with his mighty wit.

Of course, it hadn't panned out that way.

Dave stormed into the pub bang on time, full of nervous energy. Ian was sitting with his back to him in a wing-backed chair by the fire like a Bond villain, seemingly unaware of his arrival. Dave ordered a whisky from the barman – he never drank whisky, but this was a showdown, and it seemed the right thing to do. There was no one else in the pub and the barman, obviously sensing danger, poured Dave his drink and then left through a back door.

Dave knew it was Ian in the chair because he recognized the back of his head; he had the most ridiculous floppy hairstyle, obviously attempting to emulate Hugh Grant's early Nineties look, but always looking more tramp than movie star. Dave resisted the urge to run up to Ian and pull his hair with all his might, and instead, he walked calmly to the chair opposite Ian and sat down.

The two men stared at each other for a few seconds. Ian was wearing his usual ridiculous tweed outfit, a yellow neckerchief, knotted at a jaunty angle, around his neck, and a flat cap resting on the table. He held a glass of something clear – water or G&T – and his hand was trembling. Dave felt a rush of pleasure. No one had been scared of him before. Ian obviously hadn't got a clue that Dave couldn't hit a golf ball with a tennis racket.

Ian didn't waste any time. 'Thanks for coming, Dave. Good to see you.' A slow and horrible grin started to materialize on his perfectly stubbled face and in that moment, Dave realized that he had been mistaken. Ian wasn't scared: he was angry.

Dave looked round to see if the barman had reappeared but the room was empty. He suddenly felt vulnerable in the presence of Ian's overwhelming testosterone and instinctively bent forwards, making himself a smaller target.

'Nervous, are we?' Ian asked, suddenly showing too many teeth.

Dave, whose bravado was fast disappearing, forced himself to straighten up, and attempted a smile which he hoped came across as confident and self-assured. 'Fuck off,' he said shakily.

Ian crossed his legs and took a sip of his drink. 'Very droll, Dave. I will, as it happens, "fuck off" in a minute, but first I want to say something.' He uncrossed his legs and leaned

forward, lowering his voice. 'Rose told me – after some persuasion – she'd been to see you last night. You can imagine how
upset I was, Dave.' Dave gripped the arms of his chair, his
knuckles whitening. 'And do you know what?'

Ian leaned closer, till Dave could see the veins in his eyes
and smell the gin on his breath. 'Rose deserved what she got
when I found out.' He smirked, flexing his fingers, a movement
which drew Dave's eyes to what looked like faint bruises across
his knuckles.

Had he – this . . . monster – hurt Rose? *His* Rose? The
blood rushed away from Dave's head and he swayed slightly
in his seat.

Ian's voice brightened. 'Anyway, if she sees you again, I
wanted to let you know that it will be worse for her. So if she
calls you, just tell her you're busy – OK?'

Dave had never understood the expression 'to see red' until
that moment. A surge of rage was building in him, starting
in his stomach and whirling upwards towards his brain, and
before he was able to stop himself, he launched out of his
chair towards his enemy, hands raised towards Ian's throat.

At exactly the same moment, the door to the pub crashed
open and a crowd of twenty-somethings blew in, loud and
raucous, their arms round one another, singing Ed Sheeran
and Ariana Grande and other unrecognizable songs, all mixed
up in a cacophony of tunelessness. Dave froze, hands an inch
from Ian's neck, Ian's grimace fixed in a moment of shock.
A young woman, last through the door and the only one
who appeared not to have had a skinful, looked at them both
questioningly. In an instant, the red mist in Dave melted

away. He let his hands drop and stepped backwards in retreat, and the young woman looked elsewhere, joining the others at the bar.

Ian took advantage of the moment by springing from his chair out of Dave's reach. 'It's time for me to go, anyway,' he said, 'back to the little woman.' Dave bit his tongue. 'Oh – one more thing,' Ian said, as he put on his ridiculous cap and headed towards the door. 'Rose—' he was shouting now, over the noise, 'she slept with me whilst she was still with you. Did you know? Of course you didn't!'

And with that he was gone, leaving Dave in the middle of a party of strangers, alone and betrayed.

Dave sat on his bunk, head in his hands. He hadn't said any of this out loud, but of course it didn't matter, as Arial could read his mind and had followed the story as the memories poured back. Arial, not always brimming with emotional intelligence, noticed that Dave's fingers were pressed so hard to his skull that the knuckles were white, and his fingertips were wet with tears. Thanks to watching three complete series of *Baywatch*, he knew exactly what to do. He sat down next to Dave and gave him the most enormous cuddle.

Dave, his nose pressed against the angel's breastbone, felt the hot tears drop from his left eye. Arial pulled away and looked curiously at Dave's face, and then down at the small wet patch on his white robes, where the tears had fallen and spread. He touched it, gently, with his finger, and then looked back up at Dave.

'I know something about Ian that I shouldn't really tell

you,' he said softly. He lowered his voice even further. 'Ian tells lies. The switchboard told me.'

'The switchboard?'

'It's our . . . computer. At that moment, when he told you that thing about Rose? His spreadsheet numbers fell by twenty-seven. He lied, David. Don't worry – he never hit Rose, not once, but he knew exactly how to upset you. That man is not to be trusted.'

Dave was stunned. He moved backwards on the bunk and wiped his eyes so that he could focus properly on the angel. Was Arial lying to him just to make him feel better?

'We never lie, David. We just can't do it.'

A tidal wave of relief flooded over Dave, hitting him so hard that he had to grip the sides of the bunk for a few seconds, his head spinning. A small smile formed on his lips.

'Arial,' he said. 'If you were a woman, I would kiss you.' He paused for a second and then said, 'Ahhh, sod it,' and leaned over to kiss the angel's pale cheek. It felt like kissing a mixture of feathers and tissue paper, and as his lips touched Arial's skin, his nerve endings felt like they been lit up; for a moment he felt bright and full of energy, almost superhuman. When he pulled away, everything returned to normal and he was just a dead human again, sitting on a nylon sleeping bag with a surprised angel dressed in a white smock.

Arial got up, rubbing his cheek where Dave had kissed it. He was smiling. 'I will leave you that,' he pointed at the camera. 'I have a few spares in my collection. Over a hundred, actually.' He waved and shouted 'Bye, everyone!' to the others, and then with a pop, he was gone.

23

Purgatory

After Arial left him, Dave lay in his bunk with his arms over his head, a smile on his lips. He felt more alive than he had ever done when he was – well, alive. The relief when he knew Rose was safe had sparked a whole rainbow of small Rose-related memories, and he allowed himself to float through them, as if on his own extremely comfortable magic carpet. His murder felt like a distant memory.

'Laura! David! Is "bootybrow" a word?' Freda's loud voice cut through his daydream. He sat up to see her frowning at the Scrabble board. 'Evie is trying to cheat again.' Laura and Dave both shrugged. 'Let's ask Wilf. Wilf—' Freda twisted round to Wilf's chair.

'Bugger me!' said Freda. 'Wilf's gone!'

Wilf, who had been sitting peacefully in his chair for the last who-knew-how-long, had disappeared. Louis took off his headphones. 'What's going on?'

Edie laughed. 'That's it!' she exclaimed. 'He's off! Heaven

165

bound, I'll bet. He was the best repenter here!' And then, under her breath, 'Lucky shit.'

'We can all hear you, Edie,' said Laura.

Dave gaped. So it happened like that. One minute you're here, minding your own business, and then suddenly your time is up without warning, and you're whisked off to another dimension. Just. Like. That.

'And then there were five,' said Freda.

'Isn't that an Agatha Christie?' asked Edie.

Freda thought for a moment. 'No dear, you're thinking of *And Then There Were None.*'

'Oh,' said Edie. 'That's depressing.' She turned to the Scrabble board. 'Another game, Freddie?'

Laura interjected. 'Well, let's hope he's off enjoying himself in his own version of heaven – on his farm, or in a pub, or . . . whatever.' She turned to Dave. 'That means we'll probably see Angel Gobe again soon. He usually pops in for a pep talk when someone "moves on".'

Dave put the collection of photographs in his pyjama pocket and moved closer to Laura. 'How do you know where they've gone?' he whispered conspiratorially. 'I mean, do you get a sense? Any clues from the angel?'

She shook her head. 'Nothing from Gobe. He tells us what he can but he absolutely won't reveal anything like that. Believe me, we've tried to squeeze information out of him, but he just won't have it.' She paused. 'He's all right though, Gobe. It's a good job too because there's no other link with anything outside this room apart from him.'

Dave looked over again at Wilf's chair. He thought he saw

something on the fabric and got up to have a look. What was that? It was just a small black smudge on the blue cotton of the back cushion, around heart-height, but it reminded him of the mark on his bed sheets that he'd tried to hide from his mother when he'd been illicitly smoking in bed, aged sixteen. He bent down and sniffed. Was the fabric burnt?

'Ummm . . . there seems to be—'

'EXORCIZE!' shouted Freda. 'Seventy-six points! My game, I think. No point carrying on.' and she started to swipe all the tiles back into the bag.

'But Freds, we only just started to play. Give me a chance!' Edie was trying to put the tiles back on the board as fast as her sister was catapulting them away.

Louis was back to his wall-watching, headphones on.

'Laura. *Laura*,' Dave hissed in Laura's ear. 'I think Wilf might have gone to—'

A startling white light in the centre of the room stopped him from saying anything more, and everyone instinctively raised their hands to shield their eyes. 'Fuck!' said Edie. 'I wish he would just create a door, open it and walk in once in a while.'

'HELLO EVERYONE!' And there he was, crisp, white and glowing, in the middle of the room. All five of them stopped what they were doing and stared at him. He looked different. He was brighter, taller and radiant. Luminous, even. He was surrounded by an aura – like the Ready Brek kid – but instead of an orange glow he seemed to be emitting purple UV light. His suit was shining white, and his colourful tie was dancing with disco lights.

And now Dave looked properly, was Gobe . . . hovering? Dave glanced at Laura and she too was looking hard at the space between the ground and the angel's white, laced up shoes.

'Why are you all staring at my feet?' Gobe looked down. He took a deep breath and made a conscious effort to calm himself, and his feet lowered gently to the floor. His brightness dialled down a tone or two, and the lights on his tie dimmed.

'Sorry about that. Tiny bit anxious. Always go a bit OTT when that happens. Now then! I see that our friend Wilfred has moved on. Splendid!'

Dave attempted to interrupt. 'Excuse me, but I think there's something on his chair and I wond—'

'Excellent! We'll take a look later. In the meantime – David, my boy, I need a little word, if I may.' Gobe ushered him away from the others. 'Look at me for a second, please,' he said to Dave, when they were standing together in a corner of the room. Dave looked into his eyes and he was suddenly reminded of a Disney sky, with white puffy clouds like legless sheep, and hypnotizing Monty-Python rays of sunshine. He felt Gobe take his hands.

'Keep looking at me, David. That's it. That's a-fella.'

That's a – what now?

'Brilliant. Thank you, David. We're here.'

With some effort, Dave broke Gobe's gaze and looked around.

'What the . . .?' They were no longer in the youth hostel. They were now in a small white room, standing next to two white, chipped dining chairs. A lime-green mop and bucket stood in the corner. There were no windows or doors but the soft light in the room reminded Dave of an autumn morning.

'Take a seat. We need to have a little chat.' Gobe sat and offered the other chair to Dave.

'Where are we?' Dave asked, bewildered, gingerly sitting on the chair and hearing it creak a little.

'Heaven. Sort of. Heaven's broom cupboard, really. Not many people know about this place. It's sort of . . . off the map.'

Dave made a small noise. This was it! He was actually in Heaven. He had made it! 'Does that mean that I've done enough to – you know – move on?'

'Beg pardon? Ah,' Angel Gobe began to laugh. 'Oh no, David. No! Sorry. Purgatory is a slow process. You'll need to be there for an awful lot longer to make any progress, I'm afraid.'

David's face dropped and Gobe immediately leaned forward, concerned. 'I'm sorry David. I should have explained. Wrong of me.' Gobe paused. 'The thing is – we have a bit of a problem. I needed a quiet place to chat.'

'Problem?' Oh Jesus. So it's not Heaven. It must be Hell.

'No, no, my boy – you're not going to Hell!' (*Yes.*) 'Well, you're not going to Hell *yet.*' (*Oh.*) 'Thing is, David – are you quite comfortable? Good, because this might come as a bit of a shock.' Gobe sat back in his seat and picked a shard of white paint off the arm of his chair. 'It's about who murdered you.'

Dave sat bolt upright.

'You know? You're going to tell me who murdered me?'

'Well,' hemmed Gobe. 'You see, the thing is – well . . . the long and short of it is . . .'

Dave waited, very literally on the edge of his seat.

'I'll just come straight out with it. I'm afraid – well, the thing is . . .'

He's not coming straight out with it. Anyway, it's Ian, I know it's Ian.

'The thing is . . .' Gobe expression was pained.

Just SPIT IT OUT.

'I AM TRYING TO SPIT IT OUT,' snapped Gobe. Dave sat back in his chair and tried to make his mind blank.

Gobe took a deep breath and said quietly, 'We don't know who murdered you.' He sagged a little, obviously relieved. 'There, I've said it.'

Dave didn't know quite how to react, and so he laughed uncomfortably. 'Ah-ha! This is a test, right? You're testing me to see how I react. Well, I'm not going to. I'm not going to react. I'm just going to sit right here and do nothing.'

The two sat in silence for a few moments. Gobe didn't move.

This wasn't a test.

'You don't know? *You* don't know? But you know everything!'

'Yes, well, normally that would be true but you see – we're having some . . . *issues*.'

'*Issues*?' Dave was incredulous.

'Mmmmmn. Not ideal, I grant you. But the good news is, I went to your funeral and . . .'

'Hang on – you went to my funeral?'

'Yes, David. Also – please stop saying what I've said and making it a question. It's irritating.'

Dave was silent. It was as though someone had rummaged around in his undercrackers drawer, then logged into his emails and shuffled his folders about, and finally licked all his cutlery, carefully putting it all back ready for use, each knife, fork and spoon covered in a thin layer of spittle.

'Oh, don't be so sensitive, David. Besides, I have some good news for you.' Gobe crossed his legs and leaned back a little, as if he were a headmaster about to tell an errant student that they weren't going to be expelled after all. David leaned forward expectantly.

'I found out *how* you were murdered!'

Dave leaned further forward, to the point where he was almost tipping out of his chair. Now this was interesting. 'And?'

Gobe moved his face very close to David's, so that the tips of their noses were almost touching. He smelled of bakewell tarts. Dave wondered if the angel had stopped off at a bakery whilst on Earth to purchase his favourite pastries.

'Cyanide!' Gobe whispered.

'Cyanide?' Dave rocked back on his chair. Wasn't that used during the Second World War?

Gobe sat back. 'Yes. I smelled it on you. Whoever used it on you had a penchant for tradition.'

'Did you say you . . . smelled it on me? But how?'

'David, honestly, you should have seen me. I was like . . . Hercule Poirot. Without the ridiculous moustache. When the funeral ended, I snuck behind the curtain and opened your coffin.'

'You did WHAT?'

'It's fine, absolutely fine. The funeral director was having a cup of tea in a side room complaining to some other chap in a suit about his broadband speed at home. He seemed to be on a roll so I took advantage. Obviously coffins are nailed down but I have a bit of a gift of strength when I put my mind to it.' He smiled modestly and waved his hand. 'I don't like to brag. Anyway, I managed to get it open and had a good look. I must say, they did a splendid embalming job on you, David. Although of course it could have been a side effect of the cyanide. Whichever – you looked positively radiant.'

Dave smiled weakly.

'Your cheeks! Like plums, David.' Gobe was effervescing. 'I bent down to have a closer look – I always like to know what sort of make-up they've used – and then it hit me.'

'What did?'

'The smell, David! The whiff of Agatha Christie! I'd say you were given a pretty hefty amount, probably mixed in with your main course.'

A touch paper was lit in Dave's memory. 'Yes,' he said. 'I remember – it was prawn curry. I thought the prawns were off. I think I said something . . . they encouraged me to keep eating.'

'"They"?' Gobe leaned forward. 'Who, David? Who are "they"?'

Dave desperately clawed into his consciousness to retrieve more, but everywhere he explored was frustratingly blank and dark. It was as if a virus had eaten away at his memories of that night, leaving a cavernous void.

'I can't remember,' he said simply, shrugging his shoulders. 'I'm sorry.'

'No need to apologize, my good man. Death is ruinous to recent memories. They may come back. They may not. The dead brain is not an easy animal to predict.'

Dave relaxed a little. He suddenly felt very tired and had a peculiar desire to get back into his bunk, close his eyes and let Gary Barlow's soothing voice wash over him. He was just about to ask Gobe if they were all done when there was a loud knock from the other side of the wall. Not just one knock, but a group – three slow thumps, followed by five much lighter taps.

'Come in, Arial,' Gobe shouted. And suddenly, Arial was in the tiny broom cupboard with them, the space so cramped that he was standing with his back pressed against the wall, and his foot in the green mop bucket.

'Hello, sir! Hello, David!' Arial was twitchy with excitement, and completely unaware that he had transported into a bucket. 'Sorry for the interruption, but I've found out something important. *Really* important.'

'Spit it out then, my boy!' said Gobe. 'Don't keep us waiting – Dave here is getting a little claustrophobic.' Gobe was right – he was. He'd never been great in small spaces.

Arial was effervescing with excess energy. 'The thing is . . . I managed to find a key to dismantling one of the Blocks in Jess. And when I did that, it unlocked the same Block in you, David, and your brother. And guess what I found? Guess!'

David had no idea what was going on, but it felt like he was expected to say something. 'Umm . . . have you by any chance found out who murdered me?'

173

Arial looked at him as if he was an idiot. Which, to be fair, he probably was. 'No, David. *No!*' He looked at Gobe, ignoring Dave, and cleared his throat. 'Beleth possessed them when they were children. David, Andrew and Jess. Ann cast the spell thinking it would protect them all against some sort of evil – which it did, partly – but it also allowed Beleth to inhabit them all.' He looked at Dave cautiously. 'And a piece of him is probably still there.'

24

Beleth's Second Coming (Cont.)

Ann muttered the last words of the spell and looked at her boys on the sofa. Andrew had spread his legs as wide as he could and was saying, 'Exterminate! Exterminate!' in a gravelly Dalek voice to no one in particular. David was fiddling with his zip on his trousers.

Nothing was happening. Come on, come on. Had something gone wrong?

Suddenly, Jess burst into the room, waving a colourful piece of paper in her hand. 'Look, Ann! Look what I made for you!' Elle followed hot on her heels, hissing, 'Come back, Jess! Ann is VERY BUSY and can't see you at the mo—'

But it was too late. Jess had sat down on the far side of the boys and was the first one to spot it.

'Mummy?' she said. But then went quiet.

Ann saw it next, in her peripheral vision. A hint of a shadow, creeping. The room fell darker and colder. Something smelt rotten, much worse than before, like that time they had found a dead rat under one of the floorboards that they couldn't reach. She felt his breath on her face.

'He's here.'

'But . . .' Elle made as though to move towards her daughter.

'It's too late, Elle.' Ann took her hand and pulled her back. Elle was shaking. 'He's wrapped around her. Around all of them.'

The three children were frozen in exactly the same position as they were thirty seconds ago, and yet their previously active bodies were now stiff, like mannequins. Their wide eyes were following something that was moving from their right to left, invisible to their mothers.

Elle tried again to move towards Jess but Ann held her back. 'Jess!' Elle was crying now. 'JESS!'

'It's too dangerous, Elle. You can't pull her back now. She'll be OK,' she said, but she really wasn't sure. 'Just wait. Trust me.'

It was like watching someone else watching a wasp, when you couldn't see the wasp. Or like playing Spot the Ball. Although he was invisible to them, the women could tell where Beleth was from their children's stares. The room fell darker still. Ann thought she could hear a low, deep hiss from somewhere.

Ann felt a long-forgotten fear. 'It's OK, everyone!' She tried to sound jolly, comforting, but her voice was shaking. 'Don't be scared. It's just like taking medicine. One gulp and you'll all feel amazing!' She lowered her voice and said to Elle, 'It will only last a few seconds.' She gripped Elle's hand.

Beleth took David first.

'Mum?' he said. 'There's a man. He – I can't see him properly. I don't like him.' His voice shook.

'It's OK, darling. He won't hurt you. Just try to relax.'

David leaned in heavily towards the other two children, backing away from the invisible force. 'Mum! He's really close! I don't like it! I DON'T—'

Suddenly, his little back arched and he started groaning – a low, deep, animalist growl. Ann grasped Elle's hand and squeezed it to stop her own tears. She told herself, 'It's good for him, it's good for him, it's good for him,' over and over. David's eyes snapped shut and he started to claw at his own body. And then, suddenly, his body relaxed, the moaning stopped, and he opened his eyes.

But as he did so, Jess, who had been watching David with horror, started to wail. Her body stiffened and her hands gripped her skirt.

'He's hurting me! Get out!' she screamed. Elle threw off Ann's hand and rushed forward.

'Wait, Elle! Be careful!' said Ann.

'It's OK, it's OK, Mummy's here,' Elle said, kneeling in front of Jess and trying to bring her close. Tears streamed down Jess's little face. 'He's inside my bones, Mummy,' she shrieked. 'I can feel his fingers in my head.' Her palms were up and pushing Elle away, her arms straight, as if she was a policewoman, stopping traffic.

And then it abruptly stopped. Jess brought her arms down to rest on her knees. 'He's gone,' she said simply.

Everyone turned to Andrew, who was already backing away. 'I don't want it, Mummy. Is it . . .?'

Too late. Andrew's tiny hand flew to his mouth as if to stop himself from screaming. His face purpled and his eyes were fixed and wide. His breathing became shallow. Of the three, Andrew's possession was longer and more intense, his small body struggling to cope with what was happening to him.

Elle looked at Ann, who appeared to be in an exalted trance. 'Ann. ANN! Do something!'

Elle's words snapped something in Ann and pulled her out of her reverie. What was happening? Why had she ever suggested putting their children through this? Her motherly instincts returned, and she immediately went to Andrew and scooped him into her body.

'AWAY! GET AWAY!' she screamed. For a few seconds, it was like cradling stone. What had she done?

And then, just as she thought she couldn't stand it any more, suddenly, Andrew was back. The darkness was gone. His little body relaxed and he looked up at his mum.

'My head hurts,' he said, rubbing his pale temple. 'I'm hungry. Can I have ice cream?'

Ann sobbed with relief, stroking Andrew's hot forehead. 'Take them in the kitchen for me, Elle? I need to check on something.' She cocked her head towards the curtains. 'There's some rum 'n' raisin in the freezer.'

At the mention of ice cream, Andrew ran full pelt into the kitchen, seemingly none the worse from his ordeal. Jess and David followed at a more leisurely pace, David rubbing his tummy and Jess temporarily struck dumb.

'Will they be OK?' asked Elle on the way out. 'He seemed to stick around in Andrew for a while.'

'They'll be fine. It's like – it's like stubbing your toe. It hurts for a while and then the pain eventually disappears.'

'Unless you've actually broken your toe,' Elle muttered, as she disappeared into the kitchen.

Cautiously, Ann looked through a minute gap in the curtains. There he was, just two houses away now on her side of the road, studying Mrs Belmarsh's front door. Jimmy the Mod picked up a pot of geraniums on the front step and looked underneath. He was taking risks – if Mrs Belmarsh saw him doing that, he'd have caught a hefty right hook. She waited for him to cross over to the opposite side of the road and then quickly opened the curtains, staying to the side of the window. She watched him zig-zag back to her next-door neighbours, and then again to the opposite house. This was it, she thought. The litmus test.

Clasping the hazel wand, she took half a step backwards to make sure she was in the shadows. Two can play at cat and mouse. He was out of sight now, and she would only see him if he came right up to the window.

Which he did.

His pale face loomed right up to the glass, his breath misting the pane. She turned away, terrified, back flat against the wall, in the hope that he hadn't caught sight of her. Shit! She'd left the casserole dish on the table. Would he spot it? Could he *smell* it? She could see the mist pulse on the window, as it evaporated and then returned with each exhalation. Ann's legs were shaking so violently that she was afraid she was going to fall. It felt like he was going to punch his way in, that they were all unprotected, that he was going to destroy them all. Beads of sweat dripped down her cheeks.

And then, the mist on the window disappeared. She moved the curtain aside very slightly, and saw Jimmy moving slowly back down her drive, heading across the road. She breathed out, heavy with relief. Wiping her eyes, she realized that what she'd thought was sweat was actually tears.

Still trembling, she walked back into the kitchen where Elle was keeping the kids occupied with huge bowls of ice cream and as many cookies as they could fit into their mouths at once.

'He's gone,' she said wearily, and slumped down in a kitchen chair. She placed the wand carefully on the table.

Elle managed a weak smile. 'Have you got any whisky?' she asked. 'I don't know about you, but I need a little something.' Ann smiled and opened a cupboard door close to her knees. 'As it happens . . .' she said, bringing out a bottle of amber liquid and two glasses. She poured them both a good couple of fingers' worth. And an extra thumb for the road.

'Mummy, who was that man, the shadow man?' Jess asked, between spoonfuls.

'He was scary,' said David. 'Well, I wasn't scared, but Andrew was.'

'My head hurts,' said Andrew.

'Don't worry, you lovely lot,' said Ann, getting up from her chair and kissing them all on the forehead, one by one. 'You might feel ropey today, but you'll feel great tomorrow. Like superheroes. I know he was scary, but he's given you all a gift.'

'Like Father Christmas?' asked David.

'Kind of,' said Ann. 'Except that you can't see the gift. And he doesn't have any reindeer. And he's not quite so jolly.'

'That's rubbish,' said David, going back to his ice cream. Andrew nodded, and then rubbed at his head.

Elle leaned towards Ann. 'Will Jess be all right?' she whispered.

Ann refilled her glass, and nudged it back to her. 'She'll be fine. Look at me – thirty-ish years later and I'm as strong as an ox!'

Elle smiled weakly and looked at her daughter.

'Listen, Elle, this is what I think. Beleth leaves a small trace of himself inside you after he visits. Like if someone with terrible BO drops in for tea and you can still smell them hours after they've left. But the smell doesn't last forever, does it? Same with the "superpowers" that the kids will have been left with. They'll fade over time.' Ann gulped back her whisky and enjoyed the burning sensation at the back of her throat, and the relaxed, warm feeling that was starting to radiate from her stomach.

She put her glass down heavily on the counter. 'But the main event is, I believe, that Beleth has "protected" them from being . . . investigated . . . by other beings.'

Elle looked unconvinced. 'What do you mean, "other *beings*"?'

'Well,' she tried not to think of Jimmy the Mod. 'Perhaps . . . angels.'

Elle snorted, spitting out her drink. 'Hang on a minute,' she said, wiping at her top. 'Why would Beleth want to stop angels poking around inside us?'

Ann lowered her voice. 'If you think about it, it makes perfect sense,' she said conspiratorially. 'I talked to my mum about this before she died, and she told me that . . . well, she believed that God sends angels down to spy on us all, and they regularly report back to God. So that we can be funnelled into Heaven and Hell at the Reckoning or whatever they call it.'

Elle looked incredulous. 'That's one massive monthly report. Can you imagine how long it would take God to read it? How much paper would it use?' She smiled. 'Think of the ink!'

'I'm pretty sure that Heaven has come up with a solution to all of that. Maybe they don't have paper? Maybe they transmit it all via a big screen? Like those screens on *Bladerunner*? Or . . . maybe God only listens to the headlines.'

Elle looked down at her empty glass and wiped the inside edge with her finger. 'So, let me get this right.' She licked the last remnants of whisky from her finger. 'You think that our children – and you – are now "protected" from other "beings", including nosy angels?'

Ann shrugged. 'Maybe.'

'But that's not really a problem for Heaven, is it? I mean, there are plenty of the rest of us for them to snoop about in.'

'Yes, but think what would happen if we all let the demons in? Heaven wouldn't have a clue what was going on. It would lose control. Well – if it had control in the first place.'

'Blimey.' Elle picked up the whisky bottle and poured herself a generous measure. 'Heavy. Far out.' The two women were quiet for a while, considering Ann's hypothesis. 'I like it, by the way,' Elle said. 'This witchy stuff. If it pays off for Jess – I might look into it further. Get a spell book. And a wand.' She smiled. 'And a broom, maybe.'

Ann laughed. 'I'd pay good money to see you on a broom.'

'I'll let you know how I get on,' said Elle. 'So – what happens now? With Jess, I mean. Do I need to give her some paracetamol? Or a hot water bottle? Keep her off school?'

Ann poured a generous dollop of Colin's treasured Glenfiddich into their glasses and handed Elle's back to her. 'They're not ill, Elle. They haven't got the plague or the pox or anything like that. In fact, I'll bet you anything that Jess will feel good tomorrow. And even better the day after. I bet you that she will work harder than you've ever seen her work at school and she'll also be diligent at home. You almost won't recognize her.'

Elle half smiled and fiddled with her glass. She looked deep in thought.

'Do you have a suspicious mind?' said Ann.

'Don't be cruel,' said Elle, smiling. 'I'm just worried that we've summoned the Devil in disguise.'

'If we did,' said Ann, 'our children are going to benefit from him.' She held up her glass. 'You'll see.'

'Cheers,' said Elle. They clinked glasses, and the crystal rang out like a church bell on a gloomy Sunday morning.

As Ann predicted, the three children were fine by the morning. Better than fine – Andrew slept through the night for the first time in months and instead of sobbing on the school run, he walked contentedly alongside his brother, happily holding his hand. David tied his own shoelaces without any instruction and didn't complain about the hand-holding, even when that meant that David had to walk in the ditch by the side of the pavement for a while. Neither of them mentioned the demon that had inhabited them the previous day, but they did talk in great detail about *Grange Hill* and the rum 'n' raisin ice cream. As the children were ready earlier than usual, they left for school early, which Ann was relieved about as it meant that they were less likely to see Jimmy if he was on another recce. Which he didn't appear to be, as they didn't see him at all.

Back at home after the school drop-off (Andrew ran straight in with a big 'HELLO MISS MACMANUS I HAD RUMNRAISIN LAST NIGHT'), Ann went into David's room and was astonished to see he had actually made his bed. Andrew's room was as untidy as ever, but he had attempted to fold up his pyjamas and had placed them in the middle of the carpet, like an offering, or a sacrifice.

It was as if their brains had matured overnight somehow.

Was this a good thing? Perhaps she had inadvertently sliced off their childhood by inviting the demon into their lives. But then she remembered how she had felt after her possession, and all the positives that it had brought to her. It had to be a good thing – didn't it?

There was no going back now.

25

Heaven's Broom Cupboard

If any of them had been alive, all you could have heard in the broom cupboard would have been the sound of their heartbeats, and perhaps their breathing if one of them had a sinus issue. But as they were all either dead or celestial, there was complete silence in the broom cupboard. Dave's head was bowed and he was trying to make sense of the last thirty seconds by replaying it in his brain.

Eventually he looked up at Arial and said, 'Wait.' And then he said, more urgently, 'You mean . . .?' And then he looked down at his body, touched his chest gingerly and said, 'Are you saying there's a demon inside me?' He paused, still processing Arial's news. 'No, it's worse – are you saying that my own *mother* put a demon inside me? Inside all three of us?'

Arial nodded slowly, suddenly wary, realizing that maybe his method of delivery could have been more tactful and that the news might make Dave behave even more irrationally than normal. Gobe, on the other hand, sat calmly with his eyes closed stroking his chin, and appearing to be lost in thought. He said quietly, 'Of course. This explains everything.'

'It explains NOTHING,' shouted Dave, suddenly animated, standing up but having nowhere to go, so sitting down again. He rubbed frantically at his chest and his arms and his legs. 'Is it still here? Did it die when I died? Get it out!' He stood up again and shouted at Arial, who was the only one in eyeline and just a foot away. 'GET IT OUT!' he shouted in Arial's face.

Arial, although unperturbed, wasn't enjoying the high decibel level so close to his sensitive angelic ears, and tried unsuccessfully to remove his foot from the mop bucket so that he could make a hasty exit.

Gobe, finally lifting his head to see what the racket was about, held out his palm towards Arial and said commandingly, 'STAY.' Arial stood still immediately. And then in the same tone Gobe said, 'DAVID! You have had a shock. Sit down.'

Dave, still with his eyes fixed on Arial, took a step back and sat down heavily.

'That's good, David. Look at me. I want to say two things: one, I'm almost one hundred percent sure that Beleth doesn't live inside you, despite what my friend here', he shot an icy look to Arial, 'might have said. He most likely inhabited you for a short while, it's true, but he's not there now. When he departed your body, he'll have left a mark, or a scar – a kind of remnant – inside you. You've been unaware of it, but this "remnant" will have affected your life in some ways, particularly straight after you were possessed.' David winced at the word.

'I don't remember.' But even as he said the words, he thought he recalled something; the television being on, a strange smell and . . . an emptiness. But why would his mother do that to them? Arial had said it was a protection spell – but protecting them from what?

Gobe squeezed Dave's hand and looked at Arial. 'Arial – David has questions. Please redeem yourself by telling our friend here what you know.' And then he added, under his breath, 'Sensitively.'

Arial coughed. 'Certainly.' He smoothed his robes and tried to remember his training: *think like a human. Try to put myself in David's shoes – what would I want to hear?*

Gobe, ever the teacher, was reading Arial's mind. He smiled.

Arial coughed again. 'You mustn't worry, David. About your mum, I mean. My research suggests that she wasn't a Satanist, and she wasn't summoning a demon to harm you. She honestly thought that you were under threat, and that the demon would protect you. Protect you from what – we really don't know. But my . . . er . . . *feeling* is that she had no idea that it would cause problems in the future.'

Dave, sat right on the edge of his seat, looked up. 'Problems?'

'The remnant that Beleth left made it easy for him to implant Blocks into you.' Dave's forehead furrowed. Gobe explained, 'Blocks are like "No Entry" signs, placed at junctions within your subconscious.' Dave's forehead furrowed so much that his eyebrows knitted together. 'They stop Heaven seeing what you're up to.'

Ariel continued, 'He's also fogged up your murder so we can't see the perpetrator. Putting it simply, David, Beleth

187

doesn't want us poking around in your important thoughts. And he has also been fiddling about with Andrew and Jess. They have Blocks, too.'

Gobe interrupted. 'Please close your mouth, David.'

Dave's mouth had swung open in bewilderment. He quickly snapped it shut and looked at Arial. 'I have a question.' Arial looked at Gobe and Gobe nodded. 'Out with it,' he said.

'How did my mum cast the spell? Did she have like . . . a wand, and a spell book, and a black cat and a broom and all that jazz?'

Arial smiled. 'Your mother wasn't a witch, David. But she must have had a wand. A powerful one, too. As far as I can tell, she never used it again. Either she found a way to destroy it, or she has hidden it somewhere. Or passed it on to someone she trusts.'

Dave sank in his chair. How was he supposed to process all this? It was too much. He needed a lie-down. He needed a drink. He needed to change the subject, get out of this claustrophobic room and back to his bunk.

'Not yet, David. We have work to do.'

26

Sunnyview Care Home,
a month before Dave's Murder

Ann

Ann wasn't sure what had woken her. Everything was silent now, but there had been a soft thud somewhere close by. She was sure of it. It was very, very dark – damn those blackout blinds – and she couldn't even see her fingers in front of her face, despite her knuckles being the size of fat plums.

Another sound – that was definitely the clunk of her door closing – followed by a soft, slow footstep on the carpet. She hadn't imagined it. There was someone *in the bedroom with her*. Thank God she'd left her hearing aid in.

She wondered how he had found her. Had the protection spell worn off, finally, after all these years? She'd felt something shift over the last few weeks; she'd put it down to losing her marbles, but now she knew. It was comforting, in a way, that she was still compos mentis – but not so reassuring, she supposed, that there was a murderer in the room.

Think, Annie, think. You've practised this a thousand times.

Keep your breathing steady. Pretend to be asleep. Get ready for action.

Her left hand silently found the switch for her table lamp. *Not yet, Annie . . . not yet.*

She could just make out an outline now. A figure, moving slowly and erratically, towards the bed. Each footstep gave away a soft crump on the carpet, along with the rhythmic click recognizable as the osteoarthritic grating of bone on bone. *You are ten years older than me*, she thought. *I'll have a fair chance, should it come to it.*

The figure came closer, now almost within touching distance. *Wait for it, Annie, wait until you can feel his breath on your face.*

It was sour, when it came, covering her in a fine mist of rot and torment and despair.

Now, she thought.

She'd been holding on so tightly to the switch of her lamp, that when the time came, she struggled to move her fingers to press the button. Eventually, with a gargantuan effort, she managed to flex her fingers just enough to flick the switch and illuminate the room. The intruder, caught in the sudden light, froze just inches from her face. The impression she had was of a skull on a stick wearing a pork pie hat, so smooth and tight was his pale skin, stretched to the point of translucency.

'I've been expecting you, Jimmy the Mod,' she said softly. 'I won't hand it over without a fight, you know.'

Ann didn't exactly recognize Jimmy, the old man standing over her, but that was understandable given that so many years had elapsed since she had last seen him. She did, however, remember his grasping and covetous expression, as well as the clothes he was wearing. She had to admit it – Jimmy still had style.

'How did you find me?' she asked.

'I've got friends in low places,' he said with a tight smile.

'That's not true though, is it, Jimmy? We both know that you're working alone. Because it's actually me who has—' He lunged at her suddenly, clutching her neck with his hands and squeezing, cutting off her airway. *He's nimble for eighty-four*, she thought, *despite his arthritis. I wonder if he does chairobics?* She raised her hands to try to hook her fingers under his, and managed to squeeze the little finger of her right hand under his grasp, giving her some small relief.

'*Where is it?*' he hissed, right into her hearing aid.

She wasn't afraid. When you've been possessed by a demon, an octogenarian Mod wearing Hush Puppies and a frayed pork pie hat barely raises an eyebrow. But, to be fair to him, he did currently have the upper hand in that he was strangling her to death.

She gesticulated with her left hand to her neck. 'Can't . . . speak. Can't . . . tell you . . . when you're . . . throttling me,' she croaked.

He relaxed his grip very slightly, enough for Ann to take a decent gulp of breath, and for her lungs to re-inflate.

'Over there,' she pointed to the mahogany chest of drawers on the other side of the room. 'Top drawer.'

He looked at her suspiciously, but she also detected a hint of cruel triumph on his thin lips. He started to back towards the drawers, eyes still on Ann.

'You should have destroyed it, little Annie,' he muttered. 'You must have known I'd find you eventually.'

'You're probably right,' she sighed, as he turned away from her to face the chest. 'It's just that I wanted one . . . last . . . aha!'

She whipped out the hazel wand from under her pillow and pointed it at him, shouting the chant she had practised and practised over the years:

> Vade, satana, magister fallacie;
> Sod abi, pediculator, redi sub pedibus meis
> Humiliamini et tremite sub manu Dei
> Et effing jeff off, senes Mod.

A trickle of bright orange sparks dribbled horizontally from the tip of the wand, like a disappointing roman candle from the supermarket that's fallen over in your back garden. To Ann's horror, the light didn't even reach Jimmy's shoes. And even if it had, his chairobics flexibility meant that he'd have been able to deftly step out of the way with plenty of time to spare.

What had she done wrong? She was sure she'd got the words right. But perhaps, given that she was recently prone to forgetting things, she'd got them muddled up somehow? Jimmy smiled sadistically. 'Nice try, kiddo. But next time, don't try fancy Latin and stick to the spell book.' And, after a cursory look in the top drawer, which was empty except for a bottle of Yardley perfume, he walked quickly back towards the bed, his knee clicking loudly on every alternate step.

Ann, still holding the wand tightly, weighed up her options.

One was to be killed and, old though she was, she strongly felt that being strangled by a demonic, arthritic OAP wouldn't be her first choice of how to die.

Which left the other option. She'd hoped she wouldn't have to use it – it's so embarrassing to have to rely on others – but when it comes to it, needs must. She reached up over her head and pulled the long red cord which hung from the ceiling. Instantly, the alarm sounded at the front desk, just a few metres down the corridor.

Jimmy stopped in his tracks, horrified. He could hear footsteps approaching and muffled voices.

'Did you think this was a light switch, Jimmy? Easy mistake to make. Living in a care home can be irritating at times – so many people around – but, my word, sometimes it has its advantages.'

The footsteps were louder now and sounded very close to the door. In an instant, Jimmy was over at the window and had snapped open the blind. Lucky for him, the key was in the lock and he was able to undo the catch easily and throw it open. Also lucky for him, Ann's room was on the ground floor so his jump into the flowerbeds was more of a gentle leg-over rather than a crippling leap. He was through the box hedge and into the geraniums before you could say 'Quadrophenia.' As Emma and Joe, Ann's kind and gentle carers, burst through Ann's door, Jimmy was velcroing on his helmet and revving up the engine.

'It's an intruder!' shouted Joe, who had reached the window. 'And he's on a Vespa!' He sounded very excited.

'Get the reg!' called Emma, who was stuck behind him,

jumping up and down, unable to see what was going on. 'Ann – are you OK?'

'Oh yes, dear, I'm tickety boo. Don't you worry about me. I think he was after my purse,' she nodded to where her handbag lay on a chair nearby, 'but you scared him off.' She smiled gratefully, and held out her hand. 'Thank you,' she said. And she meant it.

Emma called the police, who said because there was no damage and no one was hurt, they would pop over in the morning. Joe hadn't been able to get the registration of the bike because it was so dark, so the only description they were able to give was 'an old man in a tiny hat'. Ann chose not to reveal that she knew who he was, preferring to keep her past locked down, and away from the public glare.

'But how did he get in?' asked Emma. 'He must have walked right past us!'

Ann wondered if Jimmy had had some inside help, but she said nothing. It was 3 a.m., and she was tired.

'I'd like to go to sleep now, please,' she said to them both.

'Are you sure?' Joe asked, concerned. 'You're a tough old bird, Annie. Most people – including me – would be terrified out of their wits.'

'It helps to not have much short-term memory left, dear. He's already started to fade around the edges.' This wasn't strictly true. Her memory *was* generally in tatters, but many things from her childhood seemed to stick to her with startling clarity – including, of course, Jimmy the Mod and the rest of the First Dunstable Satanic Society.

She patted Joe on the arm and looked at them both. 'Off

you go now, back to reception. Best thing you can do for me is keep your eyes peeled in case he comes back for a second go.'

They both looked unhappy about leaving her. 'Go!' she ordered. 'I can't sleep with you two looking at me as if I'm the bleedin' Mona Lisa.'

'All right, Annie,' said Emma. 'Don't hesitate to pull the string again though, if you need anything. Anything at all. Promise?'

'Yes, yes, yes.' Ann let out a yawn. She was exhausted. 'See you in the morning. Don't wake me up too early.' And with that, she clicked off her light and pulled her duvet up to her chin. Emma and Joe reluctantly stepped out of the room and quietly pulled the door to.

'I'll pop in during the night,' whispered Emma to Joe.

'YOU WILL NOT!' shouted Ann, who still hadn't taken her hearing aid out.

The two carers smiled and padded back to reception. Ann lay in the dark, clutching the hazel wand to her chest. She knew why the spell hadn't worked, of course, deep down. She was dying, and the wand knew it. The wand was slipping away from her, like an errant teenager pulling away from their parent. She didn't blame it. What use was she now? She couldn't even fight off a wizened octogenarian.

Perhaps now that the wand wasn't aligned to anyone, she could . . . Ann grasped the stick firmly and tried with all her might to squeeze the ends together, struggling to snap it, or at least bend it. She pushed and pulled, holding her breath and feeling her heart push out of her chest. But the wand was unyielding, rigid – just like Elle's loaf cake. The memory brought a small smile to Ann's lips.

The wand seemed to be getting warmer in her hands. *It probably doesn't like being manhandled like that,* she thought. *I don't blame it.* She touched the knots in the wood gently, tracing the ridges with her fingertips.

'I know what you want me to do,' she said softly. 'But who can I trust to look after you? And who will be protected from Jimmy and anyone else who comes looking for you?'

There were only three people she could consider becoming the next guardian of the wand. She just needed to decide who to choose.

Still clutching the hazel wand to her chest, Ann fell asleep and dreamed of three children sitting on a sofa watching TV, each with the number six marked on their forehead.

27

Heaven's Broom Cupboard

There are too many bodies in this room, thought Dave. It wasn't built for meetings. The two angels were deep in conversation; Arial had finally rid himself of the mop bucket and was standing at one end of the room. Gobe had stood up and was at the other end, book-ending Dave, who was sat in the middle looking at each angel in turn as he spoke, as if watching a tennis match.

They were talking very quickly about him, but Dave wasn't listening. How was it possible that he could have been possessed – that all of them had been possessed – and not remember a thing about it? He looked down at his body and prodded his stomach. Despite Gobe's reassurances, he wondered if the demon was still resident inside him and was going to burst out any time now, like the creature in *Alien*. He considered for a moment what it would look like, this monster. An enormous pink squid, perhaps, its tentacles reaching out for something to smother. Or like the fittingly nicknamed Mr 'Leg' Braker, his PE teacher from school, who used to force them to climb to the top of the ropes with no safety mats.

And then there was his mum. He still didn't understand. How could she possibly do that to them? Did she not love them?

He said softly, 'I can't breathe.'

The angels didn't hear him above their own chatter.

He said again, louder, 'I can't breathe.'

This time, Gobe heard him and turned round. 'David! David. It's OK. You don't need to breathe. It's a memory from your old body – a reaction that you would have had, were you alive.' He crouched down next to Dave and held his hand. A warm sensation travelled up his arm and throughout his body, making Dave feel like he was lowering himself into a hot bath on a cold day. 'Forget your old body, David. You're safe.'

Dave felt his muscles unclench and his throat relax. He looked up at the angel. 'I still don't understand. Why would she do that to us?'

'David. Listen to me. I couldn't see the context; I can't tell you the precise reason why. But I can tell you that she loved you and I agree with Arial – she did it for your own good. It might be that she felt like she was in danger – or you were in danger – and she needed some protection. Beleth would have given you that.'

Dave looked again at his own unremarkable middle-aged body which had apparently housed a demon. He looked up at Arial. 'Please tell me he's not still there. Promise.'

Gobe stepped in. 'It's unlikely, but David – even if a piece of him is still there, a lot of people are part demon, you know. Not because they've been inhabited by one, but just because – well, they're a bit inherently nasty. But the Blocks are still there – they remained long after Beleth had left.' He paused. 'A bit like moving house and leaving a couple of old mattresses behind.'

Dave nodded sadly. Well, that was something at least. Although the thought of having a couple of old mattresses inside him didn't fill him with joy.

Gobe was talking to Arial again. 'This explains everything, of course. That rotter left his mark in those children when he possessed them – and he's been popping back willy nilly, blocking certain events to make our lives difficult.'

Arial was nodding very fast in agreement.

'But to block a murder . . .' Gobe continued. 'He's gone too far this time.'

'Right, sir,' said Arial, still nodding. And then, 'If I may, on a related note . . .' Gobe gestured for him to continue. 'We need to talk about the suspects. I've put the full playback report on your desk. I'm sorry it took me so long. It's 3,879 pages.'

'Good grief, Arial. We've already been stuck in here for an eternity. Can you just cut to the chase?' Gobe's tone was clipped and harassed. Dave looked at him with surprise.

Arial, who appeared not to have noticed, cleared his throat with just a touch of self-importance. 'Certainly, sir. There wasn't much more that I could access – relevant stuff, I mean. Just a couple of items.' He made a swirling motion with his hand towards the far wall and a projection appeared of two people, sitting in their lounge. It was Ian and Rose. There was no sound, but they appeared to be arguing. Ian was standing over Rose, who was cowering on the sofa. He was gesticulating, pointing, throwing his hands in the air. Doing everything he could to make himself look big and manly. She was crying, her head in her hands. Dave felt his skin prickle.

'There's no sound, I'm afraid. I can't risk transmitting the full clip here in case any of the other angels in the Hub pick something up. But he's just told her that you, David, had multiple affairs while you and Rose were together.'

'What?' Dave was enraged. 'But that's ridiculous! It's a lie! Surely she didn't believe him?'

Arial just shrugged. Dave felt a rise of nausea. She can't have believed him. They loved each other! 'Wait! When was this?' he asked.

'Two days before your murder,' Arial said. Two days before. So after she'd said she still loved him. It was clear what he was up to: Ian was trying to manipulate her into staying with him. Surely she could see through him?

'There's something else,' Arial said. 'The day after Ian did this,' he gestured to the moving picture on the wall, 'Andrew made a phone call to Jess in the morning, and he left work immediately to pay her a visit.'

Dave tore his mind away from Ian. Andrew never took time off work for social stuff. Why had he gone to visit Jess at such short notice? What had been so urgent that it couldn't wait until the end of the day?

Arial continued, 'I couldn't dismantle the Blocks, so I couldn't hear the call or see the meeting. But I accessed Andrew's phone records – I've seen them do that on *The Bill* – and I was able to connect to Jess's flatmate's playback so saw Andrew arrive and leave. He was only in there for about ten minutes.'

'Very thorough, Arial,' said Gobe. 'Although – there's a huge piece of the jigsaw missing and it's shaped like Hannah. What have you found out about her?'

Arial looked uncomfortable. 'I'm really sorry, sir. I couldn't make any headway; the Block is incredibly well constructed.' He shook his head and looked down at his trainers. He said in a low voice, 'It's beaten me, I'm afraid.'

Gobe immediately softened. 'Now, now, don't be blue about it. It's not your fault; you've done brilliantly. In fact, if we can ever tell God about what we've done, I will put you forward for a commendation.' He paused. 'And if we can't tell God, I will make you a certificate myself to hang on your wall.'

Arial smiled beatifically and his skin seemed to illuminate for a second, as if someone had switched on a standard lamp inside him. It made Dave want to reach out and touch him to see if whatever it was would flood through him, too. But before he could do anything, Arial said, 'There was one other thing I found out, sir.'

'Hit me with it,' said Gobe.

Arial looked at Dave unsteadily. 'Jess visited Ann in her care home a couple of weeks before the murder.'

Dave suddenly stopped thinking about Arial's skin and his focus snapped back to the conversation. 'What?' he said. 'That's not possible. Jess hadn't seen my mum in . . . I don't know, maybe ten or fifteen years.'

Arial took a biro out of his pocket and started to click and unclick it rhythmically. 'It's true, David. I could see her walking in, carrying flowers. But I couldn't view anything else – play-back turned foggy from the moment she went through the door.'

Dave made a gesture towards Gobe as if to say – this is nonsense, right? But Gobe just shrugged and said, 'Arial never lies, David.'

Jess visiting his mum? Why would she do that? Was his mum so lonely that she wanted someone to talk to? Dave and Andrew hadn't been the most attentive of sons, it's true, but to invite Jess to see her after all these years . . . Or had Jess just turned up of her own accord? And if so – why?

28

The Guardianship of the Wand

Two Weeks Before the Murder

Jess stopped at the front door of Sunnyview care home, a bunch of supermarket tulips in her hand. She tasted something metallic and put her hand to her lips; the red stain made her realize that she'd been unconsciously chewing the inside of her cheek. She'd never been in a nursing home before, her own mum having died suddenly at home just a year ago. Elle had been found lying on her bed in a white, crystal-encrusted jumpsuit, the 'All Elvis' channel playing on the radio, and a smile on her face. The doctor had said she'd had a brain haemorrhage, but Jess had wondered if her mother had found a way to choose how and when she passed on. She couldn't blame her – wouldn't we all do the same, if we could? – but she missed her mum. Sometimes she felt that Elle had been the only person who had understood her.

Jess hadn't spoken to Ann for years, so it was a surprise when, a couple of days ago, she'd got a phone call from her. 'Please come and visit me,' she had said, in an unfamiliar, cracked voice. 'I have something important for you.' Jess agreed, of course, curious as to what Ann had in mind. Ann gave her the address and was about to hang up when she said,

'Oh! I almost forgot. Don't tell the boys. You'll understand why when we've talked.'

Jess rang the bell at reception and while she was waiting, peeked through an open door on her left. The room beyond was bright, a huge conservatory, filled with the hustle and bustle of a National Trust tearoom on a Sunday afternoon. Elderly people sat at tables for four, eating and chatting and laughing and generally, thought Jess, having a much better time than she'd ever had. She wondered what the minimum age was to get into the place.

A young woman with a badge that said 'EMMA' appeared and checked her in. She had a kind smile and she said that Ann had been really looking forward to her visit. Jess didn't know how to respond, so she just smiled back and sort of waved the tulips in the air. She died a little inside – why was she so bad at social situations?

The woman didn't seem to notice, or was too polite to mention it. She just said brightly, 'Follow me!' and Jess found herself trotting behind Emma, down a brightly lit and colour-fully painted corridor, and stopping at a green door with a shiny brass '7' nailed to it. Emma knocked.

'Ann? Annie! Jess is here!' She opened the door and stepped aside. 'I'll get a vase for those flowers,' she said, and headed off back down the corridor.

The room was small, but neat and welcoming. An imposing mahogany chest of drawers dominated one wall, cluttered with silver-framed family photos. There was no wardrobe, but a large bookcase stood to her right, stuffed with a mess of paperbacks. A wide window let in welcome light, the rays catching flying dust in silent glitter storms. There were homely touches: a glossy Swiss cheese plant in a golden pot sat on the windowsill, a rag rug brightened the utilitarian green carpet and a doorstop in the shape of Hagrid stood next to Jess's feet; a nod, Jess supposed, to Ann's witchy past. In front of her, a white-haired woman was sitting up in a single bed with her eyes closed, covered in a patchwork quilt. She seemed to be asleep.

Was this really Ann? Jess didn't recognize her at all. The lines on her face were so deep, like the rivers you see on a map.

Why hadn't she been to visit? The last time she had seen Ann must have been ten or so years ago, when Jess had surprised her mum with an unannounced visit. Jess had walked into the kitchen and Ann had been sitting at Elle's table, surrounded by jars of unmentionables – things that Elle had collected over the years in her quest to cast just one spell that worked. Ann and her mum had looked so happy. She remembered feeling a bit envious of their easy friendship. Jess had struggled to make friends in adulthood – the only friends she could really count on were Dave and Andrew.

The old woman in front of her looked nothing like the vibrant woman she had seen that day. This version was pale, her cheeks sunken and her eyes so hooded they were almost invisible. Was she even alive? Jess watched for signs of breathing. The quilt was motionless, and Jess started to feel anxious. She moved closer to the bed and slowly leaned over towards Ann's face. They were almost cheek to cheek when Ann spoke.

'Hello, Jess. It's been a long time.' Jess jumped backwards in surprise, tripping over Hagrid and almost bringing the bookcase down with her. As she straightened up, she became aware of a guttural croaking sound coming from the bed. Ann was laughing at her.

'I'm not dead yet, my dear. Things to sort out first.' She patted the bedclothes. 'I've been so looking forward to seeing you. Let me have a proper look at you.'

Her lips look so thin that they're barely there, Jess thought. She sat down on the bed carefully, making sure not to sit on any part of Ann's frail body in case it snapped.

'Hello, Ann,' she said. 'These are for you.' She waved the tulips around and Ann nodded and smiled and whispered a hoarse 'Thank you.'

'You look well.'

'Of course I don't!' said Ann, with surprising alacrity. 'I'm on the way out.' Her chest rattled like a machine gun as she breathed in and out.

'Do you . . . do you want me to get someone?' Jess asked nervously. She'd never had someone die on her before. Except for Charlie, of course, her hamster, when she was five. Hard cuddles can have consequences.

'No, no – I won't pop off today.' Ann paused. 'At least,' she looked away for a moment, 'I don't think I will. I'm not quite so sure of anything any more. Anyway . . .' she turned back to Jess. 'I need to give you something. Now what was it?' Ann looked confused and then, to Jess's alarm, she started to hit her own head with her frail hands.

'This damn brain! No sooner does one thought fly in than another flies out. It's like the tiniest bird cage which can hold just one bird at a time. Wait – ah yes!' She reached under her pillow and brought out something long and thin. Jess blinked. A stick?

'It's not a stick, Jess. Well, it is, or was once. Don't you recognize it?' She offered it to Jess, double handed, as if presenting a crown to a queen on a cushion. Jess, bemused, took it, and held it up to the window.

At first, she felt nothing. Just a little bit foolish for holding a stick up to the light. But when she looked more carefully, she noticed something oddly familiar in its patina and its knots, and the way it bent at about twenty degrees two-thirds of the way along. And when she looked more closely still, she noticed how cool it felt and how dark it was, despite her holding it in direct sunlight.

And then, as if she had invited it in by opening up a door in her mind, a memory stepped through. A sofa, and a telly, and Andrew and Dave. Then a figure – or absence of a figure – and a sudden, fleeting sense of immense loss and despair.

She shivered and offered the wand, open palmed, back to Ann. 'I . . . I remember,' she said. 'I haven't thought about this since I was a child. It's the wand that you used when you cast that spell on us,' she said. 'You kept it, all this time? Mum said that you'd turned your back on all that spell stuff – I'd assumed that you'd destroyed it.'

With some difficulty, Ann pushed herself forward to come

closer to Jess. 'I tried to destroy it, believe me. But it is unbreak-able – at least to me.' She paused, catching her breath. 'Please, be my guest. Snap it in two! Or three!' She closed Jess's hands around the wand. 'Do it!' she said eagerly.

The poor old woman clearly had dementia. Jess sighed inwardly. If she snapped this ridiculous stick in half, hopefully that would calm Ann down – and then she could leave. She grasped the stick at both ends, surprised at how the wand was warming up in her hands, and pulled each end downwards. Nothing happened. There was no give in the wood; it didn't flex or bend at all. This was absurd. It was only a couple of centimetres thick, and dry as a bone – it should snap like . . . well, like a twig. She applied more pressure, and more, putting it over her knee, then under her foot and finally pushing it as hard as she could against a wall. Nothing happened.

'I told you,' said Ann. 'It's unbreakable. I've tried it all – I've set fire to it, squashed it, put it in a washing machine, oven, tumble drier . . . it always comes out pristine.' Jess looked at the wand, astonished, turning it over and over in her hands.

'How does it feel?' asked Ann.

'It was cold at first. But now it's very warm,' said Jess. 'Hot, even.' Ann was looking at her closely.

'There's something else,' said Ann. Her sunken eyes were wider now. 'Isn't there? Tell me. Tell me how you feel.'

Jess considered the question before answering. She did feel different – the change was small, but it was there; the wand, initially dormant, now seemed electrically charged somehow, and it was passing some of that energy to her. Through her. 'I feel . . . different. More . . . I don't know . . .'

'Powerful?' asked Ann.

Did she feel powerful? 'Not exactly,' said Jess, who didn't really know what powerful felt like. 'More . . . in control.' *But it's growing*, she thought. *This new feeling.*

Jess dragged her eyes away from the wand and looked at Ann. The old woman's face was full of life now; her deep creases were less defined and her eyes shone. In this moment, she was completely lucid.

'I've chosen you to become the new guardian,' said Ann. 'You must protect it, but listen to me because this is important: you must never use it. It's too powerful. If you try to use it, it will consume you.' She took Jess's hand. 'I don't know its history for sure, although I think the Devil is at the root of it. It was only when the wand had been brought into our family that we were able to summon his demon, Beleth, and we still don't truly know the consequences of what we have done. Others are looking for it. Hide it. Hide it from yourself and others. Try not to think of it.' She paused for a moment. 'Even your mum recognized the wand's power and coveted it; I had to tell her that I had destroyed it, for her own good. To release her.' She squeezed Jess's hand. 'I think – I hope – you are stronger.'

Jess tried to process everything that was being said. On the face of it, Ann's story was the rambling tale of a lonely old woman – but there was no doubt about it, Jess felt stronger, clear-headed, focused. If the wand could do this in just five minutes, what could it do to her in a day? A week? Her hand was shaking, and Ann caught hold of it, as though to hold it steady.

Ann looked at her. 'Have I made the wrong choice?' she asked. 'Will you be able to resist it?'

'I . . . I don't know,' Jess said. 'Why not give it to David? Or Andrew? Surely that makes more sense?' The wand was very hot now, and she could feel every fibre of the wood beneath her fingers.

'I want it out of our family,' said Ann. 'It's a curse to us. And besides – I don't think either of them are strong enough to keep it without using it. You are the only other person who would understand.' She let go of Jess's hand and fell back against her pillows, her eyes closing. Her breath resumed its rattling.

'I need you to keep it safe,' Ann muttered. Without letting go of the wand, Jess pulled the covers up under Ann's chin and smoothed them down. 'And,' Ann continued, 'get me a vase for those bloody tulips.'

29

Heaven's Broom Cupboard

Photographs

'I just don't understand it,' Dave said to the angels, looking from one to the other. 'Why on earth would Jess visit Mum?'

Arial shrugged. He gave his pen two final clicks before putting it away neatly in his top pocket. 'We were hoping that you might have an idea, or perhaps . . . *a clue.*'

Dave made a gurgling noise and shook his head. 'No! I don't have a clue! Not one. I can't remember anything about—'

'Try the photographs,' Arial interrupted.

'But they're back in Purgatory – on my bunk.'

Arial shook his head and pointed at Dave's pyjama bottoms. Dave patted himself down and felt something papery in one of his pockets. Of course! He'd slipped the photos in before he'd left. He brought the photos out; Rose's was on top, and he begrudgingly put it to the back, giving it a little stroke with his thumb that he hoped the angels hadn't seen. Jess's hooded eyes stared out at him from the next photo. Where on earth was that kitchen? He looked harder and something nudged at his subconscious.

And suddenly, he had it. The memories surged back so powerfully that he dropped both photographs and gripped the chair for support. About Jess. About how they'd lost touch and how they had reconnected after many years. And about the visit he'd made to her just before his murder.

At primary school, Dave, Andrew and Jess had stuck together like glue. Their mothers had been the best of friends and they treated each other's house as their own. Andrew had doted on Jess, and followed her around as if on a lead, nodding and agreeing with everything she said. Dave had been more aloof but would happily sit with Jess in the playground when he wasn't playing football, counting the number of skips she was doing or tutoring her in the art of marbles.

Being older, Jess and Dave had gone to secondary school at the same time. At first, they'd sat together on the bus, sharing bubble gum or TV reviews, or writing in the dirt on the window. But one day, Dave had got on the bus and found their usual double seat empty.

He'd looked around and saw that Jess was sitting with Milly and Trisha on the back seat, giggling over a photo story in a magazine. Dave had moved down the aisle towards Jess, but as he'd approached Trisha had noticed him and whispered something in Jess's ear. Jess had looked up at Dave, a brief smile on her face, and had been about to say something when Milly spoke first.

'Get lost, creep!'

Jess's smile had instantly evaporated and she'd looked away, whispering to her two new friends, something that made all three of them laugh. The bus took a sharp right and Dave had been thrown off balance, toppling him into the lap of Tanya Heard, a bespectacled first year, who had screamed. Everyone in the back half of the bus turned round to see what the commotion was about. Dave, his face turning scarlet and tears pricking at his eyes, had hauled himself up with a thousand apologies, and slumped into his usual seat, alone.

And that had been it.

Dave's embarrassment stayed with him like a scar, but over the next few weeks he'd found some other friends, and before they knew it, secondary school was over and they went to university – and he didn't speak to Jess again for almost ten years.

It had been Andrew who had re-introduced them. He'd kept in touch with Jess throughout their twenties; she'd gone to art school and after that, had ignored the rat race, choosing to live in a squat with no running water, pinching electricity from their neighbour's supply. Whenever Andrew had brought Jess up in the conversation, Dave changed the subject. He still hadn't forgiven her for that incident on the school bus, all those years ago.

Dave very clearly remembered the night Jess came back into his life. It was 2015, Rose was somewhere in Europe and he'd been facing another evening of being home alone. Andrew had used his powers of persuasion to convince Dave to go to a club, even though the last time Dave had danced anywhere was when he was seven, to his mother's Abba LP. Now aged thirty-three, he had not been looking forward to it, had not known what to wear, how to act, what to drink, how to dance. They had arrived and had immediately been surrounded by hot, sweaty young people, all slopping their cocktails over Dave's shiny work shoes. And it was so loud. Andrew had said something to him which he'd pretended to hear, and he'd nodded. It was only after Andrew had disappeared that Dave realized he had gone to join some other people. Dave was left at the bar, holding a pint of something warming rapidly, and shuffling his feet side to side almost to the beat of the music.

He'd just made his mind up to leave, when someone tapped him on the shoulder.

'Hello, Dave,' shouted the black-lipped, kohl-eyed, Quant-bobbed woman, over the music.

Dave knew her immediately, even in the semi-darkness of the club. Something about the way she held her head to one side – a kind of sinister Lady Di look – or maybe it was something to do with her smile, which was close-lipped, tight, and didn't reach her eyes. Or maybe it was the middle finger she was holding up, four inches from his face.

'Jess!' shouted Dave.

Jess lowered her finger and for a second, her smile broadened. She stepped closer and beckoned him to bend down so that she could say something in his ear.

'I saw you come in – have to admit I was a bit surprised. Didn't think this was your kind of place!'

Dave shrugged. 'Don't know what you're trying to say,' he shouted. 'I've got all the moves.' He did a little shuffle with his feet.

Jess looked at him. 'Was that a . . . tap dance?'

Dave straightened up and took half a step backwards. She was wearing black leather trousers and not much of a top. In the flashing half-light he thought he could make out a dragon tattoo curling down her left arm. She had come a million miles from the girl he had known at primary school.

'You've changed,' he said, bending over again to get closer to her ear.

'You haven't.' She gestured to his shoes, so shiny they were reflecting the moving shapes of dancers a few feet away.

Despite himself, he smiled. She was right – his shoes were an awful choice for a club. But she didn't exactly fit in here either. She said, 'Are you here with someone?'

'Only Andrew,' he said. 'Although he seems to have disappeared with his cronies.'

Another fleeting smile. 'Do you fancy walking me home? Full disclosure – I live four miles away.' She looked again at his shoes.

'Don't worry about me,' he said. 'These babies are wide-fitting with non-slip soles and padded insoles. I could walk to John O'Groats and back and my feet would still be fresh as daisies.' He looked at her feet – she was wearing knee-length boots with towering heels.

She waved him away. 'I'm a woman,' she said. 'I can walk in anything.'

It was drizzling when they left the club. Jess only had a flimsy jacket, and Dave wondered whether he should be offering her his coat. He started to take it off, saying, 'Do you . . . ?' but she shot him a withering look and he quickly put it back on. They walked in silence at first. There was a huge elephant in the room; he desperately wanted to ask her why she had been so cruel to him all those years ago but wasn't able to formulate the words. He was worried that they would come out of his mouth accusingly, and he didn't want to frighten her away. Despite himself, he was enjoying her quiet company.

After a couple of minutes, he stopped walking and turned to her. 'Look—' he said, just at the same time that she said, 'I want to—' They both smiled awkwardly and then, together, said, 'You first.' Then they laughed. Proper, uninhibited laughter, like they were kids again.

'I think Andrew set us up,' she said. 'I've been asking him about you for years and I think he got tired of me banging on about you, so he invited both of us to that godforsaken place.'

Of course! It did feel strange that Andrew had been so adamant he come with him to the club, and then immediately left him on his own. 'Why that little shi—'

Jess cut in. 'I'm glad he did. I wanted to say sorry, Dave. Really. I've wanted to say sorry for years.' Her eye make-up was running in the rain and she wiped it with her wrist, smearing it across her cheek.

'Thing is,' she continued, 'I didn't know who I was when I was a teenager. Who am I kidding? I'm still not sure.' She looked up at him. 'I know I caused you a lot of pain.' She paused, and he wondered if she was waiting for him to say something. He said nothing.

'So anyway . . . I always ask Andrew about you – I was sorry to hear about Rose but, you know, from what I've heard, she's not—'

'Please don't talk about Rose,' Dave interrupted. 'You don't know her.'

Jess bit her lip. 'Yes, sorry. Again. You're right.' She dipped her toe into a puddle that was growing by her feet, and dragged a line of black water out onto the pavement. 'Anyway, if it makes you happy, those girls at school – the ones I hung around with? They're all bored housewives now, full of Botox and dressed in designer gear.' She flung her arms out. 'I mean, look at me! I don't exactly fit in with them anymore.' And then, 'I never did, truth be told.'

Dave looked at her, this small, spiky woman, bedraggled and vulnerable. He wondered if she was as lonely as he was. 'Your make-up's running,' he said. 'Want me to fix it?'

She looked confused. 'Yes – OK then.' He stepped towards her and with one sweeping movement wiped his palm all over her face, smudging white foundation into black eyeliner into purple lipstick into brown eyeshadow. When he had finished, he stepped back to admire his handwork, wiping his hands on his trousers.

'Do you feel a bit better now?' she asked, her whole face a storm of colour.

'Funnily enough, I do,' he said.

They walked in silence for a while. After about two hundred yards, he nudged her elbow, sending her off balance. She pushed back, a little harder than she meant to, cartwheeling him back into a pile of wet bin bags. Dave lay there, cushioned by discarded coffee cups, plastic wrapping and, happily, an old mattress which broke his fall. He was wet, bruised and cold. But he couldn't remember being happier.

They didn't walk arm-in-arm like lovers, but they walked close to one another, giving each other a little push or nudge when the other said something funny. It was like being ten again. He told her about Rose and the troubles they'd been having, and she told him about her failed romances and financial difficulties. He asked her if she was OK – financially – and was about to offer her a loan when she said, 'I don't want your money, Dave. Just your friendship.' And he smiled and offered his hand up for a high five. She left him hanging and ran off, laughing.

They got to the corner of Jess's road and she convinced him to leave her there, not wanting him to see where she lived. 'It's a tip,' she said. 'I'll be all right here.' Reluctantly, he left, but changed his mind and ran back to the top of the road, only to see her disappear into a house about a hundred feet away from where he stood.

They'd kept in regular touch after that, at first mostly by phone but eventually meeting for coffee, or an after-work drink. Jess always seemed to have some drama going on in her life, usually to do with men, or money. Sometimes she seemed a little detached, unable to keep eye contact, nervy or just plain sad. Dave wondered whether she took drugs, but never asked her about it. He preferred to keep things light and always tried his best to cheer her up when he saw her, with his terrible jokes and memories of when they were children. They'd spent the next few years gradually rekindling their friendship: pub quizzes, Sunday lunches, after work drinks, walks in the park. At one point they even tried jogging together, but Dave laughed so hard at Jess dressed in fitness gear that their first run was also their last.

When Rose returned, Dave invited Jess round so that they could meet. The two women got on reasonably well but Dave noticed that Jess wasn't her usual sparky self; he put it down to her being out late the night before. With Rose back on the scene, Dave saw less of Jess, and the times he did see her, she seemed keen to get away. He came to the conclusion that she must be seeing someone else, and felt happy for her that she'd found someone.

And now, Dave remembered how he had felt after Rose left him for Ian. He'd sunk into a fug. It wasn't depression but much sharper, more like the feeling he'd had when his dad had died. Grief. He had been with Rose for so long after all – on and off – and although they'd never married and hadn't been able to have children, he'd nevertheless thought that this was it for him – the woman he'd live with and die with (the irony being that she'd been present for his death, even if it had been decades earlier than he'd imagined and that twat Ian had been there too). But this second departure had hit him much harder than the first, and in the immediate aftermath, he'd found it difficult to get up, to get dressed, to make himself something to eat. His boss had signed him off from work and he'd spent pyjamaed days watching bad films, crying into one of Rose's jumpers that she'd left behind, drinking in the remnants of her scent.

Jess had been such a wonderful friend to Dave during this

time. She seemed to find new reserves of energy and had phoned every day, entertaining him with gossip from her office. She had popped round twice a week to tidy up his pizza boxes and listen to him sob about the unfairness of life. And she had organized Thursday pub nights for Dave, Andrew and herself at the Three Johns, opposite the Angel Tube station, presumably in the hope that getting Dave out of the house and amongst people would cheer him up.

Dave hadn't been keen at first. He didn't want to leave the house, never mind step on to the Tube. But Jess told him not to be such a pussy (her word) and that, if he didn't want to use the Tube, he could damn well use his legs to walk because it was only a mile and a half. So, reluctantly, Dave put his trainers on and found himself amongst people again.

Jess – a socialist – had suggested meeting at this particular pub because of its links to the Russian Revolution. Apparently, Lenin and Trotsky had met there in 1903 with a group of agitators. When Dave arrived early for their very first 'Thursday Socialist Club' (her words), he found a round table free, and sat down wearily. He looked at the friendly bar staff, and the small groups of happy people gathered around him. This wasn't too awful. He could just about bear it. He flicked through the menu and absent-mindedly picked up one of the beer mats on the scarred table. Underneath, he saw that someone had scratched 'I LOVE HITLER' into the wood. Given the pub's history, this made him laugh. And when he'd stopped laughing, he reflected that this was the first time he had laughed in ages.

They had met at the round table every week, without fail,

for months. For a while they thought it would be funny if they pretended to be the three Johns, and to call each other John, and whenever someone forgot, they had to drink. And at some point in the evening, Jess would always say, 'Do you think Trotsky sat here?' and the other two would say 'yeeeessss' in a very bored way, and then they could get on with their evening. Jess would occasionally try to steer the conversation round to politics, but Andrew and Dave would deftly steer it back towards pale ale or TV or office chatter.

It was Andrew who had first suggested inviting Rose to the Thursday Socialist Club. He had kept in touch with her after she'd left Dave and knew that her new relationship with Ian wasn't panning out well. She missed her friends and wanted to build some bridges with Dave. To say that Jess wasn't keen was an understatement. In fact, when Andrew had tentatively brought it up in conversation one evening at the round table, Jess had thrown the remains of her pint at him and stormed out – only to storm back in a couple of minutes later because she'd forgotten her phone. Dave remembered exactly what she'd said, before her second stormy exit.

'He hates you, you know.' She nodded towards Andrew who sputtered with (fake? Genuine?) laughter. Dave had been confused about what she'd meant. Surely she wasn't referring to his brother? She must have meant Ian.

Andrew didn't hate anybody.

30

Heaven's Broom Cupboard

Dave thought he had been in this tiny room longer than his entire time in Purgatory. Or longer even than his entire time on Earth. However, given that he'd been sitting on the same hard-backed chair with no cushion for what seemed like an eternity, his body was holding together pretty well. Back in the good old days of being alive, by now his back would have seized up and his bum would be completely numb. There had to be some upsides to being dead, he supposed.

His mind, unfortunately, was another matter. He was still reeling from everything that had been thrown at him. He knew that Gobe and Arial were telling him the truth about his mum and about Beleth's possession of himself, Andrew and Jess. But he was finding it all very hard to accept.

He zoned back into the angels' discussion. Arial was talking softly and hesitantly. 'Actually, sir, there was one other thing. But it's . . . well, it's to do with feelings.'

Gobe looked surprised. 'Feelings, Arial? Right, well, out with it.'

Arial looked at Dave sheepishly. 'It's Jess. I think – well, I think she's in love with you, David.'

Dave was gobsmacked. 'Well, yes,' he stuttered, 'as a friend. We've got a lot of history together, you know.'

'Not as a friend, David.' Arial was firm. 'Despite the Blocks, I can tell how she felt. It's as plain as day. The little gifts she gave you. Regular phone calls. The way she looked at you, the way she steered clear of you when you were with Rose – remember?' Dave looked blank. 'Glory be and hallelujah, David – I'm probably the least emotionally intelligent being you will ever meet, and even I can tell that she was besotted!'

Not for the first time, Dave felt his jaw slacken. Jess? Raven-haired goth Jess, who he'd climbed trees with and played knock-down ginger with and watched *Going Live* with? He knew she hadn't had many boyfriends but he'd always assumed that for whatever reason she just wasn't interested in a relationship or maybe even was gay. Jess? In love with him? Ridiculous!

'Arial is never wrong,' said Gobe, sounding like a proud parent. 'Well, this is a turn up for the books, isn't it?'

'You could say that,' said Dave, still reeling. He turned to Arial. 'Are you absolutely sure?'

'Oh yes. And another thing. She was unhappy about your wish to rekindle a relationship of sorts with Rose. In short, she was jealous, David.'

Dave stood up forcefully, pushing his chair back, and found himself inadvertently nose-to-nose with Arial. 'Now that is preposterous! She was happy for me.' He shuffled around 180 degrees to face Gobe. 'Wasn't she?'

'Apparently not,' said Gobe. '"A tranquil heart gives life to the flesh, but envy makes the bones rot." Isn't that right, Arial?'

'Exactly, sir. Proverbs 14:30, I believe.'

Gobe continued, 'The question is though, did she think, "If I can't have him, no one can?"'

31

One Week Before the Murder

Jess

After Jess had stormed out of the Three Johns, Dave and Andrew sat in silence for a while. It had been months since he and Rose had split but still, every time her name was mentioned, Dave felt odd and anxious. He had come to love his Thursday evenings, and he wasn't sure how he felt about someone who had betrayed him so terribly joining their safe, happy circle.

But he did still love Rose. Which was a bit of a curse.

Jess's reaction foxed them both and they agreed it was best to let her calm down before broaching it with her. But when she didn't turn up the following Thursday, Dave began to worry.

'She'll be fine!' Andrew said. 'Give her another week. I won't say anything to Rose yet.' They spent a pleasant evening in the pub together, talking about their mum mostly, and what they should be doing now that she had been diagnosed with dementia. They discussed power of attorney, which Andrew seemed to know about in great detail, and they agreed that

Andrew should arrange it as Dave couldn't organize a piss-up in a brewery. But it felt odd having just two Johns at the table, rather than three.

The following day, Dave took the day off work, saying he wasn't feeling too well. Which was true – he'd only had a couple of hours' sleep as he'd been so worried about Jess. He'd called her three times the previous evening, and left messages, each increasingly concerned. This was so unlike her; usually, she'd pick up in an instant.

She'd moved into a new flat share just a month earlier, not far from Highbury Fields. Dave hadn't been round yet – as usual, she hadn't been keen on visitors – but he knew the address, so he set out, pausing at the florists to buy a bunch of something pretty from a bucket.

When he arrived at her house, he understood why she hadn't been keen to receive guests. The front door only had one hinge and the paint had long ago dried up and skulked off. The front garden was full of bins and tarpaulin and a couple of old dining chairs with five legs between them. Music seeped out from gaps in the downstairs window. He checked the address on his phone. Was this right? Did Jess really live here?

He knocked tentatively on what was left of the door, and had to fight the urge to run away when it was opened by a giant man with a spider's web tattooed over his entire face. The man laughed uproariously as Dave stuttered,

'H . . . he . . . hello. I'm here to see J . . . Jess.'

Tattoo-face-man offered his hand and said in a surprisingly sing-song voice, 'Alreet! Reet good to see you, fella. My name's Thomas. Dinna shat yesen. I'm just a lover of nature from the North.' He pointed to his face and laughed. Dave tried to rearrange his face into something that looked less terrified.

'Oooooh. From the North? That far?' What? What was he saying?

Thomas smiled, showing his perfect teeth. 'Aye. It's a long way to walk but only a nanosecond by Facebook Messenger!'

Dave smiled back and they both stood there in uncomfortable silence. Dave didn't trust himself to break it with any ridiculous attempt at social pleasantries.

'Anyways,' said Thomas, who was used to filling the conversational gaps of terrified strangers. 'Jess then, is it? Aye – ye look like ye come from the same stock.' He opened the door wide on its one hinge and gestured him inside. 'Second floor. Mind the gaps in the stairs as you go.'

Dave squeezed past and found himself giving Thomas a half-hearted salute. *Jesus,* he cringed – *he must think I'm a total cock*. Straight in front of him was a flight of dusty stairs which he ran up, two at a time, avoiding the holes and not looking back.

The landing was shabby but full of light from a floor-to-ceiling window at the back of the house. He counted four scratched doors, all with locks, and there was something large next to the banister, covered in a blanket. He was just about to lift the blanket when one of the doors opened.

'I've been expecting you, Mr Bond!' There was Jess, resplendent in the sunlight, wearing black leather trousers and a black hooded top. Give her a cape and she'd look like a supervillain.

'I've just escaped from a literal monster!' Dave panted as

he hugged her, her leather trousers creaking in the embrace. Jess laughed.

'Thomas? He works at Morrison's bakery. He's an absolute wonder at bakewell tarts. You should see his room – covered top to bottom in Nigella recipes!'

Dave wasn't sure if she was joking or not. Thomas didn't look the baking sort. But he had to agree that Nigella was marvellous and resolved to try to engage Thomas in culinary conversation, should he have the pleasure of meeting him again.

'I expect you want to know why I left the pub in such a flounce.' Jess took a step backwards and gestured inside. 'Come in. I'll put the kettle on.'

He proffered the flowers from the bucket. 'Happy new home,' he said, walking through the door. The first thing he noticed were huge paintings propped up against the walls, all of them monochrome, with thick black and grey globs of paint covering the canvases. The room was multipurpose; a shabby sofa bed stood squat in the middle of the room, and a short row of beige kitchen cupboards lined one side. There was a tiny Belling stove in the corner and an ominous patch of mould on the ceiling that Dave thought at first was just another piece of art. The room smelled like a men's changing room.

'Thanks, Dave,' Jess said, taking the flowers. 'Aren't lilies symbolic of death? My favourite!'

'I thought you'd like them.'

'I'll have to put them in a saucepan for now.' She smiled apologetically. 'I'm out of vases, I'm afraid.'

'No bother,' Dave said. 'Jess—'

'Just sit over there, Dave' she interrupted. 'Shove the books on the floor – I'll bring the tea over and I'll tell you everything. OK?'

Dave nodded dumbly and walked over to the sofa, pushing a small pile of books carelessly on to the carpet. He felt a bit unnerved by the whole situation. Why was Jess living here? He couldn't understand why she always chose to live in such squalid places. Sure, rentals in London were expensive, but this . . . the bright tie-dye bedsheets covering the sofa and the odd jolly houseplant couldn't disguise the dingy, damp little room for what it was – a right royal dump.

'Your paintings are . . . interesting,' he said, while Jess made the tea. 'They kind of . . .'

'Suck up all the joy?' Jess was deadpan, putting teabags into mugs.

'That's it exactly.'

He looked at the pile of books on the floor. A vegan cookbook, an Agatha Christie, a Michael Palin and . . . wait, he used to have a copy of this! *Fungus the Bogeyman*. He picked it up and was just about to shout over to Jess when something stopped him in his tracks. There was something very familiar about the book – the pattern the creases made on the cover, the waviness of the paper and the peeling Woolworths sticker on the back. But it was the stain just under Fungus's nose that clinched it.

That was *his* blood, from *his* nosebleed, right after he'd walked into the kitchen cupboard, aged nine. This was *his* book.

So why did Jess have it?

Dave quickly shut the book and returned it to the pile, just as Jess turned around, holding a tray with two mugs of tea and a plate of custard creams.

'My favourite!' said Dave, grinning.

'I know,' she said, settling herself down next to him and handing him a mug with 'I AM A TWAT' on it. 'Why are you grinning?' she asked.

'Oh, am I?' He never did have a good poker face. 'Sorry,' he mumbled, covering his smile with his hand until he managed to flatten out his mouth.

'So,' said Jess, 'before you start, I know you have questions. Correct?'

Dave helped himself to a biscuit. 'Correct – it's just that we're a bit—'

'Worried about me?' she interrupted. 'I'm OK. Well, I'm dealing with some shit, but I will be OK.' She caught Dave looking at the mouldy patch on the ceiling. 'I know this place is a bit of a change from where we grew up.'

'Jess – I hope you don't mind me asking,' he said hesitantly. 'But your mum died a year ago, didn't she?' Jess gave a curt nod. 'Well – didn't she leave you anything? The house or some money or . . . something that might improve . . .' he looked around '. . . this.'

Something flashed across Jess's face. Pain or anger or something else that Dave didn't recognize. 'She left me nothing. Well, that's not quite true. She did leave me the house, but it turned out that she had nothing else but debts. One cancelled out the other. So I was left with nothing except the house contents. In other words, a lot of jars full of . . . weird stuff.'

Dave didn't know what to say. He knew Elle was a bit different, but he'd always thought she'd make sure that Jess was looked after. He started to stutter. 'Well, I'm sure she didn't mean . . .' but left it hanging, because he wasn't sure of anything at all. Why did he find this sort of conversation so hard? Andrew was always much better at emotional stuff. He couldn't even look Jess in the face, staring instead at a spot just over her left shoulder.

A glass jar on a shelf above them caught his eye. It had a jagged lightning bolt crack and an unusual glass stopper in the shape of a shell. It was a quarter full of a pale blue liquid.

'Hey,' he said. 'That looks like one of the jars my mum had when we were kids. You know – the ones that held herbs and things.'

Jess turned to look, and then turned back to Dave. 'Ah. Bullseye. Trust you, Dave. You always get to the heart of the matter!'

Did he? What on earth was she talking about?

'I think that did used to belong to your mum. She must have seen how much my mum loved it, and given it to her.'

'Yes, I remember. My mum gave her all her books, too. They'd been in our loft for years. She had so many of them – not that I ever really took any . . .' He trailed off – Jess didn't seem to be listening. She was biting her nails, and Dave couldn't help noticing that she'd got down to the quick on almost all of them. A drop of blood by her thumbnail expanded slowly, like a tiny balloon, before bursting and snaking its way down her hand.

'What's the matter, Jess? Listen, if it's about Rose . . . it's really kind of you to be worried about me but I think I'm OK with it, you know?' He paused and then said, 'You've got . . . something dripping . . .' He pointed to her hand.

Jess gave her head the tiniest of shakes and her eyes refocused first on Dave, and then on her thumb. She mumbled something which Dave didn't catch and quickly rubbed off the blood, then sucked the last of it away as if she was drawing out poison. She took her thumb out of her mouth and cradled it on her lap. After a few seconds of uncomfortable silence, she looked up at Dave. 'I need help,' she said, simply. Her eyes were glistening. 'I can't cope.'

Dave's mouth dropped open. He didn't know what to say. 'Can't cope? With what?' was all he could manage.

'I've been given something and I – well, it's making me ill. I can't sleep any more. I worry about everything.' She sat down suddenly, very close to Dave. He could feel her breath on his face as she spoke. 'And I've started to have hallucinations. Graphic, scary ones. I—' She put her hand to her mouth. 'I think I'm going to be sick.' She got up and ran through a small door behind the sofa into what Dave assumed was the bathroom.

This was weird. 'Jess?'

'I'm OK!' A thin voice fed through from the bathroom. 'I think I just need to sit here for a minute or two. Just in case.' A pause. 'Sorry. Help yourself to biscuits.' Another pause. 'I'm OK.'

Dave did as he was asked and took another custard cream. What was wrong with her? Was it women's problems? His mum had talked to him about the menopause once, and it had made his eyes water. But surely Jess was too young for that? And what was all this about her being given something?

His eyes wandered round the room and settled again on his mum's old jar on the shelf, holding the pale liquid. It was such an unusual pastel blue colour. Now that he looked properly, he could see something long and thin wedged behind it. What was it? He stood up, stretched his arm up and was just about to move the jar when—

'DON'T TOUCH IT!' Jess was out of the bathroom, looking pale and weak but sounding very loud and strong indeed. Dave snapped his arm back.

'I was just going to have a look,' he said sheepishly. 'What's that in the jar? It's an extraordinary colour. And there seems to be something trapped behind—'

'It's nothing. You should . . . Sorry, Dave, I think it's best if you go now,' she said. She had positioned herself between him and the jar and was walking towards him with her arms wide, shepherding him towards the door. Her eyes were so wide that the whites were showing all the way round her iris.

Dave instinctively took a step backwards. 'Wait . . . what?' He frowned. 'But I've only just . . . I wanted to know why you left last week. I don't care about the jar. I just wanted to know if you were all right.' He softened his voice. 'Look – you said you'd been given something. Shall I take it if it's upsetting you?'

'NO! No, don't worry. I'm fine. It's all fine. I'll be there next week. I just need to . . . to be alone right now.' She was pushing him out of the door. Actually pushing him.

'Right, well, I tell you what, I'll get Andrew to come round. Perhaps he can help. Is that OK?'

'If you like.' Dave was almost on the landing now. 'Mind the holes in the stairs on your way out.'

And she slammed the door behind him.

Well – that threw up more questions than answers, Dave thought, as he picked his way carefully down the stairs. Thomas was painting in the hallway.

'Lovers' tiff?' he asked, winking.

Dave didn't know what to say, so he just winked back in what he hoped was a knowing way, and quietly left.

He'd talk to Andrew about it all. Andrew was much better at things like this – he'd know what to do.

32

Heaven's Broom Cupboard

'I think we've lost David,' Arial was saying to Gobe. The angels had been discussing Jess – whether her being in love with Dave was a motive for murder, or a de-motive (Arial's phrase) – when Arial noticed that Dave had slumped in his seat, apparently looking at some spot on the wall over Gobe's left shoulder.

'All right, my boy?' asked Gobe, shaking Dave's shoulder gently. And then, whispering to Arial, 'He's been through a lot, poor chap. His mind must be an absolute sea of spaghetti.'

'I am still here, you know,' said Dave loudly. 'I haven't completely lost it. In fact, I was just thinking,' he shuffled himself back upright in his chair, 'you should bring people here instead of sticking them in Purgatory. It's so much more . . .' he looked round at the tiny space and the walls that seemed to inch interminably towards him '. . . gruelling.'

Gobe clicked his fingers. 'Glad to hear you're tickety-boo, David. I know you've had a lot of information to take in, but

235

focus is what's needed now – we need to keep our eyes on the prize. And what is important here is that we solve your murder. What has happened to you is highly irregular – unheard of, even. We are very concerned about it here in Heaven. Actually,' he paused, 'God is very worried.'

David wasn't sure if he could take yet another round of disbelief and it took a great effort to keep his mouth closed. God was worried? About him?

Gobe continued. 'Yes, God is aware of you and what has happened and has tasked me with "cleaning things up". You see, it's important that we know who committed your murder because – well, put simply – they'll need to be punished. We cannot have a murderer slip into Heaven; it would destroy us. The last time we had a bad nut almost led to our ruination and we have been at war with him ever since. We can't risk that happening again.'

The light in the room fizzed, and Gobe looked up.

'That's odd. We are definitely protected here. Must be a glitch somewhere.' He got up and touched the walls at different points, seven or eight times, his head tilted, as if listening for something. Dave wanted to ask what 'protected' meant, but Gobe was rolling on.

'So, my boy, my friend Arial and I have arrived at a plan. It's an unusual plan for an unusual problem.' Gobe got up and started to pace around the tiny room, Arial having to press himself tight into the wall to allow his master to stride past. Dave thought Gobe got brighter, shinier as he walked. He was stoked.

'Yes, I am unusually on edge, David. And I'll tell you why.

I've decided to fly under God's radar. Go rogue. Maverick, if you will.' He sat back down and clasped his hands together on his lap. Dave noticed that the angel's legs were shaking and Gobe immediately gripped his own knees to quieten them.

'The only course of action we can think of involves a bit of . . . rule-bending. We know that God wouldn't agree to it, but there's simply no alternative. And if our plan works, we will identify the murderer and curse him to an eternal burning afterlife.'

Dave nodded encouragingly. 'Go on.'

'Arial and I have found a way – a loophole, if you like – to send you back down to Earth before you were killed.'

'Alive? Will I be alive?'

'Of course alive, David! There'd be no point if you were dead, would there? You wouldn't be able to do much if you were a corpse. Please engage your brain.' He paused and looked around the tiny room, as if checking for intruders. 'David,' he said, leaning forwards, his voice low but urgent. 'We're sending you back to Earth to solve your own murder.'

Dave leaped up. 'You're giving me a second chance! A second coming. Like Jesus!'

'For goodness' sake, don't get carried away. It's nothing like Jesus. First – and we're pretty sure about this – you're not the son of God. Second – if you don't solve and avert your murder, you're going to get murdered – again – and will bounce straight back to Purgatory. Third – God doesn't know. Bending time is really not allowed. Have you never watched *Dr Who*?'

'Of course I have! I grew up on it!'

'Very good. Well then, you'll know that you cannot interfere with time. In this case, it means that when you're back on Earth, you can't reveal anything about what you know about the dinner party, the murder, Purgatory, me . . . anything. You have to be rigorous about that. Because if you do reveal something – whether by accident or on purpose, a light will be lit on God's switchboard and our secret will be out. And then we'll both be – excuse the terminology – in the shit.'

Surprised as he was by the angel's cursing, Dave had something else on his mind. 'How did the *Dr Who* writers know about how time works? Seems a bit complex to be a coincidence.'

Gobe paused. Dave thought he detected a half-smile on his lips. 'I had occasion to visit Steven Moffat once, and I might have been a bit . . . loose-lipped.' He saw a thousand questions breeze on to David's lips and said, 'Not now, David. In fact, not ever. An angel carries more secrets than you could ever count in your lifetime. If you were alive, of course. Which you're not – yet.'

No, not yet, thought Dave.

'Hang on,' he said. 'Why don't we just wait until I remember what happened to me? My memories have started to come back, you know. You've said that I need to spend a long time in Purgatory. So why don't we all just sit tight until it all floods back? And then I can tell you exactly what's happened. Job done.'

Gobe shook his head slowly. 'You might never recover all your memories. Death shoves your mind through a strainer and it is, quite frankly, addled. And in addition – memories are tainted with all sorts of subjective matter. They're never quite true, no matter how confident you are about what has happened. You might end up accusing the wrong person.'

'Oh,' said Dave. 'OK.'

Gobe patted him on the back. 'We'll stick with plan A. There is, however, a bit of a catch,' he said.

Of course. There had to be a catch.

'It's a silly little thing, really. To do with time. You see, we need to avoid a time flag.'

'A time flag? What's a—'

'A time flag is a warning signal that comes through to the Hub if there's a time anomaly on Earth. God put it in place after the Dark Ages.'

'Why – what happened in the Dark Ages?'

'Precisely, David. Nothing happened in the Dark Ages because they never actually took place. Well, not much of them. The Devil found a way to play fast and loose with time and fast-forwarded a couple of hundred years. You wonder why *Time Team* never dig anything up between AD 600 and 800? It's because *it never happened.*'

Dave let this sink in. Finally he said, 'Blimey.'

'Quite. So after this, as you might say, "balls-up", God put a variety of safety measures in to stop it happening again. Firewalls, if you like.'

Now this was more like it. As a software engineer, firewalls were things that Dave could understand.

'But there's always a way to bypass a firewall, isn't there? Even the really well-crafted ones,' Dave asked hopefully.

'Arial,' Gobe waved at Arial, who was standing ramrod

straight against the wall, 'says that there is a way. The good news is that it's quite simple. The bad news is that it involves you doing an awful lot of running around.'

Arial stepped forward and explained to Dave what he needed to do.

'So,' Dave said five minutes later, looking from one angel to the other. 'Let me get this straight. I have to run round Hannah's house like a maniac, find all the clocks, and stop them – as well as solving my own murder?'

'Not all the clocks, David,' Arial said. 'Just the old-fashioned ones that aren't linked to satellites. We can do the modern ones from here.'

Dave was dubious. This didn't seem to conform to the laws of physics *at all*. 'And this – stopping time thing – that will be enough, will it? I won't trigger a time flag?'

'I know it sounds low tech, but that's how God likes to work. Sometimes.' Gobe added, just a little irritably, 'And remember that the laws of physics were created by God and so bending them is really not an issue.'

Dave still wasn't convinced. 'OK, so you put me back down on Earth . . . when? A month before the party? A week? I'll need to do so much groundwork on my so-called "friends"; scout out the houses of them all, follow them, go through their bins – then I'll need access to Hannah's house, of course, maybe the day before, to search for clocks . . .'

Gobe shifted in his seat. 'Ah. Not quite. Arial?' He looked at Arial who looked shifty, then sighed and shrugged apologetically. 'I'm sorry, David. We'll put you down outside Hannah's house at 8 p.m. On the evening of the party.'

'Wait, what? So if we sat down to eat at 9 p.m. – and that's being generous, time-wise – you're giving me A WHOLE HOUR to stop all the clocks AND solve my own murder?'

Arial wrung his hands. 'I'm sorry,' he said again. 'It's all I could manage.' And then, 'To be fair, Columbo manages it in ninety minutes, and he's much older than you.'

Dave was just about to launch himself at the angel when he noticed that Gobe was smiling. 'Desist, David – Arial was just trying to lighten the mood.'

'I think he needs practice with that,' said Dave. 'I suppose – I suppose it won't be too bad if I've got a team of angels behind me. Where will you all be? In a van down the street, tuned in like the FBI? I suppose I will be wearing a wire? And a special vest?' He was warming to his task.

'Ah. Well, I'm glad you've raised that. First thing – we're not exactly a huge team. There's me, and then there's Arial. That's it.' Dave's face fell.

'Look, we have to keep it small because we don't want a . . . mole . . . feeding back to God. Arial is the best angel to have on our team, David. He is bright, knowledgeable, humble and – well, if I had a life, I would trust him with it.' Arial suddenly brightened, a huge smile sweeping across his face.

'Right,' said Dave. 'So there's you, and there's Arial. And that's it.'

'Yes, David, but let me assure you, we are the crème de la crème of investigatory angels – isn't that right, Arial?'

'Absolutely, sir. We are your Starsky and Hutch, your Cagney and Lacey, your Mulder and Scully, if you like. We are the "A" Team – that's right, David, but this time, "A" is for "Angel".'

Dave had to admit that Arial's knowledge of US detective dramas from the Eighties and Nineties was pretty comprehensive. 'Fine, OK. So you'll be there too – what? In disguise? Invisible? Next door?'

Gobe looked uncomfortable. 'It's not that we don't *want* to be there, David. But at the moment, we can't figure out a way that we can do it. If either of us appear at the dinner party out of the blue, we think our cover will be blown. You'll be dragged straight back to Purgatory – if you're lucky – and Arial and I . . . well, we'd be immediately exiled.' He shuddered at the thought. 'And we still wouldn't know who your murderer was.'

Dave was trying to square all this in his mind. 'So, let me get this straight. You and Arial have gone rogue in order to find a bad apple. I will have an hour to find out who the bad apple is. If I fail, I will have to die all over again – which I am by the way not looking forward to, as I'm sure it hurt considerably the first time around – come back to Purgatory and not mention the secret mission to anyone, ever.'

'Oh, you needn't worry about that, David. You'll have absolutely zero memory of it. You'll be completely empty headed. Just like—'

'Yes, thank you, no need to say it. Carrying on, then. What if I succeed? I mean, if I find out who is trying to murder me – what? Do you swoop in like MI5?'

'David, I know this is all very difficult for you, but have you not been listening? We haven't found a way to appear whilst you're replaying time. I'm really sorry. But we will arrange a rendezvous when the dust has settled so we can "debrief". We'll be in touch.'

'Oh, that makes me feel so much better.'

'Does it? Jolly good. Now, Arial and I have some technical details to see to – a case of dotting i's and crossing t's – nothing to worry about, so I'm going to pop you back in Purg for a little while. And mum's the word. Don't tell a soul.' Gobe paused and look steadily at Dave. 'And when you're down there, eyes and ears open. No pre-judging.'

'Brilliant. Already looking forward to it,' said Dave. As the angel picked up his chair to place it back against the wall, Dave noticed a large sweat patch on the back of Gobe's shirt. He glanced at Arial, who put a finger against his lips. Dave was just about to ask why he was doing that, when Arial made a sudden hand gesture, forcing Dave's eyes closed. When he opened them again a second later, ready to splutter complaints at Arial, he found himself lying on the scratchy but oh-so-comforting nylon of his sleeping bag, the zip reassuringly cutting into his back. The now familiar sounds of Edie and Freda arguing washed over him like the most soothing of lullabies. He touched the underside of the thin mattress above him, feeling the sharp springs on the tips of his fingers.

Ahhh – there's no place like home.

33

Purgatory

As Dave prepared to get up from his bunk and tell everyone about his time in the broom cupboard, he heard Gobe's voice inside his head.

'ON NO ACCOUNT TELL ANYONE ANYTHING OR WE SHALL BE – AS YOU MIGHT SAY – UP A CERTAIN CREEK WITHOUT A PADDLE.'

Dave looked around to see if anyone else had heard, but they were all going about their usual business, seemingly oblivious. Freda and Edie were arguing again. Loudly. Laura was refereeing. Louis was busy wall-watching, with his head-phones on. And the small mark on Wilf's chair still looked remarkably like a burn.

Gobe's voice sounded again in his ear, softer this time. 'I have a few things to take care of. Get yourself prepared. Be ready to go at a moment's notice.'

'How can I get myself prepared?' Dave whispered back. 'I haven't got anything to prepare myself with.' He waited for a response, but none came. Ready to go? It wasn't as if he had anything to pack – or even a bag to pack it in. What was he supposed to wear? Was he going back down to Earth in his pyjamas?

And if that wasn't bamboozling enough, their conversation in Heaven's broom cupboard had rocked him to the core. For starters – his own mum had possessed him with some sort of demon. Not just him, but Andrew and Jess too. What was she thinking? And where was that wand? And then, closer to home – what effect had Ian's lies had on Rose? Did she hate him? And Jess, in love with him? They had known each other since they were kids, and not once, not one single time, had he got any whiff of her liking him in that way. This Arial, this supposed whizz-kid, had completely got his wires crossed. Perhaps there was something wrong with the Hub. Perhaps he should offer to look at it for them. He was pretty good at wiring.

Anyway, the whole thing was absolutely preposterous.

Dave sat on the edge of his bunk, hands clasped in front of him. Perhaps, before he left for his mission, he should run through what he had learned in the broom cupboard and try to make sense of it all. Make a list of priorities. Make a pla—

'Coooeeeee! Dave! Fancy a game of Scrabble?' asked Freda.

Dave hesitated. 'Why not?' he said, but as he swung himself out of his bunk, happy to have some time away from the workings of his own mind, there was a blipping noise and—

34

The Murder

Back to the Start

There was no standing on ceremony. No holding hands or golden keys or making a wish or saying a fancy word. Just the blip, a sudden blankness, as if the lights had been turned off, and then a faint 'pop'. And there he was, standing in front of Hannah's house on the night of his murder.

Dave's head span and he put his hand out to the laurel hedge to steady himself. The touch of a leaf, and a twig – such a normal thing on a normal day – startled him. He drew his hand back quickly, as if burnt. He could feel again. How weird. He reached out again and rubbed the leaf between his fingers. Cool and smooth and of the Earth.

It made him smile, though he wasn't sure why.

His clothes felt different. Itchy. He looked down and realised he was dressed in his favourite gently unthreading jumper, a Bowie T-shirt and a pair of old jeans – exactly what he had worn the first time around. The jeans were tight around his crotch and the label of the T-shirt was digging into his neck, and despite himself, he found himself missing his soft Purgatory-issue PJs.

He forced himself to think about the task ahead – Gobe had told him not to 'pre-judge' – well, that was unfortunate, because currently 'pre-judge' was his middle name. He knew Ian had killed him. He just had to stop him from doing it.

He had a plan, of course. It was beautifully crafted, detailed, thought through to the nth degree. It was this.

1. Stop all the clocks
2. Stick like glue to Ian and stop him from putting anything in his food
3. End of plan.

Admittedly it was simple, but simple plans were so often the best, weren't they? Look at the cardboard tanks they made in the Second World War. Simple. The development of penicillin by accidentally growing mould. Simple. Adding salt and vinegar to flavour fried bits of potato. Simple. Don't ever overcomplicate something that can be done better by sticking to the basics.

There was a tightness around his right wrist that seemed at the same time familiar and unfamiliar. He looked and saw his dad's watch, its black leather strap a little too snug, as it had always been. Well, before he'd died, anyway. The gold hands shone: it was 7:58 p.m. He pulled out the winder and the watch stopped.

It was already dark and mist hung in clots around the house. When Dave turned his head to look at the front door, water droplets clung to his face.

Gobe? Are you there? He wasn't sure if he'd said that out loud, or whether the words had stayed in his head. Either way, there was silence. He was on his own, and it felt unexpectedly lonely.

The detached Edwardian house looked imposing in the blue darkness. It wasn't of mansion proportions, but the fact that it was set back a little from the road with a gravel drive made it appear grander than it really was. It looked like the sort of symmetrical house you would draw as a child: front door in the middle, flanked by two large bay windows downstairs. Four smaller windows above, and two chimneys, one of them puffing out white smoke into the night sky. Light leaked from the bay window to the right; the curtains were closed but the burble of noise inside made something inside Dave vibrate – a memory, or a shadow of a memory, or a shadow of a shadow of a . . . Whatever.

The sense of déjà vu was extraordinary. It made him nauseous. He wondered briefly whether all déjà vu was linked to a previous life. *Good grief – now is not the time to be contemplating the nuances of how an afterlife seeps into living. Pull yourself together, Dave, and concentrate on the job in hand.*

He checked his watch – still 7:58 because, *GODDAMN (stop swearing) you stopped your watch about thirty seconds ago. Right*, he said to himself, *I've got an hour to solve this thing and start living again.*

It's Agatha time, he thought, as he strode down the path towards the door.

*

'So lovely to see you, Dave!' Hannah welcomed him, hugging him warmly although he was damp from the mizzle outside. Why was she so bright? Her golden hair seemed back-lit, like an aura round her face. Something was wrong with his eyes. He had to squint to see her properly. Was it something to do with coming out of the darkness and into the light?

'You're looking . . . well,' he said, turning sideways so that he could look at her without his retinas burning. She was still holding his right hand and staring at him.

'You look . . . different,' she said, her thumb pressing into his palm, her eyes holding his. She looked concerned.

'I feel a bit odd, to be honest,' he said, shrugging. *Don't reveal anything. Don't reveal anything.* 'It's my eyes, Han. Everything's a bit . . . contrasty. Maybe I'm just getting old!' He laughed as best he could. It sounded hollow to him.

She let his hand fall and wafted over to the light switch. 'Hang on – let me try something,' she said, and fiddled with the switch for a second. The light in the room remained the same but suddenly, somehow, Hannah wasn't so bright. Was it just that his eyes were compensating? He looked around. The room hadn't changed – still the same waxy, ivory wall-paper, but Hannah – Hannah was more subdued. Her hair had gone from full-on halo to blonde shoulder-length bob. Normal.

More human. Less extra-terrestrial.

She must have noticed that Dave was staring at her because she said brightly, 'Just the new bulb!' and gestured upwards towards the pendant light. 'Something whacky that I bought online.' She looked at him strangely for a moment before turning on her heels.. 'Come on! You're missing the party!' And with that, she glided through an open doorway towards the sounds of a drinking game in full flow.

Pull yourself together, Dave. You've got fifty-nine minutes. Look for clues. Look. For. Clues.

'I'll just take my jumper off!' he called to Hannah's disappearing back. He heard a faint, 'Right-o!' from Hannah, and then general sounds of people having too good a time to notice he wasn't immediately at Hannah's heels.

Now he had a slice of time to get his bearings. He was alone in the lofty hallway, next to the coat hooks and shoe rack. The shoes were paired and tidy, and Dave surmised that they must belong to Hannah and her parents. The coats however were a mess; perilously hung up on top of each other like a grown-up's Buckaroo, threaded through with a long, cream, knitted scarf. Rose's scarf. *Don't sniff it, you weirdo.* He tore his attention away, focusing instead on the layers of pockets in front of him. He glanced towards the living room door to make sure he wasn't being watched, and then started to peel back the coats, looking for Ian's poxy old leather jacket that he wore everywhere. Work, weddings . . . Dave had even seen Ian wearing it to his own mother's funeral.

Of course, it was right at the bottom. He had to get into the coats, like a gateway to Narnia, to be able to get a hand in its pockets. If anyone saw him now, how would he explain this? His hand slid into the right side pocket, felt something cold and smooth; my God, was that a scalpel or something? He clasped it carefully between thumb and forefingers and then—

'Dave? Dave! What you doing, *mate*?'

Ian's weasely voice made him jump and the mystery object slipped from his fingers back into the depths of the pocket. He turned around quickly, his hackles raised, ready to spit fury at his nemesis. It was only when he got a mouthful of bomber jacket that he realised his top half was still hidden by coats, and that Ian was probably sniggering at the sight of his noodle-legs sticking out from underneath. By the time he had fought his way out, Ian was snorting with laughter.

'Something wrong?' Ian asked, taking a tissue from his pocket and pointedly wiping his eyes. Dave stood stock still for a moment, paralysed with embarrassment and anger, briefly considering whether murdering Ian there and then would be a fair exchange for an eternity in Hell.

After a second or two, he breathed out slowly and with difficulty said, 'Nothing at all. I was just looking for my jumper.' He turned back to the coat hooks. *Go. Away. You. Prat.*

'But mate – you're wearing it.'

Dave looked down and groaned. Only five minutes in and he was already way out of his depth. More Clouseau than Poirot. He really, really wanted to swear.

He shrugged at Ian. *I hate you.* 'What can I tell you?' Dave made a sterling effort to keep his voice level. Pleasant, even. 'It's been the longest of days.'

Ian curled one side of his mouth in a half smile, aiming, Dave thought, for sympathy but in fact achieving world-beating condescension. He held out his hand as if he was Dave's dad, and Dave was six. 'It's OK, mate. Come with me. We'll get you a drink.'

Dave reluctantly took off his jumper and threw it on a vacant chair by the stairs. He looked at Ian's hand as if Ian was holding the biggest dog turd in the world, and walked straight past him into the sitting room. *You may have won this battle, but I will win the war*, he thought. *You utter bastard.*

And then he wished he hadn't thought 'you utter bastard' because he could almost hear the points ticking away from his celestial spreadsheet.

'DAVE!' A collective, joyful greeting shook him out of his torpor.

The sitting room was large and comfy and old-fashioned and perfect for a party. An immense bottle-green velvet sofa was lit by orange standard lamps, standing like bookends. A glass coffee table with a map of the world on it was strewn with papers and books and half-drunk glasses of wine. An ornate iron fireguard hid a crackling fire. The wallpaper was a shiny cream colour, embossed with . . . what were they? Bowls of grapes? Difficult to tell in this light. Faded photographs drooped from a picture rail.

Wonderful cooking smells of frying garlic and something in the bready department were floating through from the kitchen, where Hannah was banging about with pots and pans. The Human League played softly from a karaoke machine.

Andrew and Jess were standing by a window at the far end of the room in a heated conversation about something. As he watched, Jess handed Andrew something, half hidden by her jacket, and Andrew bent down to put it carefully in his duffle bag. Dave half wondered what it was before catching sight of

Rose, who was sitting on the sofa. She looked like an angel and was smiling up at Dave – that was a good sign – but as he moved forward to kiss her on the cheek, Ian dumped himself next to her, pointedly putting his arm around her and drawing her towards him – a move that screamed 'mine'. Rose's smile faltered and she looked down, suddenly interested in something invisible on her dress.

The man was full of smug dirt. Well, Dave was going to hoover up that dirt and put it in God's waste bin.

'Bro!' Andrew was suddenly by his side, a firm hand on his shoulder. Dave turned and hugged him, tight. A bit tighter than was strictly necessary, truth be told.

'Whoa, Dave – I can't breathe!' Andrew pushed him away. 'I only saw you last week. You can't have missed me that much!' Andrew was red faced, and Dave noticed a single bead of sweat running down the centre of his forehead.

'Sorry, mate. You have no idea how much I long for you when you aren't with me.' He gave Andrew a playful punch on the arm. Andrew manoeuvred Dave's head into a headlock and they tumbled round the room like oversized toddlers, eventually falling on to a rug at someone's biker-booted feet.

'Hi Jess,' Dave panted.

'Stop looking up my skirt,' Jess said. She was half leaning out of an open window and Dave could smell her cigarette smoke from the floor. She looked tired, he thought.

Without warning, the smell of nicotine triggered off a sudden wave – a tsunami – of memories. It was as if Jess had hooked up a couple of jump leads, attached them to Dave's brain and flicked a switch. He'd walked into this room before.

He'd seen Ian being a twit. He'd seen Rose embarrassed. He'd rolled around the floor with his brother. And he'd tried to look up Jess's skirt.

That stain on the rug by his right temple – he'd wondered what had caused that before. He'd thought it was red wine, but now he was sure it was blood. The mud on the toe of Jess's right boot. It had been raining, of course. The tear in her tights behind her left knee. The strange, flocked wallpaper that had gone out of fashion in the Seventies, but somehow fitted right in here. The ceiling rose that was off-centre, and peeling.

He'd seen it all before. He was in this exact position. Nothing had changed.

A shabby grandfather clock stood in the corner. Golden hands pointed to 8:05.

'Is that the right time?' he called out to no one in particular.

Rose and Andrew looked at their watches (both digital, Dave noticed). 'Coupla minutes slow,' they both said, in unison.

'I'll fix it,' said Dave. He heaved himself up and walked over to the clock, trying to appear nonchalant. Standing right next to it, he could hear it gently ticking.

'You don't know anything about clocks!' his brother sneered.

I know how to stop them, Dave thought. He opened the glass casing carefully and pretended to fiddle about with the hands. Behind him, he could hear that Andrew and Jess had lost interest and were talking in hushed tones about something – presumably picking up the conversation they'd been having before he had arrived. Ian was trying to cosy up to Rose, but she had her back to him and was edging away. Dave desperately wanted to talk to her, to make things right with her, but he knew that he couldn't. Time wasn't on his side.

Hannah was in the kitchen next door, opening and shutting cupboard doors. *All clear*, he thought. He carefully opened the mahogany case and stopped the pendulum, then shut the case quickly before anyone noticed. The clock was silent.

He closed the glass case a bit more forcibly than he should and proclaimed, 'ALL DONE!'

No one was listening.

Step one done. It was around 8.07 p.m.

He looked around the sitting room for other clocks. No sign. Not even one on the fireplace – a stroke of luck. This was all going jolly well so far. Now on to the kitchen.

He was about to leave the room when something hit him. The fault in his plan. The gaping wound of a flaw that he hadn't thought of until now, the dim-witted muttonhead that he was.

Who was going to watch Ian whilst he was running around the house stopping the clocks?

35

The Murder

Stop All the Clocks

'Andrew! Andy!' His brother turned to him, looking annoyed at the interruption. Quite right too – he had just got to telling Jess the crux of why the Commodore 64 trounced the ZX series back in the day. Jess shot a grateful look at Dave before returning to her smoke.

'Sorry Andy, listen,' said Dave furtively, taking Andrew by the elbow and leading him into a quiet corner. 'I need you to do me a favour.'

Andrew suddenly perked up, interested. 'Sure. Of course. Anything.'

Dave whispered, 'I'm going to go into the kitchen and I need you to watch that mug,' he gestured at Ian, who was still attempting to engage Rose in conversation. 'I don't trust him with Ro.' *Don't tell a lie*, he thought. *Stick to the truth and you won't get penalized.* 'I don't trust him one little bit.'

'Why, mate? Have you seen something?'

'Yes,' Dave nodded. 'Yes, I've seen something.' Well, that was true. He had seen something. A lot of things, in fact.

'Well, what? What is it?'

Dave hesitated. 'I can't say at this time. Only that . . . I'm concerned.' That was true too. He WAS concerned.

'No need to say any more. My Action Man Eagle Eyes are on the case.' Andrew moved his eyes from left to right to left to right to show exactly how eagle eyed he was. 'I've got this.' He slapped Dave on the back good-naturedly.

'Thanks, Andy. I really appreciate it.' More than you know.

Andrew winked broadly and sloped back to Jess, but angled himself so that he could watch Ian whilst continuing his chat about Eighties hardware. Feeling satisfied that he had his best (only) man on the case, Dave left the sitting room for the kitchen, in his quest to temporarily stop time.

He passed back through the hallway and missed the step down into the kitchen. Stumbling into the room, he saved himself from a painful nosedive by catching the corner of a cupboard on his way down. *Calm down,* he thought. *It would be pretty stupid if you had an accident and killed yourself now.*

Hannah was standing on the far side of the room and had her back to him. She didn't turn, so Dave assumed that the sounds of rattling pots and pans had covered the noise of his not-so impressive entrance. That was something, at least.

He was struck with something else. He had no memory of that step, of falling. This must be new. He had not been in the kitchen before – probably because he was a lazy git and hadn't offered to help first time around. This was all new territory

257

to him. It felt good. It felt like he was *properly investigating*.

The room was opaque and hot, like a steam room. Dave suddenly wished he wasn't wearing a jumper. A strip light ran the length of the room, giving off a violet glow. Cooking mess covered all the surfaces; mountains of peelings, dirty bowls, cutlery, plates, whisks . . . every implement seemed to have been taken out of the drawers, used and added to the disarray.

'Are you cooking a curry?' he asked, pushing up his sleeves absent-mindedly. Was it a huge five-course affair? Some sort of tasting menu? He remembered that he'd had prawn curry, but couldn't recall anything else about the meal.

Hannah turned around and Dave tried to make out her expression through the purple mist. She was all soft around the edges like a . . . well, like a ghost. Or an angel. In fact, if Dave hadn't actually met an angel he'd have been convinced that she was, in fact, an angel.

She must have stepped towards him because she suddenly snapped into focus, and became Hannah once again.

Shame, Dave thought.

'Yes, it's a prawn curry,' Hannah said, wiping her brow with a dishcloth.

'Just . . . a prawn curry?' Dave asked, looking at the wreckage around them.

'I've had a few goes,' she said, smiling. 'I haven't cooked much before.' She glanced up at him. 'Well, actually, I haven't ever cooked.'

'Haven't *ever* cooked? How have you managed to get away with that?' Distracted, he leaned against a pinboard hanging on the wall. *Servants*, he thought. *She's had servants all her life. Cut-glass accent like that, big house – I'll bet she's an aristo.*

'Servants. I've had servants all my life,' she said, flat, as if it was just a normal thing to say.

'That's funny, I was just thinking those exact . . .' but as he was talking his shoulder slipped, and the shifting weight tore the pinboard off the wall. It hit the floor with a crack and a dozen bits of paper and postcards and calling cards and Lord knows what fluttered into the air.

'Oh no – I'm so sorry,' he cried, sinking to his hands and knees, trying to locate all the different scraps, most of which had settled under the kitchen table.

'Don't worry – it needed a sort-out anyway!' Hannah said cheerily as she joined him under the table.

Dave spied a postcard right at the back corner underneath a chair leg, and stretched to reach it. As he slid it towards him, he noticed that it had a picture of KITT, the car from *Knight Rider*, on the front. *That's odd*, he thought. *Does Hannah have an unlikely Hasselhoff obsession?* He glanced up at her but by this point she'd gathered up as much as she could and was in the process of standing up. Dave turned the card over. There were five words scrawled on the back with blue crayon:

DAVID
GET ON WITH IT

Dave dropped the card in shock, and then quickly picked it up, folded it in half and slipped it into his pocket. He checked to see if Hannah had noticed anything, but she had turned away and was clanking with something at the sink.

Gobe! I thought he said . . . Anyway, no time to think. Gobe was right. He needed to crack on.

'So sorry about that,' he said, standing again and dusting himself down. 'Shall I pop it back on its hook?'

'No need,' called Hannah. 'I only bought it a couple of days ago and I've already decided I don't like it.'

'Really?' It had collected a lot of paper over just a couple of days. Dave looked for the bits of paper that Hannah had cleared up, but they seemed to have disappeared.

'Hmmmmm. Sorry – could you pass me that spoon? Thanks.'

She's probably thrown them all away, thought Dave. *She probably can't bear clutter.* But the surrounding chaos didn't support that theory at all.

'Ummm . . . Hannah?'

'Yes?' She was distracted, tasting something that looked like it had lumps of potato in it.

'Do you have many . . . clocks? In the house, I mean. It's just that I've got a bit of an obsession with . . .' he hesitated, 'clockwork. Things. Clockwork things. Actually, not just clock-work things – battery clocks too. As long as they tick. Just . . . things that tick.' This wasn't going well.

She paused, spoon in mid-flight, and he thought he saw something pass over her face. A shadow or a thought or maybe a realization of something. But it may have been the steam playing tricks with his eyes.

'Well now, as it happens, we do have a handful of clocks.' Dave felt his heart sink. 'A couple of them are antiques – are you looking for something in particular? A maker? Or a style?'

Dave was feeling uncomfortable and out of his depth. He knew he should have watched a few more episodes of *Antiques Roadshow*. Having some fingertip knowledge of antique clock workings would have been invaluable in a situation such as this.

He decided to plump for a different route.

'It's more the . . . engineering. I'm writing a report comparing the . . . timekeeping ability of clockwork timepieces, compared to battery-operated clocks.'

'But I thought you worked in IT?'

'Ah! Yes. I'm being . . . seconded. To engineering.'

'But you work for a software development company, don't you Dave? Not a clock manufacturer.' He thought he saw her smile. How did she know so much about him? She must be one of those people who's actually interested in others. How unusual.

'Yes, but . . .' the lies were flowing more smoothly now. 'It's for a clock-making client. They're called . . . Folio Handface.'

'Who?'

'Folio Handface.'

'I've never heard of them.'

'They're new. Retro. Don't bother googling; they're not even on the web yet.'

She looked at him for a few seconds.

'OK,' she said, turning back to her potato. Thank God, he thought. 'Let's see. The clocks we've got are . . . the grandfather clock in the sitting room – that's been going strong ever since it was made in 1778. We're always so careful to wind it, and it's never once stopped.' Dave gulped. 'There's my dad's old travel clock. It's kept in his bedside drawer. You can go in there but please be quiet – he's very unwell and he needs all the sleep he can get.' She started cutting the potatoes and throwing them into a pan. 'Respiratory failure. Not long now.' She turned and smiled at him.

'Oh – I'm sorry to hear it,' said Dave, a little perplexed at how un-sorry Hannah sounded.

'Not to worry. Ah yes, and I've got a little carriage clock in my bedroom – you're welcome to take a look at that, it's only a cheap thing. And there's the clock above your head, of course.'

Dave looked up in surprise, to see a flat, dinner plate-shaped clock above him. It was one of those clocks made to look as if it had been lifted off a church steeple: roman numerals, some fake scratches and chips, a traditional maker's name (*Jonathan Lloyd* – not as creative as *Folio Handface*).

'Nice clock,' he said. 'Did you get it from that shop on the Edgware Road?'

'No, we lifted it from Bath Abbey in the Fifties.' She said this flippantly, as if she'd just told him what colour socks she was wearing.

'You did what?' Dave was incredulous.

Hannah turned around. 'I'm just teasing. It's got a battery. We got it from John Lewis.' She smiled.

'Oh! Ha ha! Funny.' *She unsettles me*, thought Dave.

'Listen, Dave, it's lovely to chat, but as you can see, it's eight twenty-three and you've got a lot of clocks to find before dinner. Hadn't you better get on with it?'

Get on with it?

'Besides, I've got so much cooking to do! Much, much more mess to make.' She waved him away. 'Go!'

She turned her back once more and he felt dismissed. She was right. Time was condensing and he had a lot to do. He reached up and un-hooked the clock from the wall. It was heavier than expected and for a moment he wondered whether she had been telling the truth about Bath Abbey – but then he turned it over and saw the Evacell batteries in their plastic casing. He glanced at Hannah to make sure she wasn't watching, and then quickly pocketed the batteries. The clock was stopped at 8:24.

'Just one more thing,' he called to Hannah.

'Hmmm?' She was distracted with chopping and didn't turn round.

'Has anyone else been in here this evening, apart from you, I mean?'

'No. Just me. Oh wait – Jess came in for some wine. But that's it.'

Dave hung the clock back on the wall and left, remembering the step this time.

The impressive oak stairwell ran from the hallway to a half-landing, and then split to the left- and right-hand sides of the house. The stairs were blanketed in a sage-green carpet with shiny brass stair-rods, and Dave's foot sank as he climbed the first step. *What a lovely pile*, he thought, *but I bet it's a bugger to vacuum.*

A strange reinterpretation of *The Last Supper* hung as a centrepiece on the wall where the stairs separated. Dave hadn't noticed it before but now he looked – there was something about it that made him pause. All the characters were wearing modern dress. The food on the table was fast food – burgers, fries, milk shakes. A couple of the men were looking at phones. There was a big flatscreen TV in one corner. And in the window, right at the back of the painting, two men were looking in. They were far away but . . . surely that couldn't be . . . was that Gobe? Dave stood on tiptoe to get a better look. He couldn't make out his features but it was something about the way he was standing. And if it was him, who was the short, nerdy-looking guy with him? Arial?

Get on with it.

He reluctantly tore his eyes away from the picture and clambered up the right stairwell. At the top, he took his bearings. The landing ran around the top of the central hallway, with five plain white doors leading off. He carefully opened door one to his right, and found himself looking at a bathroom from the Seventies with a coral-pink suite. In the half-light, he saw what looked like photographs pegged to a line running from one wall to another, and a row of plastic bottles and trays on a shelf above the sink. A dark room? He looked closer at the photographs. The figures, although blurred in the semi-darkness, looked familiar. Wanting to examine them, but realizing that time was not on his side, he backed away. *No clocks here,* he thought. *Move on.*

Remembering what Hannah had said about not waking her father, Dave trod lightly around the landing to door two. It was slightly ajar and he pushed it open gently, holding his breath.

The landing light illuminated a triangle of cream carpet

and a hint of a wardrobe. Smooth shadows across the bed gave Dave some assurance that there was no one sleeping here. The luminous dial of a clock shone clearly from the left-hand side of the bed. 8:26.

He flicked on the main light. The room was light and airy, but starkly furnished. The bed was neatly made with a rose printed cotton duvet and plump, white pillows. It was flanked by two old-fashioned side tables, painted white, but chipped. A small white wardrobe stood in one corner. A plain white desk sat against a wall, with a matching piano stool. *This must be Hannah's room*, he thought – *but where's all her stuff?* There was no make-up, no books, no jewellery boxes, no hairbrushes and no mirror. Not even any curtains. How did she sleep without being woken by the morning sun?

It was like a really rubbish hotel, Dave thought. Perhaps she'd just moved in. Or was soon moving out.

There was only one personal item on show – a small, white carriage clock, which squatted proudly on the side table to the left of the bed. He picked up the clock to examine it, surprised by its weight. *Feels like a brick*, he thought. The face was white but the hands were painted orange and Dave could quite clearly see some form of luminescence painted on each one. A second hand ticked away mercilessly.

Carefully turning the clock in his hands (*don't drop it don't drop it*) he was dismayed to find seven different brass knobs and buttons on the back. He squinted at them and wished he'd brought his glasses with him. Wait – perhaps he had? He put the clock back for a moment and patted himself down, only to find his pockets empty, save for a small lump which, upon further exploration, turned out to be a blue rubber band, the sort that postmen use for bundling letters together.

He must have picked it up in a different life.

He sighed, slipped the band back into his pocket and picked up the clock. He had no idea what he was doing, and he was starting to feel panicky. Perhaps that was the winder, he thought, picking out one of the larger knobs and turning it anti-clockwise. The knob came off in his hands. OK, maybe not, he thought, and he tried to re-attach it without success for some time, before giving up in frustration and moving on to the next little brass prong. Dave pushed and pulled this for a while with his now sweaty hands, with no effect. The third brass protuberance, a tiny button not quite flush, held little promise. Dave gave it a prod, and without warning, Annie Lennox filled the room with vocal rapid machine-gun fire:

'LA DA DO DA DA DA DO DAAAA, DA DAAA, DA DA-DA-DA-DAA'

In a normal situation, on a normal night, in a normal house, Dave would have been easily able to cope with a surprise rendition of 'There Must Be An Angel', played at a normal volume. He might even have enjoyed it. Had a little wiggle to it, perhaps. But in this house, which Dave thought would be a perfect set for a British remake of *The Shining*, with a very ill man sleeping just feet away and the fact that he was ABOUT TO DIE – well, it spooked him a bit.

He wildly pressed all the buttons at once, hoping that one of them would mute Annie.

One of the buttons eventually did the trick. He didn't know which one, and he didn't care. Silence mercifully returned in the bedroom, punctuated by the dull thud of a bass line from the party downstairs. Dave paused for a few seconds, listening out for moans from the old man nearby, or calls from below. Nothing.

He breathed out, his panic subsiding, and looked at the clock. To his horror, he saw that the glass face and two of the three hands had disappeared – just the hour hand was stuck fast. He realized that all his shaking and pummelling must have resulted in the glass face falling out, along with the hands. The unwelcome but familiar feeling of panic started to rise to his chest once again. He'd destroyed Hannah's precious clock! The one personal object that tied her to this room! What on earth was he going to tell her?

But hang on – on the other hand, his mission here was accomplished. Time had stopped. He would come up with an excuse for Hannah later. Surely, it was more important now that he solved his murder?

Without giving it another thought, he put the clock back carefully on the side table and strode manfully to the door. *Just one more to find*, he thought, as he turned off the light and closed the door behind him.

If he had stayed just a few seconds longer in that room, lit only by the streetlamps outside, Dave would have seen two things: 1: the missing tiny clock hands, illuminated orange, and a glittering circle of glass, sitting together snugly under the bed. And 2: shadows cast on the opposite wall by the leafless trees outside, which quite clearly said

BE MORE CAREFUL, YOU TWIT

Blissfully unaware of this latest piece of celestial advice, Dave was motoring onwards towards the next door. Downstairs, it sounded like they had fired up the karaoke machine; he could hear the introduction playing of '9 to 5' and Jess was making typewriter noises into a fuzzy microphone. He wished he was down there heckling and drinking beer, rather than up here, looking for a sick old man's travel clock so that he wouldn't get in the eternal shit with God (*sorry, God*).

Door three – locked or immovable for some other reason. No point lingering, Dave thought. The old guy's not going to have locked himself in. Is he?

Door four – a tiny room with space only for a desk and chair, and shelves crammed with old books and pamphlets. Dave touched one of the books longingly. It was brown with gold lettering, its dust sheet long gone and the leather spine cracked and brittle. He'd never really thought of himself as a book lover, but this space reminded him of his grandparents' house: books at all angles, balanced Jenga-style on top of each other, and the fusty smell of damp pages and leather covers. He wished he had just a few minutes to dawdle in here. Taking one last look, he backed out of the room and closed the door gently.

Dave stepped up to The Final Door. *This is it*, he thought. *Quiet as a dead mouse. Don't trip over anything, spill anything, bump into anything. Don't be scared. It's just an old man in there. He won't even know you're in the room. In and out with all possible dispatch.* He glanced upwards. 'Wish me luck,' he said.

36

Heaven's Hub

'Good luck,' said Gobe under his breath. Arial crossed his fingers behind his back.

Both angels were squinting at the screen as Dave opened the door. Beyond Dave's shoulder was the shape of a bed, an unexpected and human-shaped lump in the middle of it. But that wasn't the biggest surprise, because surrounding the bed . . .

'What in Glory to Goodness are those . . . things?' asked Gobe.

'I think they're . . . oxygen tanks?' said Arial, who had just a few hours before been watching early episodes of *Casualty*.

'And who's the old man? I didn't see any record of him on the report.'

'I . . . well. The thing is.' He coughed. 'Well.' Arial closed his mouth and looked down at his shoes.

'Arial.' Gobe was impatient. 'Do I look like I have all the time in the world? Out with it!'

'Right, sir. The thing is . . .' he looked directly at Gobe. 'The thing is – it looks like he doesn't exist.' Arial braced himself for one of his master's outbursts.

Silence. And then:

'Realllllly? That's very interesting indeed.'

Gobe turned back to the screen and said nothing more.

37

The Final Room

Dave opened the door carefully, slowly. The bottom of the door stuck on the heavy carpet, so he had to push harder than he would have liked. The door made a *SHHH* sound, gliding over the heavy pile carpet. He paused, to check if he could hear anything from inside, then pushed a little more. Eventually he had opened up a crack big enough to slide into the room.

It was very, very dark. The thin squeeze of light from the hallway meant that Dave could make out the outline of a large bed, surrounded by . . . Dave stepped back in horror. Were those unexploded shells? A wall of large torpedo shapes was just visible in the dim light. He forced himself to step towards them, his eyes gradually adapting to the darkness. Now he looked closely, they were too small for torpedoes, and they had some sort of valve at the top. He was pretty sure bombs didn't have valves (although he was no expert). They were more like air tanks for divers.

An unsettling, rhythmic sound was coming from the far side of the bed. It reminded Dave of the noise that Ivor the Engine, an animated steam train that he'd watched as a child, made when he was firing on all cylinders.

This must be what a ventilator sounds like, he thought.

Dave stepped closer to the bizarre barrier of what he was now pretty sure were oxygen tanks. There must have been fifteen tanks running in parallel to the edges of the bed, forming a perfect defence blockade. Each tank was about four feet tall. They were massive, like turrets around a princess. The old man was Sleeping Beauty and he, Dave, the handsome prince.

Well, I am not kissing the old bugger.

Dave was only a couple of feet away now, and had started to be able to make out other forms in the bedroom. Within the blockade, he could identify the silhouette of a bedside table. On the other side of the room stood a large wardrobe, and he could just about trace the outline of a fireplace and mantel shelf, crammed with strange objects in shadow. Thick curtains that let in not an ounce of street lighting. And a figure in bed, still as any stone.

The first thing Dave thought was – is he dead? The second thing was – why has someone arranged the oxygen tanks around him, forming some sort of tomb? The third thing was – I don't care; just find the bloody clock.

Hannah had told him that the clock was in her father's bedside drawer. 'Don't wake him,' she had said. Well, that wouldn't be difficult if he was, in fact, dead. Dave briefly wondered if the old man was currently in Purgatory having a nice chat with Gobe. He was a bit envious, truth be told.

Dave's eyes could now make out pretty much everything in the room. Weren't eyes miraculous? If only *he* was able to adjust to change as brilliantly as a pair of eyes. Maybe if he got through all this he'd be better at adventure, at travel, at taking risks. Maybe he'd go backpacking in Thailand. Did they still do Interrailing? Perhaps he'd quit work and get an open ticket. Perhaps—

The wheeze of the ventilator interrupted his trail of thought.

He could now make out the features of the old man's face, and the curves of his body under a tightly tucked bedspread. He was wearing an oxygen mask, the thin straps cutting into his hollowed and papery cheeks, and a tube from the mask led out into the gloom, presumably hooking up to one of the canisters on the other side of the bed. The mask overwhelmed the old man's face, like a parasite or an alien that was sucking him dry. Except it wasn't – presumably it was keeping him alive.

Was his chest moving? It must have been, but it was so dark that Dave couldn't tell for sure.

Concentrate on the job in hand.

He reckoned that he would have to move three tanks to make a hole big enough to squeeze through to the bedside table. Those tanks looked heavy. He grabbed the top of the one closest to the bedside table and tipped it towards him, testing its weight. An 'oof' escaped from his lips before he had a chance to trap it. No movement from the old man. How was the floor supporting all these? Fabulous. Something else to worry about – the floor collapsing and the contents of the bedroom ending up in the sitting room below. Mind you, Ian might be squashed by one of the canisters. Silver linings.

There was no way he was picking this bad boy up. Instead, Dave bent his knees and, with the tank at an angle resting against his body, he started to spin it towards him and away from the figure in the bed. Spin, spin, spin. He was a circus performer, balancing and spinning, walking a tightrope between this realm and the next. When the canister reached the wall, he made sure it was secure and wouldn't topple – then he started on the next. It was back-breaking work. Dave couldn't remember the last time he had taken any actual exercise, and he was about as flexible as a piece of chewing gum left in the playground on a hot day. After he had carefully leaned the second tank against the wall, he had to take a moment to stretch. He put his hand on his lower back and was sure he felt something protruding that hadn't been there before. Great. If he survived the next few minutes he'd be a hunchback for the rest of his life.

He closed his eyes and had a word with himself: *come on – one more to do and you're practically on the home straight. All that's left is to solve your own murder and, well, happy days. Happy days bent double, but happy days nonetheless.* He braced himself, took the weight of the final canister, and spun that muddy funster for all it was worth – his technique honed now – until it was safely parked up with its gassy siblings.

The pathway was clear. He was Indiana Jones, obstacles conquered and anticipation in his fingertips, as if he was about to take the golden idol from its pedestal. Stepping

274

forward through the gap in the aluminium fortress, he opened the bedside table drawer carefully. He realized he was holding his breath and forced himself to exhale slowly.

There were a handful of objects in the drawer which Dave couldn't quite make out in the low light. Some nail clippers, perhaps; an earplug; something that could have been a row of teeth. But there was something else – it looked like a large clam shell with gold edges that glinted in the hallway light. Two brass balls fastened it together, like the clasp of an old fashioned purse. It chimed with Dave's memories of the case of his father's travel clock that he used to take away on business trips. This must be it. The clock must be inside.

He picked it up gently and cradled it in his palm. The case was covered in cream leather, with some cracks that Dave could feel under his fingers. It had, as the experts from *Bargain Hunt* might say, 'some age to it'. Just for a moment, Dave was a child again, holding his dad's travel clock in his tiny hands and pleading with his father to let him pop the clock up, just one last time. His dad always said yes.

Another hiss from the ventilator. *Stop thinking, start doing!* it seemed to say. He pressed the gold button and popped open the case to reveal the clock. Bingo. He held it to his ear and heard the soft, malevolent *tick . . . tick* of its workings, then angled the face towards the hallway light in the gloom. The gold hands glittered, and he could just make out the time: 8:50. What the – where had the time gone? Frantic now, he ran his fingers around the edges to find the winder. *Come on, come on*, he thought, *this should not be so difficult.* There – thank goodness – there was the little lump of brass on the right-hand edge. He gripped it and slid his torn fingernails underneath, and pulled.

He imagined that the action of pulling out the winder would trigger an enormous event – the sky would fall in, or the earth would swallow him up, or the curtains would fly open and there would be a hundred police cars outside. But there was nothing. He held the clock to his ear and listened. Silence.

The relief he felt was immense. *Thank goodness*, he thought, as he stepped back to lean against the wall for support. *Now I can get on with the real task ahead.*

But Dave had forgotten about the canisters behind him.

Oh Dave.

38

Heaven's Hub

'OH DAVE!' yelled Gobe and Arial, simultaneously.

They both watched as Dave backed clumsily into one of the canisters, unbalancing it, just a touch. The canister rocked from side to side – tiny movements at first, but gathering momentum – and eventually making contact with its neighbour. And then the middle canister fell into the third, and they all toppled like enormous dominoes, making an almighty, thunderous crash.

They saw Dave's face frozen in horror. And then the screen went black.

'We've lost signal,' said Arial.

Gobe turned to him. 'Did you see . . . ?'

Arial gulped. 'Yes, sir. Just before the signal cut out. The man in the bed – he woke up.'

39

Out of Time

In that tiny patch of time after the thundering cacophony, two things happened. The first was that Hannah called up the stairs. 'Dave? Is everything OK?' The second thing was that the old man woke up. Not only that, but when Dave turned to check on him, he was sitting bolt upright, staring at him. His mask obscured most of his face. What little light there was caught in his eyes and the deep contours of his skull.

'I . . . I'm dreadfully sorry to wake you. I was just . . .' At this point he realized he was still holding the man's clock. '. . . just giving your clock its . . . annual service, and good news! It's all w-working swimmingly.' He put the clock down on the bedside table. The old man continued to stare.

'I'm coming up!' called Hannah.

'No! I mean, there's no need! Everything's under control!' Dave called back frantically. His eyes were on the old man, unsure what, if anything, the pyjamaed skeleton was going to do. He could hear Hannah's soft tread on the stairs.

'It's OK,' he whispered, with his best bedside manner. 'I'm not here to steal anything. Your daughter – Hannah – she said it would be OK to take a look at—'

Hannah's face appeared around the door. 'You OK, Dad?' she said. Her father nodded, just once. She came into the room, picking her way around the fallen canisters.

'You were supposed to be quiet,' she hissed at Dave.

'Sorry, Hannah. I wasn't really expecting . . .' he gestured towards the oxygen tanks. 'I'm really sorry.'

'Well . . . no harm done – right, Dad?' she said cheerily. Her father continued to stare at Dave. He was giving him the heebie-jeebies. 'I'll tuck you in again.' She gently laid her father back down in bed and pulled the covers over him again. He whispered something in Hannah's ear. She looked at Dave.

'He wants a quick word,' she said. 'Don't be afraid – he won't bite.' *I know he won't*, thought Dave, *because his teeth are in that drawer*. She moved aside to let him through.

He approached the old man nervously. Dave saw in the half-light that the man's eyes were wide open. His cracked lips were parted and he seemed to be preparing to say something. Dave leaned over the body, their faces a foot apart. *Is he going to tell me to leave his house? I wouldn't blame him. He probably thinks I've come to rob him blind.*

'He wants you to move closer,' said Hannah, although how she knew that, Dave wasn't sure. He lowered his face so that their noses were almost touching. Dave could feel the old man's shallow breath on his face. It smelled like . . . like . . . well, if he was going to be honest, it smelled a bit like Marmite.

Dave turned his face so that his ear was a sucked aniseed

ball's width from the old man's puckered mouth. He could hear rasping sounds in the man's throat. And then, suddenly, he started to cough uncontrollably. Wait – he wasn't coughing. Was he . . . laughing? Hannah rushed forward to calm her father. 'Dad. Dad! What's so funny? Calm down.' He looked at her and his breathing softened. She gently lowered his arm. The old man closed his eyes. The ventilator returned to normal. It was as if nothing had happened.

She turned to Dave with a questioning look.

'Before you say anything,' he panted, 'what time is it?'

Hannah shrugged. 'All the clocks seem to have stopped. But I imagine it's around nine o'clock.'

'No!' cried Dave. He grabbed Hannah's wrists. 'Listen – this is important. Who was in the kitchen when you left?'

'No one,' she said. 'Why do you . . . ? Dave?'

But Dave was already thundering down the stairs.

40

Heaven's Hub

'What do we do now, sir?'

Arial and Gobe were standing in silence, watching the blank screen. Gobe was aware that he was sweating again. He wondered fleetingly whether angels went through the menopause and, if so, why no one had told him about what to expect.

'I'm not sure there's anything we *can* do, Arial,' he sighed, fanning himself. 'We can't reach him again until—' he paused. 'Wait. Wait a minute.'

'What is it, sir?'

'Shhh. I'm thinking.'

Arial stood obediently quiet, staring at his magnificent mentor. He loved these times when Gobe was cooking up a plan; he was so impressive, so cognitively quick and clear, his mind fizzing with the power of a thousand computers all working together to solve the most astonishingly complex riddle. Gobe was his Sherlock Holmes, his Confucius, his Han

Solo, all wrapped up in one cloaked, ecclesiastical, slightly damp package.

Arial felt a tear pricking his eye.

He was brought back down to earth by Gobe clapping his hands together with a God-almighty CRACK. 'I have it, Arial! Of course! I've been so stupid!'

You could never be stupid, thought Arial. *Never.*

'Dave's stopped all the clocks, right? Which means that I . . .' His voice faded away as he looked at his apprentice. 'Look, Arial, I have to go away to do a – thing. You're not to worry, OK? Keep watching the screens. I won't be long.' And with that, he winked, and vanished.

'Stop! Can I help?' But Arial was left alone in the Hub, which suddenly seemed vast and very, very empty. He drew up a chair and sat directly in front of the screen, and waited.

41

The Murder

The Kitchen

Dave ran down the stairs at full pelt, taking them two at a time. He careered through the hall and catapulted into the kitchen, remembering the step at the last moment and skidding to a halt, road-runner style, at the feet of someone he knew well.

But it wasn't Ian.

The plates were laid out on the counter top – six of them – all piled high with curry and rice. Hannah had obviously been in the middle of plating up before Dave's blunder upstairs called her away. The steam that had given Hannah an ethereal air had disappeared, and the kitchen air was clear and crisp. A duffle bag sat next to the plates, and there was no mistaking its owner who had been caught red-handed pouring out something from a jar into a plate of food.

It was his brother, Andrew.

'Andrew?' Dave said softly. 'What are you doing, mate?'

Andrew looked up, eyes wide. He quickly put his hand behind his back.

'I . . . er . . . well . . .' Andrew tilted his head from side to side and rolled his shoulders. *He's preparing for something*, Dave thought. *He always fidgets like this when he's getting ready for a fight.*

'Thing is . . . *bro* . . .' Andrew laughed nervously. 'A friend of mine gave me . . . gave me some of these g-great – you know, *edibles* – and I wanted to share some with you. I didn't want to tell you because I knew you'd say no.' His tempo was accelerating, finding its rhythm. 'But it's brilliant – you'll love it, Dave! Make you feel less anxious about life. And of everyone I know, you're the most anxious. I mean, you really are, Dave. You'll love it.' He pushed the plate of food towards him. 'Try some!'

Dave was still for a second, processing the scene. His brother was still, too, frozen, his smile set to a waxy grimace. Also, he didn't know what the word 'edibles' meant but he assumed that Andrew was trying to pass off what he had behind his back as marijuana.

The karaoke was still going next door and Ian's version of The Human League's 'Mirror Man' floated around them both.

'Andrew. I'm no drugs baron, but even I know that marijuana doesn't come in a jar. And why are you wearing plastic gloves?'

'It's my eczema.'

'You don't have eczema.'

Silence crept into the gap between them.

'You,' Dave whispered. 'It's you.'

'C'mon, Dave, you know I smoke the odd bit now and then. No biggie.' But Andrew's eyes were wild. He tore off the gloves, threw them to the floor and stepped backwards, finding himself trapped between the cooker and the fridge. *He looks like a cornered animal*, Dave thought, *with haunted, red eyes.* Suddenly, Andrew lunged towards the table and picked up a fork, his knuckles whitening around it.

Dave was floored. A hundred scenes from their childhood flashed through his mind: him and his brother playing Risk; riding bikes together in a storm; both cheating at Yahtzee; eating banana splits on holiday together; club dancing terribly with their arms around their shoulders; sharing relationship advice . . . they loved each other, for Christ's sake. Or maybe they didn't. Because now his brother, his truest friend, was trying to poison him AND skewer him with a piece of IKEA cutlery. Where had it gone so wrong?

'Give the jar to me, Andrew. Or is it a bottle? The poison.' He wanted to see it. Not that he was a poisons expert. But he'd picked a few things up from reading whodunnits over the years, and he needed to see some tangible evidence.

Andrew was still for a moment, then shrugged. He brought his hand from behind his back and rolled the small glass bottle along the worktop towards his brother.

'Have it! It's empty anyway. I gave it all to you.' He gestured at the plate of food. 'Ever the generous younger brother!'

Hannah's distant voice filtered in over the top of the backing track. 'Everything all right in there?' It sounded like she was coming down the stairs.

They looked at each other. 'All fine!' Dave called back. 'We're just dishing up. We can handle things here – you can join the others!' And then, as an afterthought, 'Put your feet up!' His voice was catching in the back of his throat.

Keeping his eyes firmly fixed on Andrew, he picked up the bottle carefully, took out the stopper and smelled it. Almonds.

'Why do you want to hurt me, Andy? What have I done?' Dave was finding it difficult to process what was happening. Tears welled up in his eyes and his vision blurred. The man standing in front of him, who he had grown up with, had thirty-five years of shared experiences, memories, family, in-jokes . . . this man hated him. How could he have fatally misunderstood their relationship?

Andrew was suddenly all smiles. 'What? No, Dave, don't be a dick! You're totally overreacting! It's just a little treat from the street for you.' He looked again at the plate of curry.

'You eat some then,' said Dave. He wiped his eyes. 'From the middle. Eat it.' He stepped towards his brother. 'Eat. It.'

Andrew's smile faded. His skin, already the colour of parchment, greyed.

'I'm actually not that hungry,' he mumbled.

'But we're here for dinner. You haven't eaten yet.' Dave took a step closer.

Andrew growled, 'Don't come any closer.' The brothers were just inches apart.

Dave, keeping his eyes nailed to his brother, bent over the plate of curry and inhaled.

'Now then, *bro*. Tell me this. Why would a prawn curry smell like a Bakewell tart?'

Andrew shrugged. 'Maybe Madhur Jaffrey likes a touch of marzipan in her recipes?'

The brothers glared at each other, eyes locked, each silently daring the other to move. They were children again, fighting over Top Trumps, or train tracks, or Lego. They each wanted the biggest ice cream, the latest trainers, the loudest speakers.

Dave was first to break. He backed towards the door to the living room and quietly closed it, all the while keeping Andrew under his glare. The music and chatter stopped abruptly. When the door was safely shut, he allowed himself to explode.

'YOU UTTER BASTARD. WHY ARE YOU TRYING TO KILL ME?'

He flew at his brother, who was taken completely by surprise at Dave's sudden wrath. Dave grabbed Andrew by the throat with both hands, and watched as Andrew's eyes bulged and his face reddened.

'Was it that time I beat you at backgammon? Yes, I cheated, but I know you did too. I saw you throw those dice again and move the counters when you thought I wasn't looking.'

Andrew tried to say something but as his voice box was being crushed, he sounded like radio static. Dave relaxed his hands slightly to allow his brother to speak.

'It wasn't the backgammon, you complete twat!'

Dave was so preoccupied with board games that he had forgotten about the fork. But releasing his brother's throat had thrown Andrew a break; before Dave could react, Andrew had lifted the fork high above his head and thrust it downwards, aiming for his brother's neck. Fortunately for Dave, hand–eye coordination had never been Andrew's strong point, as proven in the infamous rounders match of St Christopher's Primary School versus All Saints, when Andrew had aggressively swung at the oncoming ball, missed it, and then been unable to stop the swing in time to avoid hitting himself on the head with his own bat. Now, as then, Andrew's aim was off; although this time it wasn't an entire miss – the prongs of the fork skimmed the skin of Dave's neck, leaving four small scratches.

The fork slipped out of Andrew's hand and skittered over the floor tiles. Andrew cursed. 'Jesus Christ. I can't even hit a stationary target.'

But the scratch was enough for Dave to loosen his grip further on his brother. Andrew forced his fingers under Dave's and managed to thrust him backwards towards the opposite kitchen counter. Dave, off balance, put his hand out to steady himself and accidentally swiped an expensive-looking wine glass into the sink, where it shattered. The brothers paused, listening for concerned voices next door, but the karaoke party had moved on to Spandau Ballet and Jess was deafeningly, painfully, belting out her own version of 'Gold'. Their argument remained unnoticed.

Dave saw Andrew look to his right and followed his gaze. Andrew's duffle bag. What had he brought to the party? Hang on – hadn't he seen Jess pass him something earlier? Surely they weren't in league with each other?

Simultaneously, both Dave and Andrew rushed for the bag, but Andrew was far closer and able to reach inside before Dave was anywhere near. Dave saw that he was beaten and was already looking for something to defend himself with when Andrew drew his weapon and pointed it at his brother.

'Is that . . . a stick?' said Dave, taken aback and suddenly wanting to laugh at the absurdity of the situation.

But Andrew wasn't listening, and he certainly wasn't laughing. His face had gone a remarkable shade of puce, and his hand was gripping the stick so hard that his knuckles bulged white and red. When he spoke, his voice was deep and guttural.

'It's not a *stick*.' He spat out the word. 'Don't you recognize it, Dave? The hazel wand? This is it! The wand that our own mother used to invite the demon in.'

Dave stared, mute. Was this really the gnarled bit of wood that had started it all? The summoning of Beleth, the Blocks, the angels, his journey back in time? And if so, how had Andrew got his hands on it? And more to the point, what was Andrew capable of, now that he had it in his grasp?

'You and I had forgotten about it, hadn't we?' Andrew paused, breathing heavily, and Dave thought he saw tears in his brother's eyes. 'Mum gave the wand to Jess– can you believe it? She didn't trust either of us with it.'

She was wise, thought Dave. *Look at us.*

'But it was driving Jess nuts – she couldn't stand it. You went to see her, didn't you? Because you were concerned about her. Well, you were right to be concerned. The wand was crippling her, Dave. She loves you, you know that, right? She couldn't cope with the idea of you and Rose getting back together. She was planning to kill Rose with that.' He pointed to the glass jar. 'She said she couldn't control herself, said the wand was making her do things that she didn't want to do. She begged me to take the poison away. Put it right in my hand, like a gift.' His eyes were wide now and his pupils dilated, unfocused.

Oh Jess, Dave thought. *Why didn't you tell me? Why didn't you give the wand to me? I'd have saved you from it. From yourself.*

Andrew wiped his mouth and went on. 'She wouldn't give me the wand at first though – was worried how I would use it. But I persuaded her to bring it tonight. I've done her a huge favour; listen to her now, singing karaoke, not a care in the world.'

She was indeed singing tunelessly in the other room and sounded, for Jess anyway, happy. Dave had no idea what to say, or what to do. To be held at 'wand point' by his brother in Hannah's kitchen was not one of the options that he had prepared for. He found, unexpectedly, that he wasn't concerned for himself – he was dead already, after all – but for his brother. Andrew had obviously lost his mind.

Dave tried to think rationally through the soupy stress that was slowing down his brain. His own mind wasn't running anywhere near as clearly now that he wasn't in Purgatory. He needed to find a way to snap his brother out of – whatever this was. *Come on, Dave – think!*

And then he had it.

Dave whipped out the rubber band that he'd picked up in Hannah's room, stretched it between his thumb and forefinger and flicked it with practised precision at Andrew's ear. Bullseye.

'Ouch!' yelled Andrew, dropping the wand in surprise.

Dave ran towards his brother and kicked the wand away, just like he'd seen Bruce Willis do in countless films. It rolled away from them, stopping only when it hit the skirting board on the other side of the room.

They both looked at it in silence. Dave said, simply, 'Don't.'

They stood there together, aware of each other's tiniest movements, for what seemed like hours. Dave was taut, ready to spring at his brother if he moved towards the wand, but Andrew stayed where he was, motionless. Dave wondered whether his brother was weighing up his options, or whether he'd given in, or was playing some sort of cunning bluff to coax his brother towards him. What he did not expect was for Andrew to suddenly open his mouth wide in a silent scream, covering it with his hand. Andrew's face turned from pink to white to deep purple, and his eyes became fixed and wide.

'Andrew? Andrew!' What was happening? Was he having a heart attack? The last few minutes forgotten, Dave ran over to his brother and half shook him, half steadied him to stop him from sliding to the floor. Had he taken some of the poison? He didn't think so – a memory, long forgotten, was resurfacing. There was something familiar about what was happening to Andrew, a reaction he'd seen long ago.

Dave was wondering whether he should call for help when his brother's body suddenly stiffened and then almost immediately relaxed into Dave's arms. Andrew exhaled audibly. Colour returned to his face and his eyes softened.

Andrew spoke first. 'So,' he said, panting, 'the old rubber band flick trick, eh? Always a winner.'

Dave couldn't help smiling. His brother's voice was back.

It was Dave's turn to breathe. 'It all got a bit serious there for a moment. Can we stop fighting now? Please,' he said. He touched the scratch on his neck. It felt oozy.

Andrew shrugged. Non-committal.

'Andrew.' Andrew looked up. Dave searched for something meaningful to say. 'I don't want to die yet. I'm thirty-seven. Life's still got something to squeeze. I think I might want children.' Was that true? Saying it out loud had taken him by surprise. 'I want to go to Iceland. I'd like to do a sponsored swim. And I want to take up jogging.' Jogging? Really? 'But most of all, I don't want to die yet because I really, really want to know why my own brother is trying to kill me – first, with a shedload of poison, and then, with a . . . stick.'

'It's not a stick, it's a wa—'

'I don't give a flying fuck what it is, Andrew,' he said. 'The point is, you were trying to kill me. Jeez, I thought it was going to be Ian.'

Andrew looked up, surprised. 'You thought what was going to be Ian?'

'What? Oh, nothing. I just meant that I'd always thought Ian was jealous of me and Rose.'

Andrew snorted, suddenly animated. Back to the old Andrew. 'Have you looked at yourself recently, mate? You're not exactly God's gift.'

Dave's cheeks burned. He looked down at himself. Admittedly, he hadn't been able to see his feet in recent years but that was one of the benefits of being middle-aged, wasn't it? You could let yourself go a little bit? Andrew was skinny as a whippet, but that was just a case of him getting the thin genes. Wasn't it?

'And don't pretend it's genetic,' said Andrew. (*How does he know what I'm thinking?*) 'It's because you drink too much, eat three packets of salt and vinegar crisps a day and don't do any exercise.'

'Fine. You're right, I'm disintegrating.' He took a step closer to his brother. 'Look – why are you doing this, buddy? I thought we were mates. I mean, you behave – behaved – as if we are. Were. Bloody Hell!' (*Don't swear!*)

Andrew looked genuinely surprised.

'You don't know? You don't remember?'

'Remember what?' Dave shook his head subconsciously. Had the journey to and from Purgatory interfered with his memories more than he'd realized? Maybe he still had some amnesia over recent events. Perhaps he had offended his brother in some way. Or stolen from him? Or worse? What on earth could he have done that would make his brother want to kill him?

Andrew was mirroring Dave's head-shaking. 'Unbelievable. You've repressed it. I knew you had. All these years and there was no sign you had kept it with you.'

Dave held his hands in front of him, palms up, an expression of helplessness. 'I honestly don't know what you're talking about, Andrew. If you could just give me a clue . . .'

Andrew took a step forward, and Dave pressed himself back into the countertop. 'The holiday!' he said angrily. 'The holiday to Cornwall, when we were kids! When you tried to kill me!'

42

The Holiday

After David had apologized for destroying Andrew's sandcastle *and* hurting his arm, Colin forced them to shake hands 'like gentlemen' and then suggested that they build a sandcastle together – which they did, at first under duress, but then out of choice as they became more and more enthused about their creation. When it was finished, and they had pressed the last shell into the roof, David leaned forward and grasped Andrew's hand. 'Come on,' he said. 'Come with me for a swim?' Andrew looked up at his mum. Ann felt something odd in her gut which she'd later recognize as a mother's instinct, but in the moment, put it down to yesterday's Battenburg. She looked at Colin, who shrugged.

'Fine,' she said. 'But put your arm bands on properly, nice and tight. David – make sure you keep an eye on him.'

'I don't want to go with him.' Andrew looked nervous, and eyed his brother suspiciously.

'It will do you both good,' interjected his dad. 'Bury the

hatchet. Boys together. Brothers in arms. Brothers in armbands!'
He guffawed at his own joke.

Andrew stood silent whilst his mum half blew up his orange
armbands, carefully inserted his arms, and then inflated them
as much as she could before popping in the valve.

'They hurt!' cried Andrew.

'Stop moaning. They'll get looser when you go in the water.
They have to be tight. And you—' she directed this at David,
'just because you can swim in a pool with your pyjamas on,
it doesn't mean that you can go out of your depth here.'

David hopped from foot to foot, impatient to go. 'Yes,
Mum.'

She crouched down, put her hand on David's shoulder and
looked him in the eye. 'Look after him.'

David looked back, defiant. 'Of course.' Ann hesitated; there
was something about him that made her uncomfortable. She
strengthened her hold on his shoulder.

'MUM! You're hurting me!' David squirmed to get away.
He looked round for his brother, but Andrew had already left
the scene and was running as fast as his little legs could take
him towards the waves. As David threw off his mum's grip
and raced to catch up, she thought she could hear Andrew's
delighted squeals travelling up the beach as his feet hit the
surf.

'BE CAREFUL!' shouted Ann, as Colin adjusted the windsock and settled back down in his deckchair to find the folded
corner in his copy of the latest Stephen King novel.

Ann watched them for a little while. The waves were perfect
for jumping over, breaking at knee height and rolling into

the beach with just enough power to knock the boys off their feet if their leaps were mis-timed. Squinting, she could make out Andrew's bright orange armbands, still firmly fixed to his skinny arms. The tide was going out, but she could see that both boys were laughing and she relaxed, allowing herself to sit down and occasionally glance at her well-thumbed copy of *Men are from Mars, Women are from Venus*.

About five minutes later, she realized that she'd been swept up, thinking about Colin's man cave, and hadn't been watching the boys. She looked up and tried to focus on the figures in the retreating sea. She scanned the waves back and forth, silver against the sun, looking for the two orange armband beacons.

Colin was snoring, Stephen King in his lap. She shook his arm. 'Colin. Colin! I can't see them.'

'What?' Colin looked up, bleary eyed.

'They're not there. I can't see them.' Colin could hear the rising panic in her voice and he suddenly sat up, joining her in scouring the sea. Ann threw down the book and ran full pelt to the water's edge. 'ANDREW! ... DAVID! ... ANDREW!'

Parents close by looked up and turned to the sea. Ann waded in, still dressed in chinos and linen shirt, frantically looking left, then right, then out to sea and into the sun in the hope that she would see the two small silhouettes, and all the panic would be for nothing.

'Ann, don't go in like that, you'll bloody drown.' Colin growled next to her, stripping off his T-shirt, throwing it to the ground and striding into the waves. 'Where the hell are they?' he said, now with the water up to his neck. 'Christ, Ann, where are they?' he said more urgently, now swimming full pelt out to sea, frantically looking both over and under water for any sign of his boys.

'There, Colin – there!' He turned to look at Ann and followed the direction of her index finger. About twenty metres away he caught sight of the top of a small, brown-haired head bobbing between waves. As he started to swim towards it, he saw the head come up and a mouth opening, then a faint cry, before he lost sight of him entirely. *That's him*, he thought. *That's Andrew.*

He's drowning.

Colin, normally not the strongest of swimmers, ploughed through the water so fast that he created his own wake. When he got to the spot, Andrew was almost motionless. His arms were still and only tiny leg movements were keeping him from being sucked under. Colin, treading water, took hold of the small, limp body in his arms. He had never had lifesaver training but had watched *Baywatch* many, many times, so he knew what he had to do. Lying on his back and cupping his son's head to his chest, he became aware of his own tears rolling into the sea as he swam back to shore.

Staggering back on to the beach, he was aware of younger men – lifeguards – surrounding him and taking Andrew from his arms. 'We'll look after him,' they were saying. 'He'll be OK.' Colin let go unwillingly and watched them take his little boy to a waiting ambulance. He suddenly thought – why wasn't he wearing his armbands?

He could see Ann and David running over the sand towards him, and heard David asking his mum, 'What happened? I just lost sight of him. He swam off and the waves were too big – I couldn't see him. Is he OK? It wasn't my fault, I . . .'

Colin felt a sudden, sharp pain in his chest, so severe that he sank to his knees, as if he'd just been punched, hard. He saw Ann, already alarmed, double her speed.

'I'm fine,' he gasped, unable to catch his breath. 'Go with Andrew. It's nothing.' And with that, he toppled over face first into the surf. He was vaguely aware of Ann turning him over and climbing on top of him, then thinking, *this is a bit* From Here to Eternity – *typical that she chooses the moment I'm having a heart attack to re-invigorate our marital relations.*

She kissed him like they were eighteen again. Or maybe she was blowing in his mouth. He couldn't really tell. For some reason she was pinching his nose. He wanted to say, 'I'm not dead yet!' but nothing came out of his mouth except for a gurgle and some grit.

'HELP! HELP US!' he heard Ann shriek. And then, nothing.

43

The Kitchen

'Don't try to deny it, David,' Andrew said. 'We all knew what you'd done. If it hadn't been for Dad . . . for fuck's sake, I nearly drowned!'

Dave was stunned, stupefied. His Purgatory. His Point of Decision. Throughout his time in Purgatory, he'd never scrutinized why he'd ended up in that youth hostel. Why? Maybe because he'd been afraid of facing the obvious conclusion – that his POD, aged ten, was the decision to murder his own brother.

He felt sick. 'I need some air,' he said, opening the back door and tumbling out into the garden. He saw a pair of wooden chairs and sat down heavily in one of them, crumpled and confused, his head buried in his hands. The seat cracked as his weight settled into it.

It was true, he thought. He remembered. He'd always had the memory, of course, but had stored it in the understairs cupboard of his mind, locked, cobwebbed, hidden.

Too ashamed or lazy perhaps to search for it and bring it out into the light of day. And now the memory of that holiday flooded into him, making it difficult to breathe.

Before the holiday, Dave had been so jealous of his younger brother. Andrew, with his sunny disposition and winning smile – the Favoured One, who always had the backing of his parents, no matter how obvious it was that Dave was in the right.

Of course, Dave had thought about revenge. Ways to take Andrew down a peg or two in the estimations of their parents, or get him off the scene for a bit. He planned to steal money from his mum's purse and hide it – sloppily – under Andrew's mattress. Or to cut Andrew's bike cables so he would have some terrible accident. Or to eat Mum's Sunday best fruit cake and place the crumbs on Andrew's pillow.

But in the event, he did nothing. Andrew, possibly realizing that his brother was about to take action, became more conciliatory. Weeks passed, and life carried on. The brothers rubbed along like two pieces of fine-grade sandpaper for a while. Until the holiday, that is.

Then there was the incident with the Silver Surfer in the car on the way down.

Dave had been so enraged that his brain had felt out of control, red-hot, on fire. He'd wanted to pummel Andrew to death, to push him into the traffic, to take the wheel and run him over, to break his neck with his bare hands. His brother had destroyed the thing that he loved most in the world – on purpose – and justice had to be served. Outwardly, he had remained calm, but in the frenzied hothouse of his head, he had been planning his revenge.

Dave's reaction wasn't normal for a little boy of ten. A *normal* little boy would have been upset, and kicked and screamed, and shouted 'it's not fair' and 'he did it on purpose' a lot. A *normal* boy would have been placated by chocolate and promises of 'it was an accident' and 'we'll buy you a new set of Top Trumps when we get home.'

But instead, Dave had been plotting murder. And nobody had been the wiser.

Except . . . Angel Gobe. He knew now that Gobe had visited them in the youth hostel because he'd had some inkling of what was going to happen. And thanks to Beleth, he, Dave, had been 'red flagged' in Heaven ever since.

44

The Back Garden

The back door opened and a triangle of soft, orange light fell on to the paving slabs. Andrew's silhouette appeared, a can of beer in his hand. 'Want some?' he asked, holding it at arm's length in Dave's direction. Dave smiled tightly and reached for it. Andrew drew backwards, just out of Dave's grasp. Yesterday, they would have laughed and bantered and slapped each other on the back. Today, Dave just sat back in his chair and shrugged.

'This is when you say you didn't want it anyway,' said Andrew.

'Oh,' said Dave. Buffoonery after attempted murder didn't really appeal.

'Can I sit?' Andrew asked.

'Be my guest. It's only fair to warn you though that I picked up that rubber band, so if you try anything . . .'

Andrew sat down in the seat next to Dave, separated by a small wooden side table. The wood was old and splintered. He put the beer down. 'Have some if you want.'

Dave looked at the can and extended his arm, remembered what had just transpired and withdrew it again. 'On second thoughts, I'll pass,' he said.

'Understandable,' said Andrew, picking it up and taking a noisy swig, sucking the liquid through his teeth.

Dave looked sideways at him. 'That's always been bloody annoying, you know.' Andrew looked surprised. 'I remember when you did that when we went to see *Godzilla*. You were swishing your Coke about in your gob so loudly that the front four rows couldn't follow the film.'

'To be honest, the plot was pretty incomprehensible. Even without my slurping.'

'Fair point.'

They sat in silence for a minute or so.

'When we were on holiday in St Ives,' Dave began, 'did you know what I'd . . . done?'

'Not straight away. I thought that my arm bands had just slipped off. That Mum hadn't blown them up properly, or that she hadn't plugged the stoppers in properly, or that the waves had dragged them off me. I had very skinny arms, so, you know, they could have just slid off.

'But when I was in hospital and they were checking me over, a nurse brought one of the armbands over.

'It was just me and Mum – I think you'd been taken to see Dad. She showed Mum that the plastic had been split by something sharp. Said it looked like it had been done on purpose. Mum didn't say a word to me about it. Must have stuffed the armband in her handbag or chucked it in a bin. I think we both knew that it had to be you that had sliced it.

Can you imagine what that does to you, as a parent? Knowing that one of your sons has tried to kill the other?'

'But it might not have been me!' Dave protested.

'Of course it was you,' Andrew replied softly.

It was me, thought Dave. *I remember.*

They had built sandcastles and Andrew's had been better than his. He had knocked into one of Andrew's turrets deliberately, pretending it had been accidental. Andrew hadn't been fooled, though, and took it for what it was – an invitation to start a war. Andrew's subsequent kicking of Dave's castles was inevitable.

On top of everything, this had been the final, humiliating straw.

While his parents had watched Andrew's frenzied attack on Dave's motte and bailey, Dave had picked up a broken mussel shell from his brother's model of Hampton Court and tucked it carefully into his swimming trunks. Once they were in the water and Andrew was distracted with wave-jumping, it was easy for Dave to use the sharp edge of the shell and pop each armband.

Back in the garden, Dave suddenly felt very ill indeed. He leaned over, away from his brother, and was sick; his vomit looked like moon rock in the twilight. He looked at his brother's pale face, illuminated from orange light shining through the kitchen window. 'It was me,' he admitted. 'I cut holes in your armbands.'

'I know,' said Andrew, looking directly at his brother. He sounded exhausted. 'I've known for twenty-seven years.'

45

Gobe's Visit to the Underworld

Gobe knocked at the front door. As front doors went, it was pretty perfunctory, being made only of roughly patchworked human skin. It was very bleak this far down, and although he didn't feel the cold, he did feel a little underdressed. He pulled his robe tighter around himself.

A grunt from inside – the usual warm welcome. He picked up the flap and went in.

There were the familiar elements of interior design, such as the inside being larger than the outside, of it being lit by candles, of it suddenly being very hot. 'I wish you'd get on the National Grid,' he called out to the shadows. 'Electricity makes all the difference – trust me.' He covered his nose. 'And it reeks in here. Why don't you clean up a bit? We're not savages, you know.'

WHAT DO YOU WANT? I'M BUSY.

'Well, what a charming welcome. Look – can you please come out? I need to talk to you. It's important.'

WAIT A MINUTE. I'M PUTTING THE RECYCLING OUT.

Gobe shuddered to think what this meant. Who knew where he'd put his rotting corpses once he'd finished with them? He absent-mindedly wiped his finger over the seat of a nearby stool.

'Have you ever thought of getting a cleaner? You could really do with some help.'

I'M PERFECTLY CAPABLE OF LOOKING AFTER MYSELF, THANK YOU. Beleth came out of the gloom, carrying something. EXCEPT I CAN'T FIND THE OPENING ON THIS BIN BAG.

'Oh, give it to me, old ham hands,' said Gobe. Perhaps Beleth had been doing the recycling, after all. He rubbed the edges of the plastic together to separate them. 'There you are, Belly. Don't say I don't do anything for you.'

Beleth snorted and flame shot out of his nostrils, forcing Gobe to step back in alarm. SORRY, he said. SOMETIMES IT JUST SLIPS OUT.

Gobe nodded, wiped the stool with the inside of his robe and sat on it, carefully. Beleth leaned against a wall, which was puckered with bones. Like a climbing wall, Gobe thought. After a short while—

'Well now, this is nice.'

WHAT DO YOU WANT?

'Why should I want something? I thought it would be lovely to come and see you.'

YOU NEVER COME TO BE SOCIAL. YOU'RE ALWAYS LOOKING FOR FAVOURS. ONCE IN A WHILE IT WOULD

JUST BE NICE IF YOU CAME FOR DINNER, YOU KNOW?
BRING SOME CHOCOLATES.

'You know it's not that easy. Officially I'm not allowed. The
rules say—'

RULES SHMOOLS.

Gobe coughed. 'Quite. Well, as it happens, I would like to
ask a small favour.'

I KNEW IT.

'Now, don't be like that. Actually, it's in both of our interests.'

Beleth snorted again and this time Gobe, seated, was a
sitting duck.

'You singed my robe!' he exclaimed, fruitlessly trying to
rub it clean.

Beleth shrugged. IT'S NOT MY FAULT. IT'S JUST BIOLOGY.

Gobe sighed. 'Sit down, please. This is important.' He
paused, and Beleth sat opposite him in a grand, red leather
winged-back chair. 'I'm in a spot of bother.'

The red leather squeaked as Beleth tried to get comfortable.
SORRY. MY FUR STICKS SOMETIMES.

Gobe waved his hand dismissively. 'Don't worry. Thing
is . . . look, Belly, I'm just going to lay it out for you and trust
you, OK? This is between us, within these four walls – and,'
he said, looking at the bones sticking out of the plasterwork,
'them, I suppose.'

OH, DON'T WORRY. THEY CAN'T HEAR ANYTHING.
I DON'T KEEP THE EARS. HAHAHAHAHAHAHA.

Gobe took a deep breath. 'There's a human. He's called
David. You've . . . visited him in the past. He's been murdered.
We can't see who did it and obviously, we need to.'

YES. I KNOW. I GOT DEMON OF THE WEEK FOR THAT. AND A HAMPER.

'Congratulations. Thing is, Belly – God got angry.'

EXCELLENT.

'Incandescent, actually. And I didn't want any retribution to come your way. I wanted to protect you. So I – well, I sent Dave back in time. To solve his own murder.'

Beleth leaned forward, suddenly interested. GOBEY! I ALWAYS KNEW YOU HAD A TOUCH OF THE DEVIL IN YOU!

'I couldn't stand to see the might of Heaven brought down on you, Belly.' Gobe thought he saw a touch of a smile haunt Beleth's lips.

There was a pause. Gobe heard faint screams, coming from somewhere deep in the darkness.

DON'T WORRY ABOUT THAT. IT'S MY MINDFULNESS TAPE. IT HELPS ME RELAX.

'Ah. Of course.' Gobe rearranged his robes. 'Thing is . . . I'm not sure he'll make it. David is . . . a trier . . . but I think this may be too much of a challenge for him.'

YOU KNOW I CAN'T REMOVE THE BLOCKS, DON'T YOU?

'Yes, yes, but – I think there's something else you can help me with. I need to get down there. I have a feeling that he might need my help.'

Beleth absently-mindedly picked at his hooves. I SEE. AND YOU DON'T WANT TO ASK YOU-KNOW-WHO SO YOU NEED ME TO BEND THE RULES.

'It's for the good of both us, though, Belly.'

HUMPH.

Gobe paused.

HAS HE STOPPED ALL THE CLOCKS?

'I hope so.'

WELL THEN – HOW CAN I REFUSE? He smiled broadly, showing his three rows of teeth.

Gobe asked Beleth to get a paper and pencil. Beleth didn't have a paper and pencil, but he did have some dried sheets of lung and a hypodermic syringe, which actually worked pretty well, considering. As there was no Excel to rely on (or a computer, or electricity), Beleth had to help Gobe out with the mental maths. He had always been best at sums.

They worked together on the floor, both on all fours in the dirt. Gobe tried not to worry about the state of his robes. Beleth rolled around occasionally just because he enjoyed it so much. *Like a pig in muck*, thought Gobe – although he didn't say it out loud.

Time didn't exist in this place but if it had been measured by an earthly yardstick, they would probably have been in deep discussion for about half an hour. When Gobe was sure that the final details were in place, he got up and brushed himself down.

'I think that will do,' he said, picking something unspeakable off his gown. 'Shall we go? Is the timing right?'

WE HAVE A MOMENT OR TWO. I'LL JUST MAKE A QUICK SANDWICH. DO YOU WANT ANYTHING?

'You know I don't eat,' said Gobe.

JUST CHECKING. Beleth had disappeared once again into the darkness. I CAN SEE YOU'VE BEEN SWEATING. LOOKS

LIKE YOU'VE BEEN GETTING MORE HUMAN AGAIN. YOU'LL NEED TO KEEP AN EYE ON IT.

'I'll address it properly after all this,' Gobe called out. 'I don't have the headspace at the moment.' He turned and picked his way carefully through the candles (such a terrible fire risk) to the front door.

And there it was. Seeing it pinned up on the back of the flap like that took him by surprise. He felt something strange in his chest – a velvet punch – and his eyes stung.

'You've put it up, then,' he said, quietly.

YES. Beleth was beside him. I WANTED . . . TO BE REMINDED.

Together they looked at the frayed tapestry.

GOB<u>BE</u>LETH

Each letter was beautifully cross-stitched in a different jewelled colour, apart from the B and the E, which stood out in gold. Flourishes and swirls surrounded the letters and a baby magpie sat on the B. Tiny musical notes poured out of his tiny beak.

It couldn't have looked more incongruous in Beleth's sordid den.

They both stood for a moment in silence, shoulder to shoulder (even though Gobe claimed to be the tallest).

'Clever of her to link us like that,' said Gobe.

I MISS HER.

Gobe nodded. 'So do I.'

YOU'RE CRYING.

'No, *you're* crying.'

I'M NOT.

'Yes, you are.'

NO, I'M NOT.

Beleth pulled the flap aside and pushed his brother out.

'You are.'

NOT.

'You could really do with a wash.'

DON'T START.

And squabbling like toddlers, the brothers trotted off happily together, up to the terrestrial world.

46

The Garden

Somewhere overhead they both heard a magpie's harsh, fast chatter. It was faintly overlaid with Jess's sweet rendition of 'Shaddup You Face', seeping outside from the living room.

Dave's head was on fire. How could he have tried to kill his own brother? Was he fundamentally evil? Had he had some sort of breakdown as a child? Jesus. He was repulsed by himself.

'I'm so sorry, Andrew,' he said. 'I know it's a ridiculous thing to say. It goes no way to repairing anything. I . . . I can't believe that I did that to you. Well, I can believe it, because I remember it, and I did it. I definitely did it.'

'It was like polarized sibling rivalry – magnified. You hated me,' Andrew said. 'And, to be fair, I hated you. I just wasn't imaginative enough at that point to plot my own brother's murder.' He stretched his legs out in front of him. 'It ate away at me though, Dave. Especially when I was younger. Considered seeing a therapist, but bloody hell – do you know how much they cost? I could have a weekend in Barcelona for the same price as a session with a shrink! So I just trudged on, you know? And as time went on, and we were getting on really well, I felt lighter and less intense about the whole thing. But then, Jess told me about the wand and . . . well, it was weird. Things got out of hand. In my head, I mean.'

'You didn't tell me you'd gone to see her.'

'No. But you phoned me – remember? And asked me to do something. So I did. I didn't tell you because, by that point, I thought that if you knew about the wand, you'd want to steal it. For yourself, I mean.'

'Nothing could be further from the truth,' Dave said. 'I wouldn't want that stick if you presented it to me on a purple pillow.'

'Encrusted with diamonds?'

'Even then.'

They sat in silence for a moment, listening to the birds.

'I wasn't lying about Jess loving you, you know. Don't blame her for the poison thing. I don't think she'd really have gone ahead with murdering Rose.'

Dave wasn't so sure, but said nothing. If he'd been told six months ago that his best friend was in love with him and was plotting to kill his ex-girlfriend with poison she'd inherited from his own mother – well, he'd have dismissed it in an instant. But now, after dying and coming back to life, after seeing and befriending angels, after watching old women playing Scrabble in Purgatory – anything was possible.

'I took the poison, Dave. I took it with the sole intention of stopping her from poisoning Rose.' Andrew looked Dave in the eye. 'I promise you.' He broke off the gaze. 'But when I got home, I had the idea that perhaps I'd been given an opportunity – a gift – to try to silence that worm that I'd carried for years. Because it did feel like a worm, Dave. I started to remember how it had felt and suddenly I was being eaten away by it, and that part of me was replaced by something dark and hateful.'

Dave found himself holding his brother's arm. Occasionally, when he'd been low or alone, he'd felt something similar. A gnawing sensation. A calling of some kind. 'It was the wand, Andrew. Sometimes, I feel echoes of what you just described. But I think it was the wand that made you want to act on it.'

Andrew nodded. 'I hope so,' he said.

Dave sat back on his damp, splintered seat. 'We never spoke about the protection spell, did we? The demon spell, I mean. I'd forgotten about it, but now I think of it, I'm sure Mum regretted doing it to us. After that day, she got rid of all her magic stuff, didn't she? Either packed it away or gave it to Elle. Dad was pleased. I don't think he'd ever come to terms with the fact that she'd come from a family of Devil worshippers.'

'It wasn't that simple though, was it?' said Andrew. 'I felt great afterwards. For a good few weeks. Do you remember, I broke all the school running records on sports day? And you know as well as I do how rubbish I am at sports.' He glanced at his brother, a broad smile on his face. Dave hadn't seen him this relaxed in a long time.

Was that because of the spell? How could he have forgotten? Everyone had been sure they had cheated; some had thought that they'd been on performance enhancing drugs – or whatever the early Nineties equivalent had been. Mrs Vaughn, the dinner lady, had demanded to see Andrew's trainers because she was convinced he'd modified them in some way. Dave laughed at the memory. 'What did Mrs Vaughn say again? That you'd fitted your trainers with wings?'

'She made me take them off so that she could examine them before they would declare me the winner,' Andrew said. He took one of his trainers off and brought it to his eye-line in mock examination. 'Now then, Andrew,' he said in falsetto, 'what's made you into a little Hermes? Have you installed those new fangle-dangled dynamo things?'

Dave made snorting noise which made Andrew choke on his beer, which in turn made Dave guffaw, which in turn made Andrew laugh until his insides hurt.

The fun eventually fizzled out. The two men sat in their chairs, legs stretched, and sighed at the same time. It was dark now, and colder. A single magpie was cawing somewhere out of sight.

Dave broke the silence.

'Andrew?'

'Hmmm?' Andrew seemed lost in thought.

'That protection spell. Did it ever leave you feeling . . .'

'Possessed?' Andrew said.

Dave was taken aback for a second. 'Yes. Because I have felt like that, in the past.'

'Me too.'

'Really? For me, it felt like I wasn't fully in control of my thoughts, or behaviour. I felt like . . .' Dave struggled to find the words. 'Like an *infested puppet*. It's as if the core of you still exists, but somebody is overriding it, or flooding it, with their own plan, their own . . . rules.'

A magpie screeched somewhere and he had to raise his voice. 'I felt *possessed* when we were on that holiday. I'm not trying to use it as an excuse – well, I suppose I am, a bit – but now that I think about it, it all makes sense.' Dave was animated now. 'Mum invites him in. The demon. Beleth, or whatever his name is. She invites him in, to protect us – you, me and Jess – if only for a minute, but when he leaves us, a part of him remains. This part of him makes us strong for a time, but this . . . physical advantage . . . fades. He is still there though, like a piece of . . . shrapnel, surfacing when we are vulnerable, pulling our strings. Encouraging us to be corrupt.' He turned to Andrew, pleased with his speech. He'd never been so articulate.

Andrew simply said, 'I know.'

'And also – look at us. The three of us, I mean. We're all in our mid-thirties. But none of us have a long-term partner. We don't have kids. Surely that must be to do with Beleth's influence?'

'I dunno,' said Andrew. 'Could just be us. Perhaps we're just rubbish at relationships.'

They sat again in companionable – brotherly – silence. The magpie with a voice like a cymbal had either flown off or settled down for the night. Even the dreadful karaoke burbling inside the house had stopped. A sickle moon had just edged from behind a cloud and was throwing down just enough light for the brothers to see the outline of each other's faces.

The remnants of a breeze tickled the leaves on the shrubs nearby. Dave fancied he saw the reflection of a fox's eyes towards the end of the garden, but when he looked properly, it was gone.

'Andrew?'

'Yes?'

'Do you think that Beleth has been visiting us our whole lives? We let him in as children and it's like he has a key; he comes to visit whenever he wants, puts the kettle on, and has a good rummage in the sock drawers of our psyches. Licking our spoons. Egging us on. Whispering. No wonder I find it so hard not to cheat at the Pub Quiz on Thursday nights. Do you think that, in fact, we are sons of Sa—'

But Dave was interrupted by the back door bursting open and Jess running out, shrieking.

'It's Ian! Come quickly! Something's wrong!'

47

The Other Poisoning

They all rushed into the brightly lit kitchen.

'The food, Dave,' Andrew panted, his eyes like saucers. He gestured to the empty countertop where he'd left the poisoned dinner. 'It's gone.'

They careered after Jess into the dining room and saw unfinished plates of food laid out on the table, chairs pushed back or knocked over. In one corner, Ian lay on the orange carpet, legs drawn into his chest, cradling his neck. His skin was the colour of clouds, and his breath rattled. Rose and Hannah were crouched on either side of him; Rose was on the phone, presumably calling an ambulance. She looked pale and very beautiful in the low light, Dave thought.

'My chest . . . it's my chest,' Ian grunted and rolled from one side to the other, as if he was trying to rock himself to sleep.

Andrew looked at Dave. 'Shit,' he said.

This is it. This is my chance, thought Dave. *This is my chance to make a difference. To save a life. To be a good person.* (*And yes,* thought the self-centred slice of Dave, *if I can pull this off, it will top up my Purgatory rating very nicely indeed.*)

'Hannah!' Dave said urgently. Hannah seemed mesmerized by Ian's crooked body, and didn't respond. 'HANNAH!' She looked up, her face peculiarly blank. 'Your dad's oxygen cylinders. Do you have any downstairs? We need one.'

She looked at him and smiled beneficently as if they were having tea together and he had asked her to pour. 'There's one under the stairs,' she said calmly. 'I'll pop and get it.'

'And a mask! And anything else we need to make it work!' called Dave after her, as she disappeared through the door.

Andrew clutched at Dave's arm and hissed in his ear. 'He ate your plate of food! I've killed him, Dave!'

'Not yet you bloody haven't,' mumbled Dave, and he moved to help Hannah drag the oxygen cylinder across the carpet towards Ian. It made a line in the pile of the carpet, Dave noticed. Hannah expertly hooked up a mask and placed it over Ian's greying face. He wasn't moving any more, or making any sort of noise. She turned on the tap. Everyone waited in silence for something to happen.

Nothing happened.

'Is he still breathing?' asked Andrew.

'I think so. The mask is misting up,' Hannah replied.

'Are you sure the oxygen is on? I can't hear anything,' said Andrew. *He's panicking,* thought Dave. *I wonder how he was after he'd killed me in round one? Regretful? Guilty? Jubilant?*

'Shush a minute,' said Hannah, and she lowered her ear to

the oxygen canister. 'Yes, it's hissing.' She turned to Dave. 'How do you know if this will do any good?'

'I ... er ... well, I think I saw it on telly. Ill people are always given oxygen, aren't they, on those hospital programmes?'

'Michael Jackson had it,' said Andrew helpfully. 'He slept in an oxygen chamber to prolong his ... life.'

They all stared at Andrew, who decided not to speak for a while.

Rose, who had been hanging back, knelt next to Ian. 'Ian. IAN. Can you hear me? It's Rose.'

A muffled sound came from under the oxygen mask.

'Thank God,' muttered Andrew. 'I haven't killed him!'

'Yet,' said Dave, under his breath.

'I just wanted to say,' continued Rose, 'whilst everyone is here,' she looked round at the assembled company, who were standing around Ian as if at a burial, 'that I don't want to be with you any more. You are a self-centred, controlling and jealous man and I'm moving out.' She paused. 'I don't want you to die – I don't think – but I don't want to see you again. Ever.'

Silence. *She is magnificent*, Dave thought.

'Do you understand?' She poked Ian in the stomach. He made a gasping noise to show that he did.

Rose, apparently satisfied, got up and walked over to an armchair in the corner. She sat down, took her phone out of her pocket and started scrolling, apparently uninterested that her ex-boyfriend was dying just feet away.

There was a scuffling noise in the hallway and Hannah, who was closest to the door, went to investigate. The others heard her whispering urgently to someone but couldn't make out what she was saying. Next, they heard soft, uneven foot-steps heading unsteadily towards the dining room and everyone apart from Rose, who was busy on her phone, and Ian, who was busy trying not to meet his maker, looked expectantly towards the door. There, leaning against the frame, was Hannah's dad, resplendent in just pyjama bottoms. His bare chest was proudly on display, his clavicles sticking out like door handles and his skin slipping down his body, but looking much more alive than when Dave had seen him a few minutes previously.

Hannah was standing behind him, looking annoyed, and saying, '*Dad*, what are you doing up?' and '*Dad*, go back to bed' and '*Dad*, everything here is FINE.' She put a strange emphasis on the word 'Dad', Dave noticed.

But Hannah's dad looked bright and perky and perfectly capable of making his own decisions. His sallow skin was still spotted and lined but there was a new light behind the very bluest of eyes that caught Dave's attention. He looked like a totally different man to the corpse-like body he had seen just a few minutes before. But then, it had been very dark upstairs, and Dave had been terrified out of his wits.

'SURPRISE!' Hannah's dad said to them all, smiling broadly, showing a mouth of missing teeth. His voice was familiar to Dave. Sort of comforting and rakish, all at once. Everyone responded with a shy 'hello', as if they were living in a student house, and somebody's parents had come to visit. Even Ian tried to do a little thumbs up from the floor.

Hannah, meanwhile, stood behind her father with her arms folded, looking remarkably pissed off.

Jess stepped forward.

'Hello, Mr . . .?'

'Just call me,' he faltered a little, 'Mr . . . H.' That voice, thought Dave. It doesn't fit with the old man's body. It's too . . . smooth.

'OK, Mr . . . H,' said Jess slowly. 'I'm sorry for all the noise. It's just that I think our friend here has had some sort of heart attack. We used one of your oxygen – things – to help him breathe. I hope that was all right.'

Mr H walked calmly over to Ian and bent down with surprising ease to hear what he was trying to say through the mask.

'He says – has someone called an ambulance?'

'Yes, I did,' said Rose, glancing up. 'And they're sending the police, too – said it's standard practice.'

Dave, Andrew and Mr H shouted 'NO!' and 'WHY?' and 'UH-OH' at exactly the same time. Andrew looked particularly horrified.

'Why not?' said Jess. There was an uncomfortable silence. Andrew looked at Dave and silently mouthed, 'I can't go to prison. I'm too . . . artistic.'

Mr H jumped up with a surprising energy. 'Right. No time to lose. Hannah! Stop sulking and get me some sodium thiosulphate. I think you've got some in the dark room upstairs? We've got to try to transform the you-know-what into a non-toxic stable derivative.' Hannah rolled her eyes and reluctantly sloped off towards the kitchen.

'Sorry – are you a doctor?' said Jess.

'I never quite qualified,' said Mr H, 'but I *have* seen a lot of dead people in my time.' He walked calmly over to Dave, raised his hand and cradled Dave's cheek – a tender, fatherly gesture.

'David,' he said softly. Dave looked in Mr Hannah's eyes, and remembered. These were the pale blue eyes of the man he'd fallen in love with as a child. *He's come to help me,* Dave thought. *Even though it wasn't possible, he's found a way.*

'Hello, Gobe,' he said quietly. 'I'm so glad to see you. But how did you—'

Gobe smiled, and waved his hand nonchalantly at the others. All sound and movement stopped and he and Dave were left in silence.

'I had some help getting down here without being "under the eye", so to speak,' said Gobe. 'I was worried about you, my boy, and I thought that you might need a hand, but to be honest I can see that you've coped marvellously. Apart from him, of course.' Here he gave Ian a small kick. 'Bravo!' Dave's heart swelled with pride.

'Remember, pride is a sin, David.' Dave immediately deflated. 'And your brother is not out of the woods, you know. But listen – Hannah and I will save *him,*' he gave Ian another small kick, 'so at least Andrew won't be looking at a murder charge.'

'I can't let him go to jail,' said Dave. 'Andrew and I talked tonight – I mean, really talked, for the first time in for ever. He reminded me what I did on the beach that day, when we were kids. This,' he looked around at the detritus of the dining room – the half-eaten food, the upended chairs and Ian spread-eagled on the floor attached to an oxygen canister – 'is all a consequence of what I did when we were young.' He turned to Gobe. 'It's all my fault.'

'Perhaps,' said Gobe, softly. 'So – what are you going to do about it?' He paused, arched an eyebrow, and waved his hand again. Movement and sound returned to the room.

Jess was saying something to Gobe. 'So if you're not a doctor, what are you?' Hannah re-appeared carrying a hypodermic needle and gave it to Gobe with a tut and something that sounded like 'I'm not your servant, you know.'

Rose, galvanized by the sight of a needle, began to show some interest in the welfare of her ex-boyfriend, and put down her phone. 'Isn't this a bit risky?' she said. 'I mean, shouldn't we wait for the paramedics? Do you really know what you're doing?'

Dave watched the tableau unfold in front of him. Rose and Jess, emotions heightened and voices strained, questioning Gobe as he injected Ian with a drug that Hannah 'happened to have' in a room upstairs. Andrew, still next to him, pacing and sweating. Hannah leaning against the sideboard, bored, scratching some food off her skirt. Her demeanour had changed since Gobe arrived, Dave thought. He wondered why.

The doorbell went. 'Paramedics,' said Jess and Rose together. 'Police,' said Andrew weakly.

'I think not,' said Gobe, as Jess went to answer the door.

48

An Unexpected Guest

An elderly man wearing a paramedic's uniform and carrying a large bag walked slowly but purposefully into the sitting room. He was also, Dave noticed, wearing a pretty cool hat. But it was only when the man stepped over Ian, who was obviously very sick, and made his way towards the kitchen that Dave twigged there was something wrong.

Gobe and Hannah were hot on his heels. The others all just stood there, open-mouthed.

'Don't worry!' called Hannah, as she sped after her dad.

'Stay where you are, everyone!' called Gobe. 'Nothing to see here!'

Dave thought on his feet. 'You lot stay here in case the paramedics arrive. I'll go and see what this is all about.' And he rushed into the kitchen, slamming the door behind him.

The old man had walked straight to the wand, which was still tucked against the skirting board. Gobe made to rush forward but Hannah put her hand out and stopped him with surprising strength. Gobe looked at Hannah in surprise. She simply put her finger to her lips and said simply – 'Watch.'

The old man picked up the wand, his hat falling off as he did so. Now unshrouded, Dave could see his face and it was maniacal, his Joker-like grin so wide that his face was all teeth and wrinkles. He held the wand high, pointed it at Hannah and spoke, his voice high and thin like scraping teacups,

'I see you! I know you. And you underestimate me.' He turned to Dave. 'You almost led me to this, once, when you were a child. Your mother was one step ahead then, but you boys turned out to be not so sharp. Your stupidity is my gain! I have been searching all my life for this. It doesn't belong to your family any more!' Eyes wide, he turned back to Hannah and shouted, 'IT IS MINE!' He started to mutter incoherently under his breath.

Hannah, who had stepped protectively in front of Gobe, stood magnificent and defiant, her golden hair loose, her hands on her hips. She said nothing, but her amber eyes were focused on the tip of the wand. As Dave and Gobe looked on, the wand in the old man's grip started to change colour – from brown to umber, to yellow and finally to orange. He stopped muttering and looked at the wand, his expression changing from supreme confidence, to wonder, to one of severe pain. The wand now glowed hot like an ember in his grasp.

'This can't be happening,' he said, as much to himself as anyone else. He tried to let go but it had attached itself to his hand, like mistletoe on a tree. He shook his arm violently but as Dave watched, the wand appeared to grow roots, small at first but quickly lengthening, and the roots started to wrap themselves around the man's arm, then his torso. He screamed in agony as they gradually engulfed his small, wiry body. After just a few seconds, he had become a glowing tree, his torso the trunk, with only his head sticking out of the top. He just managed to gurgle the word, 'help', when the roots grew into his mouth and his head disappeared into the knot of embers.

Out of the corner of his eye, Dave saw Gobe trying to move towards the man, but Hannah was still blocking him. She said another single word – 'Wait.'

The tree was shrinking. Fiery roots were retreating, revealing no sign of the man they had consumed. In no time at all, all that remained was the wand, left in exactly the same place by the skirting board, as if it hadn't been touched.

Hannah walked forward and picked up the wand. With one swift, fluid movement she lifted a knee and brought the wand down on top of it with force. It snapped cleanly in two and from the broken pieces, a light flashed so bright that even Gobe had to put his hands to his eyes. At the same time, a strong wind blasted through the kitchen, crashing plates and saucepans to the floor and forcing everyone to hold onto the nearest wall to steady themselves. It lasted just a second. And when it was over, Hannah said quietly, 'I think it was *you* who underestimated *me*.'

There was complete silence in the kitchen. All they could hear was Ian's faint moans coming from the other room.

'Wh-who was that?' asked Dave. He looked at Hannah. 'And who . . . are you?'

Hannah sighed. 'Ah. Well, thereby hangs a tale. You see—'

The doorbell chimed. Nobody reacted. The kitchen door opened and Jess appeared.

'Everyone all right in here?' she said, looking in wonder at the broken crockery all over the floor. 'There's someone at the door. Again.'

Gobe hurriedly brushed himself down and said breezily, 'Well, that probably *is* the paramedics. Or the police. So that's me done. Lovely to meet you all. Smashing, in fact. See you all again, hopefully.' He practically ran out of the room, heading for the stairs. 'Best not to mention me to the old bill!' he called down from the landing.

The doorbell went again.

'Ummm . . .' said Rose. 'Shall I get it?'

'W . . . wait!' Andrew said. 'Before you answer it, I've got something to say.' Jess stopped and turned back; everyone went quiet. 'Thing is – I need to tell you all before the police come in – the thing is—'

In a moment of clarity, Dave knew what he had to do.

'You don't need to say it, Andrew,' he said. Andrew looked at him with surprise. 'I'll confess. It was me. I did it,' he said to everyone calmly. 'I poisoned Ian.'

Andrew looked at him, agape. In fact, they all looked at him, agape. Even Ian, who by this time was looking better and had taken his mask off.

'I mean, I know what we just saw was . . . weird . . . but this is a joke, right Dave?' said Jess, unbelieving. 'You can't have . . . I mean, you're one of life's good guys.'

'It's all a bit Midsomer Murders, even for you, isn't it Dave?' Rose said. 'In fact, have you set this whole thing up for us?'

she added. 'Smoke and mirrors? Flashes and bangs? It's right up your street!'

There was an aggressive rattling at the front door. 'POLICE!' came the shout from outside. 'Is everyone OK in there?'

'I really had better let them in,' said Hannah, and walked past Jess to open the front door.

'Sorry, mate,' said Dave. Ian started to mumble his reply. 'Not you,' said Dave sharply. Ian stopped mumbling abruptly. Dave looked at his brother. 'I'm so sorry. For everything.' He hugged his brother hard, and slipped quietly out through the kitchen and the open back door.

49

The Escape

Dave had never felt so alive, as he clambered over Hannah's picket fence, snapping off the top of a fence post. He felt a splinter burrow into his thigh and he enjoyed the pain. This is how he should have lived his whole life – taking risks, owning stuff, saying sorry and meaning it. Actually *feeling* things. It's time to start really *living*. It was as though he'd just lifted himself out of the muck, like he was holding onto a hundred helium balloons and floating away from indifference and boredom. Like the old man in *Up*. He was *just* like the old man in *Up*.

The houses began to peter out and he made out a sign to a footpath leading between two high fences. He took the path which led to open scrub, with what looked like a small copse of thin trees, black against the thin moonlight, about 100 feet away. He ran for the trees, thinking they would shield him from any search lights and helicopters, and snagged his shirt on a branch. He continued to run, looking behind at the piece of cotton trailing in the wind. *Come and get me*, he thought. *I'm ready for you. All of you.*

He kept running. He'd had no idea he had all this energy balled up inside him. He probably could have been an athlete if he'd tried harder. All those Olympic events, missed. Wasted opportunities. He would be a different person from now on. He'd be slippery and clever, like Moriarty or the Pink Panther. He'd avoid the long arm of the law by travelling by night, keeping off grid, using only cash.

He slowed his pace, realizing for the first time that he had no idea where he was. The watery light from the moon barely showed him the path under his feet, and he had to strain his eyes to avoid tree roots, or uneven rocks, or large puddles. He shook his phone to activate his torch and picked up his pace again. Just like Bear Grylls, he thought. He could hitch to Scotland and lie low for a bit, in a cave or a bothy or whatever they're called. He'd live off berries and nuts and . . . heather.

He was free. Finally, he was free.

And with that thought, he ripped at his Marks and Spencer checked shirt, pulling off the buttons, shedding it like a skin and throwing it to the ground.

'I'm alive!' he shouted, to Heaven, to Hell, to anyone who could hear him. 'I am reborn! I AM ALIVE!'

Dave threw his arms upwards in a state of ecstasy, and as he did so, he stumbled backwards off the path and tripped over the strut of a child's swing. He fell straight and hard, everything happening too quickly for him to realize that he had wandered into a child's playground not far from the North

Circular, and not the wilderness that he had imagined. The back of his skull caught the edge of a climbing frame with such force that his occipital bone shattered, driving fragments directly into his brain, and causing a fatal haemorrhage.

And with that, Dave died. Again.

50

Heaven's Gate

'Sir – all I'm saying is, to die once might be a misfortune, but to die twice looks like carelessness.'

'Did you just make that up?'

Silence.

'Remember God knows everything, and doesn't like lies. Even tiddlers.'

Pause. 'I might have read something similar, somewhere . . .'

Dave heard the voices, familiar but unplaceable, as soon as he woke. He didn't want to open his eyes as he could tell the light was very bright beyond his closed lids, and he felt like he'd been in darkness for a long time. Was he in hospital?

A loud creak interrupted his thoughts.

'Shush with your blathering. He's waking up. David? David! Open your eyes!'

Dave slowly, unwillingly, opened his eyes, blinking in the white light. 'Have I had an operation, Doctor?' he asked.

'Oh, for goodness' sakes. Arial – I thought you said he'd be a bit brighter this time around.'

'Well, to be fair, sir, this sort of situation is unprecedented. I thought that, as he'd been through it before, he might need less adjustment time.'

'Are you a doctor?' asked Dave, looking at Angel Gobe. 'You look . . . familiar.'

'It's me, David. Gobe. Angel Go-between. Remember?' Gobe bent over so his face was inches from Dave's. 'You've had an adventure, my boy,' he said gently.

Dave rubbed his eyes. 'You look like Michael Palin,' he said. 'Am I at a book signing?'

Gobe turned to Arial and sighed. 'Do we really have to go through all this again? I'm not sure I've got it in me.'

Dave sat up suddenly. 'Am I in the hostel? Where's Laura?'

'Finally,' said Gobe to Arial. He turned back to Dave. 'You are dead,' said Gobe.

'Again,' interrupted Arial.

Gobe stared hard at Arial, who retreated and busied himself with a lightbulb he'd found in his pocket.

'David,' he said softly. 'You had an accident. Your own fault, of course. The situation seemed to run away with you. The good thing is, you died happy. Ecstatic, actually. And that cannot be said for many people.'

Gobe could see that Dave's eyes were coming into focus, and that his memories were returning, albeit slowly, as if through stretched chewing gum.

'It's brighter here than the hostel room,' he said weakly. 'Am I outside? By the sea?'

'Well, David,' said Gobe luminously. 'Not quite. But I've got a surprise for you. Are you ready?'

Dave gave a small nod, trying very hard to focus on Gobe's face. As he did so, Gobe drew back, revealing more of Dave's surroundings. The light suddenly got stronger, and Dave unconsciously brought his hand to his face to shield his eyes.

'You'll get used to it. We control the brightness from the central core – we like to keep it cheery, don't we, Arial? Good for vitamin D production. Not that you need it, now you're dead. Nevertheless it seems to help keep away the demons.'

'Central core?' said Dave, who was rapidly feeling more like himself.

'WELCOME TO HEAVEN!' they shouted together, both beaming broadly.

'Wha . . . but . . . I mean . . . why?' stuttered Dave, whose eyes had finally settled into the light.

'Sit back, my very best of boys, and I'll tell you all. Have a sip of coffee – I think it's your favourite mug.'

Dave noticed a mug with steam rising from it on a small white bedside table next to him. It was a mug from his kitchen. The one that said 'This tea was stirred with my balls'. He mouthed a silent apology to the angels as he brought the mug to his lips.

It was only now that Dave felt able to take in his surroundings. He was lying on a park bench which was unexpectedly comfortable. He couldn't tell if he was inside or outside; if inside, the room was monumentally huge, because he couldn't see any walls. If he was outside, everything was terrifically clean and bright. The overwhelming sensation was one of light and, now that he was properly awake, he found it restorative rather than overwhelming. Gobe and Arial were standing in front of him looking very pleased with themselves, and about fifty feet away was a five-bar gate, standing up on its own, and definitely not attached to a fence. It appeared to be studded with something, although he couldn't quite make out what. A man in a toga was squatting next to it.

'Ah, yes,' said Gobe, following his gaze. 'We'll come to that in a sec.'

'Did you say I'm in Heaven? Really?' Dave's brain was catching up with the news. Actually, his brain felt in pretty good working order, like a clean engine running in cold air. His synapses – or whatever they were now that he was dead – were firing like crazy.

'Arial – please fill our friend in,' said Gobe.

'Certainly, sir,' said Arial, stepping forward. He had a clipboard in his hands and was flicking through sheets of paper.

'Ascension to Heaven report on David Walsh. Unusual case – save to Celestial Library.'

'What does that mean?' whispered Dave to Gobe.

'It means that your case will be studied by thousands of angels, David! You'll be famous!' Gobe seemed very excited by this. 'Anyway, I think we can skip the preamble, Arial. Just move on to the meaty bit.'

'Right, sir. Of course,' said Arial. He flipped a page over on his clipboard. 'In summary, Dave, and in layman's terms: you know that we keep a scoresheet on all your doings down below? Well, in the last few hours, you smashed it. You started well by apologizing to your brother once you had confronted what you had done to him, as a child.'

'Absolutely!' said Gobe.

Arial smiled gratefully, and coughed. 'Thank you, sir. Anyway, you got . . . 1,240,487 points for that excellent work. Which would have still left you in Purgatory when you died, but it would have significantly shortened your time there.'

Dave was following this so far. He wondered how long he would have had to spend there had he not been offered the chance to solve his own murder. It didn't bear thinking about.

'So, then we come to the big one. You took the blame for Ian's poisoning.' Arial seemed very excited by this. 'You have no idea how rare this is, David. If we look down at the boxes, you've got Self-Sacrifice, plus Good Samaritan, plus the Paying (or over-paying) of a Debt, Love Thy Neighbour . . . I could go on, but in short – you ticked them all. With this one action, you got yourself a fast pass to Heaven.'

Gobe turned to Dave. 'Do you see, David? It's "Advance to Go" for you, my boy. You've made it!'

Dave couldn't quite believe it. 'You mean – this is it? I'm in Heaven? It looks a bit . . . bleak.'

'Ah, quite, well spotted. You're actually at Heaven's Gate. It's a sort of . . . *debrief* place. Where we break the news. It takes a while for most people to get used to the idea of being dead, even if they have made it to Heaven. Not you, of course! You're an old hand at it!'

'Hmmmm.' It felt impolite to argue the point. 'Is that Heaven's actual gate, over there?' He pointed to the five-bar gate which stood independently in the middle of . . . well, nothing at all.

'Why does it look like it's just been lifted out of a farmer's field? And what are all those . . . nobby bits stuck on it?'

'Oh, is that what you're seeing?' said Gobe. 'Make a note, Arial.' Arial started scribbling furiously. 'Heaven's Gate is as personal to each individual as your own Purgatory was. You've invented that in your imagination, David. Most people go full on, enormous wrought-iron gates made of solid gold, encrusted jewels – and pearls, of course. Always pearls. St Peter is usually hanging around too, of course, the box-ticker that he is.'

'Is that St Peter in the toga?' Dave asked, squinting at the figure, who appeared to be stroking the top bar of the gate lovingly.

'Him?' Gobe spluttered. 'My dear boy, no! Peter's on his break. That's Janus, Roman God of . . . what is he God of, Arial?'

'Gates, Sir. Doors. Stiles . . . any sort of openings, really.'

'That's right. Openings. He's a very good stand-in when Peter's not around and I seem to remember that he has a particular *penchant* for five-bars. Hence why he's . . . snuggled up to yours.'

They all looked over at Janus, who was now sitting astride the gate and trying to ride it, like a horse.

'I can't see the gate, but is he riding it, like a horse?' asked Gobe.

'Yes,' said Dave.

They were silent for a few seconds.

'Well,' said Gobe. 'Let's hope that Peter's back by the time we've done our debrief.'

Dave closed his eyes. So he'd died twice. That was pretty impressive. He was a very impressive person. He'd never felt impressive before. And he was tall. Very, very tall. The tallest person called Dave he'd ever met. Probably the tallest Dave in Heaven. He was so tall they'd probably ask him to be an angel. All angels were tall, weren't they? They were probably stretched. Did they have a stretching machine in Heaven? What did they call that? A rickle? A rick? A rack?

He'd made it. After everything that had happened – finally he could relax. A warmth was travelling slowly up his legs and torso, as if he was lowering himself into the most perfectly run bath. Would he always feel this happy now? It was really very nice indeed; he felt content and peaceful, at ease with himself. The hazy glow within him reminded him of the time he'd woken up after a knee operation, still high on morphine and giddy and bouncing on blancmange. He was aware of Gobe and Arial chatting to him, but he didn't feel any need to respond.

They can wait. I'll just close my eyes again for a min – oooh, those bubbles are nice. What do they mean? Shame my legs don't work or my arms oh dear what's that sinking feeling I am not figuratively I mean I am actually sinking and the sun is down and the night is shining in and I must be on a beach or in an oven or underground and gosh it's hot ugh what's that awful smell I think I'm going to be sick and who is screaming my ears this is un—

'Arial. ARIAL. What's happening?' That voice sounds distant. Foggy.

'I'm not too sure, sir. I've never seen it before. It looks like . . . I think we're losing him.'

Who's that? Is that Arial? He sounds different. Echoey. Hey. HEY! I'm here! Arial! It's me! Dave!

'But how can that happen? We did everything we could! We thought of everything, didn't we? Quick, Arial, pick him up. We need to get him through the gate.'

Can you hear me? I'm still here! Oh. I can't see my fingers. What the—

'Yes, sir. Sir, he's slipping. He's slippery. I can't hold him by myself.'

'Janus. JANUS! Leave the gate and get over here. NOW. Pick him up. Arial, take a leg. You too, Jan. Quickly! That's it. I'll take the head. DAVID! You've just got here, don't you dare leave us now. Through the gate, boys. We need to get him in to God. Yes, God. I don't care, Arial. There was always going to be a day of reckoning. It might as well be today. Now, one . . . two . . . three . . . LIFT.'

51

The Last Chapter

He didn't want to open his eyes immediately. It felt like there'd been way too much eye-opening recently with unexpected consequences. Fiction Factory was playing softly somewhere, far away. He could smell Christmas; cinnamon, or mulled wine, or minced pies, or all of those things. It made him smile. It reminded him of the best bits of his childhood, of presents in pillowcases and candles in oranges and Granny putting that Quality Street tin on her head and making everyone laugh. People he loved, now long gone.

He opened his eyes.

He was in the most amazing bedroom. The walls were mahogany panelled, highly polished, red and splendid. A gun-metal spiral staircase led up to a mezzanine, lined with mahogany bookcases with glass fronts and drawers with traditional gold handles. There were enormous double doors at the far side of the room, flanked by bright copper side tables. On top of a handsome chest of drawers was a

341

collection of cut-glass tumblers and what appeared to be decanted whisky.

He was propped up in a huge round bed, like one he'd seen in *Dynasty* once and entirely peach-coloured, from the studded leather headboard to the satin sheets. He shifted his weight and holy moly, yes – he heard the soft gurgle of water. A waterbed. The bed of his dreams.

'Nice bed.' He looked up to see Gobe, sitting in a wicker rocking chair by the side of the bed. 'Nice room, actually. I didn't know you had it in you. Not what I'd expect, but I'm learning that you're a little bag of revelations. Also – I'm loving this rocking chair. Where's it from?'

Dave scratched his head. 'I'm not sure – maybe *High Noon*? I always fancied the idea of sitting on my porch with a cigar, waiting for some action to start.'

Gobe smiled and nodded briefly.

'Am I dead? Again?'

'Well, much as I would love to spill the beans, dear boy, I defer to someone much more able than me. They've been desperate to meet you and I don't want to steal their thunder. Ha! As if I could.' Gobe suddenly stood up attentively. 'They're on their way.' He treated Dave to a broad wink. 'Get ready.'

Dave looked apprehensively at the double doors. A few seconds passed and Gobe coughed nervously. 'Any time now,' he said reassuringly.

The music stopped. Abruptly, the doors flew open and a strong blast of warm air whipped into the room. Dave had to hold onto his sheets to protect his modesty and he could see Gobe gripping onto the rocking chair to hold it down. One of the beautiful cut glass tumblers fell onto the floor but Dave couldn't see if it had broken or not. 'Don't worry!' shouted Gobe above the noise. 'They like to make an entrance. We'll clear up the mess later!'

As quickly as it had come, the wind died down.

The figure at the doorway, backlit by golden light, looked like everyone you've ever loved: your ancestor, your parent, your lover, your friend, your sibling, your child. They were all things at once, and also every individual element. Their smile was the world, their kind eyes the universe. They were at once strong and powerful, but also welcoming and benevolent.

They held their arms out in warm greeting, offering comfort and contentment. And Dave thought:

That's God.

And then he thought:

She's a woman. That's unexpected.

And lastly he thought:

She's wearing a purple velour tracksuit. That too takes me by surprise.

'Hello, David,' she said, as she sat on his bed next to him.

David didn't know what to say, so he just said the obvious. 'You're a . . . woman!'

'Of course I am, David. Would a man have given you a second chance?'

'But you didn't know about me being sent down to Earth to solve my own murder.' She raised her eyebrows. 'Did you?' He looked at Gobe for reassurance.

Gobe looked studiously at his feet and said nothing.

God smoothed the wrinkles in Dave's bedspread. 'I like what you've done with this room. It's very . . . Bond meets Eastwood. Am I right?'

Of course she was right. She could see into Dave's mind as easily as if it were made of glass. He nodded slowly.

'You're wondering why I look like this. You're asking yourself – has she always looked like a middle-aged, middle-sized woman? Or can she change shape, depending on who she is seeing? Am I in control of how she looks? And now you're wondering – if she can look like anyone at all, why has she chosen to look like *that*?'

David was ashamed. Even though he was aware she was inside his head, he couldn't stop his mind from processing thoughts.

'I . . . I'm sorry! I'm so sorry. It's just that—'

She waved her hands. 'Don't worry at all. I'm just showing off. It's a valid question. And the answer is: I have always been a woman. I am also a man, of course.' Dave was confused. This really was an awful lot to take in. Gobe, seeing that Dave was struggling, stepped in.

'Look – you think of her as an old white man with a beard and a robe, but that's only because of skewed theological translations and mis-gendering and because your world has been a man's world for the last few thousand years.'

God was nodding along. 'But the wind is changing, David! Ariana Grande said that God is a woman and she's at least half right.'

Dave didn't really know what to say. Was he really talking to God? In a waterbed?

'Anyway,' said God, tucking her hair behind her ears absent-mindedly, 'I like looking like a woman when I meet incomers. It makes people challenge what they know. Or what they think they know. And I wear tracksuits because – well, because they're comfy.'

'I can relate to that,' Dave managed to squeak, realizing suddenly that he had no idea what he had on under the bedclothes.

'Let's just have this quick chat, and then you can explore your pyjamas,' she said. 'Gobe? Come up here, would you, and finish off the explanations? I'm sure David would like us to fill in the gaps.'

Gobe, who had retreated to the end of the bed, stepped forward. 'Of course.' He cleared his throat. 'The truth is, David, it didn't really go to plan. Not your fault, as it turns out. Entirely mine.' He looked at God. 'I shouldn't have gone behind your back.'

'Now, now, Gobey, don't start all that again,' God patted his hand. 'We've been through this, you've said sorry, and it's no big deal. I won't have any more apologies.'

Gobe smiled. 'I have an extremely forgiving boss, David.' He sat in the rocking chair, but this time at the very edge of it, leaning forward, his elbows on his knees. 'Remember I asked you to stop all the clocks at the dinner party? I thought it was a way we could . . . circumnavigate . . . Heaven's monitoring.' An unreadable look passed between Gobe and God.

'Well,' Gobe continued. 'You did a great job there, my boy. Arial and I watched what you were doing – up to a point – and we were so proud of you. You stopped all the clocks and that should have been enough.'

'Wasn't it?'

Gobe looked at the floor and cleared his throat. 'I made an error of judgement.' He paused. 'It concerns Beleth.'

Dave remembered something. 'Is it something to do with you coming down as . . . Hannah's dad?'

Gobe sighed. 'I went to see Beleth to try persuade him to drop the barrier – I knew he wouldn't let us see who had murdered you, but I asked him to help me to visit Earth during the party. Second time around, as it were.' Here he looked guiltily at God. 'Without God's knowledge, of course. It's not that I didn't have the utmost faith in you of course,' Dave thought this unlikely, 'but I sensed that you might need a helping hand.'

Gobe looked again at God who nodded approvingly. 'Go on, Gobey,' she said.

'Anyway, the thing is – and this may come as a shock to you, David – Beleth is my brother. I'm a demi-angel, really, and he's a demi-demon. The same human mother, you see? We were taken up to Heaven when we reached adulthood, but Beleth . . . Well, let's just say that he fell from God's grace a long time ago and turned to evil. A very . . . regretful business. The trouble is, we are two sides of a coin.

'I went to see him and I told him that I was protecting him by hiding his involvement in this whole thing from God. As it turns out, she knew everything, of course, and she *was* pretty angry, but only with me, and only because I didn't tell her what I was up to.

'I've never lied before, David. I've been spending so much time in the company of humans that their habits – good and bad – have been rubbing off on me. I blame myself, of course, and should have spotted it earlier – the sweating should have been a dead giveaway. It's just that you lot are so . . . alluring.'

Dave had never, ever felt alluring.

'So that *was* you? Hannah's dad?'

Gobe smiled. 'Beleth is an expert in possessing people and I have to admit that he gave me one or two "hot" tips. But I didn't quite realize what he wanted in return.'

Gobe looked so melancholy that Dave wanted to fling his arms around him.

'What happened? It can't be that bad. Everything worked out in the end, didn't it?'

Gobe was silent and shook his head, once again looking at the floor. He made a choking noise – the sort of sound that's made when you're trying to hold back tears. God took Gobe's hand gently, like a mother with a sad child, then gave Dave a tight smile.

'Beleth betrayed him. He tricked him, Dave. Gobe didn't know that you can't ask a demon for help without a consequence. Even if the demon is your brother.'

Dave felt a wave of empathy for Gobe. 'I'm so sorry,' he said. He knew how it felt to be deceived by your brother.

Gobe sniffed and appeared to pull himself together. 'Thank you, David. Anyway, the consequence of this – betrayal – was that when you died, Beleth attempted to take your soul.'

Dave gulped and glanced at God, who was making wavy lines in the sheets with her fingers.

'Holy mo—' Gobe glanced sharply at Dave who stopped abruptly. 'Is that what happened when I was at the five-bar gate?' he asked.

'Yes, we nearly lost you there. But God stepped in and saved you. Luckily for us, it turns out that God knew what we were up to all the time.' He turned to God. 'Of course she did. She sees everything.'

'Weeeeeeellll . . . I had some help,' said God. 'I couldn't do this on my own, you know.' She smiled and turned to the door. 'Gab! GABBY! Come in please, pet.'

The doors opened again. This time there was no wind, no bright light, no pomp or circumstance. Just a woman with long, chaotic, golden hair, plainly dressed entirely in white, barefoot.

She looked exactly as Dave remembered when he last saw her, except for the gold halo that hovered above her head, and two enormous gossamer wings.

'Hello, Hannah,' he said. 'You look . . . different, somehow.'

'Hello, David.' She smiled and approached the bed.

And now that she was closer, Dave could see her gold halo wasn't gold at all – it was fizzing with colours, like light through a prism: turquoise, lime, scarlet, orange. He was transported back to the discos at weddings he'd gone to as a child; lights spun and tumbled around the room, her halo a disco ball. Her magnificent wings sparkled with the same deep colours, as if they were covered with a thousand cut-glass sequins catching the light.

'"Hannah" is the Angel Gabrielle, David. I'm sorry we couldn't be honest with you. We're rarely honest with humans who are still alive, to be honest – we tried it a few times in the early days and it didn't end well.' God got up from the bed and brushed herself down. 'If it makes you feel any better, we weren't even honest with dear Gobe, here. When he popped up as Hannah's dad, Hannah – or Gabrielle here – had "a bit of a pop" at him in the hallway. She revealed who she was and poor Gobe got the fright of his life.'

God looked fondly at both of her angels.

'Well, lovely as this reunion is, I have to get on. This universe won't run itself, you know. I'll let my two beautiful angels explain things to you.' God swept out of the room and the doors closed automatically behind her.

The two angels stared after her adoringly, for what seemed to Dave a very long time, until he made a small coughing noise to bring them both back into the room.

Hannah/Gabrielle took God's place on the bed. Dave couldn't stop looking at her: she was a version of Hannah, or a thousand Hannahs, or had Hannah somewhere inside her. Her halo and her wings were so extraordinarily beautiful that Dave couldn't tear his eyes from them. He could feel himself start to cry.

'They're a bit off-putting, aren't they?' she said apologetically. 'Also, they aren't the most comfortable things when you're sitting down. I only really put them on to show off.' In an instant, the wings and the halo were gone. And she was more like Hannah again.

Dave wiped his eyes and croaked, 'Thank you.' Then, worried that might come across as rude, he added, 'You look amazing.' Then, in case she thought he was chatting her up, he topped it off with, 'I mean, for an angel.' And then he decided to be quiet for a while.

She nodded at Gobe, who began to speak. 'You know, David, that Lucifer was once an angel like me and Gabrielle?'

Dave, who didn't, nodded.

Gobe smiled. 'Well, he was. He wasn't evil in the beginning, just proud and jealous. But evil started to slip into his heart and, eventually, God had to cast him out. Other angels followed him, and became demons. Some of these demons walked the earth and had – relations – with human women.' He looked unflinchingly at Dave, and Dave could see that he was fighting back tears. 'My father is a fallen angel, Dave. My mother was a human, like you. And Beleth is my twin brother. We grew up together, on Earth.' He breathed out slowly. 'He will always be in here.' He gestured to his heart. 'Even if he doesn't feel the same.'

Dave could feel his eyes pricking again. He couldn't help comparing Gobe's situation with his own. A brother who he had loved, who had hated him and tried to bring about his downfall. He reached out and took Gobe's hand. Gobe smiled and gave Dave's hand a reassuring squeeze.

'Now,' Gabrielle continued, 'that leads me on to why we've taken such a special interest in you and your ancestors over the years. Have you guessed?'

Dave considered the question. 'Because of the protection spell? The Blocks?'

'Well, that certainly added to our . . . attentiveness. But it didn't start with that. Do you want to tell him, Gobe?'

Gobe nodded and sat back in his rocking chair, his fingers touching to form a pyramid. 'I told you my mother was human. Well, her mother had a sister. And you, David, are descended from her.' He looked at David, who looked blankly back at Gobe. 'This means that we are related! We are cousins!'

Dave's jaw dropped. Related? To an angel? And not just any angel – but to Gobe? This was incredible!

'Don't get too excited, David. Many thousands of people are related to angels if you go far enough back. Lots of us started as humans, you know.' Dave's face fell. 'Although I admit that being related to me *is* rather exciting. However, that's not all.'

'Oh?'

'First of all, the wand found you. Well, it found your grand-parents. We'd known of its existence, of course, but it had lain dormant for centuries, until a friend of your grandfather happened upon it on a dog walk and brought it to a Satanist society meeting. Coincidence? I think not. Your family were its guardians; anyone else who attempted to use it would suffer one way or another.'

'Is that why Jess went mad? And why that man got . . . eaten?'

'"That man", David, was present when Beleth was summoned for the first time. He saw how powerful the wand was, and has been hunting for it ever since.'

'You are kidding me,' Dave said softly.

'I never kid about man-eating wands.' Gobe allowed himself the smallest of smiles. 'But there's more, David. Apart from the wand, I mean.' Dave leaned forward. 'Did you know that each generation on your mother's side, for over a thousand years, had only one child? Very unusual. That is, until you and Andrew. The first siblings in that family – a family of satanists – since me and Beleth, in fact. So when you two were born, we thought you might be a bit – special – and wanted to keep a careful eye on you both.' He paused. 'We failed though – *I* failed – and for that, I apologize.'

Dave threw back the covers, got out of bed, walked the couple of steps to Gobe's rocking chair, bent down and gave him a huge hug. Gobe, who wasn't sure if he'd ever hugged a human before – or indeed, anyone – haltingly put his arms around Dave and closed his eyes, allowing his human-self free rein, for just a few seconds.

Gabrielle watched the two of them with scientific interest, as though a pig had just stood up on two legs to walk. 'How . . . charming,' she said.

As Dave pulled himself away and got back into bed, she continued, 'Anyway, we've been popping in and out, keeping an eye on your ancestors over the last few hundred years to make sure it didn't all get out of control. I had a great time as Miss Plotts the Postmistress with your grandparents. And then checking on you as Hannah over the last few months has been amusing in its own way too.'

Dave glanced at Gobe. 'Gobe didn't know anything,' Gabrielle continued. 'We're pretty good at cloaking ourselves and I could tell he suspected something, but he couldn't quite put his finger on it. Isn't that right, Gobe?'

Gobe nodded. 'You looked different to the others,' he said. 'But I just couldn't tell how. I should have been able to tell but I suppose I . . . lost sight of myself for a while.'

'Well, G – if I say so myself, I'm pretty good at illusion.' She turned back to Dave. 'The upshot is that we didn't have the faith in Beleth that Gobe did.' Gobe was silent. 'We suspected that he would try to foil Gobe's plan so we just had to be ready to scoop you up when you started your descent into Hell.'

Dave shuddered. If that had just been the start of a descent – that oppressive heat, those screams, that overwhelming feeling of dread – he wondered how anyone endured it.

'Because they have to,' said Gabrielle flatly. 'For eternity.'

'Oh,' said Dave.

'Well now, it's been an absolute delight to meet you properly and honestly, David,' she said, getting up. 'I hope this all wasn't too much of a shock for you.' As she said this, her halo and wings appeared, and lights once again shot around the room. 'I'll be in and out to check on you.' This could either have been a warm promise or an ominous threat. It seemed safer to take it as the latter.

'Wait! Don't go yet – please. I have questions!'

She sighed impatiently. 'Quickly then. I've got a huge pile of admin waiting. And I haven't done my trumpet practice yet today.'

Dave gathered his thoughts. 'I don't get it. You were there – at the first murder scene, I mean. You would have been able

353

to see who murdered me right from the start. So why couldn't you just report back to God? It would have saved all of this . . . mess.'

'Clever thinking, David! I can see why Gobe likes you. Except that I wasn't actually in the room for the first one. We didn't know that a murder was going to take place. There was no prophecy, no foretelling. We're not *palm readers*. So I was having a lovely time in the sitting room singing "Mirror Man" by The Human League, as I remember, when Andrew must have gone into the kitchen to slip the poison into your food. I think his excuse was that he needed the toilet. And second time around, I was upstairs, reacting to your oxygen canister . . . event.'

Dave winced. How embarrassing.

'I have another question,' he said.

'Hmm?' She looked bored now.

'Who was the old man – I'm assuming he wasn't your actual father – and why had you built a fortress around him?'

She smiled. 'The man is a dead actor from Heaven – marvellous chap, several RSC roles – who we convinced to come along to add some credence to my earthly persona. Poor old chap got a shock when Gobe booted him out of his body. Still, all fixed now and no long-term damage caused.' She gave Gobe a sidelong glance. 'And the canisters. They were Her idea, actually. She *loves* challenges, doesn't she G?' she smiled at Gobe and he nodded. 'A bit like *The Krypton Factor*?' she added.

'Or *I'm A Celebrity*, perhaps,' interrupted Gobe.

'Bravo, Gobe. Your up-to-date knowledge of the terrestrial

world remains unbeaten!' Gabrielle spoke warmly and Dave saw Gobe blush – although it might just have been a shadow cast from Gabrielle's enormous wings. 'Anyway, Dave, consider it God's interpretation of *I'm a Celebrity*.' She gave them both a brief smile. 'I really must go. That papyrus work will not sort itself out.'

And with wings flashing and lights dancing, she glided out of the room with a backward slung message:

'Oh, and welcome to Heaven!'

The disco lights snapped off, and she was gone.

After a moment or two of silence, Dave asked Gobe, 'So is she the Angel Gabriel? From the Bible?'

'The very one.'

'So is she a woman and a man, too? Like God?'

'Ha! No, no – she's very definitely a female angel. Always has been.'

'So why did they say in the Bible that Angel Gabriel was male?'

'Well . . . I suppose they saw an important figure and assumed it was a man in a dress.'

'Ah yes, right.' A moment's silence. 'Gobe?'

'Hmm?'

'I'm sorry I got you into trouble.'

Gobe smiled warmly. 'There is absolutely nothing for you to apologize about, my dear boy. I did it for my own selfish reasons. Of course, I wanted the best outcome for you – we all do, here, for every human – but it was my mistake, and I am very grateful to have been forgiven.'

'What will happen to Andrew?'

'I can't see into the future, David. I'm sorry.'

'Oh.' And then, 'He's still got a chance, then?'

'He has.'

Well, that's something. He looked up, and caught Gobe looking at his pyjamas. 'What is . . . that?' asked Gobe, pointing at Dave's top.

Dave looked properly for the first time at what he was wearing. He realized with a lurch that his nightwear had the diamond-shaped 'S' on the chest, just as it had when he was ten years old.

'Did I choose to wear these? In my version of Heaven?' Dave asked. But even as he asked, he knew the answer. These pyjamas had been the best Christmas present he had ever had. He remembered running wildly around the house in them, makeshift tea-towel cape flapping in the breeze behind, non-stop from Christmas to New Year − save for one airing when his mother forced him into the bath.

Gobe smiled kindly. 'You can wear them for a good while yet. Now − about Andrew. I feel that, together, we might be able to reach him. I have the beginnings of a plan which I think that you—'

They were interrupted by loud, excited voices outside the room, and then a knock at the door. 'Can we come in yet?' a male voice shouted.

The door flew open and there was a rush of familiar, friendly faces and goodwill and relief. Arial rushed up to Dave and offered him his hand, rather formally. Dave took it and Arial, beaming, pumped his hand up and down shouting 'my first proper handshake!' at anyone who would listen.

Then there was Freda, all the way from Purgatory, looking resplendent in a beautiful floral tea dress ('it was the only dress I had for dancing,' she said shyly, when Dave commented on it). She approached the other side of the bed from Gobe where miraculously a comfortable armchair had appeared. 'I brought my own,' she said, sinking into it, and winked. 'Can't be doing with other people's odd ideas of furniture. Oh – I brought you something, too,' and she gave him an oblong package, wrapped in brown paper and string.

'It feels like my birthday!' said Dave, pulling at the string and ripping apart the paper. He laughed. 'Scrabble – could it have been anything else? Thank you so much, Freda.' He leaned over and planted a gentle kiss on her surprisingly youthful cheek. 'Where's Edie?'

Freda's smile sank, just a little. 'Turns out she'd been swearing under her breath a lot more than we thought in Purgatory. She's going to be stuck there for a while.' Despite himself, Dave let out the most uproarious laugh, and Freda joined in. 'She just couldn't help herself!' Freda gasped. 'Oh, and by the way – I have another little surprise for you.' She looked back towards the door.

Dave looked up and, despite being dead, his heart leapt. There, resplendent in a long, midnight-blue sequinned dress straight from the Eighties, was his mum. And behind her – his dad, dressed in his best work suit with a colourful kipper tie.

'Come in!' said Gobe, gesturing them to come forward.

Dave couldn't believe it. It had been so long since he'd seen his dad that he had almost forgotten what he looked like. But now it all came back to him in a rush: his dark, slick-backed hair, his Tom Selleck moustache, and his gangly frame that, unlike Dave's, had never seemed to gain an ounce. And the last time he'd seen his mum had been in the home, propped up in a lounge chair, and he had been helping her to drink cold coffee through a straw. She had become agitated, the carers had said, and they'd had to give her tranquillizers to calm her down.

But now, Ann and Colin looked like a couple again, each looking about fifty – happy, glowing and full of vigour. He tore off the bedclothes and ran towards them, almost bowling them over with the fierceness of his embrace.

'Hello, David,' said Ann.

'Hello, my boy,' said Colin. They were all weeping.

'I'm sorry I didn't come to your funeral,' Ann said. She smiled. 'Either of them. It appears I died straight after each one.' She kissed the top of his head and cupped his face with her hands, as if he was a child again. 'David – I'm so sorry for everything.' She spoke softly but urgently. 'For casting that awful spell on you all and for everything that followed. Angel Gobe told me about the holiday. You mustn't blame yourself. It was my fault for inviting Beleth in; he twisted everything inside you, encouraging you to do what you did. And you were only a child.' She gathered him up again in her arms and hugged him tight.

He heard his dad's voice, muffled through his mum's blue sequins that were pressed around his ears. 'We're proud of you, David. We heard what you did for Andrew. That was a decent and brave thing to do.' He sensed Colin's hand ruffling his hair, and he felt like he was ten years old again. It made him smile.

Dave would happily have stayed like that for a long time but after a while, he heard Gobe clearing his throat.

'Anyway, Dave, did you notice that we redecorated for you?'

'Redecorated? But I've only just . . .' He looked up to see that his Bond boudoir had been radically – some might say obscenely – festooned with colourful balloons and 'Welcome to Heaven' banners. Glittering streamers and paperchains looped their way high across the walls and over the dark furniture. In one corner, a trestle table had appeared, covered in a bright, wipe-clean tablecloth. Dave could clearly see a pineapple hedgehog, its spines made from cocktail sticks, cheese and pineapple cubes, as well as pyramids of cupcakes with swirled icing and jugs of what looked like weak blackcurrant squash.

He looked back at his friends – because he did consider them friends – and they were all suddenly excited, putting on colourful cone-shaped party hats, each with a froth of crepe paper fountaining from the top.

Freda was getting help from Ann with her elastic, which Freda had somehow got knotted around her nose. Arial had been given a party blower and was merrily blowing it, loudly, half an inch from Gobe's face. Gobe, patient and benevolent, allowed four full toots of the blower before throwing Arial a warning glance, whereupon Arial moved on to Colin, who was in the process of putting three hats on, plus an extra one under his chin. Gobe clapped his hands together, just once, and the crickets, engine and footsteps of Wham's 'Club Tropicana' started up. By the time the Eighties bass had kicked in, Arial and Ann were disco dancing, hands in the air, shrieking with delight, on Dave's enormous bed.

As Dave climbed up to join them, he shouted over to Gobe, 'WILL HEAVEN ALWAYS BE THIS COOL?'

And Gobe replied, 'Cool, David? My dear boy, you ain't seen nothing yet.'

52

Epilogue

Mercia, AD 682

The village of Caeginesham, set at the confluence of two rivers, was small and unremarkable save for one thing – its production of exquisite cloth. The village weavers – Edyo, and her husband Uhtric – were highly skilled. They kept a small flock of sheep and their beautiful daughter, Cwen, spun yarn from their wool of the finest quality. Cwen was an expert in dyes, using complex compounds of ground woad, madder and weld which all grew wild close by. She created the most vivid, jewelled colours of blue, red and yellow, and mixed them to make bright purples and greens. With this yarn, Edyo and Uhtric created tunics and dresses that brought in much needed trade to the village.

The village leader, Wigheard, was a greedy man. For years he had watched rich lords wander in and out of his village to buy cloth. He envied the lives of these prosperous men – their clothes, possessions and confidence – and wanted that life for himself.

Wigheard made a plan to get rich quick. He started by organizing small raids on neighbouring villages, instructing his men to wear disguises so that they wouldn't be recognized. First they targeted sheep and cattle, but as their confidence grew, they began to steal personal possessions; furs, jewellery and silver.

The neighbouring villages joined together to find a way to tackle the raiding parties. They set a trap and captured one of the raiders, exposing his identity as a villager from Caeginesham. Gathering their best warriors, the combined villagers launched one almighty raid on Caeginesham, taking back what belonged to them, and more. A new village council was put in place and Wigheard was put on trial. He was publicly flogged and banished from the village.

The new leader of the village, a much wiser man called Godheard, knew how important it was to bring the neighbouring villages together. He ensured that the new council had equal representation from all villages, spread taxes fairly, and looked to share practices within the new community. Inevitably, his eye fell on the weaving family of Edyo, Uhtric and Cwen.

Godheard decreed that Cwen must become a 'peace weaver'; she must marry a warrior of his choice from one of the other villages, to cement the new conciliation, and to teach him and his family the skills of weaving and dyeing. Cwen, fiercely independent, sank into despair. Sweatling, the man she was to marry, was a beast, a barbarian, who barely spoke her language. As the wedding day came closer, Cwen stopped eating, fell ill and became feverish. Her parents tried every medicinal remedy they knew; hens' eggs in vinegar, pounded herbs, honey and blackthorn, and more. Nothing worked.

The evening before the wedding, Cwen's breathing became hollow and rattled. Uhtric and Edyo knew she was close to death. Uhtric, desperate to save his daughter, saw only one avenue left open to him. He left Edyo asleep next to Cwen, and went out of the village to summon the dead.

Uhtric walked purposefully to the riverbank, to a place surrounded by old oak trees, long thought to be bewitched. Standing in the moonlight, he raised his arms and uttered the unutterable words taught to him long ago. The slow and shallow river started to quicken, and out of the blackened water rose a tall and powerful figure, twice as tall and three times as broad as a normal man. The figure drifted towards Uhtric on the riverbank, bringing with it a sense of despair. Uhtric felt suddenly cold, his breath fogging in front of his face. Frightened now, he stepped backwards and then fell to his knees in piety.

'Do not be afraid,' the figure said. 'I will make a deal with you. Your daughter will not have to marry Sweatling. I will see to it. But in return, I will claim her second child as he reaches his thirteenth year. Are we agreed?'

Uhtric nodded in terror. 'Yes, my Lord!' he shouted. The figure nodded once, and sank back into the river, which immediately returned to its tranquil state as if nothing had happened.

The following morning, the day of the wedding, Uhtric and Edyo were woken by screams from their daughter's bed. Cwen's belly was swollen, huge and round, and she was going into labour.

Despite her confusion, Edyo ran out to fetch a midwife. Word spread like wildfire around the villages that Cwen, yesterday a virgin, was now giving birth. Godheard was called and he and Uhtric waited outside the hut for news.

They had a long wait. The day passed and night fell. It wasn't until the cock crowed again that they heard a baby's cry. They rushed in, to find a shocked midwife holding one baby, and Cwen holding a second. Twin boys.

The midwide was pale. 'The second boy,' she gestured to the baby that Cwen cradled, 'was delivered clinging to the leg of the first boy. He was struggling to be first born.' She looked at Godheard, fearful. 'I have never seen—'

'Twins!' Godheard interrupted. 'Truly they are gifts from the gods and a blessing for us all.'

The wedding was called off; Cwen had been celestially chosen and her body was divine, not to be sullied by any man. Cwen and her family were overjoyed. The midwife agreed never to reveal to anyone what she had witnessed.

Time passed and the bonny identical babies, Gobert – the first born – and Beleth, grew into happy and strong boys. From an early age they doted on their mother and helped to take care of the sheep and make dyes, as well as with simple weaving. The family business grew from strength to strength and they were soon able to build a second loom hut, and take on two apprentices. Over the years, Uhtric forgot about his promise to the stranger in the river.

The morning of their thirteenth birthday, the dawn broke gloomily under a leaden sky. Gobert and Beleth were up early for chores, as always, with the promise of a song after dinner in the evening. They opened the door to fetch water from the well, as they did every day, and walked the short distance through the hazel trees, where they were surprised to find a tall, dark figure blocking their path. Gobert called for his mother, but as she ran towards them, the figure approached Beleth and said, 'It is time.'

And before Gobert could speak, his brother and the figure disappeared into thin air. All that was left was a burn mark on the floor, and a hazel stick that Beleth had been playing with, glowing faintly amongst fallen leaves.

Cwen died soon after of a broken heart. Uhtric's guilt ate away at him: he lost interest in weaving and asked the gods for forgiveness every day. Edyo became old and frail, almost overnight. The apprentices were let go, and the looms fell into disrepair.

Gobert did his best to feed his much-reduced family by using the skills his mother had taught him; he continued to dye wool in bright colours and sell it to neighbouring weavers. His hands were raw from constant work; he was always up before dawn and never returned home until after dark, even throughout summer.

One morning, he found his grandparents in bed, in each other's arms, cold and still. Gobert took his grandfather's best shawl from the chest and covered them both. He knelt next to them, put his head in his hands, and howled in despair.

And that is the end of this sad, moral tale.

Or is it?

Not quite.

The night he buried his last remaining family, Gobert slept

a fitful sleep, dreaming of dark figures dripping with river water, arms outstretched. Woken by a rustling, he drew his short dagger from beneath his pillow only to find the most incredible being standing in front of him. An illuminated woman, with enormous, shimmering wings, casting bright white light into the gloom of the hut. Gobert dropped his dagger.

'Gobert?' She stared into him. He nodded dumbly. 'Great name. We won't have to change it much. I've got the perfect job for you.'

And without any further ado, Gabrielle touched Gobert on the shoulder, and brought him up to Heaven.

53

Appendix

PURGATORY DEBRIEF TRANSCRIPT WITH
JESSICA DAVIES
EARTH YEAR 2063
ATTENDEES: JESSICA DAVIES, ANGEL
GO-BETWEEN, DEMON BELETH
ANGEL ARIAL (recording)

JD: Where am I?

AG: I'm not a hundred per cent sure. Small girl's bedroom? Late Eighties by the look of it. There's Sindy's horse, unless I'm very much mistaken.

JD: No . . . I mean, it's my old bedroom, I recognize it. What I mean is – what's happened to me? Am I dead?

AG: I'm afraid so. You died [sound of notes being shuffled] peacefully in your sleep. I suspect they may have given you one too many glasses of Baileys but we won't hold it against them, will we?

JD: No, I suppose not. I felt ready to go.

AG: Jolly good. That's the spirit. You're in Purgatory. This is where we judge your performance, as it were, while you were alive. But before we do that, we just need to tie up a loose end or two.

JD: Who is that? He's very quiet. Also very big. But he seems familiar.

AG: Ah. Yes. Bit unusual. He's actually a very small part of you. This is Beleth.

JD: Oh. He's waving. That's nice. [pause] He's not saying much. Why is he here?

AG: Ah. New processes in place since the last . . . debacle. Lessons learned, et cetera. We've all decided to be a bit more . . . transparent.

JD: And why is he dressed as a jockey?

AG: Something to do with horses. I've never really understood. Anyway, introductions over – we need to talk to you about an incident that you were witness to in [note shuffling] 2019.

JD: Hannah's dinner party?

AG: Just so. How did you know?

JD: Because it was the worst day of my life.

AG: Oh. Why?

JD: Because Dave died. He was my best friend.

AG: What about Ian? Weren't you upset about him?

JD: A bit. But he didn't die. So why are you asking?

AG: Because of our friend here, we're having a problem in 'balancing the books', as it were. Since Beleth's . . . *intrusion* on you when you were a child, we've not been able to follow you properly.

JD: [pause] Spy on me, do you mean?

AG: Not spying exactly. God is supposed to be all-seeing. It's necessary for judgement purposes. So when we can't see . . . well, let's just say that it makes us anxious.

[snuffling noise]

JD: What's he doing?

AG: Laughing, I think.

JD: Oh.

AG: Hmmm.

JD: I have a question.

AG: Which is . . .?

JD: You've not been able to track me properly – yes?

AG: We have built a picture from others but you're right – your life is still . . . patchy in places. Actually, we'd like to talk to you about several instances in your life that, let's say, have been a bit opaque.

JD: What's to stop me from lying about what I've done? Pump myself up a bit? Get in God's good books?

AG: [Laughter] You're a sharp one! So glad you asked! Good to get these things cleared up. Unfortunately for you, we do know when people lie to us. Every time you tell an untruth, a small piece of your soul breaks off and gets handed to him. You don't feel anything until you're completely morally bankrupt. And then it's too late. Simple, really.

[more snuffling noises]

JD: Is he laughing again?

AG: I'm afraid so.

JD: OK. I have another question. I could potentially 'no comment' – yes?

REBECCA ROGERS

AG: [pause] Have you been watching too many episodes of *Cops in Camden*? Yes, I suppose that, theoretically, you can say nothing. But why would you do that? You want to get to Heaven, don't you?

JD: I was wondering if there's any room for . . . negotiation. Plea bargaining.

AG: This isn't really a Guilty/Not Guilty situation. More like shades of grey. [pause] What did you have in mind?

JD: I fill in some gaps for you. You let me into Heaven. Simple.

AG: Haha! You really are rather marvellous! Most people can hardly remember their own name when they arrive here – you, on the other hand, are busy trying to bribe an archangel.

[pause]

JD: Here's my deal. I've got some unanswered questions about that night, and about – well, this whole situation. Answer them, and I'll fill in any gaps for you that you want.

[sounds of AG and B whispering away from the microphone]

AG: You have a deal.

JD: Before the dinner party . . . what happened to me when I was given that . . . wand? I felt like it turned me into another person. A worse person.

AG: Ah yes! The wand. Think of it like a toddler who didn't want to leave its parents – it was bonded to a certain bloodline, apparently. Mine, as it happens.

B: AND MINE.

AG: And even those within that bloodline struggled to control it. So don't feel bad about your mind being scrambled by it. Even if you'd killed Rose, we wouldn't have counted it as murder.

B: PROBABLY.

B: PROBABLY.

JD: That makes me feel so much better.

AG: Oh good!

B: SHE'S BEING SARCASTIC.

AG: Oh.

[pause]

JD: What's Hell like?

AG: It is loud, and hot, and angry. There are no vegans. No cyclists. Knitters are rare. You're better placed to stay with me.

B: NONSENSE. CYCLISTS ARE WELCOMED AT OUR GATES.

JD: It's been a while since I got on a bike. Next question: what will happen to Andrew when he dies? And where's Dave now?

AG: Ah. Andrew. He's still got some life to live and anything could happen. We won't know where he'll end up until he actually pops his clogs. And as for Dave – well, he's with me, of course.

B: PFFFFFT.

AG: Stop being sour, Belly.

JD: Is he happy?

AG: Fill in the gaps from your history for us and you will see for yourself. Eventually.

[pause]

JD: What do you want to know?

[pause]

AG: Arial? Turn the tape over, will you? I think it's about to run out and this is going to take some tim—

[end of recording]

Acknowledgements

Unless I have the opportunity to save the lives of these people in the future, I will always be indebted to them for helping me to create this book. Martha Ashby is a queen at HarperCollins and has guided me through the publishing process with warmth and patience. Without Julia Silk, my agent, I would have been lost at sea. And of course, Helen Lederer and the Comedy Women in Print team saw potential in me for which I will be eternally grateful. There is no doubt that without this trio of strong and brilliant women, *The Purgatory Poisoning* would still be languishing unread somewhere in my bottom drawer. Thank you all so much.

Thanks also to Tim Woolf who laughed in all the right places when I showed him the story and told me to believe in myself. Rachel and Adam Ifans, talented writers and splendid people – it was your writing course that started this whole thing off. So it's your fault, really. And Al Powell, your creative early morning groups helped me beyond measure.

Thank you to you and all my fellow creative writers on Zoom and in person – yes, that's you Michele, Julia, Sarah, Pari, Tamako, David, Sara, and James.

I know every mum says this, but I've got the best children in the world. Ben and Jack – I love you. You've encouraged me so much, been open-minded and reassuring. Sometimes I wonder who the parent is, and am surprised when I realise it's me.

A big thank you to my colleagues at the job centre who encouraged me to enter CWIP, and then were even more excited than me when I won. And believe me, I was very excited indeed. Thanks particularly to Ian, who always claims, wrongly, to be funnier than me.

And then, at the centre of it all, there's Michael Palin. What can I say? I've got a picture of him on my wall, and I think that's all you need to know.